6-03

Death Row

By William Bernhardt

Primary Justice
Blind Justice
Deadly Justice
Perfect Justice
Cruel Justice
Naked Justice
Extreme Justice
Dark Justice
Silent Justice
Murder One
Criminal Intent
Death Row
The Code of Buddyhood
Double Jeopardy
Legal Briefs
The Midnight Before Christmas
Natural Suspect
Final Round

William Bernhardt

◆ ◆ ◆

DEATH ROW

BALLANTINE BOOKS ◆ NEW YORK

A Ballantine Book
Published by The Random House Ballantine Publishing Group

Copyright © 2003 by William Bernhardt

All rights reserved under International and Pan-American Copyright Conventions. Published in the United States by The Random House Ballantine Publishing Group, a division of Random House, Inc., New York, and simultaneously in Canada by Random House of Canada Limited, Toronto.

Ballantine and colophon are registered trademarks of Random House, Inc.

www.ballantinebooks.com

Library of Congress Cataloging-in-Publication Data
Bernhardt, William, 1960–
Death row / William Bernhardt.— 1st ed.
p.   cm.
ISBN 0-345-44174-5
I. Title.
PS3552.E73147 D43 2003
813'.54—dc21   2002040876

Manufactured in the United States of America

First Edition: July 2003

1   3   5   7   9   10   8   6   4   2

To Arlene Joplin
with gratitude

Rosalind: I'll tell you who Time ambles withal, who Time trots withal, who Time gallops withal, and who he stands still withal. . . .

Orlando: Who stays it still withal?

Rosalind: With lawyers in the vacation; for they sleep between term and term, and then they perceive not how time moves.

—WILLIAM SHAKESPEARE, *As You Like It* (III, ii)

Death Row

Prologue

◆ ◆ ◆

Seven Years Earlier

1

SHE DIDN'T KNOW how long she had been in the darkness when her family finally stopped screaming. She had forgotten where she was and how she had gotten there. She didn't know how long she had been trapped, chained down like an animal, dirty, helpless. She didn't know why she was naked. All she knew was that she was in great pain, that her whole body ached and her knee-cap felt as if it had been shattered. That she was alone. And that something horrible was happening to her family.

Erin Faulkner couldn't see anything, not in any direction. Only the impenetrable black. All she could feel was the stone floor beneath her, hard, rough, cold to the touch. She could hear a dripping sound, not too far away, steady, with a slight echo, making this place seem even more like a medieval torture chamber, filling her with foreboding. Maybe the man in the ski mask would come back for her when he finished with the others. Maybe that was why he had taken her clothing. Maybe that was why he had chained her to the floor.

She could hear her family—her mother and father, her brothers and sister, the baby. The words were indistinct, but she could tell they belonged to the people she loved most in all the world. She could tell that they were in immense agony, that they were begging for mercy. And not receiving any.

The screams of her father had been particularly loud. He had always had a deep voice. It carried. Despite all that had happened between them, her father was perhaps the one person she loved more than anyone else in the world. His anguished cries had reverberated, had penetrated her and rattled her skull. Her father's distress pained her more profoundly than her own injuries.

She had begged the man not to hurt her, especially not on her legs. She played soccer on her high-school team, and it was one of the few things in her short life she had ever done well. But with one swift kick to her kneecap, he had taken it all away. She had crumpled to the carpet like a boneless sack of

3

flesh, her body electrified by the lightning flashes that coursed through her. She remembered seeing the man draw back his foot for another blow. And then she remembered nothing, until she woke up here.

And that had been—how long ago? All she knew was that she wanted it to be over. The pain. The hunger. The fear for her family. Herself. She wanted it to end. If she could have made it end—any way—she would surely have done so. But she was denied even that fundamental right. All she could do was lie on the floor, unclothed and miserable. And wait. Until something finally brought an end to her suffering. Until someone—God, the man in the ski mask, *someone*—granted her mercy. Something she wasn't sure existed anymore.

SHE FOUND HERSELF missing the screams. Not that she had enjoyed listening to them. But at least it was something. Something to disrupt the horrid void that surrounded her. Something to give her a foothold on reality. A connection. A sense that she still existed.

She had no way of knowing how long it had been since the screams had died. Since all traces of others had faded away. It seemed as if it had been days, weeks, an eternity. Time didn't exist here, in this private hell in which she was the sole occupant. Only misery existed here. Misery and hunger and the hideous awful agony of not knowing. That was her life now. That was all she had left.

It had begun so innocently. Her mother had decided to take everyone out for ice cream, and had insisted that Erin come along. Being a teenager, she tried to avoid these family outings whenever possible. But once it was under way, once she had resigned herself to the ignominy of it all, she found herself enjoying it—Bernie's clowning, Louise's pathetic attempts to be just like Erin, even the baby. She would never have told them, but secretly she found herself warmed by the pleasure of being part of a larger circle, one that didn't fluctuate with the latest wave of popularity or peer pressure. Of feeling that she belonged to something that mattered a good deal more than who was on the starting team or who got picked for soccer princess.

And then they came home. The man in the mask seemed surprised when they poured through the entryway from the garage. Didn't take him long to adapt, though. Before Erin knew what was happening, her mother was crying out, her arm twisted behind her back. He forced the rest of them into the living room, where her father lay on the floor, beaten, bleeding. He was cruel to all of them, but he paid special attention to Erin, or so it seemed to her. She could barely see his eyes in that mask. She had thought that if she resisted, if she was strong, he might back off. She had been wrong. And now she had a shattered kneecap to prove it.

And she was still chained down, the pain increasing while her strength faded. Why had he done this to her? Why had he hurt her and stripped her and left her here? It made no sense, but she realized her mind was probably not working at its best. The chains that bound her, the physical anguish that crushed her, the fear that immobilized her—all took precedence over the feeble fumblings of her brain. Why did no one come to help? Why had this happened? And why could she not just die? *Why wouldn't someone show her some mercy and please just let her die?*

She knew it would be over soon. She had been far too long without food, without water. This imprisonment would kill a healthy person, much less one with a broken leg. Her eyelids fluttered with the sweetness of the thought. Soon all this misery would be replaced with the blissful sensation of not knowing, not caring anymore. . . .

No. Something inside her flashed, snapping her out of a fatigue-induced haze. She sat upright, perhaps for the first time in days. What was she thinking? Was she giving up? Was that the best she could do?

She was not a helpless baby like Bryan. She was a fifteen-year-old woman, and she was not going to die like this. She was not going to let that bastard in the ski mask have that satisfaction. She would find a way. Despite the hunger, the lethargy, the terror. She would find a way.

The handcuff around her left wrist was what pinned her down. She could feel the other cuff; it was attached to some kind of metal ring embedded in the floor. If she could get it off her wrist, she would be free.

But she couldn't. She had tried for hours, days, since she had awoken and found herself down here. She couldn't get out. Her hand was too big.

She recalled reading that wild animals caught in a trap would chew off their own limbs to escape. She didn't think she could do that. Could she?

It wouldn't have to be the whole hand. The thumb was the problem. If she could just get rid of the thumb, she would be able to slide her hand out.

She brought her mouth down to her left wrist. She smelled bad, she realized. Not a great surprise. She had been lying naked forever, on the dirty floor, in her own squalor. She had wet herself more times than she could count. But she had to put all that out of her head now.

Her lips parted. Her teeth bit into the flesh at the base of her thumb.

And she gagged. She pulled away, dry-heaving. She couldn't do it. She just couldn't do that.

But perhaps there was another way. She had discovered something yesterday, or the day before. Something hard just at the outer edge of her limited reach. A rock. Or a brick, perhaps, since it seemed more or less rectangular. She had tried to use it to break the cuffs and the chain, but they had been too hard, too solid. But maybe . . .

She reached out again and found it, just where it had been before. She carefully fingered her cuffed hand. If she could just break the bone connecting her wrist to the lower knuckle of her thumb, that ought to be enough. Get that out of the way, and she could slide her hand out. She could do that. Couldn't she? *Couldn't she?*

She took the brick into her free hand and closed her eyes. It would have to be quick. She would have to do it all at once, and fast. If she just injured herself, without breaking the bone, she would cause more pain, so much that she probably wouldn't be able to hit herself again. Worse, her hand would swell, and then she would have no chance of getting it out. She would have to strike once, hard and fast, then slide her hand out. Hard and fast.

She could do this, she told herself. *She could do this.*

She gripped the brick tightly. Her hand was beginning to sweat. She could sense her heart pounding harder, each beat feeling like a major stroke. The hollowness inside her stomach had converted to a horrible aching. The pain in her leg flared. She heard a voice inside her head trying to talk her out of this desperate plan. *Your leg is already broken. Are you going to cripple your hand as well?*

I can do this, she told herself, tears seeping out of her clenched-shut eyes. *I can do this.*

With as much speed and strength as she could muster, she brought the brick down against her left wrist. The pain was incredible. Her body began to shake. She cried out, her scream echoing around her. But she knew it had not been enough. The bone was hurt, not broken. Her hand could not slip through. And she did not have much time before the swelling began.

Once again, she brought the brick down hard. Then again and again and again, each blow harder than the one before. Her cries and screams and tears all swam together. And after the fifth blow, she felt the bone break.

She flipped onto her back, her whole body convulsing. She clenched her teeth together, trying to shut out the pain. She was going into shock and she had to fight it. Fight the pain, stave away unconsciousness. She had to—

It was a long time, or so it seemed, before she realized what she had done. In the midst of her writhing and shaking, her hand had slipped through the cuff.

It had worked. It hurt worse than anything she had ever imagined, even worse than her leg, but—she had done it.

She lay on her back, watery eyes closed, her hand lying beside her like a dead animal. She would have to sleep now. But despite the hunger, despite the cold, despite the unbearable agony, she faded from the conscious world with one certainty imprinted on her brain.

She had done it. She had made herself the woman she wanted to be. She had told herself she could do it, and she had done it.

She was free.

WHEN SHE AWOKE, much of the aching had subsided. She could still feel it, to be certain, but it wasn't the raging torrent it had been before. More of a dull throbbing, steady and rhythmic, but not incapacitating. In biology, she had learned about the body's natural anesthetics. Must be kicking in, she thought. Or perhaps she was just so broken she couldn't feel anything anymore.

She began to slowly crawl away from the spot where she had been chained for so long. She had no idea where she was going. She just had to get away.

She hit some kind of wall. She pulled herself alongside it, feeling for an opening. Eventually, she found a raised ridge. And beyond the ridge, a smooth flat panel.

A door.

Her left hand wasn't good for anything, and her left leg could support no weight, so her right side had to carry the load. Slowly, an inch at a time, she pulled herself upright. Not quite standing—more of a crouch, leaning against the wall for support. But it was enough.

Not much light came in through the open door, but by comparison to the unrelenting darkness Erin had experienced for so long, it seemed blinding. She shielded her eyes, trying to block it out. In time, her eyes adjusted. She opened them, a fraction at a time.

She had been in the basement of their home. All along. With a fragile but steady pace, she clawed her way up the stairs. Moving past each step was like climbing Everest, but she forced herself to do it. No one had come to rescue her, and there was no reason to believe anyone ever would. She would have to help herself. And that meant she had to get out of the basement.

The journey up the stairs took half an hour, although it seemed much longer. She started across the endless corridor that connected the basement to the laundry room. Then she crawled through the laundry room to the living room, the place where she had last seen the rest of her family.

And then she screamed. Screamed louder and harder than she had during the entire ordeal. Screamed longer than she had when her leg was broken, when she mutilated her own hand. Screamed for them. For what was left of them.

2

"AND WHAT DID you discover after you forced your way into the Faulkner home, Officer Marder?"

Marder spoke in calm, measured tones, trying to make his testimony flat and unemotional, when in reality it was anything but. "The first thing I noticed was the blood. Blood was everywhere. It looked more like a slaughterhouse than a suburban family residence."

"And after that?"

Marder allowed himself only the slightest hesitation before answering. "Then I spotted the bodies."

"They were all dead?"

"All eight of them. The parents, and the six children."

"Even the baby?"

"Yes," Marder whispered almost inaudibly. "Even the baby."

Sitting at the defense table, Ben Kincaid carefully eyed his client, Ray Goldman. He made no visible reaction to the testimony, just as Ben had instructed him. Whether it was an expression of guilt or of outraged innocence, reactions from the defense table always troubled the jury. Ben hadn't been sure whether Ray could keep himself calm through this brutal testimony, but so far, he had. Which was good. Because it was only going to get worse.

Assistant District Attorney Bullock paused, letting the horrific declarations from the witness stand seep into the consciousness of all those who could hear, including the jury, before he proceeded. "Was anyone left alive?"

"Only the fifteen-year-old girl, Erin Faulkner. The one who called us. She was in the passageway from the laundry room. She had crawled up from the basement. She was severely injured, but she was still alive. Barely."

"What did you do next?"

"I called for medical attention for the girl." Sergeant Marder was a trim man in his early thirties, one of the few men on earth, Ben thought, who actually looked good in a police uniform. Like all PD witnesses, he had been taught to keep his testimony brief and to the point, but Ben had a sense of hidden depths, a fire perhaps, that burned just below the surface. "She'd called the police, but hadn't the strength, or the clarity of mind, to call for help for herself."

Bullock was a tall, slightly balding man in his late forties. Ben had known him for years, since they had both worked at the state attorney general's office. "Would you please describe her injuries?"

"She'd been beaten, stripped naked. Her left kneecap was dislocated and broken. And as you've already heard, she broke her own hand to escape from the handcuffs. She was in severe shock. So I called for an EMSA team and they took her down to St. Francis's."

"And then what did you do?"

"I conducted a closer inspection of the . . . remains. The corpses. It's standard procedure in a homicide."

"Of course. You did the right thing. Under extremely difficult circumstances."

An improper comment, to be sure. But what was Ben going to do, object? The jury would crucify him. Years ago, when Bullock had been his mentor, he had told Ben: "When they put a hero on the stand, make sure you treat him with respect. Then rip him apart. But respectfully."

"Could you tell the jury more about the condition of the bodies when you found them?" Bullock asked.

"Of course." The casualness of Marder's response didn't fool anyone. This was a question he was dreading. "All eight of them were dead. With the two deceased females, there was evidence of sexual assault of . . . one kind or another. They were all in the living room, except that the baby was found in his crib in the nursery. And of course, Erin had been chained up in the basement."

"Perhaps you should describe the victims for us one at a time, sir."

Marder shifted his weight around in the chair. "The first corpse I inspected was the father, Frank Faulkner. His body was facedown, spread-eagled on a white plush rug in the center of the living room. His throat had been cut. But that was not the only injury he had suffered. He appeared to have been beaten. Quite severely. One of his legs had been broken. One of his arms had been dislocated and twisted around in an unnatural position. His shirt was off, and I could see bruises and lacerations on his chest. One of his nipples had been cut off. And his eyes—" For the first time, Officer Marder choked.

"You were saying?" Bullock prodded. "About his eyes?"

Marder swallowed, then licked his lips. "His eyes had been . . . removed."

"Removed?"

"Cut out," he said, inhaling deeply. "Right out of the sockets."

"I . . . see." Ben knew this gruesome detail was not news to Bullock—probably not to anyone in the packed courtroom. The details of this crime had held the Tulsa media in thrall—which was why the courtroom was SRO. Nonetheless, the testimony had a chilling effect on everyone within earshot. Even Judge Kearns looked shaken. And Kearns, an African-American who had been on the bench for almost forty years, was a hard man to shake. "Did you ever . . . locate the missing eyes?"

"No. None of them."

"None of them?" Bullock tilted his head sideways. "Were there . . . others?"

"All of the victims had suffered the same end, more or less. All of them had their eyes removed. And none of the eyes were ever found."

"Even—?"

"Yes," Marder said, and for the first time a note of anger, anger and perhaps something else, tinged his voice. "Even the baby."

BEN AND HIS client huddled in a corner of the corridor outside the courtroom, cradling paper cups in both hands, trying to use the heat of the coffee to warm themselves against the bitter cold that seemed to have enveloped the courthouse.

"So . . ." Ray said, as casually as possible, "you didn't want to cross that guy?"

Ben shook his head. "You have a problem with that?"

Goldman was a handsome man in his early thirties, with a tanned face and strong features. Strands of gray already flecked his hair, but they only made his appearance more striking, giving him a sense of maturity that exceeded his chronological age. "I haven't been to law school or anything, but I thought his detailed description of the crime scene was . . . damaging."

"You were right."

"Then why—"

"What would be the point? The man saw what he saw. It's not as if he were lying."

"But the jury will think—"

"The jury will think a lot worse if I spin around some poor schlep whose only crime was having the misfortune to be on duty the day the worst home invasion slash murder case in the history of Tulsa occurred. It's not as if his testimony pointed to you, anyway. Everything he said was uncontested."

"Then why did they spend so long on it?"

"Because Bullock knows that the more gruesome the crime-scene details, the more inclined the jury will be to convict."

"Then why—"

Ben placed his hand on his client's shoulder. "Ray, I promise you we will put on a defense. When the proper time comes. This just wasn't it."

Goldman nodded, but he didn't seem much comforted by the counsel. His reserved, almost intellectual demeanor reminded Ben that this alleged multiple murderer was, after all, a scientist. "Ben . . . I know this is amateurish, and defense lawyers don't like it, but—I didn't do this. I'm not guilty."

"Ray—"

"I know. It's just—this crime is so . . . ghastly. I'm trying not to let it show, but it makes me sick to my stomach just to hear about it. I want you to know— I need to know that this isn't just another job for you. I want you to know that I'm innocent."

"It doesn't matter," Ben said, not quite truthfully.

"I know. But I want you to know. I want you to want—"

"If you're thinking I didn't cross because I suspect you're guilty and I want to send you up the river, forget it. I will fight for you. I will do anything the law allows to help you."

"I know. But still, I—I—" He wiped his hand across his brow. "Oh, hell. I don't know what I'm saying."

Ben smiled reassuringly, then crumpled his coffee cup and tossed it into the trash can. "Come on, Ray. We've got work to do."

BEN SUSPECTED THAT the testimony from Detective Sergeant Murphy, the man who headed the investigation into the Faulkner family slayings, would be more damning. And he was right.

"Did you have any leads?" Bullock asked him, after several preliminary questions establishing his credentials and describing his examination of the crime scene.

"We were working on the presumption that the motive was money, and that the killer was either a psychopath or someone who knew Frank Faulkner personally. Or both. As you know, Faulkner was relatively wealthy, and there were signs that a robbery had taken place either before or after the murders. A safe in Faulkner's bedroom had been jimmied open and everything inside had been removed."

"So how did you proceed?"

"Given the familiarity the killer seemed to have with Faulkner's home and schedule, I started by trying to learn who might've been at the victims' home recently."

"Were you able to do so?"

"Yes. I found a Filofax—that's a pocket calendar-organizer—on Faulkner's dresser. Inside, I found the names of three men who had been to his home during the previous week. One was a banker with whom he was negotiating a loan to buy a piece of real estate in south Tulsa. One was an insurance sales-man who came out to investigate some hail damage to their chimney. And one was a fellow chemist he knew from his place of work." He paused and glanced in the direction of the defense table. "That was Ray Goldman."

"And did you then investigate the defendant?"

"I investigated all three of them. Goldman was the one that paid off."

"How so?"

"I found the defendant walking home from work. Apparently he lived about a mile from the plant, and it was his habit to walk to and from. I stopped him, searched him. That was when I found—"

"Objection, your honor. I renew my pretrial motion to suppress." If Ben could prevent the jury from learning the officer found a handgun when he searched Ray, it would be a big break for the defense. Of course his motion was denied, but when his turn came, Ben made that the main focus of his cross.

"Did you have a warrant to conduct a personal search?" Ben asked.

"You know I didn't." In the short time it took Ben to approach the stand, Murphy's demeanor had been transformed. Where once had sat the compli-ant, terse, unemotional witness, now was the antagonistic, argumentative pala-din for truth, justice, and the American way. "Probable cause for the search was based on his violation of Oklahoma's laws on open containers. Misde-meanor in my presence. Clear basis for arrest, then search."

Ben knew the story, having reviewed the officer's statement so many times he could recite it from memory, but he wanted to make sure the jury was with him before he proceeded. "Would you explain that, please?"

"As I drove past the witness, I saw that he was drinking a beer. Out of a can. A Bud Light, to be specific."

"You saw the can?"

"I saw the top part of it. It was wrapped up in a paper bag. Common prac-tice for people drinking in violation of the liquor laws."

"But you could see enough to tell it was an alcoholic beverage?"

"Definitely. And as you know, counselor, you can't walk down the streets carrying an open container with an alcoholic beverage. That's against the law. So I parked my car and ran after him."

"And when you caught up to him, was he in fact carrying a beer?"

"No, not then. He must've ditched it somewhere. Probably saw me coming and tossed it over a fence or down a gutter."

"But you searched him anyway."

"Of course. The man broke the law. Standard procedure."

"Were there any other witnesses to this alleged offense?"

"No, I was working alone."

"Did you ever find the alleged beer can?"

"I can't say that I ever looked. After the search, I had better things to do."

No doubt. Ironically, unlike carrying an open beer can, carrying a concealed weapon was not illegal in Oklahoma, so long as the gun was registered. And since all of the Faulkners were killed by a knife, the gun did not immediately link Goldman to the crime. But the assailant had used a gun to corral and control the family, and Frank Faulkner had a wound on his head that could have been caused by the butt of a gun. It was hardly proof positive, but it was the best piece of physical evidence the prosecution had. If Ben could get Judge Kearns to suppress it, it could dramatically alter the course of the trial.

"Pardon me for saying so, Officer Murphy," Ben continued, "but I'm having a hard time understanding how you could see a man on the street from a distance, while in a moving car, at the end of the day after the sun has begun to set, see only the top part of the can, and still know immediately that it was a beer."

"Chalk it up to experience. I've been on the police force for almost twenty years."

"Which is what inclines me to think that perhaps you followed my client, searched him illegally, then concocted this story about the beer to justify the search."

"Your honor, I protest!" DA Bullock shot to his feet, a look of outrage plastered across his face. "Counsel is desperately trying to create some impropriety where none exists. I find this grossly offensive. And I deeply resent the suggestion that this state's sworn and trusted law enforcement officers might engage in improper practices."

"If that's an objection," Judge Kearns said, "it's sustained." Ben suspected that Kearns, being an African-American in his sixties living in the Southwest, was probably less outraged than Bullock by the suggestion that a law enforcement officer might do something improper.

"Tell me," Ben said, taking a step closer, "how far away from my client were you when you first spotted the beer?"

Murphy shrugged. "About twenty feet. Maybe a little more."

"And you had no problem identifying the can he held as a beer?"

"None at all."

"Fine." Ben reached into the pocket of his suit coat and withdrew a large tape measure. "Twenty feet it is." Good thing they were in the large courtroom. Ben hooked the tape measure to the rail in front of the witness stand and started reeling the tape backward.

Murphy watched, a small crease appearing between his eyebrows. "What's that for?"

"Sorry," Ben said. "I'm the one who gets to ask the questions." He continued pulling the tape backward, taking his own sweet time about it. Let Murphy sweat awhile, Ben thought. Let the jury get interested. They've been sitting in those chairs all day. They must be ready for something a little more lively.

Ben stopped when he was exactly twenty feet away from the stand. He addressed his client. "Ray, would you come here, please? And bring that box on the floor."

Bullock slowly rose. "Your honor, I object. I don't know what Mr. Kincaid is trying to pull—"

"Well, if you'll sit patiently for a minute," Judge Kearns said, interrupting, "you might figure it out."

Ouch. That put Bullock back in his seat in a hurry. Ben positioned Ray at the twenty-foot mark, then turned away from the front of the courtroom and opened the box. He removed a can wrapped up in a paper bag so that only the top showed, then handed it to Ray.

"Sergeant Murphy," Ben announced, "I have re-created the scene just as you described it. The same man, the same distance, another can partially concealed by a paper bag—with just as much showing at the top as you say was visible when you spotted Ray on the street. The only real difference is that the lighting in here is much better than it would have been on the streets at six-thirty in the evening, and you're not in a moving car, so you'll be able to take a much more careful sustained look."

Bullock saw what was coming and did his best to stop it. "Your honor, again I object. This re-creation has not been staged under controlled circumstances—"

"I'll allow it," Kearns replied.

"Furthermore, the jury could be unduly influenced by a test that in no way indicates what happened on the evening of—"

"I'll allow it," Kearns repeated, a bit more forcefully this time. "Mr. Kincaid, you may proceed."

"Thank you, your honor." He returned his attention to the witness. "My question is pretty simple, Sergeant Murphy. What is Ray holding in his hand?"

Murphy sat silently, not saying anything. He made a few furtive glances in the direction of the prosecution table, but Bullock couldn't help him now.

"I'm waiting for an answer, Officer. What is Ray holding?"

Murphy continued to stare at the defendant intently, but he did not respond.

"He's the same distance away from you that he was on the night you searched him, Sergeant. Maybe even closer. Surely if you could tell what he was holding then, you could do so now." Ben paused. "*If* you could tell what he was holding then."

Murphy still did not answer.

"Okay, I'll make it easier for you. Consider it a yes-or-no question. Is he holding a beer? Or any other alcoholic beverage that would give you a legal right to search? Please bring your twenty years of experience to bear and give the jury an answer."

Murphy stood up and continued to stare at the bag in Ray Goldman's hand. Ben could easily imagine the thought process running through his brain. It had to be tempting to take a guess. After all, he had a fifty-fifty chance of getting it right. He could say it was a beer, just like before (and Ben hoped he would, because it was actually a can of Pepsi One). But if Murphy got it wrong, it would be a disaster for the prosecution. Ultimately, he decided to play it safe—and to answer the question honestly.

"I can't tell," he said quietly.

"Excuse me?" Ben said. "What was that?"

"I can't tell."

"Is it a beer? Or just soda pop?"

"I can't tell."

Ben turned toward the jury, a look of amazement on his face. "Officer Murphy, has anything happened to your eyesight between the day of the search and the present day?"

"No."

"Has there been some profound diminution of your mental or physical faculties?"

Murphy pursed his lips. "Not that I'm aware of."

"Is there any reason to believe your powers of perception have been reduced since the time of the search?"

"No."

"No, I thought not." Ben approached the bench. "Your honor, this was an illegal search, without probable cause. I move that the search and all evidence collected as a result be suppressed."

Kearns didn't hesitate. "Done."

"Your honor!" Bullock raced to the front. "This little courtroom prank has no bearing—"

"Don't bother, Mr. Bullock."

"But this witness is an honest, truthful servant of—"

"Mr. Bullock!" Kearns aimed his gavel in the direction of his nose. "Throughout my career as a judge, I have always shown a great deal of respect to the representatives of the district attorney's office. But if you press me on this, that could change." He slammed down his gavel. "Let's take a recess."

FOR THE FIRST time since the trial began, Ben did not have to push his way through a mob of reporters to get out of the courtroom. He assumed they were all huddled around their cell phones, calling in this surprising development.

Ray was on the other side of the hallway, joyously embracing his girlfriend, Carrie. She was a secretary he'd met at the chemical plant where they both worked. Ray was passionately in love—for the first time in his life, he said—and they had been planning to marry. Before this disaster descended upon them. Carrie had been supremely patient throughout the protracted pretrial ordeal—but Ben knew that wouldn't last forever.

Not far away, Ben noticed a teenage girl staring at Ray and Carrie. She had short black hair and was leaning on a cane. Ben didn't have to ask who she was; he'd interviewed her beforehand and had seen her sitting in the courtroom gallery every day since the trial began. She was Erin Faulkner, the girl who'd miraculously managed to escape being chained up in the basement. The only survivor of the Faulkner family.

Ben assumed she was less than delighted about the elimination of key evidence against the man accused of sadistically killing her entire family. But the look in her eyes at that moment, as she gazed at Ray, puzzled him. Was she suppressing the bitterness and hatred she must feel toward him? Ben scrutinized her face more carefully. There was definitely something going on in her head. But what was it?

She turned and, all at once, their eyes locked. Ben felt an icy twinge at his spine. He quickly averted his eyes and, without even thinking about it, wrapped his arms around himself. Defending murder cases was one thing. But this he did not need.

"Sudden chill?"

To his relief, Ben saw his legal assistant, Christina McCall, standing beside him. She was wearing purple-tinted glasses, a waist-length jacket with a fake fur collar, a short, psychedelic orange skirt, and high hip boots.

"Just in from the Sonny and Cher concert?" Ben asked.

"No. Just in from the clerk's office, where they're all abuzz about how you knocked Bullock's feet out from under him."

"I did my best."

"You did better than that. One good cross and—voilà! The prosecution case is dead in the water."

"I never make predictions. It isn't over till it's over."

"So true. And so originally put, too." She gave him a gentle jab on the shoulder. "Way to go, slugger. You hit a home run."

Ben shivered. "I always love your sports analogies."

She fluffed her long strawberry-blonde hair back over her shoulder. "So who does the prosecution have left?"

"Only the complainant. Erin Faulkner."

"Tough witness to cross. But she didn't really see much, did she? How much damage can she do?"

"I don't know," Ben said, and reluctantly he let his eyes return to the fifteen-year-old girl who would now walk with a cane for the rest of her life. "I just don't know."

"WE'RE WINNING, RIGHT?" Ray said as he reclaimed his chair at the defense table beside Ben. He kissed Carrie again, squeezed her hand, then let her return to her own seat in the gallery.

Ben wouldn't play. "I never make predictions."

"I respect that." He paused. "But we *are* winning, aren't we?"

"Ray—"

"Carrie thinks we're winning. I realize she's not impartial. But she thinks you tore the prosecutor's heart right out of his chest."

Ben tried to resist the mental image. "The last witness went . . . very well for us. I agree. But anything can happen. Juries are unpredictable."

Ray faced the front of the courtroom. "You're right. Of course you are.

That's fine." He glanced almost impishly at Ben out of the corners of his eyes. "But we are winning. Aren't we?"

Ben gave him a small smile. "I hope so."

PACKED AS IT was, the entire courtroom fell silent as Erin Faulkner hobbled to the witness stand. Ben knew her left leg had been so severely damaged in the assault that for months she had not been able to walk at all, and even now could only do so with supreme effort. Her struggle to cross the courtroom underscored the inherent drama that her presence, and her testimony, would lend the proceedings.

Slowly, painfully, she led the jury through her first-person account of the night of horror. She told them how she and her mother and siblings had returned home to find a brute in a ski mask torturing her father. How he had held them all at gunpoint, had beaten and abused and cut them, one after the other. How she had watched helplessly as her family was brutalized. And finally, how he had broken her leg and knocked her out.

The account of her time locked in the basement was perhaps even more riveting. The story of a fifteen-year-old girl, naked, disoriented, suffering from a broken leg, nonetheless mustering the presence of mind and the courage to break her own thumb in order to escape was a resounding testament to the indomitability of the human spirit. Ben knew she was making a profound impression on the jury.

At last she reached the end of the tale, how she fought her way out of the cellar and up the stairs only to be greeted by a bloody tableau worse than anything Edgar Allan Poe ever dreamed about: her entire family dead, butchered— with their eyes cut out of their skulls.

"After the police arrived," she said, in a quiet but steady voice, "they called the ambulance. I passed out soon after that and didn't wake up until three days later in the hospital."

"I see." With a solemn expression, DA Bullock closed his trial notebook. "Miss Faulkner, I know this will be painful for you, but I am required by the court to ask. Do you have any knowledge regarding the identity of the man who invaded your home? Who killed your parents and your six siblings?"

"I do. I know who it was."

Bullock paused. Ben felt his pulse quicken. "And what is the basis for your identification?"

"I was there. I saw him."

"Wasn't he wearing a mask?"

"He was. But I could still see his eyes, his lips. I have a very good memory."

"And is that the basis for your identification of the killer?"

"Not entirely, no. The main basis I have is . . . his voice."

Ben sat up straight. He hadn't heard anything about this before.

"You heard his voice?" Bullock asked.

"Of course. Repeatedly. At length. It's a very distinctive voice."

"And you remember it?"

"How could I forget?" Erin leaned forward, gripping the rail. "This is the man who slapped me across the face and said—I apologize for the language, but this is what he said—'I'll get to you later, you little cunt.' This is the man who hit me, groped me, all the while calling me names and making disgusting remarks. 'I've got something that'll cool you off but good, you li'l bitch.' That's what he said. 'I'll hurt you till you scream for me to stop. But I won't stop.' That's what he said when he pressed his knife against my throat. When he broke my kneecap." She lowered her head. "You don't forget something like that."

Ben swore silently. He'd been planning to cross on her identification of a man who was wearing a ski mask the whole time she saw him. But this voice angle complicated matters—because it made her ID seem so much more credible.

"When did you have an opportunity to make a formal identification?" Bullock asked her.

"About a week after the incident. The police prepared a lineup. There were six different men. They had them all step forward and say the same thing—about how he was going to cool me off."

"And were you able to make an identification?"

"I was. Almost immediately." She folded her hands and sat up straight. For a young woman who had been through as much as she had, she was remarkably composed. "I thought it was him as soon as I saw him. But after I heard the voice, I was absolutely certain." She raised her hand and pointed. "The man who killed my family is sitting right over there, at the defense table. Raymond Goldman."

The stir in the courtroom was audible. Judge Kearns rapped his gavel several times to quiet the gallery.

"Are you certain about this?"

"Absolutely. Without a doubt." She turned and looked directly at the jury. "Please listen to me. I know what I saw. And heard. I remember what happened. Much as I'd like to forget it, I will never be able to." She paused. "Raymond Goldman was the killer. There's no doubt in my mind whatsoever."

Ben rose slowly. "Your honor . . . I think she's answered the question."

Erin continued unabated. "I've lost my home, my family," she said, and all at once her voice began to crack. Tears streamed down her cheeks. "I've lost everything I ever had. All I have left is my faith. My faith that you will do the right thing. That you will not let my family die unavenged."

"I object," Ben said, loud and forcefully. "This is grossly improper."

"Sustained," Kearns ruled. He pounded his gavel. "The witness will be silent and wait for a question."

Erin ignored him. She rose to her feet, wiping the tears from her face. "Please. Please!" She reached out toward the jury, pleading with them, begging them.

"Bailiff!" Judge Kearns gestured toward the witness stand. "Mr. Bullock, take control of your witness!" He slammed his gavel. "The jury will disregard the last remarks from the witness. And we will take a fifteen-minute break. At the end of that time, I expect the witness to be prepared to follow the instructions of the court."

Kearns was doing his best to sound harsh, but Ben knew his heart wasn't in it. How could anyone help but empathize with a girl who had lost every member of her family? As he looked at the jurors, as he stared into their eyes, he knew that they had been as moved—and influenced—by her testimony as he had been. As everyone had been.

Beside him, Ray sat silently, not saying anything, not asking the obvious question. And Ben was grateful for that. Because he still didn't like to make predictions. But whether he did or he didn't, he knew with absolute certainty that the trial had just taken a dramatic—and irrevocable—turn. And not for the better.

O N E

The Death Watch

◆ ◆ ◆

Present Day

CHAPTER

1

THE SCENE CONFRONTING Erin outside the penitentiary both startled and disturbed her. Who were all these people? There must be hundreds of them, she guessed, people from all walks of life. Some just children. What were they doing here?

A large group of teenagers passed her, carrying candles. Some were chanting softly. A high-powered searchlight burned down from the top of the penitentiary. This would be the perfect time for a jailbreak, Erin mused. The guards are all watching the teenagers.

She moved slowly toward the building. It was still hard walking, even after all these years, especially on unpaved surfaces. The cane helped some, but not that much. The letter jackets some of the kids were wearing told her they were from Bishop Kelly High School. It was a Tulsa private school, a Catholic school. She wasn't surprised. The Catholic bishop had vociferously protested the death penalty, as had the Episcopal bishop and even some fundamentalists. An offense to humanity, they said. Legalized murder. Contrary to everything Jesus ever taught. DNA evidence has proved wrongful convictions occur, they argued. With every execution, the death penalty seemed to become more controversial, and this was the fifth execution in this state this year. Oklahoma was one of the top states in the union for executions. It was a political hot potato.

Erin didn't care about politics. She didn't care about religion, or morality, or What Jesus Would Do. She just wanted it to be over.

But did she want it to be over this way? She pressed her hand against her temples, trying to ease the pounding that had almost incapacitated her these past few days. That was the difficult question, the one that was tearing her apart.

Where was Sheila, anyway? Somehow, in this mass confusion, she had lost Sheila. Moving toward the north entrance, she saw another group of demonstrators, smaller and quieter than the anti-death-penalty crowd. A placard informed Erin that they were a homicide survivors group. Presumably that meant they were gung ho for the death penalty. So why were they here? Just to make a show of support? And what did they call themselves? she wondered. Friends of the Big Needle?

One of the demonstrators noticed her, looked once, then looked again, this time not turning away. Damn. Erin moved rapidly toward the door. She hoped she hadn't been recognized. The last thing on earth she wanted was to be proselytized by some victims-rights group. What a coup she would be for them—a young woman who had lost eight family members. What airplay they could get out of that.

As she approached the visitors entrance, she sensed another person moving behind her in the darkness.

"Kind of revolting, isn't it?"

Something about the voice gave her an eerie feeling. Which camp was this one with—the pro-deaths, or the anti-deaths?

"That all these people would turn out to be near an execution. To be a part of it."

"I didn't want to be here," Erin said quietly.

"Really? Pardon my intrusion, but—I recognized you. And I would've thought you'd be the first in line."

"I didn't want to come at all. But my friend Sheila kept saying I should. That it would make me feel better. Give me a sense of closure."

"And has it?"

"No. It's made me feel—like I can't live with myself any longer. Like I've made a terrible mistake."

"But how?"

"I've . . . done something horrible. Something—unforgivable."

"You can't blame yourself because a killer will be punished. You are only—"

But Erin never heard the rest of the sentence. She turned and headed across the front lawn, back toward her car. She couldn't do this. She just couldn't bear it.

Closure? That was a laugh. She would feel nothing but anguish and anger and . . . and guilt. Horrible, physically gut-wrenching guilt. After tonight, she didn't know if she could live with herself any longer.

And worst of all—she didn't know that she wanted to.

*　　*　　*

HE SAW THE gurney.

On the other side of the bars, in the corridor. With its leather straps stretching from one side to the other, its metal frame and thick padded wheels. Waiting for him.

Five guards and the warden flanked it, trying to look professional and relaxed. It was some small comfort to Ray to see that they weren't bringing it off. As often as they had done this of late, it still wasn't coming easy. They weren't jaded. Executions hadn't quite become mundane.

That was something, anyway.

"Ray," the warden said, stepping marginally closer to his cell, "we have some clothes we'd like you to put on. It's required, actually. That includes some . . . special underwear."

Ray glanced at the bundle of clothing in the warden's arms. The underwear looked like some kind of rubber diaper. Wasn't hard to figure what that was about. Simplified the cleanup afterward, no doubt. Made it more hygienic. Well, thank goodness for that, anyway. Wouldn't want to have a messy murder.

"Is this going to be a problem, Ray?" the warden asked. "Because if it is . . ." He glanced ever so slightly toward the guards. Because if it is, he didn't say, I've got five guards here who will put the clothes on you whether you like it or not.

"It's not a problem," Ray said. "Where's my rabbi?"

"He's waiting for you. Get the clothes on and . . . we'll take you there. I would also recommend that you go to the toilet now, Ray. Thoroughly. You'll be glad you did. You probably won't have a chance . . . later."

The cell door opened, and for a fleeting moment Ray fantasized about breaking out, knocking over the guards, grabbing the keys, and racing down the corridor. A few well-placed martial-arts kicks to the attendants and he'd be free. He'd hot-wire the prison van and race down the highway, so fast and furious no one could possibly catch him. He'd tear off into the night and soon, in no time at all, he'd be back in Carrie's arms, and she'd be holding him, and they'd tear off their clothes with animal urgency, caressing and pleasuring each other, letting the rest of the world fall away because there was nothing left but the two of them, just the two of them, together and close, forever and ever and . . .

"Take the clothes, Ray."

Silently, tears tumbling from his eyes, Ray did as he was told.

"Thank you," the warden said, looking away. "We appreciate your cooperation."

ANDREW FOWLER WAS the head man. He hadn't asked to be. He would've preferred to be the left-leg man, or the right-arm man, or anything other than the head man. But that's what he was, just the same.

Andrew was a member of the tie-down team in the unit of the Oklahoma State Penitentiary in McAlester that contained the death house. And tonight, they were on death watch. The five persons on the tie-down team were each assigned a part of the condemned man's body—the right arm, the left arm, the right leg, the left leg, and the head. It was their responsibility to strap that part to the gurney. When the warden gave the signal. When it was time for the condemned man to die.

And Andrew had the head. Which was good, in a way. A thin, wiry young man, Andrew was not renowned for his strength. Since the neck was so weak, the head was generally the easiest part to strap down. And the hardest to look at.

Andrew was a relatively new member of the tie-down team. He'd only been around a few months, only done four executions. He'd replaced Wilson Fox, a thirty-five-year veteran who'd done over forty executions—till he suffered a complete mental breakdown earlier this year.

That wasn't unusual for men on the tie-down team. In fact, Fox lasted a lot longer than most. Killing people—even people you knew were butchers and sadistic murderers—was an intense, traumatizing job. Most of them stayed calm and professional while they did their work. Stoic expressions and all that. But afterward, when they were alone, when Andrew was in bed in the dark talking to his wife, it was different. Killing shouldn't be anyone's job, he had told his wife more than once. Not anyone's.

But jobs were hard to come by in McAlester these days, and though his salary was modest, it was twice as much as any salary Andrew had ever had before in his life. If they wanted to have children—and they did—he couldn't afford to quit. Now that was ironic, wasn't it? So that he could bring new life into the world—he was helping kill people.

Andrew had gotten to know this one a little bit—a bad mistake. He tried to avoid all contact with the prisoners on death row. But Goldman had been in the library so often, and had been so courteous and . . . gentle, that Andrew had not been able to avoid talking to him. Learning what he was like. Learning to like him.

Which did not in any way mean Andrew thought he was innocent. He assumed all these guys were guilty. He had to. But it disturbed him—all these accounts of men being released from prison after DNA evidence provided proof of their innocence. It didn't happen all that often, statistically, his wife told him. But so what? If it happened once, it was too often. What if some of the people here were really innocent?

What if some of them were executed?

Goldman had asked him, during their last conversation, "Do you believe in the death penalty?" Andrew hadn't answered. He didn't really know, and frankly, it was beside the point. It wasn't about whether the death penalty was right and it wasn't about whether Goldman was guilty. It was about whether human beings, who screwed things up far more often than they got them right, had any business killing people. It was about whether killing ought to be a man's job. Any man's job.

He saw Goldman emerge from the back of the cell, fully dressed in the designated execution wardrobe. Now they would strap him down. They had learned that the moment when the condemned man saw the gurney for the first time was the hardest. That's when he knew it was really going to happen, that there was no escape. That was when he was most likely to panic, or God forbid try to make a break for it. So the tie-down team had learned to get it over with in advance, to strap him down before they got to the death chamber. It just made it easier, that was all. As easy as it could possibly be. To kill someone.

RAY FELT THE leather strap cinched tightly across his chest. He couldn't breathe. What was happening here? He wasn't supposed to die yet. Not yet!

"Can't breathe," he gasped.

"You'll get used to it," said one of the guards. Fowler, that was his name. Ray had talked to him a few times in the library. He seemed like a decent sort. How could he stand this work? How could he stand there calmly and help these people murder him?

"I didn't do it, you know," Ray said. Fowler looked away. Ray was embarrassed for himself. His eyes were streaming tears, like some six-year-old on a playground. Thank God he'd taken the warden's advice and gone to the bathroom, or he knew he'd have even more to be embarrassed about. The sick feeling inside his gut was spreading like cancer. How could anyone bear this?

"I didn't," Ray continued, choking. "I know you hear this all the time, but it's true. I didn't kill those people. I couldn't!"

Without a word, they wheeled him down the corridor. They didn't want to hear what he had to say. Pardons weren't within their control. There was nothing they could do to stop it. And nothing he could do. Except lie there, bound and immobilized, his face wet with terror, blubbering like an infant. Wondering how God could allow this to happen. Wondering how human beings could do this to one another.

And deep down, deep within him, desperate for it to be over. For the relief that would only come when the needle fell.

IN THE DEATH chamber, the phone rang.

The bell made Andrew jump a bit. He knew that would be the governor's office, calling to give them the go-ahead. A moment later, the warden, a large man with a short haircut and wire-frame glasses, put the receiver down and said quietly, "It's time."

Goldman's rabbi said some kind of prayer over him. Didn't sound like last rites, and he didn't hear any Hail Marys. Andrew didn't know anything about Judaism, but he knew what he'd be praying for if he were the one strapped to the table. Please God—get me out of here. And if You can't get me out of here, at least give me the strength to get through it without humiliating myself.

On a signal from the warden, the two members of the chemical team—that was the user-friendly name they gave the actual executioners—would each push one of the two buttons on the machine's control panel. Only one worked, and they didn't know which. That way, they didn't know for sure who had pressed the button that put the man to death. One of the buttons would cause stainless-steel plungers in the delivery module to be lowered into the chemical containers, which would force the poisons through the tubes and into Ray Goldman's vein—first, sodium pentothal, then pancuronium bromide, then potassium chloride—to put him to sleep, then stop his breathing, then stop his heart. A medical doctor and nurse stood in attendance with an EKG, but other than giving notice when the heart had stopped beating, they had little to do. There wasn't much the doctor could do, since the AMA didn't allow doctors to participate in executions. The nurse would find a vein for the IV. And that was important. Lethal injection was supposed to be a quick, humane method of execution, but Andrew was all too aware of the Texas case in which it took the executioners forty excruciating minutes to locate a viable vein on a condemned heroin abuser.

Ray Goldman didn't struggle, thank God. In the course of four executions, Andrew had seen about everything. One of the men actually told jokes before he was killed. One of them did finger exercises. What the hell he thought he was getting in shape for, Andrew couldn't imagine. All of them sweated, and all of them cried, eventually. Who wouldn't? How could they help it?

"CARRIE? ARE YOU out there? Are you there, honey?"

No one answered him, and with the tears clouding his eyes, he was having a hard time seeing anything. Was she here? Sure, she hadn't written in a while, hadn't come to visit for years, but he understood that. It was hard, waiting, hoping, when time after time their appeals failed and their prayers were squashed. But she was here with him now, even though he couldn't see her, right? She was, he was sure of it. She had to be.

"I don't want to die like this," Ray said, to no one in particular. "I don't want to die like a dog, strapped to a table. I don't want to die alone."

None of the guards would look at him. Even the rabbi didn't make eye contact.

"It isn't right!" Ray shouted. "I don't care what you call it. Killing people isn't right!" He twisted as much as he could, which wasn't much. He strained against the straps that bound him to the table. He realized now why they had pinned him down early.

He was helpless to stop this. But oddly enough, Ray felt a calm blanket him. It was over now. There was nothing he could do. Nothing anyone could do. And for once, that was okay. It was time for it to be over. Relief was on its way.

WHEN ANDREW TOOK his position behind Ray Goldman's head, the man looked up at him, right into his eyes and said, "Thank you." Andrew just about lost it. Just about lost it once and for all.

The nurse approached the table and slid the EKG pads under the neck of Goldman's shirt. She flipped a switch on the machine, and they could all hear the steady beep of Goldman's heartbeat. For now. She instructed Goldman to make a fist, swabbed the inside of his elbow with a cotton ball, and in a mercifully short period of time, managed to slip an IV needle into a vein. With two strips of surgical tape, she fixed the needle into place. For the moment, Goldman received a simple saline solution. But that wouldn't last long.

The preliminaries were complete. The warden removed the death warrant from his pocket and began to read. "Raymond Daniel Goldman, you have been found guilty of eight counts of murder in the first degree by the State of Oklahoma and have been sentenced to death by lethal injection." He paused, folded up the warrant. "Do you have anything you wish to say?"

The tranquillity that had embraced Goldman melted away. He began to wail. His voice was frenzied and desperate. "I did not kill all those people. I did not mutilate them. I couldn't!"

Andrew felt his hands trembling. Whether the man was lying or telling the truth, it was horrible. The tension in the room was all but unbearable.

"I love you, Carrie!" Goldman screamed. "I know you're out there! I love you!"

The warden removed his glasses, which was the signal to the executioners to let the chemicals flow. The chemical team looked at each other, then stepped closer to the machine and laid their hands on the buttons.

Goldman closed his eyes. The rabbi began muttering something in Hebrew.

"I didn't do it," Goldman said, gasping for air in great heaving gulps, his chest rocking. "I didn't. Tell them, Carrie. Tell them I didn't do it."

Andrew looked away.

And then the phone rang. The ring was jarring, strange. Everyone froze. The warden seemed confused for a moment, then he raced to the phone. "Stop!" he ordered. "Don't do anything."

"What's happening?" Goldman cried, his face wet with tears. "What's going on?"

The warden was on the phone for more than five minutes, most of that time just grunting or saying "I understand." Before the call ended, a clerk raced into the room waving an extra-long piece of paper.

The warden studied the document for a moment, then cleared his throat. "Mr. Goldman?"

Goldman was shaking so hard he could barely speak. "Yes, sir?"

"Mr. Goldman, it seems you have received a temporary reprieve. Thirty days, courtesy of the federal courts." He turned to his staff. "Gentlemen, you may stand down. Please unstrap Mr. Goldman and return him to his cell."

As soon as he was off the table, Goldman fell to his knees. "Thank you!" he cried out, his eyes closed, hands clasped. "Thank you!" His rabbi knelt beside him, and together they said another prayer.

Andrew felt a wave of relief so intense he could barely stand. He placed a hand against the wall to steady himself. When he finally felt he could walk reliably, he inched toward the warden.

"A reprieve from the federal courts, sir?" Andrew said. "How in the world did Goldman manage that?"

"He didn't." The warden was still staring at the paper, in particular scrutinizing a signature at the bottom of the page. "Do any of you boys know an attorney named Benjamin J. Kincaid?"

2

BEN TAPPED THE side of his head, just to make sure the old noggin was working properly. "You ate your shorts?"

"Right."

"Like . . . literally?"

"That's what I'm tellin' you."

"I mean, I've heard people use the expression. Eat my shorts. But I've never met anyone who actually did."

The young man on the other side of the acrylic barrier sighed. Clarence Brown was a long-legged white kid, almost seven feet tall, and Ben knew from the referral file that he was barely twenty years old. "Look, the cop pulled me over for no reason at all."

Ben glanced at the file. "His report says you were driving erratically."

"That's his story. I'm a good driver. Damn good driver."

"But the cop pulled you over."

"Right. And before he even gets out of his car, I can see him messin' with that breath thing, you know?"

Ben assumed he wasn't talking about Mentos. "You mean the Breathalyzer?"

"Yeah, that. He was gonna make me take that jive test. And I didn't wanna."

"Because you'd been drinking."

"Because what do I know what's gonna happen to me after I breathe into his little balloon? He says I fail, what do I do about it? Cops'll say anything to put a boy from the 'hood away."

"And so . . . you ate your shorts?"

"Well, I ripped 'em up first. Small pieces. Thought it would soak up the booze. So it wouldn't show up on my breath."

Another glance at the report. "The Breathalyzer showed you with a .12 alcohol concentration."

"Yeah, well, so it didn't work exactly like I planned."

"And the police officer charged you for attempted concealment of a crime and resisting arrest. In addition to drunk driving."

"You see what I'm tellin' you?" Brown leaned forward, practically pressing his nose against the barrier. "Them cops'll say anything to put me and my bros away. Anything!" He fell back with disgust. "So, what'ya say, counselor? Can you get me off? My main man says you're a miracle worker."

"The DA is offering to let you off with a fine, with one condition. License revoked. You can't drive for eighteen months."

"Eighteen months! No way. You gotta do somethin'!"

"Well, I can probably bounce the concealment charge. Maybe even the resisting arrest. But they've got you dead to rights on the drunk driving. Especially since you appear to confess everything in your statement."

Brown rose out of his chair. "What you talkin' about?"

"I'm talking about your statement. You gave the arresting officer a statement."

"I did no such thing."

"I have a copy of the officer's notes."

"I never did no statement, no way, no how. No, sir! I never gave them any kind of statement." He paused. "I just told the man what I did."

Ben blew out his cheeks. "Clarence, take the plea. I'm going to a party."

CHRISTINA McCALL SCRUTINIZED the business card in her hand. "You actually hand this out?"

The short man in the blue union suit nodded. "Clients, potential clients, everyone. Anyone who's in trouble with the police or likely to be. You wouldn't believe how effective it is. I've saved lives with that card."

Christina scrutinized it carefully. It was thicker than most cards because it had a shimmering 3-D surface done up in swirling psychedelic colors. Beneath the colors, set out in boldface capital letters, were four pithy statements stacked one atop the other: DON'T SAY ANYTHING. DON'T CONSENT TO A SEARCH. THE POLICE ARE NOT YOUR FRIENDS. YOU NEED A GOOD LAWYER.

She flipped the card over. In the center, above the address, it read: DARRYL COOKE. A GOOD LAWYER.

"And this gets you business?"

"Like you wouldn't believe. Oh—excuse me, Chris," Cooke said, already moving away. "I promised Charlton Colby a word."

Which was his way of saying he'd spotted someone more important to talk
to. Christina supposed she shouldn't fault him; he was just networking, like
everyone else here at the Tulsa County Bar reception. In these days of cutthroat law practice, lawyers stealing clients from one another, big firms locking
up the top corporate work, lawyers had to scurry for scraps and morsels. Any
amount of kowtowing could be justified if it led to work. Preferably with a
large profitable law firm.

Christina, on the other hand, had already been with a large profitable law
firm. And hated it. She didn't want to switch; she just wanted to see Ben start
making some money for a change. He was a fine, hardworking attorney with
a growing reputation. But as a result of a bad incident with a big firm early
in his career, his connections to the local power brokers were severely con-
strained. And his social skills were pitiful. The fact that Ben constantly took
time-consuming cases for people who couldn't or wouldn't pay didn't help
much, either. Christina had insisted that Ben attend this reception, in a desperate attempt to increase his interactivity in the legal community. This was
supposed to be his assignment, not hers. So where was he?

"Christina! Is it really you?"

She heard the voice and winced. Ohmigod. Not Alvin Hager. Anything
but Alvin Hager.

"Alvin Hager," the man said, thrusting his hand into her abdomen. "How
the hell have you been?"

She forced a smile. Alvin had been a young associate at Raven, Tucker &
Tubb back when she'd been a legal assistant there. He'd had a big crush on
her—the drooling puppy-dog kind. He was basically a nerd, but it seemed to
her at times that pretty much all lawyers were, so she tried not to hold it
against him.

"Christina, I can't tell you how good it is to see you! I'm just—I'm over-
whelmed!" As if he couldn't restrain himself, he threw his arms around her and
enveloped her in a tremendous bear hug. His faux mustache—too few whis-
kers thickened with some sort of gel—brushed against her cheek. "How did
we ever lose track?"

"Well, these things happen. So how are you?"

"Oh . . . I'm slowly recovering," he said, making Christina immediately
wish she hadn't asked. "I guess you probably heard—Candy and I gave up the
ghost. Called it quits. After a year and a half of marriage, no less."

Christina shook her head. "That long."

"Yeah, sad, isn't it? But I'm getting past the anger and, to tell you the
truth, I'm rather relieved. I feel like a free man again. Like I've been reprieved

from a life sentence. How about you?" he added, jabbing her in the ribs. "Still single? I hope, I hope?"

This would be a good time to fictionalize a lesbian relationship with a first cousin, Christina mused, but she couldn't bring herself to do it. "Yes, still single."

"And still in the law game?"

"Yes. I work with Ben Kincaid."

Hager slapped himself on the forehead. "Oh, my God, no! You're kidding, right?"

"No . . ."

"Not him! Not that chump we booted out of the firm!"

"The one and only."

"Oh, you poor dear. I had no idea! I mean, I knew you left the firm at the same time, but I never dreamed you'd still be with him after all these years."

Christina tried not to bristle. "I like working with Ben. He's a good attorney."

"Oh, but Christina—this will never do. I know times are tough for legal assistants, but someone with your skills—"

"Actually, Alvin, I'm a lawyer now."

For the first time, Hager missed a beat. "You're—what? A lawyer?"

Did her newfound status threaten him? Christina wondered. Destroy some illusion he had of overwhelming the vulnerable legal assistant with his well-educated awesomeness? "And I like it where I am," she continued. "Ben and I have handled some major cases. And won. We've helped innocent people avoid unjust charges—"

"Criminal law?" He made a gagging face. "Oh, Christina—it's just too horrible!"

Christina felt her blood pressure rising. "I like what I'm doing."

"But Christina—a girl with your smarts could work anywhere. I bet I could get you back in with Raven."

"I'd sooner die."

"Then one of the other major firms. I'm a partner now, you know. I have a lot of connections. I could put in a good word."

Christina hesitated. She *had* come to network, after all. But the thought of leaving Ben and joining some big firm just didn't appeal. "No thanks."

Alvin's brow wrinkled. "What's happened to you? The Christina I knew was a serious career woman. She wouldn't pass on a golden opportunity to move herself up in the world. Is he paying you that much?"

Christina suppressed a laugh. "No, that isn't it."

"Have you two got some kind of . . . thing going?"

"We're just good friends."

Hager spread his arms wide. "Then what?"

"I just—I—" What was she trying to say, anyway? Why *had* she stuck with Ben all this time? Why wasn't she interested in moving onward and upward? She found herself utterly unable to explain it rationally. Was that because it wasn't rational? "I like what I'm doing, Alvin. Where I'm doing it. I'm the person I want to be."

Hager took a step back. "That's fine. Don't get defensive on me. Just trying to help." He winked. "So where is this paragon of lawyering, anyway?"

She scanned the room. "There he is! I wonder how long he's been here. Sorry, Alvin. Must dash." She quickly crossed the room and grabbed Ben's arm. "Thank goodness you're here. I was trapped with Alvin Hager, of all people. Have you met anyone here?"

"I've met lots of people," Ben replied. "Most of them annoying."

"Yeah, well, you know what they say. Ninety-nine percent of the lawyers give the rest a bad name. But this soiree isn't restricted to lawyers, you know. There are some real people here, too. All kinds of big shots. Potential clients."

"Like who?"

Christina tugged her head to one side. "See the guy in the gray? Walt Helmerich, oil kingpin. The man he's talking to? Chester Cadieux. Chairman of QuikTrip. I daresay he's worth a few bucks." She adjusted her gaze slightly to a strong-looking man with silver hair. "Robert Lorton. *Tulsa World.* Gordona Duca. Real estate. Major wheeler-dealer."

"Who's the guy they're talking to? The redhead."

Christina rolled her eyes. "Ben! Don't you know anyone? He's the most prominent one in the bunch."

"You're just saying that because he has red hair."

"I'm saying it because it's true. He could buy and sell the lot of them."

"That kid? He's what? Thirty?"

"He's Peter Rothko, founder of the Burger Bliss fast-food chain."

"He looks more like the top fry cook."

"He owns the whole outfit. He's a billionaire. Fortune 500. And insanely handsome. He's got it all." Her gaze softened. "Generally considered to be Tulsa's most eligible bachelor."

Ben blinked. "I thought I was Tulsa's most eligible bachelor."

"But of course you are. What was I thinking?"

Without warning, Ben lunged sideways and ducked behind her. "Hide me!"

"What on—?" Christina turned her gaze in the other direction. "Oh."

Not ten feet from them, an attractive man in his early fifties strolled across the room jingling a glass. Some dark liquor or other, straight up. "Derek."

"Damn right. Don't move!"

"Ben . . . doesn't this strike you as just a wee bit juvenile?"

"I don't care if it is," he hissed. "The man hates me, and the feeling is mutual. I don't want to have a big scene."

"You're overreacting."

"Easy for you to say. You didn't have to work under him back at Raven."

"Actually, I did."

"Well, he didn't fire you. You didn't watch him become a federal judge just so he could humiliate you at every possible opportunity."

"If you'll recall, Ben, I was more than a little bit interested in that first trial you had before Judge Derek myself."

"The man is venal, arrogant, and vicious," Ben continued. "And he hates me. Just being in the same room with him gives me the shakes. I'm leaving."

"Ben, you're being ridiculous!"

"I don't care if I am. This is a waste of time, anyway. I'm not the networking type."

"Ben. I insist that you stay."

"Insist away. Unless you're packing handcuffs, I'm outta here."

"Ben, as your partner, I demand that you stay put!"

"Oh, look! Alvin is coming back."

Christina did an abrupt about-face. "Feets, do your stuff!"

3

WHEN BEN PASSED through the front doors to his office, he found his staff engaged in a heated discussion.

"That's the craziest thing I've ever heard," said Jones, the office manager. "Everyone knows it was the Cubans. It was payback time."

"Would you listen to me for just one minute?" Loving said. "I been readin' about this for twenty years. It was the air force, man. They had a deal with the grays and they had to protect it."

"Grays? As in space aliens?" Christina snickered. "I think it was the mob. Who else could bring off a hit like that?"

"You're all nuts." Jones pivoted around. "What do you think, Ben? Who killed JFK?"

Ben spread his arms. "Could it be . . . Lee Harvey Oswald?"

Jones rolled his eyes. Loving slapped his forehead. "Jeez, Ben. You are so gullible."

"You're right," he replied. "I'll believe anything."

"I got some stuff you could read on this," said Loving, their fridge-size investigator and resident conspiracy buff. "I could get it for you."

"Business is slow," Ben answered, "but, happily, not that slow." He paused. Something in here smelled. "Christina, did you have the office fumigated again?"

"Yes. I found a spider."

"Only one?"

"He was a monster."

" 'Bout the size of my pinkie nail," Jones muttered.

"Even the little ones can be deadly," she shot back.

"Christina, you've got to stop. All this pesticide is disgusting. Plus it's bankrupting us."

"Not that that takes much," Jones said sotto voce.

"I'm sorry, Ben, but I can't help it. I hate spiders." She shuddered. "They totally creep me out."

Well, Ben thought philosophically, Christina was a lot tougher than he was about most things. It was nice to know she had at least one weakness. "Anything going on here?"

"As a matter of fact, yes," Christina answered. "You've got someone waiting for you in your office. A young woman."

"Hey, hey, hey, Skipper," Loving said, winking. "You got a little action goin'?"

"Not to my knowledge. Did you interview her, Christina?"

"I tried. She wants to talk to you."

Ben's head tilted slightly. That was odd. Christina was the empathetic one. Usually clients preferred to spill their guts to her. "Do you know who she is?"

"Oh, yes. I knew who she was the moment she came through the door. You will, too." She looked at him levelly. "And you won't believe it."

With an invitation like that, how could he resist? "Let's do it."

Ben started toward his office, Christina close behind. He stopped at the third door on the right and pushed it open.

After he finished gaping, he stepped inside. Christina was right. He couldn't believe it.

The cane leaning against her chair was a sure tip, not that Ben needed one. It hadn't been that long, and she hadn't changed that much.

"Miss Faulkner," Ben said, offering her his hand. "This is a surprise."

"I'll bet it is," she said, taking it. "And please call me Erin." She cast a glance around Ben's sparsely decorated office. "Did you ever consider maybe watering your plants?"

"Why? They're all dead." He dropped his briefcase on the desktop. Christina sat in one of the outer chairs. "Erin, is this visit about a new matter, or . . . the previous one?"

"The same one, I'm afraid." Her eyes didn't make contact with his. "My family . . ."

Ben nodded. "Then I have to tell you, before you say anything, that technically anyway, Ray Goldman's appeal is still active and I'm representing him."

"I know that."

She looked good, Ben thought, with close-cropped dark hair and a tight-fitting sweater skirt. She had been a bit pudgy as a teenager, but judging by appearances, that baby fat was long gone. "So the prosecutors probably wouldn't want me talking to you. At least not outside their presence."

"Are we breaking any rules?"

"Christina?"

Christina edged forward. "Are you personally represented by counsel, Erin?"

"No, I'm not."

"Then we're not breaking any rules. But the prosecutors still wouldn't like it."

"Frankly, I don't give a damn what the prosecutors like."

Ben's eyebrows rose. This was certainly a new attitude from the DA's star witness. And the sole survivor of the tragedy. "Okay. How can I help you?"

"You got Goldman's execution stayed, right? I know—I was there."

Ben's heart sank. Is that why she had come—to chew him out for stopping the wheels of justice? "True, but that's only temporary. We applied for federal habeas corpus review, but due to an unusually busy docket, the court hadn't set a hearing. That's why we got an eleventh-hour stay. But that won't happen again. And a hearing has been set, in about a week."

"What are you planning to say at the hearing?"

Ben pondered whether to answer the question. He didn't normally brief prosecution witnesses on his case strategy. But for some reason, he thought he should tell her the truth. "Frankly, we don't know. Getting a prisoner released on habeas corpus is pitifully rare. One of the most common grounds—which isn't at all common—is incompetence of counsel at trial. I can hardly argue that the trial counsel was incompetent, since I was the trial counsel. Someone else could make the argument, though. Which is why I was looking for a new lawyer to take the case."

"I was at that trial every day," Erin said, and Ben could see in her eyes that she was returning to that time, a place he suspected she did not like to go. "I don't recall you being incompetent. In fact, I remember thinking if I was ever in trouble, you were the one I'd hire to get me out."

"I appreciate that. But there's no such thing as a perfect trial, and every trial attorney makes mistakes. If there's an argument to be made, we need to get someone in who can make it."

There was a long silence. Ben could tell Erin was thinking, running something through her head. Unless he missed his guess, there was something she wanted to tell him. She just hadn't figured out how to say it yet.

"I—" She started, then stopped, then tried it again. "I—would like to help. If I could."

Christina's brow creased. "You want to help us—with Ray Goldman's appeal?"

"Yes. If possible. I would."

Ben stared at her, unsure what to say. "Forgive us if we seem taken aback, Erin, but—you were the principal prosecution witness at the trial. The only one who mattered, really. To be quite honest, I thought we were winning. Until you took the stand."

"Everyone thought so," Christina added. "Erin, your testimony is what got Ray convicted. More than that. It's why he got the death penalty."

All at once, Erin crumbled forward. Her head fell into her hands. "I know," she said, barely audibly. "I know that."

Ben and Christina looked at one another. This was too strange, almost surreal. What was going on?

Christina inched forward and gently laid a hand on the woman's back. "I'm sorry, Erin. I wasn't trying to induce a guilt trip. I was just stating a fact. About your testimony, I mean."

Her chest heaved. "That's why it hurts so much."

"I—I'm afraid I don't understand. You told the jury what you saw and heard. Why does that hurt?"

"Because it was all a lie." She brushed the tears from her face and pressed against the arms of the chair, trying to steady herself. "Every word of it. A tremendous lie."

Ben was so stunned he could barely speak. "You—didn't really see him?"

"I wasn't sure what I saw." Her broken voice seemed part anger, part anguish. "I wasn't sure about anything. The killer wore a ski mask, remember? I couldn't tell what he looked like. I did hear his voice, and when I heard Goldman's voice in the lineup, I thought maybe it was the killer's voice. But I couldn't be certain."

"Then why—"

"The DA." Her lips stiffened as the letters slipped out of her mouth. "He pushed me. Pressured me. He was desperate to win that case. There had been so much publicity, you remember. He couldn't afford to lose. He was certain Goldman was guilty and he was willing to do almost anything to convict him. I was only fifteen years old and barely thinking straight. Easy for him to manipulate."

Ben didn't argue with her. He knew most district attorneys were honest lawyers who played it straight, but some of his subsequent experiences with Jack Bullock proved the man was willing to break rules to convict someone he believed guilty. "So he told you to lie?"

"Oh, he never said it like that. He just pushed. Pushed and pushed and never let up. Told me how important my testimony was. How the jury had to hear it from me. How I had to sound sure of what I was saying. That my whole family was counting on me. That I was the only one left, and it was up to me to make sure the man who committed this atrocity didn't live to do it again. He—" She turned her head, fighting back the tears. "He showed me pictures. Of them, I mean. Of what the killer did to them. So I'd see how important this was."

Ben felt as if someone had slipped a dull knife inside his heart. Small wonder Erin was traumatized—to be put through so much when she was only fifteen.

"So I did what he said," Erin continued, her voice trembling. "I testified. I told them I was certain." She paused. "But I wasn't."

Ben stared dumbly across the desk as Christina tried to comfort Erin. He had no illusions about what had happened at that trial. It was her testimony— the certainty of her testimony—that had convicted Ray Goldman. But for that, they would not have lost. And Ray would not have spent the last seven years on death row.

"You should talk to the DA," Ben said finally. "Tell him what you've told us."

"But—if I do that, won't they charge me with perjury?"

"I think it's unlikely. You were a crime victim, and a juvenile. And the prosecutors encouraged you. But I can't rule it out."

"I don't want to go to prison. And I don't want to see that district attorney. I can't face that man again. He'll try to shut me up."

"Well, Bullock isn't there anymore, but . . ." But other DAs were. And since her recantation meant they would have no legitimate conviction on one of the worst homicide sprees in Tulsa history, they had plenty of motivation to silence or discredit her.

If this mess was going to be fixed, it would have to be a defense attorney who did it.

"We'll need you to swear out an affidavit," Ben said quietly. "And the judge will want to hear from you in person. You'll be examined—and cross-examined."

"Whatever. Whatever it takes. Just stop this. Don't let it go on any longer." She drew herself up and tried to steady her voice. "I've been tearing myself apart. I've talked to everyone—my preacher, my friends, my boyfriend, my coworkers—everyone I know. But no one can help. When I thought Goldman was going to be executed, I almost died myself. That's when I made up my mind. That I had to talk to you."

Christina wrapped her arms around the young woman. A fresh wave of tears cascaded forth, but Erin continued to speak in the same voice tinged with despair. "I can't bear it any longer. I don't want that man's death on my conscience forever, damning my soul. I want it to be over." She looked up at Ben, her eyes wide and watery. "Please help me, Mr. Kincaid. Please."

"DO YOU BELIEVE her?" Christina asked, after Ben returned from escorting Erin to her car.

"Of course I believe her. Didn't you see her face?"

"I saw . . . a very disturbed woman."

Ben loosened his tie and flopped down behind his desk. "She's been carrying that guilt around for seven years."

"I agree that she's traumatized by guilt. But that doesn't necessarily mean she's telling the truth."

Ben's forehead creased. If this had come from anyone but Christina, he would find it laughable. But he knew Christina's instincts about people were sound—much better than his own, generally. "What do you mean?"

"She feels responsible for Ray's imminent execution."

"So? She is."

"A lot of people later come to regret the part they played in a case that leads to the death penalty. Witnesses, jurors, judges—even lawyers."

"What's your point?"

"She may be telling us she lied to stop the execution. Regardless of whether she thinks Ray is guilty."

"I don't believe that for a minute."

Christina sat on the edge of Ben's desk. "What if she's been born again? She said she'd been talking to a preacher. She said she worried about her soul being damned."

"I think you're stretching."

"Am I? She could've had a religious conversion experience, come to think of the death penalty as murder, and regretted her part in causing a man's death."

Ben shook his head vigorously. "I saw that woman's eyes, Christina. The only cause of her guilt is the fact that she lied on the witness stand."

"Are you sure about that? Or do you just want to be sure of it?"

"You're losing me."

"I know you consider the Goldman case your greatest failure. And I know you'd grab at anything to get him off death row."

"That's my job. Her word is good enough for me."

"It won't be enough for the judge."

"What do you mean?"

"I mean, the prosecutors will make all the same arguments I have. And no judge is going to overturn a jury verdict in a high-profile case unless he has something more than a recanting witness."

Ben frowned. "You're probably right about that."

"And there's more to consider. I know why you haven't been able to find anyone to take over Ray's case. The funding for his defense ran out a long time ago."

Ben averted his eyes. That was the problem with Christina—she always knew what was going on. All too well.

"Jones will have a heart attack if you launch a major initiative without someone to pay the bills."

"That much is certain."

"So what are you going to do?"

"I don't know." Ben rose. "Before I make that decision, there's someone else I need to consult. Someone whose opinion is a hell of a lot more important than mine."

CHAPTER

4

"I don't think that's wise," Major Mike Morelli said as two uniforms buckled his bulletproof vest and wired him for sound. "That's a dangerous man in there."

"Tell me something I don't know," Sergeant Hoppes shot back. "We're talking about a nutcase holed up in a fast-food restaurant holding twenty people at gunpoint."

"What I'm saying is, we have to be careful. When the SOT boys show up, keep them out of sight. Behind the perimeter."

"And what *I'm* saying is, let's get them right up in the creep's face. Give him something to worry about."

"He's already on the brink. And he has hostages!"

"All the more reason. We'll show him who's boss. Show him how quickly he'll be dead if he tries anything. He'll back down."

"Maybe. Or maybe he wants to die. Maybe he'll shoot everyone in sight."

"Sorry, Mike, but I disagree. We do it my way."

Mike grabbed his arm. "Excuse me? You're overruling me?"

"I'm the SOT team leader, Mike. This is my field of expertise."

"Nonetheless—"

"Mike, you're a homicide detective."

"I don't care if I'm the goddamn county dogcatcher. I'm a major, you're a sergeant. And that means I call the shots!"

Hoppes's eyes burned like fire. A million retorts must've run through his brain, but in the end, he kept his cool. "You're only here by accident, Mike."

"Consider yourself relieved, Tom."

Hoppes's lips tightened.

"You'll be my number two. But I'm in charge."

Hoppes bit back whatever he was thinking. "As you say, *Major*. We'll be in position behind the perimeter. Just in case you need us."

Mike watched Hoppes back off, his fists tightly clenched. There'd be hell to pay when they all got back to headquarters. But he had to do what he thought best. Hoppes was a superb marksman, and he knew SOT maneuvers better than anyone on earth. But his understanding of human nature was much less sure. And as a tactician, he sucked.

Not that that meant Mike had to take over. When would he learn to stop thrusting himself into these situations? He was too old and too smart to keep volunteering for trouble. But he happened to be in the south Tulsa neighborhood, on his way back from interviewing a potential witness, when the call came in about the hostage situation at the local Burger Bliss. And so he sped to it and offered Hoppes his assistance. And one thing led to another . . .

He made his way to the front lines, where Hoppes had been broadcasting through an electronic bullhorn, trying to persuade the man inside to give himself up, without luck. He took the bullhorn.

"Listen to me." Mike was startled to hear the electronics give his voice a mechanical, almost eerie, tone. Small wonder no one ever responded well to it. "My name is Mike Morelli. I'm a policeman. I want to negotiate with you. I assume there must be something you want or you wouldn't be doing this. Tell me what it is, and I'll do everything I can to make it happen. All I ask is that you don't hurt anyone. If you don't hurt anyone, no one will hurt you. You have my word on that. May I come in?"

Mike lowered the bullhorn and waited. And waited. Had the wild man with the gun agreed? Had he even heard?

Mike heard a groan of disgust from Hoppes. He tried again. "I am not armed. No gun, no knife, no nothing. You have my word. I'll come in naked, if it will make you more comfortable. I will not harm you. I just want to talk. May I come in? Please?" He waited another few seconds. No response. *"Please."*

A moment later, the side entrance to the Burger Bliss opened. An elderly woman who appeared to be absolutely terrified pushed her head through the door. "He says you can come in."

It worked! He was halfway home.

Now all he had to do was get those people out of there safely, Mike told himself. And not get killed in the process.

He slowly approached the side door, talking quietly into the microphone buried under his bulletproof vest.

"I'm going inside. When the SOT team arrives, put them into position, but keep them out of sight. I don't want to agitate the gunman."

"Yes sir, *Major*," Hoppes snapped back.

Mike kept moving. "There doesn't seem to be any resistance. Maybe he's ready to give up."

Hoppes's voice crackled in Mike's earpiece. "Maybe he's going to shoot your sorry butt the second you come through the door."

A cheery thought. Mike heard a squeal of Jeep tires somewhere behind him. The SOT team had arrived, no doubt. In a few minutes, they would be armed with sniper rifles and waiting for a clear shot. If he was going to end this mess without bloodshed, he was going to have to move quickly.

Inside, the decor and layout looked pretty much like any other fast-food restaurant, with the standard bright plastic tabletops and the efficient order counter McDonald's had pioneered years ago. Most of the hostages sat at the tables, but a few of the employees were still behind the counter. As a whole, the hostages were staying admirably calm. A few were crying, trembling, worried that this inexpensive meal would be their last. The kids were the worst. Some of them were toddlers. They couldn't possibly comprehend what was happening or why. They just knew there was a man with a gun. And they were terrified.

He heard Hoppes barking in his ear. "Can you see him? Are you in a position to shoot him?"

"No," Mike murmured. "I don't have a weapon."

"You—what? Why in hell not?"

"Because I gave him my word."

The man with the gun had barricaded himself between two large trash receptacles. His gun was out and his hand was shaking. He was a thin, long-haired man. Couldn't be more than twenty. He was wearing a solid black T-shirt and had a few scruffy hairs on his chin passing for a goatee. He was drenched in sweat. His eyes were red and worried; they never seemed to stay in one place for more than a second.

"My name's Mike." He kept a good ten feet away. "What's yours?"

The young man whipped around, pointing his gun in Mike's direction. "Why do you want to know my name?"

Mike tried to keep his voice even. This guy was worse than on edge. He was already in the midst of a major meltdown. "No reason. Just so I know what to call you."

"You don't need to know my name!"

"All right. Then I'll just make one up. How about . . . Elmer?"

"That's a stupid name!" the kid shouted, waving his gun around. "Are you making fun of me?"

"Of course not. How about . . . Bob?"

The young man inhaled deep and long, like a diver with a bad case of the bends. "I can live with that."

Great. They'd made progress. "What is it you want, Bob?"

"I want my goddamn job back, that's what I want."

Mike's lips parted. "You used to work here?"

"Damn straight. For almost two years. Till that son-of-a-bitch manager fired me. He said I was screwing around, not getting my work done. Made other people carry the slack. But he was full of it!" Watching the gun bob and weave in all directions made Mike sick, but there was nothing he could do about it at present. "I worked hard. Every day, hard. Not like some manager who sits on his fat ass and watches other people work. I didn't deserve to lose my job. And I want it back!"

And you thought the smart way to get it would be to run in with a gun and take hostages? Was he utterly insane? Or was Mike's friend Ben's theory right—that people of the modern world suffer from a societal illness more endemic than the Black Plague. Terminal stupidity.

"So, Bob . . . if I was able to get your job back, would you stand down? Let these nice people go?"

"Why should I?"

"Well . . . they didn't take your job. You have no grudge against them. Why don't we let some of them go. Like maybe the children?" Out the corner of his eye, through the windows that surrounded the restaurant on three sides, Mike spotted the SOT snipers positioning themselves. Damn Hoppes, anyway! Why didn't he keep them out of sight? Those rifles had a thousand-foot range. Why did they have to get right under the man's nose?

"I guess that'd be all right. But no tricks."

"I promise you, Bob. No tricks. Let's start with those two over by the door, okay?"

The children didn't want to leave their parents. Mom and Dad both pushed them toward the door, but they wouldn't go.

Mike bit down on his lower lip. "Maybe if I escorted them. Okay?"

"All right, but I'll be—*damn!*"

Mike knew what had happened. As Bob turned his head to look at the children, he'd spotted a khaki-clad SOT officer positioning himself by the south entrance.

"Bob, listen to me. Those men will not harm you."

"Then why are they here?" He was bouncing back and forth, bellowing. *"Why are they here?"*

"They're just trying to protect everyone. They won't hurt you."

"Make them go away! Make them go away!"

Mike spoke into his wire. "Hoppes! What the hell are you doing?"

"Taking charge, Morelli."

"Hoppes, I am ordering—"

"Screw you."

"I am your commanding officer—"

"You are a goddamn hostage! Out of commission. Therefore, I am forced to take over."

"Make 'em go away," Bob shouted, waving his gun every which way at once. "Make them stop or I'm gonna kill someone!"

"Back off!" Mike shouted into the wire.

The first shot cracked through the glass window on the south side. Everyone in the restaurant hit the floor, including Bob. Several screamed as panic spread through the room. Men and women and children cried and clutched at one another. An elderly man in the rear began reciting the Lord's Prayer.

The next shot came from the east. It ricocheted off one of the trash receptacles. Close, but not close enough to do any good.

The third shot came from the south again, and a split second after Mike heard the report, he heard Bob cry out in pain. He'd been hit—but not incapacitated.

Bob pushed himself back to his feet, bleeding from his right leg. "You lying sons of bitches! You're just like all the others. Just like all the others!"

He raised his gun and fired, spinning around in a circle. Mike dove behind the condiments counter and hugged the tile floor. The gunfire continued to rain down all around them.

Mike crawled around the edge of the table area to see what was happening. Bob had snatched up a baby with his right arm and held him close against his head to shield himself. He wrapped his gun arm around the neck of the baby's mother. With hostages flanking him on both sides, it would be all but impossible for the snipers to get a clear shot.

"Where are you?" Bob shouted. "You lied to me! You told me they wouldn't hurt me!"

I was misinformed, Mike thought ruefully.

"Where are you, you lying bastard?"

Bob whirled around the restaurant, dragging the mother and baby with him. The baby was crying; the mother was screaming. None of it fazed him.

The situation had gone from grim to dire. Ben knew the snipers wouldn't shoot as long as he was moving and had hostages all around him. The brick walls beneath the windows prevented them from shooting below the chest, and a head shot, even if it hit Bob first, could easily travel on to one of the hostages.

"What's happening in there?" Hoppes was shouting into Mike's earpiece. "Fill me in!"

Mike didn't say a word. He couldn't take the risk.

"You can't hide from me!" Bob cried.

Maybe not, Mike thought, but I can damn sure try. He crawled to the other end of the condiment counter, hoping he could flank Bob and get behind him.

"Can you get him to drop the hostages?" Hoppes's voice crackled. "Or force him closer to the windows?"

"No," Mike whispered. "I can't."

"What do you want us to do?"

"Just stay put and keep your men out of sight. There's still a chance I can—"

"All right," Bob shouted, "you won't show yourself? Fine. I'll kill someone else!"

Mike cried out, "No!" But it was too late. A second later, the gun fired and the elderly woman who had opened the door for him crumpled to the floor.

"What's going on?" Hoppes asked. "What should I do?"

"Take him out," Mike growled.

"Still won't show yourself?" Bob said. "Fine. Here comes victim number two!"

"We can't get a clear shot," Hoppes said.

Mike sprang forward, snatching the baby away and shoving the mother to the floor. "Now!" he barked.

A nanosecond later, five rifles fired at once. Three of the bullets hit Bob, making him twitch like a dissected frog. The mother crawled to safety, and as soon as she did, bullets rained down on Bob. He looked like a wind sock caught in a tornado. He was torn one way then another, twitching as if suffering from some uncontrollable spasm, until finally, mercifully, his body crumpled lifelessly to the floor.

"All clear?" Hoppes asked.

"All clear," Mike whispered back. "Get some medics in here."

Mike returned the baby to its mother and looked for the people who were hurt. There were many. Way too many. At least five people injured, maybe fatally. And the woman by the door was definitely dead.

What a stupid, pointless waste. This could've been handled bloodlessly, Mike was sure of it. But instead, blood was everywhere. All over everything. Including him.

It was a tragedy, a stupid loss of life. And he knew what would happen once Chief Blackwell got wind of this. Worse, once the press got wind of it. Every move, every action he had taken would be scrutinized. Every judgment call would be questioned. And when the investigation was over, someone would have to pay.

And he had a pretty good idea who it would be.

CHAPTER

5

"How often do you have sexual feelings?"

"I do not have . . . sexual feelings."

"None at all?"

"Not anymore."

"Not even occasionally?"

"Of course not. You know why."

"Still, there must be something."

"Perhaps once. Several months ago. While I slept."

"What were you dreaming about?"

"I don't remember."

Gabriel Aravena hated these sessions. He'd be willing to do anything to avoid them—anything except break parole, that is. Life was full of unpleasantness. He didn't enjoy his visits with his parole officer. He didn't enjoy his work. But he despised his sessions with the psychiatrist.

Dr. Hayley Bennett was a thin, auburn-haired, angular woman. She wore black-rimmed glasses although Aravena suspected she didn't really need them. More a fashion statement, he thought, or a protective barrier between herself and her patients.

He didn't know why he hated these sessions so. Objectively, she should have been his favorite. She was much easier to look at than his PA, and he didn't sense the wariness, the suspicion, he did there. Which was ironic, in a way. Given all he had done, the woman should be the one who wanted the least to do with him.

"Have you been taking the medication?" Dr. Bennett asked, crossing her legs in a manner that, at another time, he might have considered provocative.

"Do I have a choice?" A stupid question. He got a shot once a week. That was an express condition of his early release.

"Any more side effects?"

"My breasts continue to enlarge," he said, trying not to flush. It was deeply embarrassing, watching himself swell up like a woman.

"That's a common side effect of Depo-Provera," Dr. Bennett explained. "It's a hormone-altering medication. But you know that already, don't you?"

He nodded. He knew all about Depo. He knew it was a trade name for a generic drug called medroxyprogesterone acetate. He knew it was essentially an artificial simulation of the female hormone progesterone which, when injected into men, often acted as a hormone inhibitor. Among other things. It diminished the libido. Recidivism rates for sex offenders taking Depo were less than ten percent. He knew all about it.

He knew what it really did, too. It castrated him. Chemical castration. It made his head fuzzy, messed with his vision, and sucked away his sex drive. That was the price he was paying. For now, anyway.

"Anything else?"

"My hair is falling out. Not just on my head. And I feel tired all the time. Sluggish."

"I'm afraid those are also common side effects."

"Then why did you ask?" Stay calm, he told himself. You don't want to blow it. Not when you're so close.

"There's a lot about this drug we don't know. That's why we're conducting these trials. You know that."

He nodded. He'd been briefed in detail, before he signed the release forms. As if he had a choice. If it would've gotten him out of that hellhole, he'd have agreed to a real castration. He would be their little lab rat. He'd let them shoot drugs into his body that turned him into a woman.

"How is your work going?"

"Very nicely, thank you. I manage now, you know."

"Excuse me?"

"I—I'm the manager." Aravena had been in the States so long he had lost most traces of broken English. But he still occasionally had trouble coming up with the right word.

"That's wonderful, Gabriel. I know some people over at FastTrak; they won't make just anyone a manager."

No, and they won't pay them anything, either. But they are one of the few places that would hire a man with a record. Especially a sex crimes record.

"And at home? Any new developments?"

"No." What did she expect? That he would have a girlfriend? Not likely. Not while he was on this drug.

"I know your father is deceased. Have you had any contact with your mother?"

"No. I think I'm better off . . . without contact with my mother. And she lives very far away."

Bennett nodded. "Well, perhaps you're right." Aravena watched as she opened the file in her lap to the page covering Aravena's childhood. A moment later, her face paled. How is it possible that a mother could do such things? she must be thinking. And what hideous effect must that have had on her poor, defenseless son?

"You know, Gabriel . . . Depo-Provera suppresses sex drive. But it doesn't eliminate it. Nothing does."

Aravena nodded. Even physically castrated men sometimes committed rape. He'd known one, back in the penitentiary.

"And of course, it's well-established that most sex crimes aren't about sex, anyway. They're about anger. About power. Control." She paused, as if waiting for an answer to a question she hadn't asked.

"I feel very contented," Aravena said, and indeed, in many respects he was not lying. "I feel no anger toward anyone." Except you, you testicle-chewing bitch. You and everyone like you.

"That's good, Gabriel. That's very good." She flipped through a few more pages in her file. "Tell me. Does your work at FastTrak bring you into contact with many children?"

"Some."

"Young girls?"

Back to that, are we? "A few. After school mostly."

"Is that a problem?"

Aravena tried to seem sincere. "I am no longer attracted to young girls. I don't know that I ever was. That was just . . . just . . . I don't know what it was. But it will never happen again."

"You know what, Gabriel? I believe you. I really do. Do you know how long it is until your parole maintenance period ends?"

"Six days."

"Yes. And then you'll be a free man again. Of course, a condition of your release is that you continue to take the medication."

"I understand that." But I also know that you will cease to check. I will no longer be injected by an officer of the state.

"How old are you, Gabriel?" As if she didn't have that information in her file.

"I'm thirty-seven."

Bennett smiled. "You have your entire life ahead of you. I hope you'll make the most of it."

"I intend to." Indeed he did.

"Good. Well, I think that's enough for today."

They shook hands. He was almost out the door when she said, "Gabriel?"

"Yes?"

"Your crime—I want you to know—I don't hold that against you. No one will. You've served your time. You can start over again now with a clean slate. You have no reason to harbor feelings of guilt."

"Thank you, Doctor. That is very kind of you."

Kind indeed, he thought, as he made his way to the parking lot. The problem was, contrary to what she thought, she didn't know everything. She thought that stupid incident with the eleven-year-old was his most heinous crime.

But Aravena knew better. That was not the worst thing he had ever done. That didn't even come close.

6

ERIN RAISED THE joint to her lips and drew deeply, sucking the smoke down her throat and into the inner recesses of her lungs. Did it really help? she asked herself. Or was it just a home-rolled placebo? She wasn't sure, but she wanted to believe it brought her relief. Because she very much needed relief.

She lay back in the bathtub, surrounded by bubble bath and eight scented candles, Enya on the CD player. One way or another, she had to calm herself. She had to make it better. She had to make up for what she had done.

Visiting Kincaid was a start, maybe, but only that. She was haunted by what he had said. You need to go to the DA. Tell them. At some basic instinctual level, she knew he was right. But what would be the result? Most likely, they would totally disregard what she said and do nothing. As the lawyer had pointed out, the law enforcement community was never anxious to admit that they had made a mistake, much less that they came perilously close to executing an innocent man. They would be more likely to write off what she said to the histrionics of a guilt-ridden girl. A sole survivor. A born-again babe trying to do her good deed for the day. There was no way she could make them act, could force them to listen.

Wait a minute. Maybe there was. She didn't have to start with the prosecutors. What if she started at the *Tulsa World*? She could call up Debbie Jackson at the city desk, tell her what she knew. If the *World* heard that an innocent man was about to be executed, they would almost certainly run a story. Maybe several stories. The anti-death-penalty faction would take up the banner. This would be a dream case for them. A tormented young woman—and quite attractive, if she did think so herself—trying to prevent a gross miscarriage of justice. If they stirred up enough trouble, the law enforcement people would have to do something.

Now that was a plan, she thought, and she took another deep and satisfying drag. The hot water soaked into her skin. She could feel the tension—some of it, anyway—melting away. She did what she did, all those years ago, and there was no way she could justify it—not even to herself. All she could hope to do was make it better by telling the world her secret. One of them, anyway. Perhaps revealing the one would make it easier for her to live with the other.

That was the right thing to do, she realized. That's what would make her daddy proud. Daddy was not . . . a perfect man. He did things that were wrong. Very wrong. But he would never have stood idly by and let an innocent man be killed without trying to stop it. She had been silent far too long already. She would do whatever she could and perhaps she would finally—

Erin's head jerked to one side. Did she hear something? Downstairs.

She would've heard a doorbell. Did someone knock? She wasn't expecting anybody. She tried to remember whether she'd locked the door. Sheila was always hassling her about that. But she just never thought about it, not until she was locking up to go to sleep.

She sat up. The movement made the water in the bath slosh around, just enough noise to prevent her from hearing anything downstairs. But there was something. Wasn't there? She wasn't imagining it. She hit a button on the remote to shut off the CD player. Now if the water would just stop moving. . . .

It was faint, but she was certain she heard a squeaking noise. A slow, continuous squeaking.

Someone had opened the back door.

Erin pushed out of the bath, grabbed a towel, and headed for her nightstand. It was hard to walk without her cane, but she had to get there, and she had to get there fast. Because that was where she kept her gun.

It was just a little thing, a snub-nosed pistol. But after everything she had seen in her short life, she liked having it around. She needed to know it was right beside her, all through the night.

She lurched to the far end of her bedroom, water dripping from her, holding the towel with one hand—and the gun with the other. There was another noise. Or did she imagine it?

Sheila had asked a million times if she wanted a roommate. Erin had always said no, that she preferred to live alone. Which was only half the truth. She was still so messed up, so insecure and . . . downright weird, that she thought it would be embarrassing to share a place with someone, even her best friend. For that matter, if she hadn't been so screwed in the head, she'd probably have a husband by now. Maybe James, if not for his . . . eccentricities. Either way, she wouldn't be living alone. She'd have someone to protect her. But she never allowed that. Everyone who came near her got rebuffed in strong and certain terms. She didn't let them get close.

That had been a mistake.

Did she actually hear someone coming up the stairs, or was her imagination out of control? She couldn't be sure. There wasn't much noise—if there was any at all—but there was something. *Wasn't there?*

She extended her gun arm. "Look, whoever you are. I'm armed. I'll shoot."

Silence. Absolute silence.

Erin's heart was beating like a jackrabbit's. She felt so vulnerable, so . . . naked. If she could get to her clothes closet, she could throw something on. But she knew that would be dumb. If there was someone else in the house, that would give whoever the perfect opportunity to . . . do whatever they wanted to do. She would not be stupid, like some bimbo teenager in a horror film. She would be strong. She would be smart.

Then the lights went out. Erin started hyperventilating, gasping for air. She couldn't see anything, couldn't hear anything.

The breaker box was in the hallway, next to the heater. So now she knew two things for certain: There was someone else in the house. And they were not far away.

Maybe she should take the offensive, she thought—run out in the hallway, gun firing. She didn't know if she could make herself do it, though. Walking was always a challenge, and at the moment her legs were shaking so profoundly she could barely stand. At least here, in the bedroom, a tiny amount of light came through the window.

Wait a minute! How could she be so stupid? There was a phone on the night stand! Watching the door, still holding the gun in one trembling hand, she picked up the receiver.

There was no dial tone. But it had worked just fine half an hour ago.

Her visitor must have taken the phone off the hook downstairs.

She pounded her fists against the bed. Why was this happening to her? Why was it happening—*again*? What had she ever done to deserve this?

"Listen to me, you son of a bitch!" she screamed. "I'm carrying a gun. And I *will* use it!" Just to prove the point, she fired at the ceiling.

The recoil sent her tumbling backward into the night stand. She lost her balance and fell to the carpet. Her hand hurt. She instinctively dropped the gun.

After that, it was all over. A dark shadow at the other end of the room told her the visitor had entered the room. A black shoe darted out and kicked the gun away. An outstretched hand ripped away her towel.

Erin crumpled, curling up in a fetal ball pressed against the wall, quivering with fear. "Y-y-you're going to hurt me, aren't you?"

"I'm afraid so."

She moved her hands over her exposed body with frenzied, almost spasmodic awkwardness, trying to cover herself. "P-p-please don't. I beg you. I'm still a virgin. Sort of."

"It won't be like that."

Erin pressed harder against the wall, as if somehow she might dissolve through the plaster and rematerialize on the other side. She stared at the visitor, and then, a moment later, her blurred, watery eyes widened with horror. "You? I know you."

"Yes," came the voice hovering over her. "That's why I'm here."

CHAPTER

7

BEN HAD HEARD somewhere that wardens and corrections officers went out of their way to make the visiting room the garden spot of a prison—that extra cleaning details were assigned, extra chemicals were used—so that visitors wouldn't come away with a negative impression. If that was true, Ben thought as he noted the dried bloodstains on the wall, the almost tangible haze, the smell of vomit and human waste in the air, then he never, never, ever wanted to be incarcerated in the state penitentiary.

"So," Ray said, speaking into the telephone receiver, "should I get excited? Because I'm inclined here to get excited. But I won't do it unless you say so."

Ben suppressed a smile. He didn't want to mislead or create any false hopes. "As I've told you all along, Ray, getting a jury verdict reversed is a tall order. Statistically almost impossible. But having the primary witness for the prosecution recant can only help us. Her testimony was what convinced the jury."

"Hey, I testified, too. What was I, chopped liver?"

Ben didn't pull any punches. "She was the one they believed." He paused. "And none of it was true."

"They made that girl lie," Ray said. He clenched his fist so tightly his skin turned white. "Bastards."

"I don't think they made her lie. Not exactly. But she was young and easy to lead. And prosecutors like to win."

"Don't make excuses for your brethren, Ben. They're scum and you know it."

"Jack Bullock firmly believes that he had an obligation to—"

"I've been in this hole for seven years!" Ray rose out of his chair, eyes wide and angry. He gripped the table before him, his arms trembling with rage. "Seven years!"

"Ray! Cool it! We have more to talk about!"

Ray calmed himself, settling down before the guard on duty had to do it for him. He ran his hand through his thick curly hair. It was all gray now, unkempt and dirty. He was wearing the standard-issue uniform for maximum-security prisoners: green Levi's and green work shirt. His eyes had deep black bags underneath and his skin seemed loose and translucent. Prison had not been kind to this once handsome man. Not that it ever was. "So have you recorded her statement? And made a thousand copies?"

"Not yet, but I will. She was too upset yesterday. She's going to come back tomorrow and swear out an affidavit."

"I just . . . can't believe it. All these years. Because one fifteen-year-old was badgered into a lie." Ben saw his fists tightening again. "Do you know what it's like in here?"

"Not like you do."

"These past seven years I've watched them systematically take away everything that gave me pleasure in life." Ray fell back into his chair, eyes closed. "I used to love food. I mean not just to eat it. To try new things. Culinary adventures. I was a pretty decent cook, did you know that? I wasn't just some garden-variety dull-as-hell chemist. I was a gourmet chef. I specialized in seafood."

Ben nodded. "I remember. You had me over for dinner once." You and Carrie, he thought, but did not say.

"I haven't cooked in so long I can't remember how it was done. The only food I get in here is low-bid high-fat slop. I haven't had a glass of wine in seven years." He looked down, seeming to focus on the countertop. "I used to love to entertain, to have friends over, eat well, have stimulating conversations, spend the evening playing Scrabble or some other board game. You know what the hot entertainment in here is? Racing cockroaches for cigarettes."

"Not quite as stimulating?"

"No, but the happy thing is, we never run out of cockroaches. Not by a long shot. And Scrabble would never catch on here, because most of my fellow inmates can't spell. Three-fourths of the guys in here are high-school dropouts. A lot of them never finished the fourth grade."

Ben nodded silently. He knew it was true.

"Stimulating conversations? Forget it. Not going to happen. Most of the conversation revolves around women—although that isn't the word they typically use—and how they got screwed by the courts."

"Everyone is innocent, huh?"

"Actually, no. Most of the guys admit they did the crime. They just shift the blame to someone else, their girlfriend or mother or homeboys. Or lawyers. Almost everyone hates their lawyers."

"It's gratifying work. What about the guards?"

Ray raised a finger. "Be careful. They don't like to be called guards. They are corrections officers. And damned particular about it."

"Well, they do a lot more than just guard," Ben offered. "It's a fairly miserable, high-stress job, but the benefits are decent and there is the possibility of promotion. Better than some state jobs, anyway. Assuming you get out of here without being shanked." Ben paused. "How do the cons treat you? You're not exactly the typical inmate."

"I've learned to survive. You have to. You learn to look out for number one, 'cause it's sure as hell no one else will. Fortunately, the good time regs keep down a lot of the worst behavior. The cons know good time can cut their sentence by as much as half. So no one wants to get stuck with disciplinary action. The main problem is boredom. There's nothing to do. We go through the same tedious routine day after day after day." Ben watched as the light slowly faded from his eyes. "I had so many plans, Ben. So much I wanted to do. I was going to be a big name in industrial chemistry. I was going to get married, have a couple of kids. I was going to climb Kilimanjaro. And what did I get? Nothing. For seven years. Down the drain. Totally wasted. And I'll never get them back."

When his head rose again, Ben saw that his eyes were puddling. "I guess you know that Carrie left me."

He did, but the news still cut like a knife.

"She was faithful to me. For so long. She waited and waited, through the entire initial appeal. Two years almost. But eventually . . ." He pushed his chair back and looked away. "I kept trying to tell myself she'd come back. I even deluded myself into thinking she'd show for my execution. But it's all a fantasy. I haven't seen her for years."

"I'm sorry," Ben said quietly.

"I just—I don't know how this happened to me." Ray ran his fingers through twisted gray curls. "Do you know the story of the Wandering Jew?"

"Rings a vague bell."

"Old Hebrew myth. It was actually originally cooked up to reconcile some New Testament prophecies that didn't happen, or so the scholars say. The part where Jesus tells a group of people that some of them will still be alive when

He returns, which He obviously hasn't done yet. The story is that this one guy was punished for committing some horrendous sin—punished with immortality. Doomed to walk the earth forever and ever, never resting, never dying. Just going on, day after day, a wandering life with no meaning. That's how I feel. My life continues, but it has no meaning. It's just another twenty-four hours wasted." He threw back his head and stared at the ceiling. "And I can't figure out what the sin is I committed that I'm being punished for. What did I do?" he shouted. "What could I possibly have done to deserve this?"

"I'm so sorry," Ben said again.

"Don't be sorry. Just get me the hell out of here."

"That won't be easy. Even now. We've already exhausted our state remedies, and given all the new rules restricting death-row appeals, we won't get another shot. We do still have a habeas proceeding in federal court. But very few habeas corpus petitions are granted."

"But we've got a witness changing her story."

"Which is good. But it's no automatic pass. The court might well assume that she was telling the truth then and that for whatever reason she's lying now. I think your best shot would be to augment the actual-innocence arguments with incompetence-of-counsel arguments. But that would mean I'd have to drop out."

"No way. I want you in charge."

"I can't possibly argue that trial counsel was incompetent when I was the trial counsel. No judge is going to buy it."

"No judge is going to buy it no matter who makes the argument. You didn't do anything wrong."

"Whether I did or I didn't, the argument could be made."

"Forget it, Ben. I want you on the case."

"Ray, stop and think for a moment. This is important."

"I don't have to stop and think for a moment. Answer me one question, Ben. Do you think I'm innocent?"

Ben looked at him levelly. "I know you are."

"That's what I want. And I'm not going to get it anywhere else. No one else would've stuck with me so long, Ben. No one else would've fought so hard. You've already saved me from the executioner once. And I know it's been a good long time since you got paid. You're not doing this for money or glory. You're doing it because you believe in me." He pressed his palm against the Plexiglas screen between them. "I want you running the appeal."

Ben didn't know what to say. "You're the client."

"Good. Subject closed. Now go get that young lady's story down on paper and take it to the judge. Erin Faulkner may have done me a great disservice before, but she's going to compensate for it now. I'm sure of it. As long as we have her testimony on our side, we can't lose."

MIKE STARED AT the television screen, a tense expression on his face. The brunette telejournalist was reporting live from downtown.

"I'm LeAnne Taylor, and here at the scene of the tragedy, many questions are being asked about what happened—and why. I spoke earlier to Peter Rothko, the owner of the Tulsa-based Burger Bliss restaurant chain, about the tragedy."

The picture switched to a tall, handsome man with a thick shock of red hair. Surprisingly young, Mike thought, for a corporate CEO.

"It's a tragedy," he said, shaking his head. "A tragedy."

Mike grimaced. Someone needed to buy these people a thesaurus.

Taylor pressed a microphone close to Rothko's face. "Will the restaurant reopen?"

"I don't know about that. I think some sort of . . . memorial might be appropriate."

"What do you think of the Tulsa PD's handling of the situation?"

Rothko paused before speaking. "Well, it's not my job to assign blame. But I understand there will be a full investigation, and I support that decision. If there were any inappropriate actions taken, those responsible should be called to account. We need to make sure tragedies like this do not happen again."

Mike switched off the set, muttering beneath his breath. The quest for scapegoats had already begun.

His secretary, Penelope, entered his cubicle. Mike had worked with her long enough to know that when she came in with that expression on her face, she was not bearing good news.

"Chief Blackwell?"

"I'm afraid so."

Mike wasn't surprised. In fact, as he made his way down to the chief of police's second-floor office, he wondered why it had taken this long. In the hours following the Burger Bliss fiasco, the media coverage had been omnipresent. The papers and airwaves had been filled with reportage of the "bungled siege" and "the Tulsa PD's tragic comedy of errors." They were already comparing it with Waco and Ruby Ridge.

Which explained all too clearly why he had been summoned to Blackwell's office.

"What the hell did you think you were doing?" Blackwell bellowed, not ten seconds after Mike entered his office. He was not one for small talk. In the past six months he had given up cigars and, to make matters worse, had recently abandoned coffee. To say he was cranky was like saying Madonna was uninhibited.

"My job," Mike replied succinctly.

"You're a homicide detective, damn it. You don't have any business screwing around with the SOT team."

"I thought they could use all the help they could get."

"So you decided to barge in and take over?"

"I felt Sergeant Hoppes was making some . . . erroneous tactical decisions."

Blackwell ran his hands through the hair at his graying temples. He'd aged remarkably little in the years Mike had known him. He must be sixty, at least, but he was still in good shape and looked much younger. "Sergeant Hoppes has trained for over five years to lead that team."

"I didn't interfere with his handling of the team. I interfered with his handling of the hostage situation and a mentally unstable individual. I thought I could talk the kid down. I thought I could get everyone out of there alive."

"Well, you were sure as hell wrong about that, weren't you?"

"With all respect, sir, no. If Hoppes had held his men back, as I instructed him to do, I think I could've resolved the matter without injury to anyone. It was only when the kid saw armed snipers flanking him on all sides that he panicked."

"Says you. Hoppes tells a different story."

I'll bet. "I've submitted my report, sir. It contains everything I have to say."

Blackwell was not appeased. "The one thing your report doesn't explain is what you thought you were doing in the first place, pulling rank on Hoppes and playing James Bond on his turf!"

"Sir—"

"This isn't the first time you've done something like this, Mike, and we both know it. I've tried to cover for you, but you've become a loose cannon. I never know what you'll try next."

"I give my job one hundred and ten percent. Is that a problem?"

"No." He paused. "I suspect the problem is that you don't have a life."

"Sir?"

"If you had a wife and family you wouldn't be running around arresting speeders for jollies and interfering in hostage situations."

"Now wait a minute. That's not fair."

"Don't give me not fair." His voice hardened. "You know what's not fair? I'll tell you. Three people injured. Three dead. And why? Because they happened to go to a burger joint on the wrong day. That's what's not fair."

Blackwell began pacing behind his desk. "I guess you know I've got the press crawling all over me. And the mayor. She's furious. And who do I have to thank for that? One hotshot cop who can't keep his nose out of other people's business!"

So he'd been right; he was going to be fired. *So we'll go no more a-roving. . . .*

Fine. He wasn't going to sit still and take it like a punching bag. "Look, you want my badge? You've got it!"

"Mike . . ."

"I know how this dirty game is played. Never mind all the years I've given this force. I'll be your scapegoat." He pulled out his badge and slammed it down on Blackwell's desk. "Consider this my resignation."

"Your resignation is not accepted."

"It—" He stopped short. "What's that?"

"It's not accepted. I didn't drag you down here to fire you."

"You didn't?"

"No. I didn't. So siddown already."

Mike did as he was told.

Blackwell took his seat behind his desk and stared intently at his steepled fingers. "How long have you and Tomlinson been working together?"

Mike cast his mind back. "Since the Kindergarten Killer case."

"Right. A good long while. I wonder if maybe it's time for a change."

"Wait a minute. Tomlinson and I work well together. He's my protégé."

"That's more or less the point." Blackwell rifled through some records on his desk. "He doesn't exercise much restraint on you, does he?"

"Should he?"

"I see in his report that he advised you against intervening in the Burger Bliss siege. But you basically blew him off."

"I wouldn't put it like that."

"But why should you listen to him? He's your protégé."

Mike's eyes began to narrow. "Sir . . . where are you going with this?"

"I'm sure you've figured that out already, Mike. I'm assigning you a new partner."

"But sir, Tomlinson—"

"Tomlinson will be fine, Mike. He's earned a promotion and he's going to get it. Please don't bother arguing—I've already made up my mind."

Mike knew there was a time to play and a time to fold. He sensed this was one of the latter. So he remained calm and cool and asked, "Who did you have in mind?"

Mike continued to remain calm and cool—until about a second after he heard the name.

"Jesus Christ, sir. No! Anyone else. Please! Anyone but *her*!"

"Mike, you're wasting your time."

"Please reconsider. Please."

"I've asked her to join us." Blackwell pushed a button on his desk phone. "Send Baxter in, please."

A moment later, Sergeant Kate Baxter entered the office. She was slender and about five feet nine, with honey-blonde hair that fell to her shoulder blades. Her skin was a trifle pale and lightly freckled. She did not wear makeup, nor did she seem to particularly need makeup. All in all, not an unpleasant package, but as far as Mike was concerned, he was looking at the Bride of Frankenstein.

"It's alive!" Mike muttered under his breath.

"Major Morelli," Blackwell said, "I'd like you to meet your new partner, Sergeant Baxter. And likewise."

As she shook Mike's hand, she stared levelly into his eyes. Mike knew she was sizing him up. Just as he was her.

"Nice to meet you at last," Mike said.

"I'm sure."

Was he wrong, Mike thought, or did he get the impression she wasn't any happier about this assignment than he was? He only hoped it was true. Maybe there was hope yet.

"Sergeant Baxter has an outstanding record, Mike. As I think you know, she just transferred from the Oklahoma City Homicide Department. Worked some major cases. Made a big impression."

"Your reputation precedes you, Sergeant," he said, still looking at her.

"As does yours, Major."

Mike arched an eyebrow. "What have you heard?"

She hesitated. "I don't like to repeat gossip."

"Relax, Sergeant. You can speak freely. After all, we're going to be partners."

"Well . . ." She held back a few more moments. She glanced at Blackwell, who just shrugged. And apparently decided, what the hell? "Well," she said, staring straight at Mike, "I've heard that you're an arrogant, authoritative, sexist pig who likes to quote obscure bits of poetry to make other people feel inferior."

Mike felt his teeth rattle. This was never going to work. Never in a million years. "Is that right?"

"I'm afraid so. But I'm sure it's all untrue."

"It is. Except for the poetry part."

"I see." She smiled, but it wasn't a happy smile. It was more like a don't-push-me-or-I'll-wring-your-neck smile. "And what have you heard about me?"

Well, why not? She started it. "Frankly, I've heard that you're a ball-busting, man-hating royal pain in the butt. That your police skills are adequate, but that you alienated so many people you had to run down the turnpike and come work here."

"Do tell." Her face remained expressionless, but Mike knew he'd gotten to her. Good. He didn't need this.

"Well, I'm glad we've cleared the air," Blackwell said, eyes on the ceiling. "Now, why don't we get to work?"

"Sir," Mike said, "I wish to formally protest this assignment."

"I don't want to hear any more complaining. If you've got problems—work 'em out." He slid a file across his desk. "Here's your first case. Get to it!"

As soon as he started back to Tulsa from McAlester, Ben punched up Speed Dial 1 on his cell phone. "Christina?"

"I'm here, faithful leader. How's life in the slammer?"

"God willing, I'll never know. I've got news."

"Really?" Her voice fell. "I've got news, too."

"Ray insists that we handle the habeas corpus proceeding."

"You explained to him about the potential viability of an incompetent-counsel argument?"

Ben crossed lanes, got out his PikePass, and took the right-hand ramp onto the turnpike. "I did. He doesn't care. He thinks Erin Faulkner is going to be his savior."

"Oh." The line fell silent for several moments. "This relates to my news."

"Something about Erin?"

"Yeah."

"Did she drop by to give a formal statement?"

"Not hardly." The crackling of static on the line gave Christina's next sentence an eerie resonance. "She's dead."

*   *   *

"ERIN FAULKNER." MIKE sat at his office desk, poring over the file. "Why do I know that name?"

"Apparently," Baxter replied, reading over his shoulder, "she was the only survivor of a fairly hideous home invasion a few years back."

Mike snapped his fingers. "Of course. How could I forget? Horrible tragedy. My pal Ben represented the perp. Not that that prevented us from sending him on a one-way rendezvous with the Big Needle." He thumbed through the file. "Ben stills calls the case his greatest failure. But the truth is, he never had a chance. His client was buried by the evidence. Particularly the testimony from this girl."

"Young woman, don't you mean?"

"She was fifteen at the time, Baxter. Don't get all PC on me. I'm an English major and I won't tolerate anyone policing my language." He continued working through the file. "Looks like suicide."

"Yes . . ." Baxter said slowly. "It looks that way."

"Not surprising, I suppose. After what she'd been through."

"How do you mean?"

Mike continued reading, not looking up. "Ever heard of the sole-survivor syndrome? She must've had it big time. Eight family members killed. I'll wager her life has been a nightmare of psychological recrimination. Guilt, anxiety, loneliness. Inability to connect with others. Most likely she never married. I'll bet she had few close friends, if any."

Baxter arched an eyebrow. "Speculating in advance of the facts? Not exactly standard detective procedure, is it?"

"Understanding people is what detective work is all about, Sergeant. If you can figure out the people, the rest of it is easy." He closed the file. "Too bad."

"That's it? Too bad?"

"I suppose Blackwell wants us to take a look at the scene, then sign off on the certificate of self-inflicted death."

"He wants us to investigate the crime."

"Yeah. All violent deaths have to be investigated. It's departmental policy. But I can guarantee you he doesn't want us to expend a lot of time and manpower on an obvious suicide."

"You haven't been to the scene. You've barely looked at the file. How can you know that it's a suicide?"

"Because I didn't just join the department yesterday, Baxter." He stood and grabbed his trench coat. "Let's get this over with. But first I think it would be best if I established some ground rules, right at the start."

If there had been a wall between them before, Mike sensed it had just become titanium-reinforced. "What did you have in mind?"

"Like, first of all, I'm in charge. I outrank you, I've got more seniority, and that means I'm the boss. I'm not going to put up with a partner who doesn't do what she's told, or is constantly challenging or second-guessing me."

"Is that all?"

"No, I'm just warming up. Second, I'm not your buddy, your friend, your counselor, or your father, so don't for a minute get the idea that I am. We work together. Period. End of story."

Baxter's voice was positively icy. "Anything else?"

"Yeah. I drive. Don't bother asking if you can drive my Trans Am. You can't. So, now that we've established our rules, let's—"

"Wait a minute. We're not done."

"And why is that?"

"Because you haven't heard my rules yet."

"*Your* rules? You don't get to—"

"First, I'm not putting up with any sexist crap. I don't care where we are or who we're with. At the scene of a crime or in the locker room. Doesn't matter. I won't put up with any salacious remarks, crude innuendos, or chauvinistic character slurs. If I hear anything like that, I'll report you in a New York minute."

"Is that a threat?"

"That's a promise, buster. Second, if you have any thoughts about trying to snuggle up to me or playing grabass in your Trans Am, forget it. I'm your partner, not your playmate. I'm not attracted to you and I never will be."

Now, that was a bit harsh. "Fine. Let's just—"

"I'm not done. You haven't heard my third rule yet."

"And that would be?"

She jabbed her blunt-nailed finger into his chest. "I do not, under any circumstances, want to hear any of your goddamn poems! I hate poems!" She folded her arms across her chest. "Any questions?"

"No," Mike said through clenched teeth. "I think we understand one another quite well."

"Good. Let's go!"

Mike unclenched his fists and jaw, wiped the grimace off his face, and started out the door. This was never going to work. Never. Never in a million *trillion* years!

8

THERE ARE CONSTANTS in the universe, Mike mused. *Our echoes roll from soul to soul / And grow for ever and for ever,* as Tennyson said. Or, *A kiss is still a kiss,* as Dooley Wilson sang. The point was, some things never changed. And one of them, he realized as he trudged into the small house on Indianapolis, was that he hated crime scenes.

Something of a handicap for a homicide detective, but he'd managed to deal with it, over the years. He'd circumvented it. But he hadn't conquered it. And he supposed he never would.

A patrolman on duty pointed a finger. "Upstairs, Major."

Mike nodded and started up, Sergeant Baxter close behind.

She'd been discovered when the cleaning lady came in this morning. Rigor had already set in. Her naked body had an ashen green color, and the smell—well, there was one. Mike tried not to focus on it.

Absolutely beautiful, in a chilling way. Except for the head, of course. Because that had exploded all over the bed.

Spatters of blood and brain tissue were very much in evidence. Other than the mess on the bed, though, there were no signs that anything was amiss. Water still in the bath. (Evidently not a very soothing soak, Mike noted.) Phone on the hook. No sign of other persons. Just one little girl—or young woman, if Baxter insisted. One very sad young woman.

On the far side of the bed, Mike spotted a familiar figure looking away, toward the bathroom. He was thin, medium height, with straight brown hair and an increasingly sizable bald spot on the back of his head.

"Freeze," Mike said. "You're under arrest."

As he turned around, Ben Kincaid's face was wide-eyed with astonishment, followed by a moment of recognition, followed by a grimace. "Very amusing."

Sergeant Baxter looked concerned. "You know this man, Morelli?"

The corners of Mike's mouth crinkled. "He turns up a lot. Kind of a murder junkie."

Baxter approached Ben, all business. "This is a restricted crime scene, sir. Unless you're with the department—"

"I'm a lawyer," Ben tried to explain.

"Is that supposed to count for something?"

Mike proved once and for all that he really did have a mean streak. "To be precise, Sergeant—he's a defense attorney."

Baxter's hand slid inside her jacket, touching her weapon. "What are you doing here?"

"Tomlinson waved me up. I just wanted to have a look around."

"Why?" Baxter said, her face cold. "So you could rearrange things? Walk off with some incriminating evidence? Taint the scene so you can later allege police incompetence? This is my case, asshole, and I'm not going to let any legal crapola screw it up."

Ben adjusted his gaze wearily. "Mike, who is this woman?"

Baxter answered for him. "I'm Major Morelli's new partner. Sergeant Kate Baxter. And you're trespassing on a crime scene in violation of—"

"Relax, Baxter," Mike said, pushing between them. "Counselor Kincaid here is a friend. What's your interest in this case, Ben?"

"Do you have to ask? Ray Goldman's appeal is still pending."

Mike rolled his eyes. "You're kidding me. Are you still beating that dead horse? How long has he been on death row?"

"Seven years. Which is seven years too long."

Mike tilted his head toward Baxter. "Mr. Kincaid is referring to the sadistic bastard who tortured and killed Erin Faulkner's entire family."

"Ray Goldman is no sadist," Ben rejoined. "He's an educated, cultured, sensitive man. He's a gourmet cook."

"Oh, well, that proves he's innocent. Give it up, Ben. Your man did the crime."

"No," Ben said firmly, "he was just convicted of it."

"We had him dead to rights."

"The only thing you had was the testimony of the late Erin Faulkner. And yesterday, she showed up in my office and told me everything she said on the witness stand was a lie."

"What?"

"You heard me. She said DA Bullock pressured her, and she was young and malleable, and she made an identification she wasn't sure about. And as a result, Ray Goldman has lost seven years of his life."

"Wait a minute," Baxter said, forcing her way into the conversation. "Now that the woman has turned up dead, you're claiming she recanted her testimony?"

"You got it."

"Any witnesses?"

"Another lawyer in my office."

Baxter turned away, shaking her head. "I've heard of some sleazy defense-lawyer tricks in my time—"

"It's not a trick."

"Bull. You're trying to take advantage of the woman's death to get your creep off the hook. That's despicable."

"I'm telling the truth."

"Right. And the day after she cleanses her soul—to a defense lawyer of all people—she turns up dead. Now isn't that convenient?"

"No," Ben said, turning his eyes toward the bloodstained bed. "I don't find it convenient at all."

"Look," Mike said, holding up his hands, "I don't know what's going on here. But I've known Ben since college and I know damn well he wouldn't make up a story like this just to get his client off." He'd come up with something more credible, Mike thought silently.

Baxter stared at Mike, outraged. "So you're siding with the defense lawyer?"

"I'm not siding with anyone. I'm just telling you the facts. Ben's no liar. Of course, even if Erin Faulkner said it, that doesn't mean it's true." He dug his hands into his coat pockets, came up with nothing. Times like this, he really wished he hadn't quit smoking. "C'mon, Baxter. Let's finish working our suicide."

"How can you be sure it was suicide?" Ben asked.

Mike stopped. "What, you, too? She was found with the gun still in her hand."

"Hers?"

"No record of Erin Faulkner owning a gun. But it's hardly surprising she would have one. Given her past, she must have suffered from . . . mental disturbances. Survivor guilt. Hell, maybe she really did think her testimony was false, and she felt bad about it. Any of those could lead to suicide."

"I'm still not convinced," Baxter said.

"Look around you. Do you see any sign of a struggle? Any indication whatsoever that anyone else was here? No. And there's a reason for that. It's because no one else *was* here."

"Or maybe the assailant tidied up afterward. He had plenty of time."

"I'm with your partner," Ben said. "How can you be so sure?"

"Listen to me, kemo sabe. I've seen you when you get that I'm-on-a-mission-from-God look in your eyes, and I know it never turns out well. I also know you've been working on this Goldman case for years and that you'd do anything to get him off death row. But there's nothing here for you."

Ben stared at the bed. "I have to explore every possible avenue."

"Fine. You do what you have to do. But at the very least, you should let Christina work on a case that has a paying client. Otherwise, you're going to end up practicing out of the back of your van."

"Thanks for the financial advice."

"I'm just trying to help. I'm your friend, remember? I'm family. Sorta kinda."

"Yeah. But the fact that you're still carrying a torch for my sister doesn't mean you're right."

Baxter's head turned at that.

"I can tell you this for certain," Mike replied. "As soon as I get back to the office, the Erin Faulkner death is going to be a closed file."

"Is that so?" Baxter said, one fist on her hip.

"Yeah. That's so."

"In that case," Ben said, "since there's not going to be any official police investigation, can we at least agree to share information?"

"You're not listening to me, Ben. There's not going to be any information to share."

"You never know. Something might turn up. Let's keep each other informed of what we're doing."

"If it will make you happy, Ben, fine."

"It will." He smiled slightly. "I'll put a good word in for you at the family reunion."

"Please don't. The only person on earth your sister is less fond of than me is you."

"Good point." He crossed the room and extended his hand. "Pleasure meeting you, Sergeant Baxter."

"Was it?" She didn't shake.

Ben drew in his breath, then gave Mike a smile. "And good luck with the new partner, Mike. I think this is going to be the start of a beautiful friendship."

9

DID THEY KNOW what he had done? Gabriel Aravena wondered. Did they know it was him?

Everyone who entered the FastTrak today seemed to be staring at him. Perhaps he was just imagining it. The delusion of a guilty conscience, that's what Dr. Bennett would say. But no matter how hard he tried to tell himself that—there were still those eyes! Those damned eyes, staring at him, constant, unrelenting. He'd like to rip them out and—

He clutched the cash drawer, trying to steady himself. Get a grip, Gabriel. You are too close. Too close to spoil it by doing something stupid now. So what if they are staring? If they're staring at anything, it's probably your great big womanlike breasts. It's probably the—

"Like . . . do you carry bras?"

Aravena's eyes narrowed as he peered down at the two blonde teenage girls leaning across the counter. "Why do you ask?"

"How about . . . because I need a bra?" the one on the left said. "Duh."

Aravena lowered his gaze, making no attempt to hide where his eyes were going. As far as he could tell, she actually had very little need for a bra.

Of course, he liked them like that.

"I'm sorry, miss. We don't carry clothing. This is a convenience store."

"I know what it is, Professor. I just thought, maybe, you might have a private stash of bras around." She began to giggle, then she and her friend skittered out the door, laughing all the way.

"Obnoxious little tramps." His assistant manager, April, had returned from the storage room. "What do they think this is, Sears?"

"I believe they were making a little joke. Or so they thought."

"I'm sorry, Gabe. Girls can be such bitches sometimes."

She would know, he supposed. April was only seventeen herself. She was five feet three and trim and athletic; he could tell from her arms that she worked out regularly. "It's nothing. Really."

"How was the doctor appointment yesterday?"

"Oh fine, fine." April had never asked, but she must suspect that the doctor he took off work to see once a week was a psychiatrist, just as she must have guessed that medication was enlarging his breasts and causing his hair to fall out. How much did she know about his past? he had often wondered. The owner knew, of course, and the flunky who had hired him. He had no way of being certain, but he suspected they had also informed April. A corporate variation of Megan's Law—inform the young female employee that the man she's working with is a former sex offender. Convicted of a crime involving an eleven-year-old girl.

If April knew, she didn't appear to hold it against him. To the contrary, she made a point of being open, casual, friendly. Joking around. Making a show of the fact that she could handle it. That he didn't make her uncomfortable. Except of course that the fact that she had to make the show proved that he did.

And she wasn't the only one putting on a show. He was performing, too, every day they were together. He also had to be open, casual, friendly—but not too. And it was hard work. Because he liked April. Very much. She was almost exactly his type. Dark hair, dark eyes. A little old, but in truth she didn't look her age. Sometimes, when he was certain she wasn't looking, he'd cop a look at her bending over in the storage room, or adjusting her sports bra in the mirror. And when he did, he'd feel something. Very definitely. Something.

Not like he used to. Not like before the medication. But the Depo didn't eliminate sex drive, as Dr. Bennett had reminded him countless times. It only suppressed it. And as long as he had gone without . . . release, all the drugs on earth couldn't suppress everything he was feeling.

"D'you do anything fun last night?" April asked.

Why did she want to know? His head jerked around. "Nothing much. Watched television. You know."

"Yeah. D'you see that deal on PBS about the spiders?" She shivered. "I hate spiders."

As she shivered, her whole torso, even those petite little titties tucked away in that sports bra, shimmied in a way that made him feel as if he must knock her to the floor and take her right now. Take what he wanted, what was his. Lick her and bite her and do her, hard. Over and over again. Do her over and over again until she was unconscious. Just rip the damn uniform off her and take her—

"Is something wrong?"

Aravena shook himself back to earth. "No, nothing. Why?"

"You seemed . . . I don't know. Lost in thought or something."

"I'm just distracted. A lot on my mind. I've had . . . some troubles, lately."

"Sorry to hear that." She reached forward and gently placed her hand against his cheek. "Is there anything I can do?"

That just about did it, right then and there. The warm, electric touch of her hand on his cheek, coupled with those magic words. Is there anything I can do? He was fully erect now. It had been weeks since he'd felt like this. "No . . . I—I'm fine."

"Really?" She removed her hand. " 'Cause you don't look fine."

Aravena took a deep gulp of air. Control, he told himself. You must stay in control. There are security cameras in here. He couldn't risk blowing everything. Not when he was so close. "No, I'm okay."

"Whatever. Want me to get the receipts?"

"Sure." An easy answer, since he wasn't allowed to handle the receipts. He could take the money and put it in the register, but he was never allowed to take it away. Not that the boss didn't trust him, as he had once explained. He just wanted to make Aravena's life easier by removing temptation. Standard procedure for all ex-cons.

She stepped beside him and popped open the cash register, then began putting most of the cash into a designated zip-top FastTrak money bag. As she reached across, her breasts inevitably brushed against him. Aravena experienced a surge even greater than before. He could feel the blood pumping, rushing through him, stiffening him even more. He had to uncross his legs, just to keep from exploding. He was sweating, and he knew he wouldn't be able to restrain himself much longer. Hurriedly, clumsily, he pushed off the stool.

"I'll just be a minute," April said.

"That's fine. I'm . . . parched. I'm going to get a drink."

"Nothing too strong now," she said, grinning. "Don't dip into the company booze."

"I don't drink liquor," he said, not adding: I'm not allowed.

Aravena entered the men's room and shut the door. He splashed water on his face. It didn't help. He was just going to have to take care of this problem the old-fashioned way. He unzipped his slacks and sat down on the toilet stool.

While he worked he closed his eyes and thought of many women. Dr. Bennett, Erin. Even that bratty teenager who asked about the bras. And April.

She was the central vision in his fantasy life, today anyway. He dreamed about the way she talked, the way she walked, the way she put bags of potato chips on the high shelf. What he had felt when she touched him. How she looked. Each and every magnificent feature.

But most of all, he thought about her eyes, her deep dark rich eyes. He loved those eyes. He wanted them. He wanted them for his very own.

10

WHEN BEN RETURNED to his office, he found his staff huddled around a desk passing Polaroids.

"Baby pictures?" Ben guessed.

Jones pulled a face. "C'mon, Boss. Paula and I have only been married a few months."

"Yes, but I know how industrious you are." He snatched one of the pics. "Somebody buy a house?"

"Loving," Christina answered. "A cabin. Out in the woods."

"Cool," Ben said, eyeing another photo. "A weekend retreat? Fishing and hunting and water sports and such?"

Christina shook her head and silently mouthed, "No."

Loving pushed himself up on the desk, flexing his considerable biceps. "It's a retreat, you got that right. But not for playin' around."

"This is where Loving plans to live," Jones explained. "After the impending global economic holocaust."

"Ah." Ben nodded. "I've been meaning to get a place for that myself."

"It's fully stocked," Christina explained. "Freeze-dried food, bottled water, and gold coins."

"Gold coins?"

"It's the only currency that's gonna be worth a damn," Loving explained. "After the holocaust, I mean."

"And when are we expecting this holocaust?"

Loving's voice dropped. "It could be any day now."

"Don't I remember you saying it was starting a few years ago, when the bottom started dropping out of all the tech stocks? It didn't happen."

Loving raised a knowing eyebrow. "Because they didn't want it to happen."

"And *they* being . . . ?"

"The international banking cabal. They sold short all those tech stocks before the crash, then raked in the money."

"How could they know the prices were going to drop?"

"Because they're the ones pulling the strings. They're the ones making it all happen."

"Do you happen to know these people's names?" Ben asked. "Because I'd like to put them in touch with my stockbroker."

"Of course I don't know their names," Loving said solemnly. "If I knew their names, I'd be dead."

Somehow, Ben suspected he wasn't going to get the best of this conversation. And frankly, he didn't have the time. "Staff meeting in the main conference room in ten minutes. I want everyone there."

"I WON'T CLAIM this case will be easy," Ben said, standing at the head of the table.

"They never are," Jones groused.

"The odds against getting a prisoner released via habeas corpus are staggering. And we have some procedural problems, too."

Christina nodded. "You mean the Antiterrorism and Effective Death Penalty Act."

"You got it." Ben passed copies of the document around the room. "This was enacted in 1996 in the aftermath of the bombing in Oklahoma City. It placed extremely tight restrictions on habeas relief. Once, habeas petitions could be filed anytime. No longer. Now there are tight deadlines. As soon as the state postconviction proceedings end, the time limits on federal relief start ticking."

"Which is why we filed our petition," Christina explained. "Even though we had nothing new to say. But now we do."

"I thought you weren't allowed to introduce issues in federal appeals that weren't presented to the state courts," Jones said.

"Technically, you're not," Ben replied. "But there are exceptions. Such as when newly discovered evidence arises. Or when there was good cause for the failure to raise the issue earlier."

"Or the *Coleman* exception," Christina added. "When the failure to present the issue would result in a fundamental miscarriage of justice."

"Right. Which the *Gilbert* case defined as arising when a constitutional violation resulted in the conviction of an innocent person. Which gives us a back door to argue Ray Goldman's actual innocence. We've got a hearing in less than a week. We need to be ready to present strong evidence that Ray was wrongfully convicted."

"How are we going to do that?" Jones asked. "Now that Erin Faulkner is dead."

"That, my friend, is the million-dollar question. What we need is a million-dollar answer."

"SHE ACTUALLY SAID that? She said, 'no grabass in your Trans Am'?"

Mike nodded. "Her exact words. And get this. When I pulled up to take her to the crime scene—she wanted to drive. Even after I warned her."

"Your Trans Am?" Sergeant Tomlinson slapped his forehead. "She must've been kidding."

"She was not kidding. She was trying to rattle me."

Frank Bolen, the third cop in the canteen, a large man with a voice as deep as a well, was equally amazed. "I woulda thought she'd rather have you drive. To keep your hands occupied." He winked. "So you wouldn't be playin' grabass."

"It's a control issue," Mike said, cradling his coffee. "She wants to prove she's on top. That she's the boss."

"And she's been here how long?" Tomlinson asked. "A day and a half?"

"Whatever."

"Don't get me wrong," Bolen said. "She's a damn fine-looking woman. I'd let her be on top. So to speak. I love the way she fills out those Levi's. She's a got a first-rate ass. Don't you think, Mike?"

"Hadn't noticed," he said, not making eye contact.

"But all the cotton candy in the world ain't gonna make me go for some chick who always wants to drive."

"I think she had some bad experiences in Oklahoma City. I don't know. But she's definitely got her panties in a twist about something."

"Maybe that time of the month," Tomlinson offered.

"From what I hear," Bolen said, "this chick's got permanent PMS. The all-year, all-the-time variety. Thank God Blackwell didn't stick her with me."

"Yeah, well, it's not going to last," Mike said confidently.

"What makes you so sure?"

"The fact that I have more vacation and sick time saved up than everyone else in the department combined. As soon as this suicide is closed, and before

Blackwell can give us anything else, I'm going on vacation. And while I'm out basking on the sunny shores of some tropical beach, darn it, I'm likely to become sick." He winked. "Bad case of the blue flu."

"You rogue," Tomlinson said.

"Yeah," Bolen echoed. "Hope it ain't terminal."

"Blackwell won't be able to let her sit idle forever. He'll have to pair her with someone else. At any rate, he won't see my butt back till he does."

"Blackwell isn't stupid. He won't like it."

"Yeah, well, he shouldn't have tried to palm her off on me in the first place."

"He had to give her to someone."

"Not me." Mike polished off the rest of his coffee. "I know Blackwell's trying to punish me for that Burger Bliss screwup. But the weird thing is—I get the impression he's trying to punish her, too."

"Then he oughta just give her a spanking," Tomlinson said. "She might like that."

"I'll punish her," Bolen said boisterously. "I'll punish her with my brush hog."

"But to do that, you'd have to get your blade up," said a voice from the back of the room. "Which I very much doubt you could do."

Three jaws dropped.

Sergeant Baxter was standing behind them, at the door.

"Baxter," Mike said, tossing his crumpled cup into the trash. "How long have you been standing there?"

"So long I've heard enough macho bullshit to fill the Augean stables."

"Aw, Baxter, we were just—"

"Could I please have a word with you, Major Morelli? *Partner?*" she added icily.

"Of course," he said, eyes and teeth clenched as if in pain. Or about to be. "If you'll excuse me, boys."

"Remember," Tomlinson whispered, "don't let her drive."

"Brush hog," Bolen muttered. "Brush hog."

"CAN'T WE PUT someone else on the stand to talk about what Erin said?" Loving asked Ben. "Like, you, f'r instance?"

"That would make things simpler, wouldn't it?" Ben answered. "But unfortunately, it would be hearsay. Even given the fact that Erin is now unable to testify, no judge would let it in. And even if one did, how persuasive would it be? The guy's defense attorney says that the recently deceased witness for the prosecution retracted her testimony? We'll never get Ray out with that."

"Then what?"

"I don't know. Yet. That's what I want all of you to find out."

"Sure thing, Boss," Jones said. "While I'm at it, I'll get you a hot stock tip from Loving's international banking cabal."

"This is not the time for sarcasm, Jones. This is the time to roll up our sleeves and work. Loving, I want you to start digging into Erin Faulkner's life. Digging deep. I want to know everything about her. I want you to talk to her friends, her coworkers, her psychiatrist. Anyone and everyone. I want to know everything she's done in the seven years since the assault on her family."

"I'll get right on it, Skipper."

"Good. She told us her testimony was false. She might've told someone else."

"She said she hadn't," Christina reminded him.

"Nonetheless. She might've let something slip. In therapy. At a pajama party, when she'd drunk too much. Even a hint. Anything would help."

"All right," Loving said. "Will do."

"Some of the people you interview may not be eager to talk to you. Especially after you tell them you're working for Ray Goldman. But I know you won't let that slow you down."

"I'll do whatever it takes, Ben."

"Good." He adjusted his chair. "Jones, I want you to dig up everything you can about the home invasion at the Faulkner residence seven years ago. Absolutely everything. We've already got extensive files on it. I want more. And I'd like it on my desk as soon as possible."

"Okay. Why?"

"It's a long shot, but there might be some clues there. Some hint of what really happened."

"Ben, what are the odds that we're going to find something seven years after the fact that the police didn't catch?"

"I'm a lawyer, not a bookie. I don't care about odds. I want facts."

Jones shrugged his shoulders. "Then you'll get 'em. But it seems like—"

"Remember, the police were certain, almost from the start, that Ray was their man. They might've overlooked anything that didn't point his direction. They might have even buried it." He gave Christina a knowing look. "Wouldn't be the first time, would it?"

"Not by a long shot."

"It's even possible Ray was intentionally framed."

"By the police?"

"By someone. We have to check every possible angle. So find out everything possible about the crime, Jones. And I'd like whatever you can scrape up about this suicide, too."

"Roger wilco."

Ben turned his chair full circle. "Christina, first and foremost, you've got to educate yourself on the law pertaining to federal habeas appeals. The attorney general's office has people who specialize in these. And most of the time, they win. You've got to go toe-to-toe with the big boys."

"Understood."

"They'll be wanting to beat you over the head with the 'presumption of finality.' *Barefoot* v. *Estelle* and all that. You have to be ready to counter them, point by point."

"Got it."

"But I'd also like you to get involved in the investigation of Erin Faulkner. I want your take on her."

"Really? Why me?"

"You're a woman."

Christina fluttered her eyelashes. "At last he notices."

"What would cause a woman to keep quiet for seven years while an innocent man sat on death row? What would motivate her to speak now, after all that time? If we had more insight on those questions, we might be able to figure out what happened."

"I'll do what I can."

"Pardon me for being the voice of reality," Jones said, "but I know for a fact that Ray Goldman's defense fund ran dry a long time ago. He hasn't got a dime to his name and he hasn't worked for seven years."

Ben and Christina exchanged a look. "Jones—"

"Forgive me for being so venal, but some of us like to eat regularly. Maybe we should let Indigent Appeals handle this. Are we going to make any money?"

"I don't know," Ben said, "and frankly, I don't care. Not at the moment, anyway. We can worry about practicalities later. First and foremost has to be the appeal. This is our last chance."

He looked at each of them, a grim expression set on his face. "Our time is running out. And if our time runs out—so does Ray's."

*   *   *

"C'MON, BAXTER," MIKE implored. "We were just shootin' the breeze."

"Bull. You were shooting off your mouths, as a metaphor for shooting off something else."

"We were only having a little fun."

"That was not fun. That was not fun for me at all."

"Well . . . I'm sorry. But it was harmless."

"It was not harmless!" She whirled around, jabbing the heel of her palm into his chest. They had walked to the stairwell between the third and fourth floors of the downtown headquarters building. The stairwell was reasonably secluded, but whenever Baxter shouted, it echoed tremendously. Mike suspected the mayor could probably hear what she said three stories down.

"It was not remotely harmless. It was damaging to my reputation."

"Aw, no one takes that stuff seriously."

"I do! I'm new here, in case you haven't noticed. I'm still trying to fit in, to make friends. And I can't do that when you're running around trashing me."

"No one was trashing you."

"Just shut up and listen. You're one of the senior men in the department. People look up to you. If you act like you like me, or at least accept me, they will, too. But if you act like I'm a joke—then I will be."

"I think you overrate my importance."

"I know how it works. I've seen it happen before. And I'm not going to let it happen again!"

Mike dug his fists deep into his coat pockets. "Could we just . . . calm down here? If I made a mistake, I'm sorry. Let's just forget it happened and—"

"Oh, you'd like that, wouldn't you?"

"I'd—what?"

"You'd like to forgive and forget, since you have nothing to forgive. Let me tell you something, buddy. It ain't gonna be that easy."

Mike's eyes narrowed. "What do you mean?"

"I told you I wouldn't put up with any sexist crap, and I meant it. You're going on report."

"Now wait just a minute!"

"Too late, chumley. Too damn late."

"I have not done anything inappropriate."

She smiled. "Then you have nothing to worry about."

"Baxter, if you file a report on me, it could screw up my whole career."

"Well, I guess you should've thought of that before you started talking about your partner's panties, huh?"

Mike threw up his hands. "Fine. Do your damnedest. No one will take you seriously."

"Wrong as rain, slick. They don't have any choice. In case you haven't heard, sexual harassment is against the law. I could sue the department for big bucks and they know it."

"Sexual harassment! We didn't even know you were in the room!"

"Doesn't matter. It's called creating a hostile environment. And you and your buddies were in there doing it big time."

"I can't believe this!" Mike bellowed. "How in God's name did I get saddled with such a miserable—"

"Go on, say it," she dared. "Give my report a blockbuster finish."

"Arrrgh!" Mike pounded his fists against the wall. "I can't believe this!" He whirled around. "Was this all you wanted?"

"Actually, no. I wanted talk about the Faulkner case."

"That case is closed. Forget about it."

"I don't want to forget about it. I think you're wrong."

"Why am I not surprised?"

"I don't know why you're so anxious to close this investigation."

"If you'd seen as many suicides as I have—"

"But this one's different."

"They're all different."

She grabbed his arms and forced him to face her. "Would you listen to me?"

"I guess that would keep you from starting your report."

"You know as well as I do that women almost never use guns to commit suicide."

"Who's being sexist now?"

"It's true. Women use poison or pills or slit their wrists in the tub. Which, by the way, she had been in, minutes before her death. There was a razor close at hand. Why would she get out, get a gun, and blow her head to bits? It's just not what a woman would do!"

"Sometimes people don't act according to the statistics. Sometimes people do strange things. And this woman was obviously not thinking clearly."

Baxter held tight to his arms. "Second, her body was found naked."

"Thanks, I picked up on that already."

"Doesn't that seem strange?"

"No. She just got out of the bath."

"And shot herself? Without putting any clothes on? No way."

"Why not?"

"Because the one thing a woman knows with absolute certainty when she kills herself is that eventually her body is going to be found. Does she want to be found naked?"

"Evidently she didn't care."

"C'mon, Morelli, work with me here. There was evidence at the crime scene that she had just shaved her legs and underarms. That she painted her nails. She does all that to make herself look better—but then shoots herself without putting any clothes on? It just won't wash."

"Once again, I will remind you that the woman obviously was not entirely rational. I'll also remind you that we found marijuana at the scene and that it was in her bloodstream. She was high. You can't expect her to behave normally."

"What is this, a scene from *Reefer Madness*? No joint is going to make a woman so strung out she forgets to dress!"

"I'm sorry, Baxter. I admire your enthusiasm—sort of—but I don't agree with your conclusion."

"The gun was still in her hand."

"And your point—?"

"My point is that, as we both well know, that's not how it works. In movies and bad TV shows, they show suicides still clutching the gun, but in real life, even the smallest gun has recoil. And a person who's just blown a hole in her head is not going to be able to marshal the strength to resist it. Consequently, in most suicides, the gun is found a few feet from the body."

Mike took a deep breath. What she said was true. But he couldn't make himself agree with her. "I grant you, that's typical. But it's not a dead cert."

"There's no such thing as a dead cert. But when all the evidence points in a different direction—"

"Baxter, the paraffin test proved she had fired the gun."

"The bullet in the ceiling."

"She missed the first time."

"Yeah, she missed, but what was the target? Herself—or an intruder?"

"Baxter, you're living in fantasyland."

"Am I? Or do you just not want to admit I'm right because that would damage your fragile ego?"

Mike fought to contain himself. "You know, you really are insufferable."

"I don't much care. Just so I'm right. And I am."

Mike felt his entire body tensing like a much-too-tightly-strung guitar. "Look—let's at least think about this, okay? Give it some calm, reasoned deliberation. Before you file a report."

"Too late. I already did."

"*What?*"

"I filed my report. Explaining my concerns about your rush to judgment."

"I'm the senior officer on the case!"

"And you filed your report. Which was totally erroneous. So I filed mine as well."

Mike turned one way then another, as if searching for a rag doll he could shred. "If you've filed a report suggesting Erin's death might not have been a suicide, Blackwell will have to keep the investigation open."

"I would imagine so." She slapped him on the shoulder. "Congratulations, partner. I think we're going to be working together for a good long while."

CHAPTER

11

CHRISTINA TOOK ANOTHER sip of her caffe latte and continued burrowing through the miserably thick file. She actually enjoyed bringing her work to bookstores in the evenings, and Novel Idea was just a mile south of their Warren Place offices. To some degree, coming here went against her natural instinct to avoid all things trendy, but hey—if you have to work late, at least you can have something to imbibe scrummier than that sludge Jones called coffee.

Although to get through a file like this one, she might need something stronger than coffee. She was wading through the police reports on the Faulkner home invasion, looking for any scrap of a hint of a detail that might lend some insight as to how to get Ray released. And it was making her sick.

Could there ever have been a more horrendous crime? This case had traumatized her profoundly the first time around, and now the nightmares were starting all over again. She closed her eyes and saw the crime-scene photos appear like some grisly slide show. Every single member of the family murdered, but for Erin, and in brutal and horrifying ways. Both parents, stabbed repeatedly. The father's leg broken, plus several ribs. Her brother, cut almost beyond belief. Her sister, crumpled on the floor, a lovely polka-dot skirt draped across her legs. The whole family in one bloody heap, except for the baby, who was in the nursery, and Erin, who had been chained down in the basement. One day, they were a happy, normal suburban enclave, and the next—they were virtually extinct. What the hell was the world coming to?

By the time she got to her third latte, Christina had scrutinized every page of the reports, photos, and tech analyses, but she was no nearer to solving any of the central mysteries of the case. Such as—why? The police called it a robbery that went bad; the Faulkners' considerable cash and jewelry had been taken (and never recovered). But surely that could have been accomplished without so much brutality, so much bloodshed. Couldn't they have gotten the goods without torturing those kids? Without killing them all?

And then there was a second mystery, the one that had drawn so much attention at the trial: Why was Erin chained downstairs while the rest of her family was killed in the living room? The prosecutor had suggested that Ray, in addition to being a brutal torturer/murderer and thief, was also some kind of sex pervert, and that he had put Erin away to enjoy later, like a chocoholic saving the last Godiva for a rainy day. But to Christina, that explanation only raised more questions. Such as: Why didn't he come back for her? The bodies were not found for several days, after Erin freed herself. There was no sign that the killer had been rushed in any way. Why didn't he return? Even if he decided against a sexual assault, why didn't he kill her as he did the others? Leaving her alive could only create a potential incriminating witness. Why?

And then there was the greatest of all the mysteries: Why had the killer cut out their eyes? Why would he take the time? All the forensic evidence indicated that it was done after they were dead (thank God). So what was the point? It didn't fulfill any need to make them suffer—they were long past it. What kind of twisted psychological compulsion would cause a person to do that? Christina couldn't understand it—and suspected she never would. Which was too bad, because she would really like to come up with something useful for Ben, something that would give him some hope that they might be able to help Ray.

She pushed her chair away from the table and stretched her arms. She needed a break. She'd been at this too long. Actually, ten minutes was too long for this kind of material, and she'd been at it for more than five hours.

She passed from the café section into the book stalls, just to stretch her legs. Maybe she could browse the new crime novels; she might get some insight there. Or better yet, she'd go back to the science-and-nature section. Novel Idea had a great one; it was like visiting a mini-museum. Where you could buy stuff. Even before she arrived, she could hear the soothing trickling sound of water working its way down a stone fountain. Nice. She could go for a little Zen tranquillity at the moment. Maybe she could pick up a little trinket for Ben . . .

Or not. He never liked her presents anyway, although he did a nice job of faking it. She wasn't even sure he liked the cat she'd gotten him, and he'd had Giselle for years now. Why she kept trying was beyond her.

Or beyond reason, as her friends would say. Her girlfriends gave her no end of grief for sticking with Ben so long. You could do better, they told her. You could be making the big bucks. Which was true, of course.

So why was she still struggling along on the seventh floor of 2 Warren Place at Kincaid & McCall? She couldn't really explain it, not even to herself. But there was something about working with Ben that she just . . . liked. As unsophisticated as that seemed, it was the truth. She'd liked him the day they met, back when he was a naive and bumbling associate at Raven, Tucker & Tubb. She sensed there was something different about him, something special. She also sensed he wasn't going to be around there long, and boy, was she right about that. Given how poorly he and Richard Derek got along, it's a miracle Ben lasted as long as he did.

After Ben started his own practice, Christina came in with him. Probably not a sensible career move, but after several years in corporate America, she was ready to do something she could care about. She'd had enough of helping multinationals weasel out of their contracts and pollute the environment. She wanted work that mattered. And with Ben Kincaid, she got it. With Ben, everything mattered. With Ben, every case was a holy crusade. He took the cases that made a difference; he represented the people who really needed help. Of course, half the time he couldn't get paid, but when all was said and done, did you want to spend your life amassing money, or doing work that was genuinely important? That helped other people, that made their lives better?

It had been a real pleasure, watching Ben mature over the years. Not that he wasn't still a trifle naive. Painfully reserved. Mildly neurotic. But at the end of the day, it was all rather endearing. He was cute, damn it. Even her most cynical girlfriends, she noticed, had more than once mentioned that they wouldn't object to going out on a double date with Ben in the package. Some of them, she suspected, assumed that she and Ben were dating on the sly. Or doing something on the sly, anyway. But they weren't. Never once. Never even close.

Well . . . maybe close. But never.

She wondered what he was doing tonight. Was he feeling just as traumatized by the case and . . . well, she had to be truthful about it. Lonely? It sometimes seemed as if he lived for his cases. Maybe he didn't mind spending the night alone, just him and the files. Maybe he liked it.

She didn't. Not that she minded working, but . . .

It had been too many years now since she'd split from her husband. She'd had a few boyfriends since, but nothing that really took. They ended all too soon, and in reality, she was rarely sorry. You're married to your work, one of them said. Well, perhaps she was. Perhaps she and Ben were married and they just didn't know it.

The flaw with that theory being that he was at his place and she was here gazing at Zen fountains. Not much of a marriage.

She headed back to the café. She was being silly, but what was the fun of being alive if you couldn't engage in a little silliness now and again? For all she knew, Ben was out on the town, a girl on each arm, doing some serious party-hardy. Well, Ben, enjoy yourself. Live it up. Have a round for me. I wish you the best.

No matter what you're doing, she thought as she retook her seat and re-opened the file, I wish you the best.

BEN HAD READ the file on Erin Faulkner's death for about as long as he could stand it, then decided to walk home, taking a shortcut through LaFortune Park. The weather outside was spectacular, and he always enjoyed dodging joggers, watching children play and lovers smooch.

But he'd gotten tired of it all too quickly. A park could be a wonderful place, he supposed, when you're hand in hand with your loved one, or pushing little Susie on the swings. But when you're on your own . . .

He thought about motoring over to Novel Idea, checking out the new books, maybe grabbing one of those flavored coffees that tasted more like hot chocolate. Was the new Anne Tyler out yet? It was tempting, but there'd probably be no one there this time of night, and he'd just end up being lonelier than he was now.

Lonely? Wait a minute. He'd meant to think bored. More bored than he was now. But somehow, that slipped out.

He needed to devote more time to his private life. He'd told himself so a million times. Every year it was his top New Year's resolution. But it never seemed to make any difference. He worked far too much and he never made enough time for anything else. And what was the result? A sister who wasn't speaking to him. He didn't even know where she lived. A mother at the other end of the state. Certainly things were better with her than they had been for years, but it would still be a gross exaggeration to say they were close. About the only people he ever saw with any regularity were Mike and the tenants in his boardinghouse and people with whom he worked.

Now, Christina—there was someone who knew how to live life. He had no idea where she was tonight or what she was doing, but whatever it was, he knew she wasn't bored and she wasn't alone. Christina knew everyone, did everything. She had more friends than a politician. She was a member of every civic organization and social club. He could learn a lot from her.

So why didn't he? Or better yet, why didn't he join her?

Mmm. There were some mysteries even the great Ben Kincaid couldn't solve.

Well, he didn't have time to wallow around in self-pity. He had miles to go before he slept. Work he couldn't put off. It was now or never for Ray Goldman. And never really did mean never.

Ten minutes later he arrived at the boardinghouse where he lived. The boardinghouse he now *owned*, courtesy of the legacy of the previous owner, Mrs. Marmelstein. Why were those cats swarming all over the place? Thank goodness Giselle can't get out, he thought. Some of them looked like major ruffians. A pampered pussy like Giselle wouldn't know what to make of them.

"Should we have this place sprayed?"

From her seat on the porch swing, Joni Singleton smiled. "For cats? I don't think that's legal, Benjy."

"Too bad. How's the house?"

"Fine. If I'm not mistaken, someone even paid their rent today."

Wonders never cease. In addition to going to TU, Joni worked part-time as Ben's handyman. Handyperson. Whatever. It was a perfect position for her. Especially perfect because Joni knew how to fix things, and Ben knew how to fix nothing. "Get everything taken care of?"

"Well, Mr. Perry's toilet threw me for a loop, but after about two hours' effort and a bucketful of parts from Home Depot, I think I've got that resolved. I rewired the electricity in the Silvermans' apartment to avoid that circuit that always crashes. I even washed some windows."

"You're a wonder woman."

"Well, yes." Joni cupped her naturally curly black hair in the palm of her hand. She was in her early twenties, perfectly thin, and in a pair of blue jeans, Ben noted, she had never looked better. "Now that you mention it."

"I do. May I also mention how spectacular you look these days? Have you been working out?"

Her face glowed. "Benjy, I can't believe you actually noticed. Mother bought one of those machines she saw on an infomercial."

Indeed. The same month she said she was too poor to make her rent. "And you use it?"

"Hey, it worked for Suzanne Somers. Speaking of which, are you still taking those martial-arts lessons? Going to the gym?"

"As a matter of fact. Why do you ask?"

"Well, I'm not sure, but I thought I detected just a hint of muscle tone." She grabbed his arm and squeezed. "Yes, I did! I felt a muscle!"

Ben yanked his arm away. "Why do I think I'm being patronized?"

"Can't imagine. You're a handsome dude. By the way, handsome dude, I'm doing this short-story reading at TU next week, and I wondered if you knew a handsome dude who would like to be my escort."

"I don't know this from personal observation, but I suspect your college is filled with handsome dudes."

"I was talking about you."

"Me? You don't want to go with an old fogey like me."

"No, of course not. That's why I asked."

"Are you serious?"

"You shouldn't be cooped up by yourself all the time, Benjy. Working all weekend. You need to get out and live a little."

Which was exactly what he'd been thinking himself. So why did he resist the suggestion so? "You don't want to be seen with me. They'd think you were dating your grandfather."

"You're only fifteen years older than I am, Ben. And it would just be for fun. It's not like we were, you know . . ." She laughed strangely. "Like we were dating or something."

"Of course not. Still . . ." Ben suddenly felt extremely uncomfortable. "Any word from your wayward sister?"

Joni had an identical twin sister, Jami, who had been "on the road" for over a year. Discovering America, or some such. "Not much. She keeps sending me postcards from exotic places."

"How exciting."

"Yeah, but I notice that the postmark is the same on all of them. Omaha."

Ben winced. "I guess this points up the value of a college education. Well, if you'll excuse me, I'd better go feed my cat."

He crossed inside and climbed the stairs to his apartment.

"Good evening, Giselle," he said as he dropped his briefcase and coat. "How was your—"

Wait a minute. No Giselle.

There were not that many constants in Ben's life, but one of the absolutes was that Giselle always met him at the door. As much out of hunger as affection. But still. She required her daily fix of Feline's Fancy, the sooner the better. And he was her procurer.

"Giselle?" He heard a faint mewling. He whipped across the apartment to the back bedroom.

"Giselle?" The panel in his closet was dislodged. It allowed access to the roof. He and Christina went out there sometimes to stargaze and gossip.

As quickly as he could manage, Ben mounted the steps and poked his head through. "Giselle?"

There she was, squatting on the edge of the roof, howling her black furry little head off. Ben had never heard such plaintive, piercing mewling.

"C'mere, sweetie." He scooped her up and carried her back to the kitchen. She howled all the way. Only when he had her silver bowl filled to the brim with Feline's Fancy did she stop, and then only long enough to eat.

"What on earth is wrong with you?" On an impulse, he opened a second can (a bad precedent, he knew), then freshened her water. When he was sure he had her stabilized, he popped open his briefcase.

He didn't know where to start. There was so much to do on Ray's case—and so little time to do it. Everything had to be checked and double-checked. They could afford to let no avenue of investigation go by, not with a life on the line and the executioner closing in on them fast. He couldn't possibly do it all himself. Thank goodness he had a staff. Thank goodness for Christina.

Christina.

He almost picked up the phone, right then and there, and called her. But of course, as always, at the last moment, he chickened out. He knew she'd be busy doing something fun, and she didn't need any pathetic calls from Ben interrupting her lively lifestyle. He'd just have to tough it out. Finish his work like a big boy.

But when this case was over, he resolved, he was going to make some changes. For real, this time. He was going to start having a life.

Because when all was said and done, the executioner wasn't that far behind any of them.

So enough of the dull and lonely Kincaid lifestyle. From now on, he was going to start living like Christina did.

CHRISTINA WAS BORED to tears. She wanted to scream, but Dee was managing the bookstore tonight and Christina suspected she wouldn't appreciate any sudden outbursts.

She closed her file and tossed it back into her briefcase. She just couldn't stand it anymore. It was all too dark, too depressing. Too devoid of human kindness. The Faulkner massacre was so horrible, it was almost inhuman. As if the killer lacked even the slightest—

Wait a minute. Something inside her head clicked. She didn't get these bursts of inspiration often, but when she did, she had learned to trust them.

She ripped open the file and began rereading the key passages until at last the idea crystallized in her mind. Of course. It was all so clear now. It made perfect sense.

She ran out of the bookstore and headed for her car. She was going to have something new for Ben tomorrow morning, after all.

And if her hunch was right, it could blow this case wide open. In a way that none of them had ever imagined.

CHAPTER

12

"YES, I KNOW a cat is not the same as a lightbulb."

Ben paced back and forth in his small private office, cordless phone pressed against his ear. "Yes, I know a cat is not the same as a radiator."

Another pause. "Yes, I know a cat is not the same as a leaky toilet."

"Well, I'm glad to hear it," rattled the voice on the other end of the line. "For a moment you had me worried."

"Look, Joni, I need some help here." Ben switched the phone to the other ear. He had no idea this was going to be so complicated. "I'm worried about Giselle."

"I got that part. What I didn't get is what it's got to do with me."

"Well, you're the handyman, aren't you? You take care of the house."

"Riiight."

"And Giselle is part of the house."

"So is Mr. Perry, but I don't take him for his weekly enema."

"Look, it wouldn't be a regular thing. I just think maybe she needs to see the vet. And I'm way too busy to take her right now."

Ben heard a heavy sigh on the other end of the line. "Tell me exactly what's wrong with her."

"I don't know exactly what's wrong with her. She's just acting . . . different. Weird."

"Like what?"

"Like she didn't greet me at the door."

"Horrors."

"And she was whining and mewling all night long."

"Cats have been known to mewl."

"And she doesn't seem to have any appetite."

There was a brief pause. "Okay, this is serious. Give me the name of the vet."

Ben complied. "I really appreciate this, Joni."

"You should. You owe me big time."

"I hope you're not thinking raise."

"I'm thinking short-story reading, Benjy. And wear a tie."

She rang off. Ben barely had a chance to return to his work before Christina bolted through the door. "Ben, I've got something!"

"Is it catching?"

She whacked him across the face with a manila file. "I'm talking about the case. Ray Goldman."

Ben's interest level increased markedly. "What is it?"

"I pored over these files last night. Studying every possible aspect of the case."

"What did you find?"

"The answer," she said firmly. "The reason the evidence never added up. The reason there are so many questions that *can't* be answered."

"Okay, you've got my attention. What's the answer?"

"The answer is this: There wasn't a killer in the Faulkners' living room all those years ago." She paused, gripping Ben by the arm. "There were two."

MIKE MORELLI WRAPPED his trench coat tightly around himself as he mounted the large stone steps. "Have I mentioned that I'm not happy about this?"

"All the way here," Sergeant Baxter replied.

"Well . . . I'm not happy about it."

"I remember. You're one of those investigative detectives who prefers not to investigate."

He pulled a crumpled sheet of notebook paper out of his pocket. "What's this place called again?"

"Harvard Organ Clinic."

"Associated with Harvard University?"

"Located on Harvard Avenue."

"Right." He glanced over his shoulder. So far, they'd made this entire trip with a minimum of conversation. Without even looking at each other. She was punishing him, he knew. And the worst of it was, he deserved it.

Mike pondered. Was this perhaps time to make some feeble attempt at reconciliation? It couldn't hurt. "Baxter, you ever eat at St. Michael's Alley?"

"Love the place. Great old English-pub decor. Dynamite baked Brie."

"Yeah. Bass Ale on tap, too." He stopped outside the revolving door. "You want, maybe, after we finish up here . . . ?"

"Love to. If you promise not to make any cracks about my panties."

Mike clenched his eyes shut. "Deal."

"Good. First round's on me."

"That works." He pushed himself through the doors. "But I'm still not happy about this."

Inside, they were greeted by Dr. Michael Palmetto. When they made the appointment, they'd established that he was the principal supervisor and also that he'd had a good deal of personal contact with Erin Faulkner.

Mike shook his hand—and was impressed. For a doctor, he had a hell of a grip. Now that Mike looked more carefully, he realized that the man was in seriously good shape. Strong muscles and a broad chest were evident, even through the de rigueur white lab coat.

"Thanks for agreeing to talk to us, Doctor."

"Not at all." He was a pleasant-looking man with a soothing creamy voice. His bedside manner must be four-star, Mike speculated. "We're all very fond of Erin."

"Of course." Mike noted that he was using the present tense. Was the good doctor in some kind of denial? "How long had you known her?"

"Almost two years. Since she started at the clinic."

"What did she do?" Baxter asked.

"Mostly clerical work. But I don't want you to get the impression that she's just a secretary. She's ever so much more than that."

"What, uh . . . are her duties?"

"Just about everything. Filing, books, photocopies, phone, coffee. But her greatest contribution is in the morale department. Sometimes our work can be . . . well, somewhat depressing. Dealing with serious disease and illness all day long. But Erin always makes us see the bright side of our work."

"Doctor," Mike cut in, "I can't help but notice that you keep referring to her as if she were still here. Even though she's . . . gone."

"Gone?"

"Dead," Mike said bluntly.

"Oh, but you see, that's where you're wrong, Officer. Erin Faulkner isn't dead. She isn't dead at all."

*　　*　　*

"TWO KILLERS?" BEN was incredulous. "There's no evidence of a second assailant."

"I think there is."

"Erin Faulkner only saw one."

"Maybe the second killer was in another room. Maybe he arrived late. Maybe he was hiding. But he was there. I'm sure of it."

"Christina . . ." Ben crossed the room, letting his fingers drift across his desktop. "If there was any evidence of a second assailant, don't you think the police would've uncovered it before now?"

"Frankly, no. That notation in Frank Faulkner's Filofax led the police to Ray almost immediately. Finding a gun in his possession convinced them he was the killer. I don't think they ever looked for anyone else, and quite frankly, if they found evidence pointing to someone else, I'm not so sure they wouldn't have buried it. You of all people know what measures law enforcement will take to prop up a case. Especially once they've convinced themselves that they've got the perp."

"Still . . . a second killer? Who's been totally overlooked?" Ben shook his head. "It's hard to swallow. What's your evidence?"

Christina opened her file folder and spread it across the desktop. "Evidence might be too strong a word. More like conjecture based on the facts."

"Such as?"

"Look at this photo of Erin's sister, taken at the crime scene." She slid it across the desk. "Notice the skirt."

Ben glanced down. "Hardly the place to be admiring someone's fashion sense."

"Don't be a stooge. Look at it." She pointed. "The skirt is lying smooth. Over her knees."

"Okay. So?"

"Think about how she died, Ben. She was beaten and stabbed repeatedly. There was evidence of sexual assault. What are the odds that her skirt would be lying down smooth over her legs?"

Ben stared at the picture. "I admit it's unlikely. But it's hardly proof of a second perp. The killer probably pulled her skirt down."

"Why?"

"I don't know. To cover up the assault, maybe."

"Look at this crime scene, Ben. Does this look like the work of someone who was concerned about appearances?"

"Okay, what else?"

"The baby."

"The baby was killed."

"Right. But not like the others. The body was found facedown, in his crib in the nursery. Tucked under a blanket."

"So what's your point?"

"Why isn't the baby in the living room with the others? Part of this grand grotesque tableau."

"There's no way of knowing. This maniac wasn't acting rationally."

"He wasn't acting with much gentility, either. But for some reason, he took the trouble to go clear across the house and tuck the baby into its crib. After it was dead."

"Maybe the baby was always in the crib. Maybe he killed the baby right there."

"Nope. No blood in the crib." She paused, letting the wheels in Ben's brain turn for a few moments.

"So you're saying . . ."

"I think the infant was killed in the living room with the rest of the family. Remember, Erin said her mother brought the baby into the house when they got home, with the other children. I think a second person picked that baby up and carried him to his crib. After he'd been killed."

Ben pushed back in his chair. "Christina, you know I've always admired your insight. Always trusted your instincts. But this time, I think you're grasping at straws. And I don't think your theory, even if it were true, explains anything."

"You're wrong. It explains the greatest mystery of the whole case."

"Which is?"

She flipped through the file and yanked out another black-and-white photo. "Why Erin was left in the cellar."

"I don't follow."

"It's obvious the killer was some kind of sadistic sex pervert. It's obvious he separated and restrained Erin because he had some vile special plan for her. But he never went down to get her. And he never killed her. He left a critical witness alive."

"He probably assumed she would starve to death in the cellar."

"If he wanted her dead, why not kill her? He killed all the others!"

Ben batted a finger against his lips. "So you're saying the second man intervened?"

"Exactly."

"Why? Because they were running out of time? They weren't. The murders weren't discovered for days."

"Look at all the evidence, Ben. There's a clear pattern."

"Pattern of what?"

Christina leaned across his desk. "I think the second man—unlike the first—had a conscience."

MIKE WAS RELIEVED when Dr. Palmetto escorted the two of them back to his office. He needed a chair, preferably a well-padded chair, for this conversation.

"So you're saying Erin isn't dead?"

"Not at all."

"Well, I've got bad news for you, Doctor. 'Cause I've seen the corpse."

Baxter glared at him.

"I'm not talking about her corporeal shell. I'm talking about her inner essence. What makes Erin Erin. Her body may have ceased to function, but I can assure you that Erin is still alive and well."

Mike felt his feet itching, a sure sign that he was becoming impatient. "Are you some kind of . . . born-again Christian or something?"

"Actually, I'm a Buddhist. We're only born once."

"A Buddhist. And Buddhists believe . . ."

" . . . that the soul is eternal."

"Cool. But you understand that Erin . . . er, her corporeal shell is no more."

"Of course."

"So let's talk about that." He glanced at his partner. "Baxter? Why don't you start?" She was the one who wanted to do this interview. Damned if he was going to spend the day quizzing some flaky Buddhist spare-parts doc.

Baxter straightened in her chair. "We wondered if you might have any insight regarding Erin's . . . unfortunate passing."

Palmetto appeared nonplussed. "It was suicide, wasn't it?"

"That's a possibility." She gave Mike the eye. "Although not the only one."

"Seems likely, though," Palmetto said. "Given her background."

"What do you mean?"

"I'm sure you already know about the tragedy in her past. I'm sure you're also familiar with the survivor-guilt syndrome. Why me? Why me and not them? It's all too common."

"And do you think Erin suffered from this?"

"I know she did. It plagued her. Part of the reason she came to work here was that, having had so much of death, she wanted to be involved with life. She wanted to be a part of our ongoing lifesaving efforts."

"She ever talk about committing suicide?"

"Not in so many words. But there were hints. Strong hints, actually."

"Doctor," Mike said, "had she attempted suicide before? To your knowledge."

Palmetto thought carefully before answering. "I believe she did. There was an incident. . . ." He paused. "Perhaps I've said too much."

"There's no such thing," Baxter insisted. "We're all just trying to learn the truth."

"Yes. Well, I heard about a time from her friend Sheila. Sheila Knight. She was often here, picking Erin up for lunch and so forth. In a private moment, Sheila told me that she had once found Erin at home alone, having consumed a bottle of vodka and far too many sleeping pills. She was able to rouse Erin— in the shower—but it worried her. She asked me to please keep an eye on Erin and to . . . well."

"Make sure she didn't have access to any pills?"

Palmetto nodded.

"Did you see Erin on the day she . . . passed?"

"I did. And I talked to her, for some time. She seemed troubled."

That would mesh with what Ben told him, Mike thought. "What was her problem?"

"I don't know exactly. But she was very depressed. I wondered at times if she might not be bipolar. When she was down, she was all the way down."

"So when you heard that she had died, a probable suicide—"

"I wasn't surprised. Saddened, yes. But surprised, no." He pointed to a large banker's box in the corner. "I had everything on and in her desk carefully stored. I thought you might want to look at it."

"Thank you, Doctor. You were right." Mike scanned the framed documents and diplomas hovering about. "What exactly is it you do here, Doctor?"

"We provide organs for those who need them. For transplants. We're the top legitimate source in the Southwest."

"And where do you get the organs?"

"Wherever we can. From those who are about to die, mostly. Those who have been generous enough to donate their organs."

"That must be rewarding work."

"It is. As Erin herself once said, it is literally snatching life from the jaws of death."

Mike pondered a moment. "You said you were the top legitimate source for organs. There's a pretty sizable black market, isn't there?"

Palmetto's eyes darkened. "I'm afraid so."

"Don't like competition?"

"Not the illegal kind. Those people don't obey the law. Often the organs are stored improperly or transported poorly. Ruined."

"Still, if I needed a kidney and couldn't get one through you—"

"You'd be willing to deal with anyone. Yes, I realize that. But you should also understand—" He stopped, reframed his thoughts. "There are all kinds of dark rumors about where—and how—the black market gets its organs."

"Was Erin involved in the procurement of organs?"

"Depends on what you mean. Some aspects still must be handled by a doctor or other trained professional. But Erin was very much involved in our work. Particularly when there was a family involved. And there almost always is, of course."

He drew in his breath. "When Erin knew there was someone out there who needed an organ, she let no path go unchecked. She made it her personal quest to find what they needed." He paused, and his voice grew silent. "You can see why we all loved her."

Mike remained silent. Professional or not, he found himself touched by the man's obvious grief. And he noticed that, at last, the doctor had referred to Erin in the past tense. But he kept the observation to himself.

BEN PRESSED HIS fingers against his forehead. "So if I follow this correctly, you're saying the second killer was basically a stand-up guy?"

"Well, compared to his partner," Christina replied.

"Then why would he be at the Faulkners' house in the first place?"

"I don't know. Maybe he didn't want to be. Maybe he was forced. Maybe he was there for some other reason. But he was there—and he appears to have been doing whatever he could to make the situation better."

"He did damn little enough."

"Granted. But he was still there. I think we should tell the police."

Ben frowned. "To what end? They're not going to believe you. And they're not going to reopen the case. They got a conviction, remember?"

"Then I'll call some of my journalistic buddies. Karen, or LeAnne, or—"

"The police are never going to admit they made a mistake. And even if you get everyone convinced there was a second person on the scene, the police will just say Ray was one of the two and execute him all the quicker. In a way, you might be playing into their hands—it's a lot easier to believe Ray was your killer with the conscience than that he was a solo psychopath. Either way—it doesn't help Ray."

"Unless we find the second person, or for that matter, the first. And find out what happened."

"Which we've never even gotten close to doing before."

"Because we never really understood what was happening before. Now we do. A little better, anyway." She closed the file. "And that, for the first time, gives us a fighting chance."

AT ST. MICHAEL'S Alley, seated in a back booth that resembled two high-backed church pews from an eighteenth-century English chapel, Mike and Sergeant Baxter began rummaging through the contents of Erin Faulkner's desk.

"Erin kept busy," Baxter remarked. Mike was impressed at how she managed to simultaneously consume the baked Brie, the stuffed mushrooms, the pâté, and her white wine—without getting any of it on the evidence. A hardy appetite had Sergeant Baxter. And good table manners, too. "Looks like she had at least fourteen ongoing seriously urgent organ searches."

"Hell of a line of work," Mike said, between beer and pretzels. "You can see how doing that sort of thing day after day could cause a serious depression."

"Are you still insisting on your pathetic suicide theory? Just because she was in an emotional line of work? You're such an . . . investigative opportunist."

"Dr. Palmetto thinks I'm right."

"Dr. Palmetto thinks she's still alive in Nirvana or whatever. I'm more interested in reality."

"The reality is, Erin Faulkner killed herself." Mike polished off his beer and signaled for a second. "Look, Baxter—I don't know why you keep pushing this. Maybe this is some feminist sisterhood thing. Or it's that you want to make a good impression in Tulsa. Or that you're just plain obstinate."

"All three."

"But you're barking up the wrong tree. You want to prove yourself—let's get a real case."

"This is a real case."

"I mean, a homicide. As in, Major Mike Morelli of the homicide department."

She rolled her eyes. "You're such a jerk."

"Did you know there was a murder in Broken Arrow last night? Some old guy on his way back from the Y. And they assigned it to Prescott. The biggest idiot on the force. Catch a murderer? He couldn't catch a cold! But he got the case. And you know why he got it?" Mike rose an inch off of his bench. "Because we were still mucking around with this suicide!"

Baxter resolutely shoved another mushroom into her mouth. "This was not a suicide, Morelli. And I'm going to prove it."

"You're delusional! I mean, it's a sad story, I grant you. But the woman was depressed and lonely and she didn't want to live anymore!"

"Really." Baxter yanked a receipt out of the box and waved it under Mike's nose. "Then please explain to me, O Master Detective, why four hours before her death, she spent a small fortune of her own money to redecorate her office?"

CHAPTER

13

GABRIEL ARAVENA STARED at the man in the tacky suit sitting across from him. Was it really polyester? Surely not. But it seemed like it. If it wasn't polyester, it was something almost as bad. Not that he was any fashion plate himself; the FastTrak salary didn't permit such indulgences. But he never looked this pathetic. At least he hoped not.

"And although many parolees find the experience liberating, some also confront serious adjustment problems, once the final tether is broken and they are full-fledged citizens once more. It's a difficult time for most. I remember a case. . . ."

Aravena could hardly stand it. How long could the man possibly rattle on by himself, without the slightest encouragement from the person to whom he was ostensibly speaking? But this was the last time, he thought, calming himself. The last time ever.

" . . . getting new bank accounts. Finding a neighborhood. Building relationships with other people. That's the challenge. But that's also the great joy. Because in a very real way, you're building your whole life again from scratch. How many people have that opportunity? Not many. I know a few billionaires who wouldn't mind having a chance to start over again. Now, I remember one case where . . ."

How many times had he been forced to come to his PA's office since his release? Two hundred? Three? He wasn't sure. It seemed like a million, trapped in this tacky cubbyhole he called an office, reeking of coffee and cigarettes. Listening to the man's interminable stories . . .

Melvin Feinstein wasn't really a bad sort, not once you got past the terminal ennui. As PAs went, it could be a lot worse. Or maybe Aravena had just gotten used to him after all these years. The food-stained shirts. The loud wide ties. He was a package. And despite some wariness, he seemed to genuinely be-lieve Gabriel was over it, that he was going to try to make good now.

Fool.

"You know, Gabe, you ought to get yourself some kind of hobby."

"Hobby?"

"Yeah. Something to do in your spare time. Something to take your mind off other things."

Like little girls?

"Like me, see, I collect snow globes. Don't ask me why or how. I just love 'em. Even the cheesy ones."

They're all cheesy ones, Aravena thought silently.

"I guess my mom gave me one when I was twelve, when she and the old man got back from some big trip to Hawaii. I've been collecting them ever since. And I take care of them. Dust them, clean them. Rearrange them. Play with them. Gives me something to do when I'm not working. Something to relieve the pressure. You oughta have something like that."

How about your daughter, you smug son of a bitch? "Well . . . I like to watch television."

"Pfff." Harvey pushed the air with his hands. "TV is for morons."

Whereas snow globes were for Mensa members. "My work at FastTrak does not leave me a great deal of spare time."

"Yeah." Harvey shifted around so he could look at the file on the table be-fore him. "I can believe that. Your supervisor thinks you walk on water, you know. He's very impressed. Thinks you're going to be considered for promo-tion again in no time at all."

"I'm glad that he is pleased."

"I'll bet you are." Harvey winked. "Wouldn't mind having a few more bucks in the basket, huh?"

Aravena tried to smile. What an utter boob this man was. And the State of Oklahoma had required him to visit this cretin once a week, ever since his re-lease. As if any possible good could come from it. At least Dr. Bennett was a doctor. This man was nothing. A fool. A total waste of time.

But, he consoled himself—a waste of time who would soon be out of his life for good.

"So, you feelin' all right, Gabe?"

"I am well."

Harvey nodded. "Medication still working for you?"

"Of course." At least he wasn't asking about erections and ejaculations. Not in so many words.

"Must be a hell of a thing. I mean the . . . the . . . you know." He waved his hands around his chest. "Do they itch?"

That again. Why did the whole world obsess over his breasts? "They did. I now . . . bind them. Both for comfort and for appearances."

"I expect that would draw a lot of attention at the FastTrak." He drummed his fingers on the table. Aravena could tell there was something he wanted to say. "You know, Gabe, what you did . . ." He drew in his breath. "We haven't really talked much about your crime. I didn't see the point. I assumed you preferred it that way. But I have to ask. Before I give you the final check mark. Do you think you might ever . . . you know . . . have any . . . feelings like that again?"

"Absolutely not," Aravena said. He tried to wear that confident, square-jawed look he knew would impress this buffoon. "I no longer have any sexual feelings."

"Nothing?"

"Nothing."

" 'Cause you know, it's still possible."

"I no longer have any such feelings . . . as I once did. I know I never will. That is all in the past."

Harvey peered into his eyes for a moment, then slowly nodded. "You know what, Gabe? I believe you. I really do. I'm going to okay your release from supervision." He began scribbling on a form in his file.

Aravena tried to suppress his elation, but it took some doing. It was finally going to happen! No more tether. No more visits to the shrink. No more injections. No more endless stories from this fool. No more unexpected visits to his apartment. Freedom. Total and utter freedom. To do whatever he wanted. Whenever he wanted.

Harvey slid the form across the table, grinning. "Congratulations, Gabe. You've passed."

"Thank you, sir. Thank you very much."

"Of course, you're still expected to take the medication."

"I wouldn't have it any other way." If the man would believe that, he'd believe anything.

"And I'd still like to drop by to visit. Just every now and again. On an informal basis. To see how you're doing."

"I would be honored." I will move. I will change the locks.

"One other thing, Gabe. I hate to mention it, but . . . you know, we're supposed to register former sex offenders. Once they're released from custody."

"What do you do?"

"Oh, some of the boys in the department go door-to-door to inform the neighbors. Just so they won't be blamed later if something should happen."

"If the police go door-to-door to inform all my neighbors . . . then I won't have any neighbors."

"Yeah. Exactly." He pondered a moment, then made a few pencil scribbles on his file. "You know, Gabe, I'm going to forget to forward this information to the law enforcement boys. I just don't think it's necessary."

"Thank you very much."

"It could do you a lot of harm. And no good at all. None that I see, anyway." He fell silent a moment. "But this means I'm trusting you, Gabe. I believe you've changed. I really do." He peered across the table, insisting on eye contact. "Don't make me look like a fool, okay?"

"Of course not," Aravena said. You do that for yourself so well already.

The two men rose and shook hands. "Thank you for everything you have done on my behalf all these years," Aravena said. "I mean that sincerely."

Harvey smiled. Aravena had a sense that he wished to embrace, but that wasn't going to happen. There were limits to what even he would do.

As Aravena left his PA's office and stepped out into the sunshine, it did indeed seem as if he had entered an entirely new world. A world filled with challenges. And possibilities. And there they were, all around him. The woman walking toward him on the sidewalk. That little piece of jailbait on the other side of the street . . .

He had regained his freedom, despite everything, despite every evil thing he had locked up in his heart. He had done his time and survived. But the best of it was—they had never learned the truth. They had no idea. The worst of it. They didn't have a glimmer. If they knew what he had done . . .

But they didn't. And now he was free.

He strolled toward the Tulsa Transit bus stop, a happy man. There were always so many women riding the bus. So many women crowded together in such a small space.

The world was filled with possibilities.

14

TEN MINUTES AFTER the hearing was supposed to start, there was no one in the courtroom other than the principal players—the attorneys for both sides and the court bailiff. Somewhat ironic, Ben mused. Every time he tried a murder case, the courtroom was packed. People thought trials were exciting (even though, in the main, they weren't), full of tricks and high drama and witness hysterics and Perry Mason–style manipulation—all leading up to that dramatic moment when the jury rendered the verdict. But no one ever came to see an appellate hearing. A bunch of lawyers talking? Who cared? But the truth was, what took place at these hearings was often more interesting—and more final—than anything that happened in a trial.

"Got your argument mapped out?" Christina asked. She was sitting beside him at counsel table, armed with three tall stacks of photocopied case law.

"I think so. I'm going to start with a few token citations to the precedents for granting habeas corpus relief."

"All five of them, huh?"

"Right. But I won't spend much time there, because I know the judge already knows all that. What I hope to make implicitly clear, as I discuss the result in each case, is that the federal courts have traditionally stepped in, on whatever grounds, when they believed there was serious doubt about the defendant's guilt. And then I start laying down all the doubt."

"Think it'll work?"

"It might. If the judge is halfway reasonable, at the very least we should convince him to postpone the execution while we continue to investigate."

"Are you going to use my second-man theory?"

He looked at her sternly. "Christina, we may be desperate, but we don't have to act like it."

From the other side of the courtroom, a heavyset man in a somewhat worn suit approached Ben. "Looks like we have some time on our hands."

"Yeah. Any idea why?"

"Who knows? Federal judges do whatever they want."

"I suppose." Ben knew Jerry Weintraub from the days when he had interned at the DA's office, before he moved to Tulsa. He was a big bear of a guy—always upbeat, impossible to dislike. He was representing the AG's office in this hearing; the attorney general traditionally represented the state in criminal appeals.

"The problem is, these appointed-for-life federal judges all think they're God. And it's hard to keep God on a timetable."

Ben half smiled. Jerry had always been one of his favorites, back in OKC, and he still was—even when he was on the other side. "I can't believe you're still with the AG's office after all these years."

"Hey—it's job security. Don't knock it."

"Don't you get tired of being the AG's gofer?"

Weintraub appeared indignant. "Who's a gofer? I've outlasted three attorneys general and four governors. I run the place. They take orders from me."

"Uh-huh."

"You should never have left the DA's office, Ben."

"After the big blowup with Bullock? I had no choice. Not that it matters. I like choosing my own cases."

"Well, if this is an example of what you choose, you were better off doing government work."

A rustling from the back of the courtroom told them the judge was making his way out of chambers. "Well," Weintraub said, "time to put on my self-righteous-law-and-order-zealot face." He skittered back to his own table.

"All rise." The judge's clerk stepped out of chambers and called everyone to attention. "This court is now in session. The Honorable Richard A. Derek presiding."

Ben's jaw fell three inches lower. "Did he just say—"

Christina nodded solemnly.

"We were supposed to get Holmes. This is Holmes's courtroom. The clerk told us it was going to be Holmes."

"It seems the clerk was wrong."

The two attorneys watched as Judge Derek, Ben's former nemesis at Raven, Tucker & Tubb, slowly walked to the bench, a grave expression on his face. He was, as always, extremely handsome. There was more gray flecking his temples these days, but predictably it just seemed to augment his underwear-model good looks.

"Why him?" Ben muttered under his breath. "Why did it have to be him?"

"Stay calm," Christina whispered.

"How can I stay calm? The man hates me. He goes out of his way to make my life miserable." He cast his eyes upward. "Why couldn't it be Ellison or Seay or Eagan—"

"Isn't she a Republican?"

"Even so. Better a judge who wants to hang the defendant than one who wants to hang the defense attorney."

Derek stopped on his way to the bench to harangue his clerk. Ben couldn't hear what was being said, but he could tell the poor underling was getting a major chewing-out. Probably forgot to pick up Derek's dry cleaning or something.

Ben sighed. The man hadn't changed a bit in the years since they had both been at Raven. This was going to be a disaster.

Derek took his seat, placing his hand against the side of his head. He made it look like a scratch, but Ben knew better. He was checking the lie of his toupee. A more vain man never lived.

Derek gazed out into the courtroom. As soon as he laid eyes on Ben, his expression soured.

"Great," Ben muttered. "Just great."

His shoulders heaving, Derek read from the papers already on his desk. "This is Case Number CJ-675-03D, In Re the Habeas Corpus Petition of Raymond D. Goldman. Are counsel ready to proceed?"

Weintraub stood. "We are, your honor."

Christina nudged Ben. "Go for it."

Ben shook his head. "No way."

"What do you mean, no way?" she hissed. "You can't back out now. Think about Ray."

"I am thinking about Ray," he whispered back. "And guess what, Christina? You just became lead counsel."

"DID I MENTION that I don't want to be here?" Mike asked.

"No," Baxter said wearily. "But I'm sure you will."

Mike watched as the mourners—and there weren't many—filed past the gravesite. Did Erin really have so few friends? he wondered. Or did the fact that her death was commonly believed to have been a suicide keep people away? Had she had so much trouble reuniting herself with the real world, after the tragedy she had endured?

A few of the ten or so people in attendance at Erin Faulkner's funeral Mike recognized from the organ clinic—Dr. Palmetto, for one. But most he didn't know. And as he watched, it seemed to him that most of them didn't know one another, either.

In the movies, Mike thought, it was always raining at funerals. But not here, not today. The sun was shining and it was unseasonably warm. Some of the attendees were probably melting in their black clothes. Didn't seem right, somehow. This was play weather. This was a day for the park. Not Bartlett Cemetery.

He and Baxter kept a good distance away so as not to be a distraction, but not so far that Mike couldn't pick up scattered words and phrases. "We need not grieve for this woman," he heard the minister try to assure those present. "Now she is home. Now she is at peace."

"I think coming to Erin's funeral to conduct interviews is in incredibly bad taste," Mike muttered.

"It wasn't my idea. Sheila Knight requested that we meet her here. And I thought that as long as we're doing one interview here . . ."

"This is the sort of idea that might appeal to a new cop, but anyone with any seasoning would know better."

Baxter's face clouded over. "I'm new to Tulsa, Morelli. I'm not new."

Mike watched as the minister with the red scarf around his neck closed his small Bible. The interment rites would soon be over. "We should've met her at her home."

"She specifically said she didn't want us to come to her home."

Really? That was interesting. "Then you should've made her come downtown."

"And if she said no? Leave me be, Morelli. Go hit on one of the mourners or something."

Mike shoved his fists deep into his coat pockets. "And furthermore, I hate funerals. I didn't even go to my father's funeral, and I adored him."

Baxter shrugged. "We all have to die sometime."

"Right. 'Send not to know for whom the bell tolls; it tolls for thee.' "

"Is that more of your poetry?"

"It's Donne."

"Thank goodness." The funeral was over, and the assemblage was beginning to break up. "I'm going to talk to Sheila. Maybe you could track down the boyfriend."

Because you don't want me horning in on your interview with Sheila? Messing up the girl talk? "No, I'll do Sheila. You find the boyfriend. He's probably the young guy in the cashmere coat."

Baxter frowned. "Sure you don't want me along? It might involve some . . . you know. Women's issues. Girl stuff."

What Baxter obviously wanted, Mike realized, was for him to tell her he needed her. That she might be useful. Which he wasn't about to do. "I'm sure. It'll save time."

"Suit yourself." She started toward the gathering, then stopped. "But try not to make any remarks about her panties, okay? That sort of thing can really mess up an interview."

DEREK'S FACE WAS so flushed and angry Christina began to wonder about his blood pressure. "Are you telling me you want this court to grant relief based upon your hearsay testimony regarding the statements of a woman who is not only not present—but dead?"

"That's about the size of it, your honor."

"Ms. McCall, the only reason I have not already thrown you in jail is that I know you are a recent graduate and that you've probably acquired your understanding of evidence law from your co-counsel." Derek's quick glance in Ben's direction was enough to send chills down his spine. "That could account for a multitude of sins. Incompetence is contagious."

"I have researched this, your honor," Christina said firmly. "There is precedent for making hearsay exceptions. For instance, the rule regarding dying declarations."

"Which this isn't."

"Granted, but it only missed by a few hours."

"You're not helping yourself, Ms. McCall."

Maybe not, but she wasn't going to let him bully her into stopping the attempt. He might terrorize Ben, but to her he was just a blowhard with an overinflated ego and a bad hairpiece. "There are also hearsay exceptions pertaining to any situation where the declarant is unavailable."

"Those exceptions presume that the statement has been made in such a way or under such circumstances as to suggest truthfulness. Here, I have only the word of counsel for the defendant—the one who's trying to escape a rapidly impending execution date. Does that suggest truthfulness to you?"

Christina looked the judge right in the eyes. "I take my professional reputation and my ethical responsibilities seriously, sir. If you're suggesting that I'm making false statements to the court, with no basis whatsoever, I will not hesitate to file a judicial complaint."

"Young lady—"

"Don't you young-lady me. I don't care if you're a federal judge or the Prince of Wales. I will not allow you to cast aspersions on my character."

Ben stared at her, his eyes wide as balloons. Did she *want* to spend the night in jail?

To his amazement, Derek backed down. "Counsel, let's return to the case at hand, shall we? I am not going to allow this pseudo-testimony into evidence, and I am certainly not going to reverse a well-reasoned jury verdict on its basis. Do you have anything else?"

Christina's voice dropped several notches. "We've made several allegations of error in our petition."

"All of which have been ruled upon previously by other courts. Do you have anything that is remotely new?"

"Not really."

"Then under those circumstances, Ms. McCall, I'm afraid I have no choice but to—"

"Wait a minute. I do have something else. Something the police missed entirely."

Ben sat up straight. Christina . . .

"And what would that be?"

"The fact that Ray Goldman couldn't be the killer who massacred the entire Faulkner family." She paused. "Because there were two of them."

"Two? Miss McCall, what do you take me for?" If Derek had been angry before, now he looked ready to gnash Christina's law diploma to pieces with his bare teeth.

BAXTER NAILED THE boyfriend—James Wesley—on her first guess. Not that there were that many candidates at the funeral from whom to choose.

She discreetly flashed her badge, introduced herself, and asked if they could talk a moment in private.

"I suppose." His expression was phlegmatic and contained. Was he really so unmoved? Or was he putting a brave face on it? "This day can't get any worse."

They moved to the shelter of a large oak tree in the corner of the cemetery. "I know this must be hard for you. I understand you were Erin Faulkner's boyfriend."

"Boyfriend may be pushing it." He was a handsome black man, well educated. Way too young for Baxter, but he had an obvious appeal. His curly black locks alone would be the envy of many a woman. "We went out maybe five or six times."

"Oh. I'm sorry. Sheila Knight referred to you as Erin's boyfriend."

"Too bad she didn't tell Erin."

"Something happened between the two of you?"

"Not that I know about." Wesley ran his fingers through his curls. "Everything went fine on our dates. They were a trifle slow or awkward in places, but for first dates, really, they were fine. I wanted to see her again."

"And you asked her?"

"Repeatedly. But she turned me down."

"Did she give an explanation?"

"Not really. Just said she couldn't do it again. Something like that."

Baxter whipped her pocket notebook out of her jeans and made a few notes. "Any idea why?"

"How would I know? Maybe I was a lousy kisser." He paused. "But I don't think that was it. I think . . ." His eyes wandered about the green expanse of the cemetery. "I think she was afraid of getting too close."

Huh. And I thought that was only men. "Why do you say that?"

"Do you know what happened to her family?"

"Of course."

"Well, she never got over it. Not in seven years. It was like after she lost everyone she had ever loved—she never wanted to love again. Wouldn't allow herself to love again."

A possibility, Baxter supposed. "Was she seeing anyone else?"

"Not that I know about. Scratch that. I'm certain. I think I was the only guy she went out with the whole seven years. As far as I could tell. And I saw her pretty regularly, when I worked at the organ clinic."

"You did? But you're not there now?"

"No. I'm self-employed now. I have a hobby that I managed to turn into a profitable business."

"So that's why you left the clinic?"

"Well . . . no." Wesley made a coughing sound, deep in his throat. "There was a misunderstanding with Dr. Palmetto. I was asked to leave."

"Care to tell me the nature of the misunderstanding?"

"Not unless I have to."

Baxter decided to let it go. For the moment, anyway. "So you left?"

"Yes. And I'm making twice now what I did then, thank you. But I missed seeing Erin every day. That was when I first got up the gumption to ask her out. After I left. I just missed her. We had worked closely together for four years. And I think she missed me, too."

"But not enough for another date?"

"No," Wesley said quietly. "I guess not."

"Where were you when she was killed?"

"At home, as far as I know."

"Witnesses?"

"I'm afraid I live alone. Housekeeper wasn't in."

Baxter nodded and made a few more notes. "Any idea what might've happened to her?"

Wesley suddenly seemed supremely uncomfortable. "I've . . . assumed she killed herself."

"Why would you assume that?"

"That's what it sounded like. In the papers. Gun still in her hand and all."

"Any other reasons?"

He pushed himself away from the tree. "She was a very unhappy young woman. Many of us at work tried to help. We talked to her, included her in after-work get-togethers. But there was always . . ." His face contracted, wrinkles outlining his confusion. "A barrier. Between her and the rest of the world. Something that prevented her from making contact."

"Any idea what that might be?"

He shook his head. "There was the tragedy, obviously. But I think there was more. I can't explain it, but—I think she had a secret. Something none of us knew. And it tormented her."

"Any idea what that secret might've been?"

Wesley turned away, staring off at the gravediggers who were finishing their work, burying Erin once and for always. "I wish to God I did. Because if I'd known, I might've been able to help her. And she needed someone to help her. More than anyone I've ever known. But as it was, I was useless." He turned away. "I was no help to her at all."

"So LET ME get this straight, counsel." Judge Derek leaned back in his black padded chair. "You're saying your client should be released from prison—because he didn't act alone?"

Christina pressed her fingertips against the podium. "He didn't act at all, your honor. He wasn't there. But my point is that the law enforcement version of what happened—upon which the conviction of Ray Goldman rested—is absolutely inaccurate. The crime has never really been investigated. Not thoroughly."

"But of course you have no proof."

"We are actively following up every—"

"With all due respect, counsel, this crime occurred over seven years ago. It's a little late."

"We have several new leads."

Derek shook his head. "Judicial decisions, at some point in time, must be granted finality. Imagine what would happen if I allowed every conviction to be overturned—or every punishment to be delayed—because seven years later someone comes up with a new theory."

Ben saw tiny beads of perspiration appearing on Christina's forehead. She was up against the wall, literally fighting for Ray's life—and she knew it. "Your honor, we could not possibly anticipate that a critical prosecution witness would recant her testimony, much less that she would die soon thereafter."

"Yes, but the problem is that all of this comes from the defense attorney. I can't make a ruling based on theories and investigations cooked up by lawyers."

"Sir, the police department is also investigating."

That caught his attention. "They are?"

"Yes. They have two homicide detectives working this case as we speak."

Jerry Weintraub rose. "Excuse me, your honor, but the AG's office has been in communication with the Tulsa PD. I believe those detectives are looking into the death of Erin Faulkner—not the slaughter of her family seven years ago."

"And we don't have any reason to believe the two are related, do we?" Judge Derek asked.

"It is certainly possible."

Ben noted the tightening of the jaw that signaled all too clearly that Derek was losing his patience.

Weintraub jumped back into the fray. "Your honor, Erin Faulkner's death appears to be a suicide, and although the police are required to investigate, nothing they've uncovered proves otherwise."

Derek looked at Christina harshly. "Is this true, counsel?"

Christina swallowed. "Your honor, if it was a clear-cut case, there would be no investigation."

"What's more," Weintraub added, "the death of Erin Faulkner was nothing like the hideous murders of the rest of her family seven years before. There was no torture, no mutilation, no sexual assault. No eye gouging. The weapon was a gun, not a knife."

"MOs could change over seven years," Christina said.

"The point," Weintraub continued, "is that there is absolutely no reason to believe a connection exists between the crime for which Raymond Goldman was convicted and the recent unfortunate death of one of the witnesses who testified against him."

"Your honor," Christina pleaded, "if there is any possibility—"

Derek shook his head. "I'm sorry, counsel, but I'm afraid you just don't have the goods."

"But your honor—"

"I have no choice but to rule—"

"Your honor, *please!*" Christina stepped away from the podium. "We're talking about a man's life here!"

"I am aware of that, counsel. Nonetheless, we must show due respect to the rulings of the state courts."

"Habeas corpus relief doesn't exist to show respect to the state courts. Pretty much the exact opposite."

"Counsel, you are not helping yourself. Or your client."

"Furthermore, your honor, if you refuse to use the powers that have been granted to you, you show disrespect to the Constitution and the entire federal judiciary."

Derek bobbed forward, as if bouncing up on his toes. "Counsel, you go too far."

"I mean, what's the point of having federal judges, totally independent and appointed for life, if they're too cowardly to intervene to prevent injustice?"

"Counsel!" Derek rose to his feet, visibly trembling. "Maybe this is how your cocounsel has taught you to behave in the courtroom, but I can assure you that I will not tolerate it!" He pointed the gavel in her direction. "Consider yourself sanctioned. You may deposit a check for five hundred dollars with the clerk of the court on your way out of the building."

Christina was unrepentant. "I'd pay five hundred thousand dollars if it would prevent the warden in McAlester from executing an innocent man."

"Ms. McCall!" Derek's voice boomed across the room. He swiveled his gavel around in Ben's direction. "Why is it I only have these problems when that man is in the courtroom?"

"She's just doing her job," Ben said quietly.

Derek was seething, practically foaming at the mouth. "I've already fired you, Kincaid. Maybe I should finish the job and disbar you as well."

Ben held his tongue. He knew the best thing he could do for Ray now was to keep as low a profile as possible.

"Your honor." Christina's voice was quieter, but no less insistent. "At the very least, give us more time. Let us—and the police—continue to investigate. That's all we ask. Just stop Ray Goldman's hourglass while it still has a few grains of sand left in it."

"The man has been on death row, at the taxpayers' expense, for seven years. I will not delay his execution date with no better cause than you have given me." He slowly lowered himself back into his chair. "I will, however, continue this hearing to a later date."

Christina's lips parted. She and Ben exchanged a quick and amazed look.

"I should simply deny the petition and end this protracted case. But since the law enforcement community is still investigating a matter that might have some bearing on this case, however slight, against my better judgment I will continue this matter to next week. We will reconvene, and I will expect to be told what, if anything, you've learned. I will make my final ruling at the time. And I do mean final."

Derek lifted his gavel and rapped it against his desk. "This hearing is adjourned. Now get the hell out of my courtroom. Both of you!"

SHEILA KNIGHT WAS stunning. Mike was not one much given to hyperbole, particularly when it came to women. His mother had been lovely, judging from the pictures he'd seen. His ex-wife, Julia, had been drop-dead gorgeous—when she wasn't drowning her sorrows in potato chips. But the woman who stood before him now was absolutely stunning. Her dark hair was a mess, her face was streaked with red, her black dress was magnificently unflattering—and she was stunning, just the same.

"I loved Erin so much," she said, her voice quavering. "I loved her like a sister. Like a mother almost."

"You can't be much older than she was," Mike said gently.

"No, I'm not. But Erin was one of those people who need someone to take care of them. Even before the tragedy with her family. And I tried to be what she needed."

"You knew her even before the deaths?"

Sheila nodded, wiping her nose. "We met in junior high school. Hit it off almost immediately. She was not an outgoing type and neither was I. We didn't care who was hot and who was not. We didn't go to football games and we couldn't care less about the pep squad. We were a good pair."

"So you were still her friend when . . . ?"

"When it happened. Yes. God, I can't tell you what that was like. Horrible. Horrible."

"I'm sure."

"I mean, I knew those people, every one of them. I'd played Monopoly with the whole family. I'd even sat for the baby."

"You must've been a great comfort to Erin."

"Not really." She removed a Kleenex from her purse and dabbed her eyes. "I wanted to be. I stayed with her when she was in the hospital. I came to physical therapy with her, when she was learning to walk again, with the cane. Something had happened to her. Something . . ." She shook her head. "I don't know. But something had changed."

"You continued to be her friend, though?"

"I tried. We became more distant, after we got out of high school. We both went to OU, but somehow, we never saw each other. Until we both came back to Tulsa."

"And you resumed your friendship?"

"Pretty much so. We'd put down a lot of miles together, and that meant something. We got along well."

"But not always?"

Her eyes darted downward. "No one gets along all the time."

True enough. But Mike couldn't let it go with that. "Were there problems?"

"Nothing serious. I thought at times she might be . . . jealous of me."

"Why?"

"Well, I had a much more developed social life. I had a boyfriend. I wasn't seeing a shrink. And didn't need to be. She, on the other hand, was all but a hermit. Till she started working at the organ clinic."

Mike thought he detected a subtle change in her eyes. "What did you think of that job?"

"I thought it was spooky. I still do. Being around all those body parts. Trafficking in organs. Counseling distraught families and dying children. Not that their work isn't important. I understand the value. But I wouldn't want to do it."

"But Erin did."

"Right."

"Dr. Palmetto seemed to think that the job was helping her get over the horror of what happened to her family."

"Did he? Huh." Again the subtle variation in her expression, her voice. "Well then."

"You don't agree?"

Sheila shrugged.

"You don't much like Dr. Palmetto, do you?"

She thought a long time before answering. "It's not that I don't like him. Exactly. It's that I don't trust him."

"Why?"

"I don't know. There's nothing concrete. It's just a feeling, I guess."

"Did Erin express any reservations about him?"

"Not to me. If anything, I wondered if she might not have a little crush on him. You know, the young girl falls for the handsome doctor. Soap-opera stuff. I thought that might be the real reason she was hanging around."

"Was she getting any help? With her problems?"

"As in shrink? Yeah, a woman. Dr. Hayley Bennett. Don't know how Erin met her. Never seemed to help. She was seeing another doctor—"

"Yes?"

"Kinda strange, actually. But I guess that's what happens. When people can't get the answers they want from conventional medicine, they turn to the weird stuff."

Mike frowned. He didn't like the sound of this at all. "I'd like that doctor's name, too, please. If you don't mind."

"Sure."

"When was the last time you saw Erin?"

"The day before she died. She went out to McAlester for the Goldman execution. I went with her."

"What was her reaction when the execution was halted?"

"Actually, she had already left. Before the call came in. She couldn't stand it there. Something about it was really eating her up. She was silent all the way home. Even more distressed than she had been before we left."

"Are you aware that Ray Goldman's lawyers are claiming Erin recanted her testimony? Said she couldn't ID Goldman as the killer after all?"

Sheila seemed startled. "No. I wasn't. I mean—" She paused, obviously deep in thought. "That might explain something she said. In McAlester . . ." Her voice drifted off.

The sun was beating down on them. It was high noon, and dressed in heavy black cotton, Sheila must be about ready to melt. "So what do you think, Ms. Knight? You must have an opinion."

"I—don't know what you mean."

"Do you think Erin lied on the witness stand? Do you think she killed herself?"

Sheila looked hesitant, almost embarrassed. "Well . . . it certainly looks like suicide. Doesn't it?"

"Yes. But some people have doubts. She had tried to kill herself before, hadn't she?"

Sheila paused, gripping her purse strap much more tightly than was necessary. "She did. With pills. I was the one who saved her, actually."

"So she owed you her life."

"Yeah. She mentioned that a lot. It brought us closer."

"Any attempts since then?"

"No. Well, not that I know about. And that was long ago. Granted, I knew she was still having trouble. I knew she had a lot of issues. Guilt. Anxiety. Loneliness. But I didn't think she was suicidal." She raised the Kleenex to her eyes. "I didn't think so."

"But you can't rule it out."

"No," she said quietly. "I can't rule it out."

"Can you think of any reason why anyone would want to kill Erin?"

Sheila looked at him incredulously. "God, no. I can't—I mean—God! Hasn't enough been done to her already?"

Mike couldn't argue with that. "Just one more question, ma'am. If you don't mind. Why did you ask to be interviewed here? At the cemetery."

"I just—I knew—" She struggled to explain. "I knew it would be hard, coming here. Finally saying good-bye to Erin. After all this time. But it has to be good-bye, you know? I have to move on. I've devoted so much time to her. I loved her so much. But now I've got to get on with it. When I go home tonight, I don't want to be rehashing the last seven years. I want to start fresh. I have—I have to forget." Tears welled up in her eyes.

"I can understand that," Mike said quietly. "Thank you for talking to me."

The gravediggers carried away the last of the chairs and the barrier cords, then raked the ground smooth. A moment later, Erin Faulkner was fully and formally interred, and there was no sign that the funeral party had ever been there.

"Sure," Sheila said, her voice broken. "Erin really was a wonderful girl. She had a beautiful spirit. But after she lost her family, in such a horrible way, everything changed. She was . . . I know this sounds trite, but—she was like a beautiful flower. Like a rose, you know? Lovely to look at, a joy to behold. But once someone breaks it—"

"It never grows back," Mike completed.

"That's right," Sheila said, and all at once, her tears streamed. "It just grows weaker and weaker. Until finally, it dies."

Two

How Time Moves

◆ ◆ ◆

CHAPTER

15

CHRISTINA STARED AT Ben. "You consider that a win?"

"From Derek, yes."

"He all but said he didn't think there was any chance we'd come up with anything that would change his mind."

"But he gave us another week to try. From Derek, that's a major victory. It means we still have a chance."

"Ben, I admire your optimism, but I think you're possibly being unrealistic."

"What else is new?"

"I just don't want you to get your hopes up. Unrealistically. You or Ray."

Ben removed his feet from the desk and swiveled his chair around to face her. "Look, that was Judge Richard A. Derek in there. *A* for Asshole. The worst judge Ray could conceivably have drawn. As far as I was concerned, the case was over as soon as Derek saw who was sitting at counsel table. I'm surprised Derek didn't volunteer to drive down to McAlester and inject the needle himself."

"I think you're overstating the case."

"Getting anything out of Derek—even the little we did—was a triumph."

Christina shook her head. "If you say so. Man, he sure hasn't mellowed any over the years, has he?"

"He's past mellow. He's ripened and rotted."

"Just last week I read that he's filed for divorce against his wife."

"Again? They were blowing hot and cold back when we were at the firm. Had some kind of sick codependent thing going. The man is seriously unstable and you know it. And snide. And self-centered. And he wears a toupee."

Christina smiled. "What I was getting at was—most people get a bit out of sorts during a divorce. And I thought he seemed a little spacey in the courtroom. I wouldn't be surprised to learn he's on antidepressants."

"So what you're saying is, we've drawn the worst possible judge—at the worst possible time."

"Pretty much, yeah." She grabbed her coat. "Come on. We've got an appointment to keep."

"THANK YOU FOR seeing us, Dr. Bennett. I really appreciate it."

Ben watched as the auburn-haired doctor with the black-rimmed glasses peered down at a tray covered with dead butterflies. She seemed absolutely absorbed by her work. He almost felt guilty, interrupting her with anything so trivial as a murder investigation.

"Not at all, Mr. Kincaid. Thank you for agreeing to see me at home. It's my day off."

"Least I could do. And call me Ben."

Christina inched forward. "How long have you been collecting butterflies?"

The doctor did not look up. "Well, I don't exactly collect them. I admire them. Lepidoptery is a science, not a hobby." She smiled slightly. "Of course, I'm just an amateur practitioner. But still."

Ben gazed at the walls of her study, which were covered with framed and mounted butterflies. Dozens of them. The myriad sizes, shapes, and colors were truly beautiful, Ben thought, even if he was basically looking at dead insects. The mounting also seemed very professional, at least to his untrained eye. The good doctor knew what she was doing.

"It must be an enormous amount of work," Christina commented.

"True. But I enjoy it."

"How long did it take you to pick it up?"

"Oh, I don't know. Years, I suppose. A little bit at a time." She set down the stiletto she was using to position a butterfly on a cork-based board. "Of course, I've spent my whole life learning to identify the butterflies themselves. Several years learning to use the tools of the trade. How to catch them. How to use the stiletto and scalpel to mount them. It's delicate work. Requires some real skill."

"Fascinating," Ben said, and for once, he meant it. "How did you learn it all?"

"Well, I'm a member of the American Lepidopterists' Society. They have meetings and such. Very detailed guidelines about collecting and exhibiting specimens. Data sharing. The handling of live material."

Ben bent down for a closer look at her work. "Mind if I ask what that is?"

"That, my friend, is a pristine specimen of *Ornithoptera victoriae victoriae*.

Queen Victoria's Birdwing from the Solomon Islands. I've been after one all my life. And now, thanks to the Society, I have one. They find already deceased specimens and preserve them." She grinned like a kid with a cookie. "You can see why I couldn't wait."

"It's beautiful," Christina said, wishing she could think of a more profound comment.

"That it is. And extremely endangered. Like all too many rainforest species, its days are numbered. The Society has tried introducing them into new environments. But it rarely takes. Unless there are some serious changes in the way we manage our natural resources, we'll probably see this and thousands of other beautiful and diverse species disappear. In our lifetimes. A tragic loss."

Staring at all the lovely examples lining her walls, Ben couldn't possibly argue with her. And he would've much rather talked about butterflies than murder. But that was not a long-term option. "Could we talk about Erin Faulkner for a moment?"

Dr. Bennett laid down her tools. "Of course. Poor Erin. I liked her. Genuinely. Not just in a doctor-patient way. She was a good person. And at one time, she was very strong, I believe."

"Before her family was murdered?"

Bennett nodded. "The way she handled herself during that crisis, the courage she showed in her escape, those were all remarkable. But the emotional toll it took on her—that was incalculable."

"Were you surprised when you heard she was dead?"

"Of course. I mean, suicide had always been a possibility for her. She was struggling with so much trauma. So much guilt. But I thought she was getting better." She sighed.

"You know," Christina said, "there's some doubt about whether it was suicide. In the police department, I mean."

"I know. I just finished talking to a homicide detective. Some big gruff guy with a Raymond Chandler fixation."

Ben's lips turned up. "Major Morelli, perhaps?"

"Yes. That was the one. I suppose they have to be thorough." Her eyes drifted, and Ben thought he caught a touch of genuine regret. "But it's hard for me to imagine it could be anything other than suicide."

"Did Erin ever discuss the source of her . . . guilt? I assume you can talk about this now."

"Yes. The privilege expires with the patient, I'm afraid." She paused. "Erin would never have used the word *guilt*. Not as such. But it was always there. It was as much a part of her as her arms and her damaged leg."

"She felt guilty because she survived. The only member of her family."

"Yes. That was certainly a part of it. But I also . . ." Her head tilted slightly. "I always had the sense there was something more."

Ben's eyes lit up. "Did she ever indicate what that other source of guilt might be?"

"No, I'm afraid she never did. Erin had not been my patient that long, you know. And she had not yet learned to speak freely. Had not learned to trust yet, not entirely. That woman should've been in therapy long before she was, frankly. If she had been . . ." She shook her head. "But worlds could be built on ifs, couldn't they?"

"Did she ever talk about the home invasion?"

"Yes, but she didn't like to. And of course, she didn't see that much of it herself. She was crippled and knocked unconscious early in the horror. When she woke, she was chained up in the cellar."

Ben nodded. He was all too familiar with the grim events of that night. "Can you think of anything she said, anything that might not be in the official reports? We have reason to believe that the man accused and convicted, Ray Goldman, did not actually commit the crime."

"That doesn't surprise me."

Ben blinked. This was a refreshing change of pace. "And we're trying to find out who did."

"Well, I could help you there."

Christina's eyes widened. "You can?"

"Oh yes," Dr. Bennett said, removing her glasses and rubbing the bridge of her nose. "I know who killed the Faulkner family. I always have."

"CAN I TALK to you?"

Mike glanced up from his coffee cup. Sergeant Baxter was bearing down on him. It seemed there was to be no rest, even during coffee breaks.

"Can it wait?"

Baxter placed one fist against her hip. "No, it can't."

Mike glanced over her shoulder. There were four other guys in the canteen, and they were already looking this way. "Not very private."

"Frankly, my dear, I don't give a damn."

Mike poured himself another cuppa. "Okay, Sergeant, what's the beef?"

"You filed a negative report on me."

"Tell me something I don't know."

"You accused me of unprofessional conduct."

"And your point is?"

Mike could feel the steam rising from the top of her head. "What the hell are you trying to do to me?"

"I think you're personalizing this, Sergeant. I'm just doing my job."

"Bullshit." She knocked the Styrofoam cup out of his hands. Hot black coffee flew across the room. "I didn't complain when you tried to get transferred to a different partner. I didn't complain when you filed reports disputing my conclusions. I didn't complain when you tried to use all your sick leave to get away or threatened to catch the Blue Flu if you didn't get transferred. But this is different! This goes on my permanent record."

"Sergeant, we may be partners, but you would do well to remember that I am also your superior officer. When I see conduct that in my opinion does not conform with the standards of this department—"

"Cut the crap, Morelli." She surged forward, giving him nowhere to escape. "You want to embarrass me in front of the other officers, you do that. You want to make me out as some kind of man-hating ball buster, fine. But don't screw with my career!"

"All I did was—"

"I know exactly what you did! And I know why you did it, too!"

"Sergeant Baxter—"

"I've been a cop for twelve years. And I've run into a lot of sexist creeps in my time. But no one ever messed with my record."

"Maybe it's overdue."

"Your screwing around could lose me my career!"

"Maybe you should lose your career."

"It's all I have!" Her voice rocketed through the small kitchen. Everyone else present instantly turned away, but Mike knew they were following every word.

Baxter retreated a step. She pressed her hand against her forehead, as if struggling to regain control. "May I ask one question? What exactly did I do that you found so unprofessional?"

Mike twisted his neck. "Well, there was no one single thing, really . . . some of the remarks you made at the organ clinic . . ."

"Like what?"

"Various things. You said the place gave you the creeps. Others overheard you."

"So what?"

"So, it's not the behavior of a professional. It's more something you'd expect from a . . . a . . ."

"Weak sister?"

"Not a member of the police department, anyway. Not a member of the homicide squad."

Baxter turned away. "This is such bullshit."

"It isn't. We're public officials. We have to maintain professional deportment."

"Bullshit, bullshit, bullshit."

"Plus, if you can't stand to be around body parts, how the hell are you going to handle yourself around a corpse? What use is a homicide detective with a weak stomach?"

Baxter's teeth were clenched so hard Mike thought her jaw might burst. "I've been around plenty of corpses, Morelli. Almost as many as you."

"You don't act like it."

"Why, because I don't go in for the macho poker face? Because I don't act like I don't care?"

"There's professional behavior, and there's unprofessional behavior. And unprofessional behavior—"

"Would be that crack you made the other day about my panties. In front of witnesses."

Mike fell silent.

"Now, that was genuinely unprofessional. That could get you suspended for a month. But did I turn you in, even though I found your behavior grossly offensive and revolting? No, I didn't. And you know why?" She leaned into his face. "Because I would never do such a crappy thing to my partner, that's why. *Even if he's a total and utter asshole!*"

"Excuse me. May I cut in?"

Mike ripped his eyes away from Baxter and saw, to his horror, Chief Blackwell standing not a foot away from them.

The other people in the canteen scattered. Show was over.

"Could I have the next dance?" Blackwell continued. "You two seem as if you may be ready for a break."

Baxter backed off. Mike tugged at the edges of his shirt, smoothing the wrinkles.

"Morning, Chief."

"And to you, Mr. Senior Homicide Investigator. Enjoying your early-morning caffeine?"

"Chief . . ."

"This isn't working," Baxter said bluntly, tossing her hair back. "Not at all."

"So I see." Blackwell looked at both of them. Mike could read the tension in his neck, his eyes. "I think it's time we had a private conference. A little heart-to-heart. One-on-one."

Mike nodded. "It's always hard to be the new kid, Chief. Don't be too tough on her."

Blackwell brought his head around slowly. "Her? I'm having a private conversation with you, Major. In my office. Now."

BEN COULD HARDLY restrain himself. "You know who killed the Faulkner family?"

"Of course," Dr. Bennett said. "I mean, I don't know his name. But I know who he was. And it was a him, by the way. I can guarantee it."

"How do you know this?"

"I'm a psychiatrist, remember? And I deal with a lot of sick miserable human beings. Frankly, Erin Faulkner was a pleasant change of pace from some of the cases I get, referred by prison or parole boards. Seriously deranged, dangerous individuals."

"So getting back to the Faulkner case," Christina said, "who was the killer?"

"The killer who almost wiped out the Faulkner family was what psychiatrists would classify as an organized nonsocial. I mean, when you think about it, the crime was really rather systematically executed. Even the eye removal was handled with consistency and efficiency. These people are usually relatively intelligent, decent looking, and well attuned to the feelings of others. Not just what they like, but what they don't like. What scares them."

"Sounds dangerous."

"Very. Combine that with an active fantasy life that allows them to dream about their crimes well in advance—which results in them being well planned by the time they are actually conducted."

"I see."

"Some experts think all children are organized nonsocials—their world revolves around themselves. But at some point in their development, most learn to care about others, about the world outside. But not organized nonsocials. They never outgrow the 'me' stage. All they care about is what they need. They are the center of their universe. They think they are never wrong, that they never make mistakes." She paused. "But of course they do, thank goodness. It's the only reason some of these monsters are ever caught."

"But—why?" Ben asked. "What would be this . . . organized nonsocial's motivation?"

"That could vary," Bennett explained. "Some of them simply like to inflict pain. They get a charge out of it—literally. Some delude themselves into believing they are scientists—conducting research into the levels of pain tolerance or some such horrid thing. For others, it's purely a power trip; they do it because they can. And for some, it's an intellectual challenge. What can I get away with? How long can I go without being caught?" Her eyes drifted to her butterfly wall. "And for some, it's purely sexual. They have a preoccupation that society doesn't condone—little girls, little boys, whatever."

"Any common denominators?"

"Just one. People who commit crimes like this can't help themselves. It's not that they lack self-control or they've consciously decided to indulge themselves. They just can't stop."

"How horrible," Christina said.

Bennett agreed. "Modern medicine has made some important strides. There are drugs now that can suppress some of the more malevolent urges. But it's always a tricky thing. Drugs can be unreliable. And if the patient forgets to take his pill one day—"

"Another family is obliterated."

"That's possible, yes."

"This may sound crazy," Christina said, "but I have a theory that there was more than one person involved in the crime. That there was a second person present. A second person with . . . well, for want of a better word, a conscience. More than the principal killer, anyway. Does that fit with your theory?"

Bennett considered for a moment. "Well, it would be extremely unusual for an organized nonsocial to take a partner. He would want to do all the planning and killing himself. But I suppose I can't totally eliminate the possibility of some kind of . . . procurer. Someone who didn't participate in the killings but was still essential in some way. Someone who suggested the crime or facilitated it."

"You expressed some doubts about Ray Goldman being the murderer," Ben said.

"Well, he doesn't really seem the organized nonsocial type, does he? I mean, I haven't met him personally, but from what I've read, he was a high-functioning, professional, highly educated man with no apparent psychological problems."

"Exactly," Ben said. "That's what I've been telling people for seven years. Would you be willing to take the stand and say that?"

"To be honest, I don't care much for the expert-witness scene. It's all a little tawdry, isn't it?"

She'd get no argument from Ben, but he could still use a medical witness at that hearing next week. "I'm fighting for a man's life here. I won't ask you to say anything you're not comfortable saying. Just tell it straight."

Bennett pondered. "Well . . . I'll think about it. But you must also remember—it's not unheard of for an organized nonsocial to be able to disguise his illness. To hide his aberration. Lots of people knew Ted Bundy—and liked him. No one thought he was a killer. Until he'd knocked off about forty people."

Ben nodded. A sobering thought.

"If there's nothing else, Ben . . ." She smiled. "I hear a rare lepidoptera calling me." She picked up her pins and stiletto.

"Of course." He and Christina headed for the door. On first arrival, he had thought the butterfly business a rather unusual hobby. Maybe even a little sick. Killing the pretties. But after hearing about what she did, what she knew, what she dealt with on a regular basis—he could see why she enjoyed her butterflies. He could see why she needed them.

"What the hell is wrong with you?" Chief Blackwell bellowed.

Mike drew himself back into the armchair. He felt about two feet tall. Like he'd been called into the vice principal's office. "I can't work with her, Chief. I just can't."

"You can if I say you can."

"No, I'm sorry, but I can't."

"You mean you won't."

Mike gripped the arms of the chair. "It's impossible, sir. She's got a chip on her shoulder the size of Sand Springs. She's bullying and domineering. A real harpy."

"Don't start with the sexist remarks."

"I didn't mean it that way."

"No? I suppose you meant to say something about her panties?"

Mike closed his eyes. "I should've known she'd go running to you."

"For your information, Major, she did not report the incident, although pursuant to departmental regulations, she should have. Happily, I got reports from about twelve other eyewitnesses who heard the whole thing. You're the talk of the department."

"Chief, it was just me and Frank and some of the boys shooting the breeze."

"I don't care what it was. And I don't want to hear any excuses!" Blackwell pounded his fist against his desk. "I don't understand this, Mike. Hell, you're

supposed to be the sensitive one on the force. The college man with the graduate degree. The English major, for God's sake. And you're behaving worse than
the worst of the old-guard male chauvinists. The difference being—they don't
know any better. You do."

Mike's mouth felt dry. "Chief, you know I don't have a problem with women
working on the force—"

"I don't know that I do, Mike. I used to. Now I'm not so sure." He leaned
across his desk. "What do you think would happen if word got around about
this? What if the press got a hold of your 'panties' remark? What if it got back
to the mayor? Huh? I can assure you she would not find it amusing."

"Sir, I have absolutely no objection to women police officers. Or even personally working with women. It's just . . . *this* woman. Baxter. I can't work
with her."

"Why? Are you hot for her?"

"Huh? What are you talking about?"

"It hasn't escaped my notice that Sergeant Baxter is quite attractive. And
I'm sure it hasn't escaped your notice, either. Is that the problem? Do you
have feelings for her? Are you suppressing your sexual frustration with open
hostility?"

"Sir, I can assure you that isn't the case."

"Yeah, I hear your mouth working. But I'm not sure your brain is along
for the ride." He rapped a pencil on his desk. "That would explain a lot. I'm
aware that your personal life has been totally screwed up ever since your divorce. Rarely a date, from what I hear. Hanging out with defense attorneys.
Perverse stuff like that."

"Sir, I give you my personal guarantee. There is no sexual attraction. If the
rest of the female population were covered with pustulant weeping boils, there
would still be no sexual attraction."

"Says you." Blackwell stared across the desk at him. Mike didn't remember
ever seeing the man look so angry. "May I remind you how this assignment
started, Major? It started because you screwed up. Badly."

"Sir—"

"Just shut up and listen. A lot of the higher-ups thought I should've
yanked your badge right then and there, after you butted into that hostage
scene where you had no business and made a mess of it. But I said no. I said
give him another chance."

"I appreciate that, sir."

"Our record as an equal opportunity employer has not always been the
best. The mayor wants to change that." He paused, looking squarely at Mike.

"You can see where she might have an interest in that sort of thing. She wants Baxter to succeed. And therefore, so do I. That's why I assigned her to you. And that's why you are going to do everything possible to make the assignment a success. Do you understand me?"

Mike's face tightened. "I suppose."

"I will not accept excuses, Mike. You will make this work."

"I'll do my best—"

"Don't give me that schoolboy crap about doing your best. *You will make it work.* Are we clear on that?"

Mike stood at attention. "Yes, sir!"

"I'm tearing up this bogus report you wrote. I wouldn't allow that to sit in anyone's file, much less Sergeant Baxter's."

"Yes, sir."

Blackwell pointed a finger. "And make no mistake about it, Mike. I don't care how long we've worked together. If you screw this up, I'll have your badge."

"Chief—!"

"I mean it, Mike. You keep that in mind as you continue to work with your new partner. You want this to work." He lowered his voice. "Because it's not just her career that's on the line here. It's yours."

16

BEN WAS ALMOST out his front door when Joni stopped him. "Got some news."

He pulled the door closed behind him and locked it. "Mr. Perry finally going to pay his bill?"

"Not that exciting."

"You got the Silvermans' air conditioner fixed?"

"Not that mundane, either." She shifted her weight, and as she did, Ben couldn't help but notice the tool belt slung low around her hips. Pretty darned appealing, as handymen go. "It's about that bundle of fur you room with."

"Giselle?"

"Yeah, that one. I took a look at her last night, before you got home."

"Did you take her to the vet?"

"Didn't need to. It's obvious."

"What's obvious? Feline schizophrenia?"

"I don't know why I didn't think of it before. All the signs were there. Moodiness. Strange behavior. Desperation to get outside. All those cats swarming outside the house. All of them male."

"Is this Final Jeopardy?" Ben asked. "Because if it is, I'm about to lose everything I wagered."

"That's because you, for all your brains, are so pitifully unaware of some of life's little fundamentals."

"Like what?"

"Like sex, Ben." She grinned. "Your cat is in heat."

Ben was nonplussed. "Then get her a fan."

Joni sighed. "Come along, Benjy. We're going to have a little talk. The one your daddy should've had with you a long time ago . . ."

*　　*　　*

THE MAN WHO greeted Ben an hour later at the front door of the laboratory was wearing a white coat with a pocket protector that held an array of pens and pencils and even a small calculator. Ben supposed he looked the very image of an industrial chemist, but for some reason he kept thinking of Sherman and Mr. Peabody.

"Thank you for agreeing to see me, Dr. Reynolds."

"Not at all." Conrad Reynolds was a short, balding man in his late forties, and remarkably convivial for someone who spent his days with test tubes and formulae. "I still remember Ray Goldman fondly. And Frank Faulkner, for that matter. Please come inside."

Ben followed him through the door. The front lobby of the building was about as stark as it was possible to be without becoming a warehouse. No attempt whatsoever had been made to meliorate the trek from the door to the elevator bank. Only a single sign that read: PRAIRIE DOG FLAVORS, INC.

"Mind if we go upstairs?" Reynolds asked. "I've got some chairs in my lab. And there are a few others you should talk to."

"People who knew Ray?"

"And Frank, yes. All those years ago. Not many employees have lasted that long, but a few." They rode up three floors.

When they stepped out, they faced a heavy iron sealed door. "I'm afraid the security around here is in the same league as the Pentagon's. Excuse me just a sec. Retinal scan."

Ben grimaced. "Can I wait outside?"

"That was *retinal*, Mr. Kincaid. Re-tin-al." Reynolds pushed a button, and a screened panel on the door flickered to life. Reynolds pressed his face against it. A red light flashed across his eyes. A moment later, Ben heard the door click open.

"Wow. That really works? I thought that was just on *Star Trek*."

"This isn't even new tech," Reynolds replied. "We've had this for more than a decade. Nowadays they're using voiceprints and DNA tests."

"Is all this necessary?"

Reynolds nodded. "Our owners are very protective of our secrets."

"Mind if I ask why?"

Reynolds gestured toward the interior. "Because the stuff we come up with in here is worth billions, that's why."

Ben stepped into what seemed to him a prototypical chemistry lab, not that he would really know. There were long tables covered with tubes and Bunsen burners and vials of brightly colored fluids held upright in wooden racks, some of them labeled with long Latinate names. It reminded Ben of his organic chemistry lab class back at OU. He only hoped he handled this case better than he had the class.

The one difference was the smell. Marvelous mouthwatering aromas assaulted his senses the moment he stepped inside. Part bakery, part steakhouse, part patisserie. No wonder Reynolds seemed so genial. If Ben worked in a place that smelled this nice, he'd probably be happy, too.

"What kind of work do you do here?" Ben asked. "What industries do you serve?"

"We specialize in the fast-food industry. Have since this lab was built." He took a chair and offered Ben the one beside it. "We serve other businesses on occasion, but that's our bread and butter."

"I see. What do you do for the fast-food people?"

"Make their food taste good." He winked. "And believe me, that's no mean feat."

"But—surely you don't cook their food."

Reynolds chuckled. "Cooking, Mr. Kincaid, has nothing to do with it. You have to realize that, in most fast-food restaurants, virtually everything has been processed and flash-frozen, then reheated for serving. If it weren't for the chem lab, it wouldn't taste like anything. Certainly nothing you'd ever want to put in your mouth."

"What do you do?"

Reynolds's eyes twinkled. "Magic." He reached for a nearby vial containing a clear liquid. "See this? This is the secret of the double whammy burger in the Bob's Burgers chain. And that one? Something we came up with last year. Made the chicken sandwich a top seller at Burger Bliss."

"That stuff is in the food?"

"Just a touch. That's all it takes."

"Doesn't sound very appetizing."

"Don't be fooled. Those burgers sell by the millions. You've eaten fast food before, haven't you?"

Ben smiled wryly. "Once or twice."

"And be honest—for the most part, it tastes pretty good, doesn't it? May not be good for you, but the flavor is generally yummy. That's why they sell so well. Up to ninety percent of a food's taste can derive from its aroma. And we provide the aroma."

"That's amazing."

"Yes, I suppose it is. It's the dirty secret that has made the fast-food industry the gigantic economic success it is. May have made the whole nation obese in the process. But it's made a lot of businessmen very rich. Last year, Americans spent more than one hundred and ten billion dollars on fast food—more than they spent on cars, computers, or college. Combined."

"That much?"

"It's a huge business. Hugely successful. For years, the taste and aroma business was dominated by a handful of chemical plants located just off the New Jersey Turnpike. International Flavors & Fragrances is the largest. They handle many of the large fast-food chains. They're responsible for six of the country's top ten perfumes. We were actually one of the first to make a success of it in the Southwest."

"Based on your fast-food formulae?"

"It isn't just that. We've devised flavors for potato chips, cereals, bread, crackers, ice cream, toothpaste, mouthwash. Even pet food."

"I'm surprised all this chemistry doesn't jack up those cut-rate fast-food prices."

Reynolds flat out laughed. "Are you kidding? Fast food is cheap for a reason. You're not exactly eating Grade-A meat, you know. Typically, the packaging costs the company more than the food itself. They can afford a chemical or two to make it scrummy."

"Where do these flavors come from?"

"Most are a combination of several chemical compounds, but often the primary aroma comes from a single component. Let me show you." He grabbed one of the vials of colored fluids, uncorked it, and held it under Ben's nose. "Close your eyes and tell me what you think."

Ben took a whiff. "Apple."

"Yeah. Except actually, it's ethyl-2-methyl butyrate." He uncorked another vial. "Try this one."

Ben inhaled. "Marshmallow."

"You'd think. But in truth it's pure ethyl-3-hydroxybutanoate. And methyl-2-peridylketone gives you popcorn. Benzaldehyde smells like almond. And 3-methyl butanoic acid gives you human body odor."

"Wouldn't that make a swell hamburger."

"No, but a hint of it might make a splendid cologne."

"How can you add these chemicals to food without telling people? Aren't there FDA rules? Labeling laws?"

Reynolds smiled. "Ever read one of those labels?"

"Only when I'm trying to diet."

"Next time you check one out, or read the ingredients on a fast-food prod-uct, look for the words *natural flavor*."

"I thought we were talking about chemicals."

"We are. But if they come from organic sources, they're called natural fla-vors. Even if we've worked for months to create those natural flavors in the lab. If they come from inorganic sources, they're called artificial flavors. Either way, it sounds pretty innocuous, don't you agree?"

"And you don't have to explain what they are?"

"Nope. The FDA doesn't make us identify the ingredients of the fla-vor additives, as long as they're GRAS—Generally Regarded As Safe. You wouldn't believe some of them. Beef extracts are commonly added to chicken sandwiches. So-called natural smoke flavor is often added to grilled chicken breasts. Is that natural? You tell me. Whatever it is, we're specifically protected from detailing the ingredients—because these formulae are considered trade secrets."

"Nice loophole."

"Believe me, it's true. The fast-food corps are constantly spying on one another, trying to swipe the other guys' formulae. They hire spies—they're called *kites* in the biz—to ferret out their competitors' secrets. Every aspect of this business is cutthroat. Did you hear about the Kraft Foods pizza case? Kraft sued Schwan's, claiming they stole their frozen pizza plans. They asked for 1.75 billion in damages."

Ben whistled.

"We're expected to do our best to keep these secrets out of the hands of kites. Which is why we have the tight security."

"We've come a long way since Betty Crocker, huh?"

"Oh, not really. Flavor additives go way back. Remember, when Colum-bus and most of the other early explorers took off, they were searching for spices. Making food taste good was big business even then. We're doing the same thing they did, except with chromatographs, spectrometers, and vapor analyzers."

"Is this the kind of work Ray Goldman did? And Frank Faulkner?"

"Frank was a flavorist. He specialized in developing new food flavor for-mulae. He was one of the best. Sort of a cross between a chemist and a poet. There was talk that he might start his own lab. Before the tragedy. He did some breakthrough work on mouthfeel."

"Mouthfeel?"

"Oh yeah. Very important. Mouthfeel is the combination of chemicals and textures in the mouth that determine how a processed food is perceived by the consumer."

"Can that be controlled?"

"You betcha. Mouthfeel men use starches, gums, fats, and emulsifiers to alter the texture of foods."

Ben considered. "Did you know anyone who might have had a grudge against Frank?"

He shook his head. "It's like I told the police all those years ago. The murder came as a complete surprise to me. To all of us."

"What about his personal life? Any skeletons there?"

"Not that I ever heard about. Frank seemed like the model of a family man. So many kids—but he loved them. You could tell that whenever he mentioned them. He'd been very successful and made a lot of money, and he liked to shower it on his family."

"What about Ray? Any gossip there?"

"Not that I recall. But I didn't hang with him much. You should talk to Chris Hubbard. He'd know more. They were pretty close."

Ben pushed out of his chair. "Okay. Is he a flavorist?"

"Sort of. He works in the biological additives department."

"Biological additives? Do I want to know about this?"

Reynolds walked him to the door, smiling thinly. "Probably not."

MIKE ENTERED THE exercise room without knocking.

"We need to talk. Now."

Sergeant Baxter was seated on the floor, legs crossed, hands pressed against her knees, eyes closed. She did not look up. She did not answer.

"Did you hear me? We need to talk!"

Baxter opened one eye. "Leave me alone. I'm on my break."

"That didn't stop you from barging in on my coffee klatch and it's not going to stop me from interrupting your—" He stopped short. "What the hell are you doing anyway?"

She opened the other eye and sighed. "I'm meditating. Was, at any rate." She pushed onto her knees and dusted off her backside.

"You meditate?"

"Every day. Keeps me centered. Keeps me from losing control."

"So that's how you do it."

She gave him a withering look. "You should try it sometime, Morelli. You could use a little tranquillity in your life."

"Actually, I used to meditate. Regularly."

"A big ol' macho brute like yourself?"

It was Mike's turn to wither. "Used to." Without thinking, he took her elbow and helped her up. Baxter appeared surprised but did not resist. "I was into the hatha yoga thing. And Zen meditation. Back in college."

"How did you ever get started on that?"

"Oh, it wasn't me really, it was—" He shook his head. "Someone else."

"But you stopped."

"Yeah. I had to make some major life changes a while back. I guess that's one of the things that fell by the wayside. Hadn't even thought about it for years. Shame, really. I always rather enjoyed that."

Baxter folded her arms guardedly across her chest. "I'll probably regret this, but . . . if you'd like, I could show you a few positions."

Mike considered for a moment, then shook himself out of it. What was he thinking? "We need to talk."

"You've said that three times now. Instead of talking about how we need to talk, why don't you just say what's on your mind?"

Good point. "We have to work together."

"Just now figuring that out?"

"God knows I've tried everything possible to avoid it, but it remains true. You may not like it. I don't like it. But we still have to do it."

She cocked an eyebrow. "So what do you suggest?"

"I suggest we behave like professionals. No more big scenes in the kitchen."

"I can live with that. If you think you can restrain that tongue of yours."

Control, he told himself. Control.

"That means you've got to cool it with the nasty reports. Partners don't do that to one another."

"Blackwell tore it up. And he told me that . . . that you didn't say anything. About what happened the other day. What you overheard. I . . . uh . . . appreciate that."

Baxter couldn't have looked more surprised if he had proposed marriage.

Mike continued. "We both know you could've gotten me into a hell of a lot of hot water. And it must've been tempting, especially after my report. But you didn't." He paused. "Thank you."

She waved her hand. *"De nada."*

Mike suddenly felt ungodly uncomfortable. Why was it so much easier to deal with this woman when they were yelling at each other? "We're going to have to find a workable compromise."

"Sounds good."

"Even if I don't necessarily think this investigation is . . . meritorious."

"What a diplomat you've become."

"Even so, I'll do my best to see it through in a professional manner. At the same time, I expect you to respect the fact that I'm the superior officer here. I have mucho years in homicide. I know what I'm doing."

"Granted." She looked at him warily. "As long as you don't try to send me for coffee or anything."

"No problem. I brew my own."

Baxter smiled, just a little. She picked up her coat and holster from the hook behind the door. "Mind if I ask what brought about this remarkable conversion experience? Did you see a light on the road to Damascus?"

"More or less. Blackwell read me the riot act."

"And?"

"And he told me to bury the bickering. He wants you to succeed here. And he wants me to help make it happen."

"I see. So I'm sort of like your charity project or something."

Mike fought back the irritation. "The only charity I'm working for is me. I'm not trying to be a great guy. I'm trying not to lose my job."

Her face hardened a bit. "I see. Basically, it's just more looking out for number one."

"Basically, yeah. You have a problem with that?"

"No," she said as she adjusted her holster. "I just—" She shook her head. "Never mind."

Mike pulled a crumpled scrap of paper out of his pocket. "I found the doctor."

"The shrink?"

"No. The other one. The doctor Sheila told us about. If you can call him that."

"What kind of doctor is he?"

"I don't think I can explain it. You'll have to see for yourself."

"How did you find him? Sheila didn't even remember his name."

"I've been a cop for fifteen years. That's how."

"Right, right." She extended her hand. "Peace?"

He shook. "Peace. Hatchet buried."

"Good."

Mike started toward the door. "Well," he said, trying to sound optimistic, "perhaps my lawyer friend was right. Maybe this is the beginning of a beautiful friendship."

"Don't push it, Morelli."

"Right."

"FUNGAL CULTURES?"

The man behind the thick glasses blinked. "That's right."

"People are eating funguses?"

"Fungi. Sure. Anytime they go into a fast-food joint, it's a strong possibility. Biotechnological flavoring is the hot new thing." Chris Hubbard was younger than Dr. Reynolds, and his youthful exuberance showed when he talked about his work. Rarely had Ben seen anyone become so wild-eyed and rapturous while talking about food additives. "Tissue cultures are used, too. Fermentation. But I think the most exciting breakthroughs are happening with fungi."

"Be still my heart."

"Although enzyme-based processes can give you some darn good dairy flavors. Any kind of butter you can imagine. Cheesy butter, creamy butter, milky butter. Anything."

"Except that none of it's real butter."

"Well, not the kind Ma and Pa made back on the farm. The fermentation processes, heating combinations of sugar and amino acids, have also resulted in some dynamite meat flavors."

"Yum, yum."

"And the best part is, all of these are considered natural flavors by the FDA."

"Amazing." In order to speak to Hubbard, Ben had to submit to more security checks, then be escorted by an armed guard into a lab maybe a tenth the size of the previous one. The only entrance or egress was through a single thick metal-reinforced door. "So if your research is so hot, why do you have such a lousy lab?"

Hubbard leaned closer. "The smaller the lab, the easier it is to secure."

"I see. Dr. Reynolds tells me you used to hang out with Ray Goldman."

"True. I considered Ray one of my best friends."

"Have you seen him lately?"

"No. I haven't seen him since . . . you know." He sighed. "I've thought about driving down to McAlester and visiting him. But somehow, I never did it. It just seemed . . . I don't know. I wasn't sure if he'd be glad to see me or not. So I never went."

"What did the two of you do? Before he was incarcerated?"

Hubbard averted his eyes. "Well . . . this is . . . rather embarrassing."

Aha, Ben thought. At last, I've uncovered the nasty. "I don't mean to make you uncomfortable, but I need to know everything that might possibly be relevant."

"Still . . . I don't see any reason . . ."

What is it? Ben wondered. Sexual degradation? Petty larceny? "I'm sorry, but I have to insist. And if necessary, I'll have to subpoena."

Hubbard drew in his breath. His teeth clenched tightly together. "Well . . ."

Yes . . . Yes . . .

"We used to play Scrabble."

Ben stared at him blankly. "That's it?"

"Yeah. Humiliating, isn't it? You probably thought we were hot young studs out on the town, carving a swath through all the beautiful babes. But no. Most nights we were rearranging tiles and figuring out a way to get rid of the Q."

"I see . . ."

"It's particularly embarrassing because people already have this stereotype that scientists—and particularly chemists—are really boring. And what do you know? It turns out to be true."

"There must've been something else. . . ."

"Not much. Mind you, we got really good, there toward the end. We were in a league."

"A . . . Scrabble league?"

"You bet. They're all over the country. All over the world, actually. We got together twice a week to play and practice. Compare strategies. Memorize word lists."

"Fascinating."

"Did you know there are ninety-six legitimate two-letter words? Knowing them is the key to the game. A well-placed two-letter word can score better than a seven-letter bingo."

"Do tell."

"Ray was one of the best. He had all the word lists down cold. He was so organized, you know? Not all that social, but very organized. And he was a master of the anagram. He once scored three bingos in a single game. That's when you lay down all seven of your tiles at once. You get a fifty-point bonus for that, you know."

"Sounds like you two took this seriously."

"We did. We were tournament-rated."

"There are tournaments?"

"Lots of them. We'd qualified for the nationals. Then Ray ran into that spot of trouble. . . ."

Being arrested for murder. Yeah, that could spoil your Scrabble career. "What did you think when Ray was arrested?"

"I couldn't believe it. I mean, sure, Ray had his eccentricities. Oddities. But a mass murderer? No way." Ben noticed that his fingers were fidgeting. "I mean, surely not."

"You don't seem totally convinced."

"Well, I mean, I wasn't there, was I? You never really know what anyone might be capable of doing, given the right circumstances. But I couldn't believe that Ray did . . . that horrible crime."

Ben shifted around in his chair. This conversation was starting to make him feel distinctly uncomfortable. "Tell me about these eccentricities of Ray's."

"Oh . . . gosh . . ." Ben could tell the man already regretted having said anything. "It's hard to explain. Once or twice we went out together. Single bars, that sort of thing. I was unmarried back then. And this was before Ray met Carrie."

"You knew Carrie?"

"Oh yeah. Wonderful woman. She really loved him."

"She dumped him."

"Well, honestly, what can you expect? When your fiancé is on death row, that doesn't augur well for the marriage. Still, I always wondered if there wasn't maybe . . . I don't know. Something else going on. Something he did or said."

"Like what?"

"I don't know. I'm just babbling."

Was the man intentionally frustrating him, or did it just work out that way? Ben couldn't be sure. But he made a mental note to follow up on this. "Tell me about these singles'-bar outings. What was so odd about Ray?"

"Maybe odd isn't the right word. He just . . . didn't react the way other people do. Particularly about women."

"Give me an example."

"Oh, like, I'd see some hot-looking chick in a slinky dress and I might wolf-whistle or make some approving remark about a part of her anatomy. But Ray would say things like, 'Yeah, I'd like to knock her down and give her what she wants.' You know, stuff like that."

Ben felt his mouth drying. "And what did you think when he said this?"

"Not much at the time. I just thought of it as one of Ray's quirks. Frankly, chemists aren't always the most socially well-adjusted people on earth. But then, after the murders, I began to wonder. . . ."

"If Ray was really the killer."

"No, no!" Hubbard held up his hands. "I'm sure he wasn't. I just . . . you know. You can't help but wonder."

"Did Ray make any other violent remarks?"

"Just more of the same. 'If I could get her in a room alone, I'd wipe the smile off her face.' Or: 'I could take that clown out with one kick to the kneecap.' Like that. I mean, I can't say I never heard anything like that from a man before. Guys will be guys, especially after a few drinks."

"Did Frank Faulkner go on any of these barhops?"

"Frank? No."

"But you knew Frank."

"Yeah, but he ran in higher circles than we did. He was older and had already become a huge success. He was the company's bright young thing. Already rich as hell, too."

"Did you know of anyone who might've had a reason to kill him?"

"No. I suppose his early success could stir up a lot of jealousy. Resentment. But to kill him? Surely not."

"What did you do on these bar outings?"

"Oh, precious little, believe me. I don't think we ever once picked up a woman. I'm not sure we ever even spoke to one. We just watched mostly. Swilled drinks and admired from a distance. Which was not so bad, actually. There are worse things than watching a parade of shapely female calves pass by."

Ben smiled a little. "You're a leg man."

"Guess my secret's out."

"It's not a crime." Ben folded up his notebook and prepared to leave. "What about Ray? Was he a leg man?"

"Oh, no." A crease crossed his forehead. "He made that very clear on more than one occasion. He went for the eyes."

Ben felt his back stiffen.

"He was nuts for a good pair of eyes," Hubbard continued. "He'd catch the ladies' gaze and follow them from one end of the club to the other. Staring at their eyes."

17

"EAR KINDLING? THAT sounds dangerous."

"Not kindling. Candling."

"Ear candling?" Mike shrugged. "Still sounds dangerous."

The doctor appeared all too accustomed to this reaction. "It's a well-established scientific technique. Dates back to ancient Egypt."

"So does trepanning, but I wouldn't want to try that either."

Dr. Harris smiled. "Totally different, I assure you."

"And Erin Faulkner went in for this?"

"She visited me once a week. More regularly than she saw her psychiatrist, I understand." Dr. Jamison Harris was a relatively young man—in his early thirties, Mike guessed. He was a trifle overweight but seemed in generally good shape, with long, brown hair that curled uncontrollably down his head and touched his shoulders. "She enjoyed her sessions."

"Do you mind if I ask—why?"

"It's very relaxing," Harris explained. "And we live in an age when people are looking for relaxation, for something to calm their nerves and relieve their stress. Simple ways to achieve an altered state. No one more than Erin Faulkner."

Sergeant Baxter frowned. "Personally, I think I'll just stick with a good hot soak in the tub."

Harris nodded. "And do you light candles when you take your bath?"

She shrugged. "Sometimes."

"Turn on some soothing music?"

"When I have the time."

"And what Erin Faulkner did with me was much the same. Only more so. And with some medical benefits."

"If you say so." Mike dug his fists deep into his trench coat. "You ever heard about this ear-candling bit, Baxter?"

"Actually, I have. I had to educate myself. We shut down a couple of so-called therapists who were doing it in OK City."

"What was the charge?"

She gave the doctor the eye. "Quack medicine."

Harris held up a finger. "But they weren't licensed to practice medicine, right? I am. I'm beyond your reach."

"True enough. But I wonder how the AMA feels about this?"

Mike gave her a stern look. Don't alienate the witness before they have a chance to interrogate him.

Baxter took the cue. "Maybe I haven't had it explained to me properly. Could you tell me what it is exactly you do?"

"I'd be delighted." Harris walked them across his apartment to a long table in the corner. It looked to Mike like something he might expect to see in a massage parlor, which, combined with the fact that the doctor was operating out of his apartment, did not elevate his opinion of the man's practice.

"It's very simple, really," Harris said, raising a long white object. "I light the wide end of a hollow conical candle made of waxed cloth. Very gently, I insert the narrow tip on the opposite end into the ear. The heat generated by the flame creates a vacuum that sucks out all the foreign matter in the ear."

"Like what?"

"Wax, obviously. But there's more. Dust, dirt. Ear mites. Sometimes even small insects. Spiders and such."

Mike cringed. "Out of someone's ear?"

"You heard me."

"You know, I've personally viewed sixty-four homicide victims, most of them violent deaths. But this is making me sick."

"It's not that bad, I assure you."

"But how do you know if you actually accomplished anything?"

"After the procedure is finished—it takes about an hour—you can cut open the hollow candle and see for yourself what came out."

"Oh happy day. And you say Erin Faulkner went in for this?"

"She said it was the high point of her week. She looked forward to it. It made her feel clean—in a way that nothing else did."

"I'd like to ask you a few questions about what Erin might've told you. When she was in for her . . . er . . . candling sessions."

"I'm afraid I can't do that. Privilege, you know."

"She's dead, Doctor."

"Yes. But I still prefer not to reveal confidences. Not unless I'm ordered by the court."

Apparently this was more than Baxter could bear. She stepped in between Mike and Harris. "Look, Doctor—if you were performing open-heart surgery, I might buy that. But this is medicine-show crap and we both know it. I'm not going to let you hide behind any so-called medical ethics."

"I very much resent that. The ear-candling technique is a tried-and-true—"

"Don't pull that crap on me, Doctor. I'm aware that this is the hot trendy new treatment for society broads who don't really have anything wrong with them. But that doesn't mean it works."

"And tell me again where you got your medical degree?"

"There's absolutely no proof whatsoever that this procedure does any good. What's more, it could lead to infection, not to mention burns on the ear canal or eardrum or hair. The FDA considers it a heath hazard."

"As if they knew anything about medicine."

"Does the American Academy of Otolaryngology know anything about medicine?"

Mike did a double take. Now he was impressed.

"Because I happen to know for a fact," Baxter continued, "that they don't think it works. They say a lighted candle could never create enough suction to draw wax or much of anything else out of the ear. They say that stuff that shows up when you cut open the candle is just melted wax."

"That's absurd! It's—it's—ear mites, and—"

"Dogs get ear mites, Doctor. Dogs and cats. Not people. And ear wax is good for you, at least up to a point. It traps dust and dirt and prevents infection. Ear canals are hard to get at for a reason—to protect the eardrum."

"It helps relieve headaches. Stress. You're totally ignoring the psychological benefits."

"What, the pleasure of lying on a table for an hour with a decent-looking guy in the room?"

"My business has been thriving."

"You've got other customers? Besides Erin?"

"I've never been so busy. Does that surprise you?"

"Well, frankly, yes. I mean, I know Erin was kinda messed up—"

"Excuse me," Harris said, cutting him off, "but I don't agree with that at all."

"You don't?"

"No, I don't."

"Why not?"

"I can't talk about it."

Mike sighed. "Dr. Harris, surely you realize that a report from us to the state licensing board or the AMA could get you shut down inside of a week. What's more"—he glanced at his partner—"it should be fairly apparent to you by now that Sergeant Baxter would really enjoy doing it. I think you better talk to us, Doctor. Don't you?"

"OKAY," JONES WAS saying to Loving as Ben entered the office, "I understand about the food and the water and the weapons. But why do you need the metal helmet?"

Ben's eyes diverted to Jones's desk, which was currently ornamented by an underwater diving helmet that had been tricked out with mirrors and an antenna. It looked like something Commander Cody might wear in an old movie serial.

Ben pulled up a chair. This was an explanation he wanted to hear.

"Two words," Loving said, his face grave. "Mind control."

Jones was not impressed. "I'm supposed to believe someone wants to control *your* mind?"

"It ain't just me, wise guy. When they come, they'll come for everyone."

"And they is—?"

"The Council on Foreign Relations. The UN. The CIA. The Trilateral Commission. The Rhodes scholars."

"The Rhodes scholars?" Ben echoed.

"Hell, yes. Cecil Rhodes was a One World nut from the get-go. What did you think he was doing out in Africa?"

"Well, as I recall—"

"The Rhodes scholars exist to implement his totalitarian dream. That's why the Trilaterals make sure they're put in positions of power."

"They do?"

"Of course they do. How did you think Bill Clinton managed to become president?"

"I've wondered about that, actually."

"It's all part of a scheme orchestrated by the CIA—but of course the CIA is controlled by the NWO."

"Of course."

"It's well documented. Just like the CIA mind-control experiments."

"CIA mind control?" Jones said. "Give me a break."

"It's a fact, chump. Ever hear of MK-ULTRA? Congress had to pay big bucks to the survivors of that early shot at LSD-induced mind control. And that's just the tip of the iceberg. There's a dozen more that Congress knows nothin' about."

"But you do."

"I try to stay informed." Loving jabbed a thumb toward his massive chest. "They've expanded their reach. Programmed suicides. Jonestown. Heaven's Gate."

"All CIA experiments?" Jones said. "And here I thought those people were just easily manipulated losers."

"I gotta friend who downloaded a top secret NATO report off the Internet. Shows how the New World Order plans to soften up America with treaties like NAFTA that suck away all our jobs, then terrorize us with operations like Ruby Ridge and Waco. When all hell breaks loose, the UN so-called peacekeepers will be sent in to quiet things down. Those troops are already stationed in our national parks. They're just waiting for their cue to spread out and take over. And our military will go along with it. You know why?"

"Uh . . . mind control?" Ben hazarded.

"Damn straight. Been setting this up for years. And the American public won't resist. Know why?"

Ben and Jones spoke in unison. "Mind control."

"Right as rain. But they won't get me." Loving patted the big round hunk of metal on the desk. " 'Cause I'll be wearing my helmet."

"Well, not in the office," Ben said. "Violates the dress code."

Loving appeared miffed. "This is serious, Skipper."

"Seriously deranged, you mean. This is the most paranoid stuff I've heard since . . . well, since the last time we talked, anyway." Ben pushed himself out of his chair. "But enough fun. I want a status meeting in the main conference room in ten minutes. Be prepared to tell me what you've learned."

Jones scowled. "And if we haven't learned anything?"

Ben checked his watch. "You've got ten minutes."

"LET'S TRY THIS again," Mike said. "Why don't you agree that Erin was pretty messed up?"

Dr. Harris pursed his lips, obviously unhappy. But given a choice between talking and facing the wrath of Sergeant Baxter, he apparently decided he could be a bit more garrulous. "I had a chance to talk with her on a regular basis for more than two years."

"And you found her perfectly normal?"

"I don't know what perfectly normal is." Harris spread his hands expansively.

"Certainly I've never seen it. But Erin was no worse than most of the women I see. To the contrary, when you take into account all that she had been through, all that she had experienced, I think she coped rather well."

"I would agree with you. Right up until she killed herself." He saw Baxter glare at him, but chose to ignore it.

"I don't believe that, either," Harris shot back. "The Erin Faulkner I knew would never give up like that."

"How can you be sure?"

"Think about it for a moment. If she didn't give up when she was trapped in that basement—alone, abandoned, chained like a wild dog, listening to the tortured screams of her family—when would she?"

Mike didn't answer.

"I think Erin had an inner strength she was only beginning to tap. She had some problems, yes. Something was eating away at her. She kept telling me there was something she had to fix. Something she had to make right."

"Ever tell you what that was?" Baxter asked.

"I'm afraid not. I tried not to push her. I wasn't her shrink, after all. I knew she'd tell me when she was ready. What I'm saying is—she was dealing with it. She was coping. There was absolutely no indication that she was at her wit's end."

Mike considered. "I got a lawyer friend who saw her the day she died. He says she made a big confession to him about . . . something she said at the trial."

"But that again is an indication that she was dealing." Harris looked down, shaking his head. "I just don't believe she would kill herself."

"Maybe that's because you don't want to believe it," Mike said. "Sounds to me as if you rather liked Erin."

"Of course I liked her. Who wouldn't? She was a survivor. A real one—not some media fool who won a game show. Someone who had been through an experience that would've killed most of us. Someone who conquered her fears and was functioning as a useful productive human being. Who wouldn't admire that?"

Mike had to concede the point. "I don't know what I'd have done if that had happened to my family. If I'd lost all the people I love and cherish most."

Harris looked up abruptly. "Well, except—oh, of course. You're right."

Baxter stepped in. "What? What was that?"

"Nothing. You're right. I agree."

She positioned herself directly in front of Harris. An obvious intimidation move, but Mike had noticed Baxter didn't exactly shy away from those. "Is there something else? Something else that happened to Erin?"

"I—I don't know what you mean."

Baxter grabbed him by the lapel. "You're hiding something. Tell me. Now!"

The proximity of her hand to his voice box made it difficult for Harris to speak. "I just—I sensed there were some . . . issues. Between Erin and her father."

"Her father has been dead for seven years!"

"I know. Before that."

"Stop playing games! What do you know?"

"Nothing! Nothing at all!"

"Listen to me, you little quack. I got a twenty-two-year-old woman dead. I don't believe she killed herself any more than you do, and if you know something that could help us figure out who did, you will tell me. Do you understand?" She leaned close, nose to nose. "You *will* tell me!"

"I don't know anything! I don't!" Given the panicked expression on his face, Mike couldn't imagine that he was lying. "I just sensed that she had some problems that she was still dealing with. Have you talked to her shrink?"

"Yes. And she didn't say anything about Erin's father."

"Well . . . maybe you should talk to her again."

Baxter released the doctor with a little push. "Maybe we'll do that." She turned abruptly. "Are you ready to go, Morelli?"

"Yeah, just about. One more question, though." He turned toward Harris. "Mind if I ask how you got started on this candling gig? I mean—I've checked you out. You're a real doctor. Graduated with good grades from OU Med. Used to work at a well-respected clinic. I found no evidence of scandal or complaint." Mike shrugged. "What the hell happened to you?"

Harris's lips remained tight. He was obviously weighing all the alternatives, evaluating whether he wanted to speak or not.

"You know that clinic I was at?" he said finally.

"Yeah. Over in Brookside."

Harris nodded. "That was an HMO. HMOs believe in many things. Health, welfare, prevention. But what they believe in most is low overhead."

"Go on."

"They decided the best way to cut costs would be to have every doc specialize. Everyone was to have one chore they did well and efficiently. That would streamline the medical examinations."

"Okay. So?"

"So . . . I drew rectal examinations."

Mike's lips parted wordlessly.

"Some career, huh? You start at the bottom—and you stay there."

Mike tried really hard not to smile.

"I'd see some forty or fifty patients a day. Think about that—fifty big hairy butts a day, one right after another."

"That would be . . . different."

"Yeah. And of course, no one enjoyed or appreciated my work. No smiles, no chitchat. It's worse than seeing the dentist. No one wants to talk when the doc is feeling up their butt. Although I did get the occasional twenty-one-gun salute."

"Excuse me?"

"Farts. They can't help themselves. They get nervous, and . . ."

Mike slapped his hands together. "Well, this is fascinating, but—"

"I was miserable at the office parties. All the other docs started calling me the Rear Admiral. Ha, ha. At cocktail parties, everyone wanted to tell me about their hemorrhoids. I mean, I went to school for years to become a doctor. I spent a fortune. And I was doing important work—colorectal cancer is a major killer. But no one else saw it that way."

"So you quit."

"I went out on my own. But do you have any idea how hard it is to get a solo practice going these days? I think some people have the idea that anyone who graduates from med school ends up rich a day after graduation. But it isn't true. Not these days. Particularly not in a competitive market like Tulsa that's already saturated with physicians. It's hard to make a living. And you're a slave to the insurance companies."

"So you started in with ear candling?"

"It was just a hook. Something different. Something to attract the attention of . . . you know. Well-to-do women."

"And it worked?"

"I'm eating regularly. I like all my clients. I can work out of my home. I have virtually no overhead. I don't have to deal with insurance companies or Medicare. And best of all, I don't have to answer to some money-grubbing HMO."

"Yeah," Baxter said. "If only your work wasn't total quackery, it would be perfect." She grabbed Mike's arm. "Okay, Morelli. We've heard the doctor's oh-so-sad story. Can we go now? This guy is stressing me out."

"I could help," Harris volunteered. "I give great candle."

Baxter flashed him a look that defied description. "Pass."

*   *   *

"FIRST OF ALL," Ben said, standing at the head of the conference table, "I want to thank you for all your work. I know it's not easy bringing fresh enthusiasm to a case that's been around so long, but you've given me 110 percent just the same, and I really appreciate it."

Jones, Loving, and Christina sat around the long table. Loving spoke first. "Why do I think there's a *but* comin'?"

"Because there is, of course. The but is, for all our work, we haven't come up with much that's new. Certainly nothing that's going to get a habeas corpus petition granted by Judge Derek. And the hearing is just around the corner."

He turned toward Jones. "I read your report on the Faulkner home invasion. Several times. So did Christina. And she has this . . . theory—"

Christina smiled. "Thank you for not making little quotation marks with your hands."

"Don't mention it. Christina has this theory that maybe there were two killers. Two people in the Faulkner home. And that if we approach the case from that angle, we might see something we missed before. Something everyone missed. So . . ."

Jones buried his head in his hands. "Don't tell me you want me to do more research on that horrible crime."

"I'm afraid so."

"Boss . . . that case is seriously depressing. Every horrible thing that could happen to those people did, or damn near. I just can't take it anymore. Paula says I haven't been sleeping well. She's says I've lost all my energy and drive and—"

Ben held up a hand. "I'm sure I speak for everyone when I say we've already heard more than we'd like of what your wife says about your drive. Just review the material. Find a trace of that second man."

"Yes, Boss," Jones said, but he didn't appear happy about it.

Ben shifted his attention. "Loving, great work on Erin's death. Between your reports and what I get from Mike, I feel as if I'm riding around in the police car with Mike. Except, from what I hear, I don't want to be riding around in the police car with Mike."

Loving grinned. "I heard 'bout some of that down at Scene of the Crime last night. He still partnered with Mad Dog Baxter?"

Ben nodded. "With no hope of parole. And frankly, that's just as well, because his partner doesn't believe Erin killed herself."

"Then who did?"

"So far, they have no answer. What do you think, Loving? Wouldn't be the first time you beat the cops to the punch."

Loving shook his head. "That's a pretty big order, Skipper."

"Well, you're a pretty big man. What do you say?"

"What I always say. I'll give it my best shot."

"You're the man, Loving. Do it to it." Ben shifted his gaze around to Christina. "Any luck on the legal-research front?"

She shook her head. "The case you want doesn't exist, Ben. In these conservative times, habeas corpus relief is a rarity. Particularly in the Tenth Circuit."

"But there have been some petitions granted."

"And believe me, I've pored over those cases. *Wiseman* v. *Cody. Horton* v. *Massie. Battenfield* v. *Gibson.*"

"Detect any pattern?"

"Nothing we haven't talked about before. We need to hit Judge Derek with all the evidence we've got indicating that Ray Goldman is innocent. And anything that points a finger in another direction."

Ben nodded. He knew that nothing they had uncovered to date would be sufficient to persuade Derek to issue such extraordinary relief. Besides being a major jerk, he was a Bush Sr. appointee. His friends back at the country club wouldn't approve.

"One more thing," Ben added. "I need someone who can educate me on fast food."

Loving shrugged. "There's a McDonald's on every street in Tulsa."

"I'm thinking more like an expert witness."

"Loving's an expert on eating it," Jones said.

"That wasn't what I had in mind. I need someone who knows the ins and outs of the business. Especially the taste-creation part that was Frank Faulkner's specialty."

Christina shrugged. "Well, the ideal candidate would be Peter Rothko."

"Who's he?"

Christina stared at him. "Come on, Ben. I pointed him out to you at the bar reception, remember? And he's been all over the news, ever since that horrible hostage situation where so many people were hurt. Peter Rothko is Tulsa's fast-food magnate. Owns the Burger Bliss chain—you know. They serve high-class fast food that tastes good and won't totally destroy your health. That's their advertising angle, anyway. He started about ten years ago with one shack in south Tulsa. Now he's got hundreds of them."

"Conrad Reynolds mentioned that they'd done some work for Burger Bliss. Sounds like the man I need. Can you set up an interview?"

"I can try. I'm sure he's a busy man. Maybe if I went out to see him personally . . ." She batted her pen against her lips. "Rothko is a darned good-looking man. And very single."

Ben arched an eyebrow. "Are you interested?"

"Let me think. A handsome hunk, never married, who's also a billionaire." She shook her head. "No, I wouldn't be interested in that."

"Just set up the interview," Ben said, pressing his hands against the table. "Remember, folks, Ray Goldman has been wrongly incarcerated for seven years. Seven *years*. He's lost his fiancée. He's lost his business. He's lost all his friends, family. And if we don't do something to prevent it—he's going to lose his life." He paused, making eye contact with each of them. "Do I need to say anything more?"

18

APRIL WAS WEARING the transparent blouse again.

She did not intend it to be transparent, Gabriel Aravena reasoned, and she would undoubtedly be shocked if she knew that it was. But when she stood directly beneath the powerful overhead fluorescent lights in the store, it dissolved. Her brassiere was fully visible, as was her cleavage and the lovely little mole at the base of her neck. He could even make out her nipples, dark and firm and pert. They were winking at him, playing peekaboo.

Aravena smiled. Off Depo for a mere twenty-four hours. And what a change it had already made in his life.

The chemical castration, the hormones that were slowly turning him into a woman, enlarging his breasts, shrinking his genitals, making his facial hair turn to peach fuzz, had been arrested. If he was not quite himself yet, he was certainly on his way.

"Did you see what that clown was driving?" April asked. She was staring through the front doors toward the gas pumps. "The pickup with the jacked-up wheels?"

"I did."

"Why do men do that? Or boys, I should say?" She turned slightly. It was as if she were pointing at him with those lovely little nippies. "Does it make them feel more manly?"

"Perhaps so," Aravena said.

"I hate it when boys think they have to put on a big show."

"All men are not alike."

"No. You don't do stuff like that, do you?" She smiled. "We've been working together at this store for—how long now? And you never do any of that macho-stud crap."

Better living through chemistry, Aravena thought. "It would not be appropriate in the workplace."

"I bet you wouldn't do it, wherever you were." She smiled, letting her hand brush his shoulder. Her touch sent his blood coursing through every part of his body. "You're just not the type."

As if you had the slightest idea what kind of man I am, Aravena thought. If you did, you would not be standing so close to me. If you knew how much I wanted you. If you knew how I would take you.

And now I can.

"I used to go out with this guy," April said, "who drove one of those rigs. And he had tattoos all over his body. And he spit and cursed and chewed tobacco. Every he-man affectation in the book. His whole life was governed by his dick."

Aravena felt himself becoming aroused. "What about the young man you are seeing now?"

"Larry? He's all right. I mean, he's kind of thoughtless sometimes. Rude. But I'm not thinking it's going to be a forever thing, anyway, so who cares?"

"You should have someone in your life who treats you well, April. Someone who takes care of you."

"Yeah, well, we'd all like that."

"You deserve it."

April's eyes darted downward. "That's very nice of you, Gabe."

"It's the truth." And about that he was not lying. He would take care of her, given half a chance. He'd take care of her over and over again, till she cried for mercy. He'd take care of her in every possible way, every position, every orifice. He'd pound her again and again till she screamed. Till it killed her.

"I'm going to pour in some more Slushee mix. Can you watch the front counter?"

"Of course." He watched as her curvy little butt sashayed away from him. It had been so long. Too long. But he was going to change that. He was going to change everything, starting—

"Excuse me?"

Aravena brought his eyes out of soft focus. There was a young woman standing before him on the other side of the counter. Tall, dark-haired, slender. Beautiful.

"Can I help you?"

"Yes. I need to pay for my gas."

She seemed familiar, but he couldn't quite place the face. "How would you like to pay?"

"Plastic. What else?" The woman passed him a credit card. Sheila Knight, the name on the card read. Sheila Knight.

He stole a few furtive glances at her while he processed the card. Her blouse was not transparent, but it was so tight it might as well have been. She had no secrets. Her body was beautiful and she knew it. She wanted everyone else to know it, too.

Maybe it was just the effect of the chemicals drying up, but it seemed to Aravena that she was the most arousing, most devastatingly desirable adult woman he had ever met. And he had seen her before. He was certain of it.

But where?

It came to him as he thrust the pen and the credit-card receipt across the counter to her. She was a friend of Erin's.

He smiled with great enthusiasm. "Thank you for shopping at FastTrak."

She nodded, grabbed the receipt, and left. Too bad.

But he would see her again.

He watched as she passed through the front doors to her car, swinging her hips, inviting everyone around to drool over her. How he would like to give her what she wanted. What she was asking for. How he would like to throw her down, knock her to the concrete, take her under the pumps, roll around in the gas and grease and—

But that would not be smart. It would be pleasurable. But not smart.

He glanced at the credit-card receipt in his hand. That was his passport. The key to whatever he wanted to know about—or to take from—Sheila Knight. He would call the credit-card company and say that she had left her card behind. They would give him her phone number. From her phone number he could get her address. From her address, he could get—her.

He smiled, feeling better than he had all day. Better than he could remember, actually.

The days of looking and talking and being a woman were over. From now on, he would be himself. Himself and no one else. The real Gabriel Aravena. Not the fake chemically induced, harmless-puppy variant. The real thing.

He would be visiting Sheila Knight. Soon. And it would be a visit she would never forget.

19

BEN WAS DOING double time across the street toward his van when he heard Joni shout. "Be-en!"

He stopped, and a moment later, she caught up to him. "Sorry, Joni, I'm running late. I have to get to McAlester—"

"The penitentiary? To see another of your glamorous clients?"

"Something like that. You can give me the maintenance update later, okay?"

"It's not about the house, Benjy. I took Giselle to the vet, like you asked."

"And you got her . . . got her . . ."

"Fixed? No, I didn't."

"But you said—"

"I know I said I'd take care of it. But there was a problem."

"I'm waiting."

Joni grinned from one high cheekbone to the other. "She's already preggers, Ben."

The color drained from Ben's face. "Giselle? Pregnant? How—?"

"Do I really need to explain that to you again, Ben?"

"I mean—she spends the whole day locked up in the apartment."

"Apparently she busted out. Or a furry friend busted in."

"But—she can't! I'm in the middle of a huge life-or-death case. I don't have time for this."

"You'll make time."

"And—I don't know anything about delivering kittens."

"Don't panic, Ben. I'll be there for the blessed event. It usually pretty well takes care of itself."

"And then there'll be all those kittens!"

"That is usually how it works, yeah."

"What am I going to do with all those kittens?"

"You'll think of something."

"This can't happen, Joni. You're the handyman. Do something . . . handy."

Smiling, Joni put her arm around him and led him to his car. "Sorry, pal, it's already a done deal." She reached into the pocket of her flannel shirt and pulled out a pink candy cigar. "Congratulations, Ben. You're going to be a father."

"YOU KNOW, I really shouldn't be telling you this," Dr. Bennett said as she artfully uncrossed and recrossed her legs. "I shouldn't."

Mike smiled. He was happy because his years of experience with interrogations told him that when the witness started insisting that they really shouldn't be talking—it was a sure sign he was getting close to something good.

"I'm afraid we have to insist," Sergeant Baxter said firmly.

She wasn't playing hardball yet, but Mike knew she was only about two sentences away. And unless he missed his guess, once Baxter started playing the big bad, Bennett would retreat and the questioning would come to an abrupt end.

"First, there's the matter of doctor-patient privilege to consider."

"That didn't prevent you from speaking with us before. You said the privilege died with Erin."

"But that was different. At that time, you were inquiring into her death. I thought I not only could speak but should speak. But this." She shook her head. "This is something altogether different. I don't know that this has anything to do with her death."

"With all due respect," Baxter replied, "we have to be the judge of that."

"I know, I know. But still . . ." Bennett's hands gestured futilely in the air. "I just don't like it."

"We could subpoena you, Doctor."

"Fine. Subpoena me. We both know what will happen. I'll claim privilege, the judge will put me in jail for a few hours, and then I'll go home. And you'll be none the wiser." She hesitated. "I just don't know what I should do."

Which was Mike's cue. He stepped closer to the interrogation table. He had deliberately staged the questioning, calling Bennett at a time when she was out of the office and claiming great urgency, forcing her to come to him. He wanted this interview to take place at police headquarters, not in the cushy comfort of Bennett's home or office. He didn't want her to be comfortable. He wanted her to be on edge, at least a little. He wanted her to feel vulnerable.

"I know what you should do, ma'am. You should tell us everything you know. Even if you don't see the relevance. You should give us unrestricted access to your files."

"I can't do that."

"You can. And you will." He leaned across the table, hunched like a vulture, his eyes burning into hers. "I insist."

Bennett drew back. "Are you trying to intimidate me?"

"Yeah. Is it working?"

"Kind of." She ran a nervous finger across her lips. "You do that smoldering-intensity thing really well."

"I've had a lot of practice."

"Seriously, some of my patients are major-league bad boys, murderers and rapists and such. But they don't give me chills the way you just did."

Mike shrugged. "It's a gift."

Bennett allowed herself a small smile. "What makes you so sure there was some dark family secret Erin was hiding?"

"I'm not sure of anything. But Dr. Harris was making some pretty broad hints, and he generally seemed to know what he was talking about."

"The man is a quack."

"But a quack who spent a lot of time talking to Erin Faulkner."

"I don't see how this could possibly relate to her death."

"I do. And believe me when I say that if you withhold evidence that might help us break this case"—he glanced at Baxter—"or put it to bed once and for all, I will come down on you. Hard."

Bennett's long-nailed fingers fluttered in the air. "I can't prove any of this."

"Tell us what she told you."

Bennett frowned, started again. "There were some indications of . . . child abuse. In Erin Faulkner's past."

"Indications from?"

Bennett sighed. "From Erin. She first revealed it to me during hypnosis. After that, she talked about it more freely."

"And her father was the molester."

"That was . . . what she said. Yes." She took a shallow breath. "Do you mind if I smoke?"

"Actually, yes. I've quit and I don't care to be tempted."

"It would really calm me."

All the more reason to say no. "Sorry. Departmental policy."

She was wearing a vivid red dress that stopped at midthigh. Very attractive, but not very professional. Certainly not the image of the icy lady psychiatrist. Mike wondered if she had been planning to go out on a date. Or maybe hit the singles bars. "Erin was conflicted, and this dark chapter in her past only made it worse. Of course she grieved for what had happened to her family, and she felt a good deal of guilt about having survived when the others did not. But I sensed there was also a certain amount of . . . relief."

"Because the man who had been molesting her was gone?" Baxter suggested.

"Perhaps."

"Did she give you any details?" Mike asked.

"She did. But do you really want to hear them? As she explained it, the abuse initially just involved touching. Inappropriate touching. But as she got older, it . . . progressed."

"To intercourse?"

"I don't think so. But there was definitely intimate contact. Sexual contact."

Baxter nodded. "And did you believe Erin?"

Bennett hesitated before answering. "I have learned to be cautious about such accusations. Especially when they originate under hypnosis. She seemed very convincing. But there have been cases of false accusations."

"Did you think Erin was lying?"

"No, I certainly didn't think she was lying. But it is possible she was . . . mistaken."

"Okay," Mike said, "did you think she was mistaken?"

"No. But I'm not a human polygraph. I can't eliminate the possibility. And in a case such as this one—when the complainant has been through a great deal of emotional trauma, when the accusations only arise years after the incident, when the accused molester is long gone and utterly unable to defend himself—there is cause for concern."

"You're being very diplomatic, Doctor," Mike said, "but not terribly helpful. Did you believe her?"

"Yes," Bennett said, raising her chin. "I did. But I'm not anxious to tarnish a dead man's memory without objective proof."

"Is there anyone else who knew about these accusations?"

Bennett shrugged. "I don't know. It seems unlikely. As I said, they only emerged under hypnosis."

"And when was that?"

"About six months ago."

"But you can't rule out the possibility that she told this to someone else."

"I suppose not. Why?"

Mike pushed away from the table. "Because it opens up a whole new world of possible motives, Doctor. That's why."

"Can you think of anyone else Erin might've told about this?" Baxter asked.

Bennett pondered a moment. "Well, she was seeing a young man for a while. James Wesley."

Mike nodded. "We've spoken to him."

"But the relationship didn't progress far. They never became intimate. Frankly, I don't think Erin was ready for that yet. And I can't imagine the subject coming up casually over dinner."

"What about Sheila Knight?" Baxter asked.

"It's possible. Sheila knew Erin for years—even before the tragedy. She could conceivably have known about the abuse when it was happening."

"Then that's our next stop. Thank you, Doctor."

The relief on her face was evident. "Am I free to go? I have an engagement tonight."

"Let me check with my superior officer," Baxter said wryly. She turned her head. "Can she go?"

"Yeah, you can go," Mike said, then added, absolutely straight-faced, "But don't leave town."

DID HE REALLY look that much worse than the last time? Ben wondered as he peered at the man on the other side of the glass. Or was this just the product of an overactive imagination, perhaps augmented with feelings of guilt and senseless responsibility? It had only been a few days. Maybe it was the harsh glare of the overhead lighting, the clouding effect on Ben's contact lenses.

Or perhaps Ray really had aged in the hours since Ben had seen him last. Think of all he had been through recently. Almost executed. Then the key prosecution witness recants. Then she dies before she can tell the authorities and the judge declines to grant his petition for relief. And once again, an execution date is looming, drawing near all too quickly. Maybe the recent developments had taken a toll on Ray's body that to anyone else would simply be unimaginable. Maybe that was the reality of life on death row.

"I wish I had more to report," Ben said into the receiver, "but it seems as if all we uncover are more questions. Interesting questions. Important questions. But damn few answers."

"I like Christina's theory about a second assailant," Ray said. "It makes a certain sense. There was so much death, so much destruction. A second person is definitely credible."

"A second person with a heart of gold? Who nonetheless participated in the torture and murder of an entire family?"

Ray hunched his shoulders. "Heart of gold might be stretching it. Some vestige of morality, perhaps. And we don't know to what degree he participated in the killing. He or she, that is."

"I'm still not convinced. Serial killing is not usually a group activity."

"I don't know from serial killers," Ray said. "But it seems to me this crime breaks the mold in several respects."

"That's what the psychiatrist thought, too. Dr. Bennett. She seemed to have a hard time coping with the idea of anyone being cruel enough to do this."

Ray grunted. "This from a woman who puts pins through butterflies."

"Well, yeah." Ben glanced at his notes. "Do you know anything about this organ clinic where Erin worked?"

"Sorry," Ray replied. "Never heard of it. I don't think it existed when I was last a free man."

"It did, actually. Although Erin didn't work there yet."

"Any reason to think her workplace has anything to do with this case?"

"Not really," Ben admitted. "I'm just trying to be thorough. I did get a tip from my pal Mike at the police department. He says the feds have been quietly taking a look at the clinic. They think Dr. Palmetto may have been involved in some black-market organ dealing."

"Shades of Robin Cook."

"Apparently it's a big-money racket. Organs are even being sold over the Internet, which makes it all the harder to catch the marketeers."

Ray thought for a moment. "If Erin was involved in something like that, it would definitely give someone a motive to eliminate her."

"The thought had occurred. Does the name James Wesley mean anything to you?"

"No. Should it?"

"He dated Erin. Said she had some . . . peculiarities."

"Another news flash."

"Granted. Although this ear-candling stuff she went in for is pretty weird. Was her father like that?"

"Not that I'm aware."

"You got along with Faulkner, as I recall. Didn't you?"

Ray thought a moment before answering. "We got along well enough. I worked directly under him, and he could be a bit of a blowhard. Especially after he started having such success with his flavor formulae and bringing in the big bucks. But there was no ill will between us or anything like that. I've told you before."

"I know. I just wanted to see if any of this had spurred any old memories."

"Sorry."

"That just about covers it," Ben said, closing his folder. "I don't have anyone left to talk to."

"What am I, chopped liver?"

"You know what I mean. Anyone who might have new information about the murders." Ben curled the phone cord around his finger. "I was thinking . . . I might talk to Carrie."

"Absolutely not."

"Why?"

"Because I said no."

"Ray . . ."

"Carrie has been through enough, thanks to me. I won't put her through any more misery."

"Ray, if she can help you—"

"But she can't. If she could, she already would have."

"Still—"

"There is no 'still,' Ben. Listen to me. You will not talk to Carrie. Under any circumstances. And if you go against my wishes on this—you're fired."

MIKE DROVE HIS Trans Am crosstown, heading south toward the home of Sheila Knight. Baxter was in the passenger seat.

"By the way," Baxter said, staring straight ahead, "thanks for letting me take the lead on the Bennett interrogation."

"No problem. You were useful."

"Useful?"

"Can't be a bad cop without a good cop."

"Well. I'm so glad I could be . . . useful." Out the corner of his eye, Mike could see her jaw clenching. "Thanks also for not trampling all over me when you decided to cut in. I mean, you could've just shoved me aside. After I was no longer useful."

Mike licked his lips.

"You didn't have to do that. After all, you are the superior officer."

"Baxter . . ."

"Sorry. Couldn't resist." She stared out the side window, giving Mike the back of her ash-blonde hair. "You believe what Bennett was saying?"

"I think she believes it. That doesn't mean it's true."

"Yeah. Hard to size up a woman who's so full of contradictions. Working with criminals by day, butterflies by night. Smart, but funny. Cold, but horny."

"Horny?"

"Oh yeah. She was hot for you."

"For me?" Mike's grip on the steering wheel tightened. "Are you making fun?"

"I'm not. She was drooling for you, Morelli."

"You're nuts."

"I know a woman in heat when I see one. When you leaned over the table and started playing the stern disciplinarian, she turned to putty."

"Go on."

"If you'd turned her over your knee and spanked her, we'd probably have cracked the case by now."

Mike rolled his eyes. "Baxter, you're full of it."

"Says you. Why do you think she suddenly started spilling her guts? She went from 'I shouldn't say anything' to 'Let me tell you everything I know' in about ten seconds flat."

"I attributed that to my brilliant interrogation technique."

"Sure, Morelli. Keep telling yourself that."

"That shrink was not hot for me."

Baxter narrowed an eye. "Why? Is that a problem for you?"

"Problem? What do you mean?"

"Why are you protesting so much? I'm no expert on women, but she seems like a pretty darned attractive specimen to me. And she's bound to be loaded."

Mike felt his palms starting to sweat. "Well . . . she's not my type."

"What is your type?"

"Never mind."

"Do you have a type?"

Mike felt his face reddening. "Yes, I have a type."

"Does it involve women?"

"Yes, but it doesn't involve Dr. Hayley Bennett."

Baxter held up her hands. "All right. All right already."

They drove in silence. Baxter didn't think she should say anything more, and Mike was almost afraid to. Until he couldn't stand it anymore.

"Look, are you just giving me more grief here? Or do you really—"

"She was on fire, Morelli. Liquid flame. Undressing you with her eyes."

"Wow." He continued driving, eyes straight ahead. "Guess I missed that. Thanks for letting me know."

"My pleasure." After a moment, she turned herself around in the bucket seat, just enough to face him. "So, does this mean I can drive the Trans Am?"

"Not a chance." He paused. "But if you keep it up, I might let you touch one of the mag wheels."

"WHAT, YOU'RE GOING to fire me after seven years because I want to talk to your old girlfriend?"

"You got it, Ben."

"Christina would say that's a good reason to do it."

"Look—just humor me on this. She couldn't possibly tell you anything of interest. Why do you think she would?"

"Well, to tell you the truth—your old lab pal Hubbard put the idea in my head."

"Hubbard? Why?"

"He told me about your social life together. When you weren't huddled over the Scrabble board, that is."

"Hubbard's full of it."

"He painted a fairly vivid portrait. Cruising the singles bars and whatnot. I know that was before Carrie, but still—"

"Did you have Christina with you? He was probably trying to impress her with his tales of macho studdom."

"Still, if there's any chance—"

"Ben—I'm begging you. I know I can't fire you. No one's going to take my case on the eve of execution. But I've caused that poor woman enough torment. Don't bother her, okay?"

Ben looked at him long and hard. "I'll have to think about it some more," he said finally.

Ray stared at him, stony-eyed. "You're going to see her, aren't you?"

"I'll let you know."

Ray grunted. He was obviously unhappy, but no doubt realized there was nothing more he could do.

"Anything I can get you?" Ben asked.

"How about a cab ride to the nearest synagogue?"

"Are you doing all right? You look tired."

"I haven't been sleeping well. I still get the nightmares."

Ben remained silent. He didn't have to ask what they were about.

"You don't know how close I came. They actually had me strapped down on that table, before the call came in from the courthouse. They had started filling the needles. I thought it was . . . was over."

Ben wished he could reach out, could touch, could offer some measure of comfort in some way. But of course, he couldn't. Ben'd had a few brushes with mortality himself, but nothing that could even come close to what Ray must be experiencing—the slow, inexorable, measured approach of an all-but-certain death.

"Now every time I close my eyes, I see that table. Right before me. The straps. The needles. The warden with his finger on the button. All of it taunting me, saying, 'We let you go once. But we're still here. And we'll get you.' "

"That must be . . ." Ben couldn't think of a word that began to describe it. "Almost unbearable."

Ray did not disagree. "I see the rabbi every day now. We get down on our knees and we say the prayers. But none of it helps. None of it makes me . . . forget. Where I'm headed. What they want to do to me. I have a burning sensation in my stomach and every day it gets worse."

"We're doing everything we can," Ben said, realizing as he said it what little help it must be. "If there's any way to stop this, we will."

Ray's dark and hooded eyes peered out from behind his fingers. "As a Jew, I should believe in miracles. But I don't. Never have. Much as I might like to delude myself with hope—I can't. Much as I might like to believe there's someone up there looking after me—I know better. When the guard closes the door at night—I'm alone in the cell. And when they strap me down to that table—I'll be alone. No more last-minute reprieves. No miracles. No eleventh-hour redemption." He shook his head with despair. "I don't think I believe in anything anymore."

Ben pressed his hand against the glass. "Believe in this, Ray. I'm not going to let those nightmares come true. Not without a fight."

Ray pressed his own hand against the other side of the glass. But he did not say anything. And the hollow, lost look in his eyes did not fade.

"YOU DON'T KNOW what you're talking about!"

"Ms. Knight, we have legitimate information—"

"From a shrink? Someone who was paid to talk to Erin?"

"Dr. Bennett seemed very certain—"

"Well, she got it wrong." Sheila Knight was wearing a T-shirt and a pair of jeans with a rip in the right knee. She was wearing no makeup and her hair was in need of a wash. Just the same, she was gorgeous.

"Apparently Erin first revealed under hypnosis—"

"That's a crock."

Mike inhaled deeply. He was tired of being interrupted. Maybe it was just him, but Sheila's protestations seemed almost too vehement. "Is it possible Erin told her psychiatrist something she would never tell anyone else?"

"It is not possible," Sheila said firmly. "Erin told me everything. If I didn't know about it, it didn't happen. So I can state absolutely and positively—this did not happen!"

Mike decided to change the subject. "What kind of work do you do?"

"I'm a tech writer. Freelance. I write all those boring little manuals you don't read whenever you buy something."

"Like what?"

"Oh, I've done almost everything. Instruction manuals for kitchen appliances. Construction manuals for children's toys. Did an employee training book for a fast-food chain. That sort of thing."

"Stay busy?"

"More than I want, actually. The first few years were slow, but once I got my name out there—wow. I have all the work I want now. I even farm some out to friends, subcontracts."

"That's wonderful."

Mike continued looking at her. He didn't want to be the one who reintroduced the subject, and he hoped it wouldn't be necessary. She knew what he wanted to talk about.

"Look," Sheila said, finally, "I know the police have to follow all their leads. But I'm telling you—this is nonsense. I knew Erin, all through school. I was over at her house constantly. I knew her father—for that matter, I knew every member of the family. If there had been something going on, something . . . horrible, I would've known about it. There's no way I could have not known about it."

"You're certain?"

"Absolutely."

"Well, if you're certain." Mike paused. "Did you know the gun that killed Erin was coated with hyperthermal luminous paraffin?"

Baxter gave him a long look, but remained quiet.

"No," Sheila said. "I don't even know what that is."

"It's like invisible paint. Rubs off on anyone who fires the gun."

"So?"

"So all we have to do is find the perp and put his hand under the luminal scanner. Unmistakable ID."

"Wouldn't it wear off after a few days?"

Mike shook his head. "Absent a special chemical bath, it wouldn't wear off for a year."

"So," Sheila said, knotting her fingers together, "that stuff must've gotten all over Erin's hand."

"It was," Mike said. "But my partner here thinks maybe . . . it got on someone else's hand as well."

"That's ridiculous."

"Yeah. I think so, too." He slapped his knees. "But if there is someone else, we'll catch him. No one can stay clear of the police for long. Did you know we can listen in on phone calls now?"

Baxter's eyebrows moved closer together, but she maintained her silence.

"We can get lists from the phone company. Tells us who called who and when."

Sheila's lips twitched. "I didn't know that."

"Yeah. Times are changing." He pushed himself out of his chair. Baxter followed. "Thank you for talking to us."

"Sure." She hesitated a moment. Mike got the distinct impression there was something else she wanted to say. "I know you're just doing your jobs. But I do hope that eventually . . . *soon* . . . you'll put this to rest. Put Erin to rest. She endured so much more than I could ever have handled. I don't know how she did it. And I understand that, finally, she just couldn't take it any longer. Thought she couldn't go on." Her eyes began to water. "I have to let her go now. I told you that before. I have to move on. But I can't do that when you people keep coming around, asking questions, stirring it all up again." She looked at Mike, tears beading in her eyes. "Please let it go. Please. Let her go."

MISS JACKSON'S WAS one of the oldest and most elite shopping emporiums in Tulsa. Technically a department store, it preferred to be thought of as a boutique (a three-story one), presumably to prevent comparisons to Sears and such. Nestled in the upscale Utica Square Mall, Miss Jackson's was a bastion of well-heeled Tulsa society, the one place you could find Bruce Webber jewelry,

Herendon china, Rolex watches, and a myriad of other lovely nonessential products linked by only one factor: they were all ungodly expensive.

Which explained why Ben never shopped at Miss Jackson's. In fact, most of Utica Square was so far out of his reach he didn't even like to visit. Well, maybe for dinner at the award-winning Polo Grill, ever since Christina got his name put on a plaque behind one of the booths as a birthday present. But shopping? Not hardly. Nonetheless, here he was on the first floor of Miss Jackson's, watching the resident cosmetologist make over a matronly woman who clearly had nothing better to do with her day than, well, be made over.

"Wonderful. Absolutely wonderful!" the woman said, when the work was at last complete. "I can't wait to show George. He's waiting in the car."

The cosmetologist blinked. "Your husband is waiting in the car?"

"My husband?" the woman said as she gathered her purchases. "George is my poodle."

As soon as she was gone, Ben sidled up to the cosmetics counter. "Got anything in my color?"

It only took her a moment to place his face. "Ben." The initial smile faded. "What brings you here?"

Ben extended his hands. "I was thinking maybe you could do my nails."

"Oh, no." She picked up a mascara pencil. "Let me do your eyes. That's my specialty. And you have such long luscious eyelashes. Most women would kill for those."

Ben grinned. "How have you been, Carrie?"

"I've been well, actually." She paused. "And you know why?"

"Because you haven't had to talk to me?"

"Very close." She glanced over her shoulder, checking to see if anyone was watching them. "I suppose this is about Ray."

"Of course."

She pushed away from the counter. "I can't talk to you, then."

"Carrie, please."

"Not about Ray, no."

"Carrie, it's important."

She wrapped her arms around herself. "I'm sure it is. It always is."

"Do you know where Ray is right now?"

"I've got a pretty good idea, yeah."

"He's on death row."

"He's been on death row for seven years."

"Well, he won't be in less than two weeks."

"Because—" The light dawned. She looked downward. "Oh."

"That's why I need to talk with you. We've only got one chance. And frankly, it's not much of a chance. But we've got to take it."

She turned away. "I still can't talk to you."

"If it's because you're working, I can come back—"

"No. It's not that. I just . . . can't talk to you."

"Carrie, Ray's life is literally on the line here. If we—"

"Are you listening to me, Ben?" The sudden increase in volume took them both by surprise. "I'm not saying I won't talk to you." Her eyes rose until they found his. "I'm saying you don't want me to talk to you."

"So WHAT DO you think?"

They had traveled in silence for the first ten minutes of the drive downtown, and Baxter thought that was long enough. "Do you believe Sheila?"

Mike didn't mince words. "No."

"You're kidding."

"She's holding something back. Or flat out lying."

"Really. Well, tell me this, super-sleuth. What possible motive could Sheila Knight have for lying about whether her deceased best friend was sexually molested?"

Mike thought a long time before answering. "When they were young, Erin and Sheila were nearly inseparable. They spent lots of time together. As Sheila said herself, she was a frequent guest at Erin's house. She came over for play dates, study nights, birthday parties." He paused. "And sleepovers."

"So YOU DID break up with Ray," Ben said. "And you did it for a reason. A reason other than the fact that he'd been convicted of murder."

After Carrie made some excuse to her supervisor, they'd left the store and begun strolling down the sidewalks of the outdoor mall. It was a gorgeous Tulsa day, and the bustling human and vehicular traffic gave them a feeling of anonymity. "It's been so long."

"But there was something else."

"Yes. Even before he was arrested. After our engagement."

Ben felt an aching in the pit of his stomach. He didn't like the direction this was taking. But he had to press on. "What happened?"

"It's not good."

Which might explain why Ray hadn't wanted Ben to talk to her. "Still—"

"It won't help your case."

"Let me be the judge of that."

"I'm telling you—"

"I know you're trying to help me, Carrie. And trying to help Ray. Or not hurt him, at any rate. But if I don't make a breakthrough soon, we're going to go down in flames at the habeas hearing. And if I have to swallow some bad information to get to that breakthrough—so be it."

Carrie looked away. Her eyes were fixed somewhere above them, in the clouds. "He hit me."

Ben closed his eyes. "Ray?"

"Yeah. We were at a club. I don't remember what the row was about. I think maybe I didn't like the way he ogled the chick at the next table. Something real important like that. Anyway, we'd probably both had too much to drink. Tempers flared. We took it outside." She shook her head. "That was my mistake. If we'd stayed inside the club, it never would've happened. But once we were alone in the parking lot . . ."

"How bad was it?"

"Bad enough. I mean, he only actually struck me twice. But it hurt like hell. Big black bruises. The doctor said he almost dislocated my jaw."

Thank God the prosecution never found this witness, Ben thought.

" 'Course I told the doctor I had fallen down the stairs or something stupid like that. But I don't think he believed it for a minute."

"Was Ray . . . sorry?"

"Oh yes. Immediately. He picked me up off the gravel and held me. Stroked me. Said he didn't know what came over him. But that didn't change anything."

Ben touched her arm gently, steering her toward Queenie's, a popular sandwich emporium.

"That's when I should've broken off the engagement. But I didn't. I already had so much invested in Ray. So much time and energy and love. I kept telling myself, it was just a one time thing. Just an accident. It will never happen again."

"And did it?"

"No. But there was never a chance. Two days later, he was arrested."

"And he hasn't been free since."

"Right." Carrie's eyes dropped. Her blunt-cut blonde hair hung like a veil around her face. "I tried to be the support he needed. But the memory wouldn't go away. How could I forget what he had done? How he had . . . violated me. My trust. And then, in the courtroom, when I heard him accused of all those horrible things . . ."

Ben could see where this was going. And as she had predicted—he didn't like it.

"After I heard them accuse Ray of that atrocity, I kept saying to people, 'Not my Ray. He couldn't do that.' But I had seen him lose his temper. I had seen him be . . . violent."

"Carrie, I don't want you to think I'm making light of domestic violence, but there's a big difference between what he did to you in that parking lot and what happened to the Faulkner family."

"I know. I know." She clenched her hands together, pressing them against her chest. "But after that, I could never be certain. That's why I broke it off with him, eventually. I felt like a heel. I know all our friends thought I was being faithless. Bailing out when the going got tough. But I simply couldn't be sure. And if I couldn't be sure—I couldn't be with him."

She brushed her hair back. Ben could see the pain this conversation was causing her, deeply etched in every line of her face. "I could've been faithful to a man on death row—I really could've," she said, as if pleading her case to an imaginary court. "But not if I suspected he was guilty."

LONG AFTER DARK, Ben tossed his briefcase into its designated spot by the coffee table and collapsed onto the ratty sofa that was the centerpiece of his living room. What a day. He was bushed. All he wanted to do now was rest. And as it happened, for once, he had managed to get inside the house and make it up to his room without being confronted by tenants who couldn't make their rent, without having Joni assault him with a host of bills and maintenance problems, without even having Giselle purr and whine and demand immediate attention. For once, they had all just left him alone.

He missed them.

A sad state of affairs, he told himself, when you're dependent upon co-workers and fussy felines for social interaction. Hadn't he resolved that he was going to get out, that he was going to start having a life? That he was going to be more like Christina and less like himself? Of course, he'd been swamped with this Goldman habeas work. It was as dire as a case could be—life and death in the truest sense. He had to give it his full attention, he had to work long hours.

But that was just an excuse and he knew it. Yes, this was an important case, and yes, he wanted to do everything possible to help Ray, to prevent a horrible injustice. But when had it ever been any different? He always had some big case going, some crusade that demanded his full devotion. Because when all was said and done, working long hours at the office was preferable to coming home and being . . . alone. Again.

He saw the telephone resting on the end table. He was staring at it, but for some reason, he had the strangest feeling that it was staring at him. That it was trying to get his attention. Beckoning to him.

What was Christina doing tonight? More than once she had suggested not too subtly that he would be welcome to join her on some engagement or another. Maybe he should call her and see what she was up to.

His hand hovered over the receiver. He had to strike the right tone, keep it casual. For starters, she had to have an escape clause. In case she was just being nice and really dreaded the thought of going somewhere with him. After all, she did see him all day, most days. She might not be that excited at the prospect of spending an evening with him as well. And he had to make it clear that this was just a fun thing, no pressure, not really like a date. I mean, it would be a date, he supposed, but not a *date* date. Not a, you know, big romantic deal or anything.

And the reason for that was . . . ? He tried to think of a good answer. Because his romantic life was so booked up? No. Because he didn't like Christina? No. So what was the problem? Well, it would certainly complicate life in the office. The two partners dating. Could make things very uncomfortable. And if it went bad, heaven forbid he should see Christina in the role of the woman scorned.

But why was he letting his brain wander down these paths? He wasn't planning a marriage proposal, for pete's sake. He was just talking about calling up a coworker and seeing if she wanted to go get a drink or something. It was a perfectly common office-worker-type thing to do. Utterly ordinary. They should've done it a long time ago.

He gripped the receiver and brought it to the side of his head. He started dialing her number . . .

And hung up. He couldn't do this. He just couldn't. He wanted to, damn it. But he couldn't.

He walked to the kitchen, poured himself a tall glass of chocolate milk, then sat down at the piano and started banging out whatever tune came to mind. It was a little late for this, he realized, but the nice thing about being the landlord was that there was no one to whom the other tenants could complain about you. He played some of his Janis Ian tunes, then a Harry number, then his favorites by Christine Lavin. He started "Old Fashioned Romance," but for some reason, it was just making him sad.

He went to bed early, planning the next day's interviews as he tucked himself in. If he was only going to do one thing in this ridiculous little life of his—work—then he'd damn well better do a good job of it.

This is so pathetic, he told himself as he eyes finally closed. Maybe I should get a dog.

A long impassioned mewling from the kitchen reopened his eyes.

Make that a male dog.

CHAPTER

20

JONES TUCKED IN his chin. "You're joking, right?"

"No," Ben said, "I'm not joking."

"You're actually going to do this?"

"It's not that big a deal, Jones. We're just going to work out."

Jones remained incredulous. "You mean—you're actually going to sweat?"

Ben zipped up the jacket of a black-and-white warm-up suit, then applied himself to his Nikes. "And why is this a problem for you?"

"You're a lawyer. Lawyers don't sweat. They . . . talk."

Ben continued lacing. "I've seen lots of lawyers sweat in my time."

Jones retreated from the doorway. "Hey, take a look at this!" he shouted down the corridor. "Ben's going to work out!"

A moment later, Christina appeared. "As in . . . exercise? Physical exertion?"

Ben grabbed his gym bag. "And why is that so unbelievable?"

Jones and Christina looked at each other. "You're not exactly renowned for your physical prowess."

"Remember the time he tried to move the copier?" Jones said, giggling.

"You should hear Mike talk about Ben's first kung fu lesson," Christina replied with equal mirth.

"You know," Ben said, passing them both, "you two are starting to annoy me."

"I'm sorry," Christina said. She looked at Jones. "This is really rude of us." And then they both burst out laughing.

"I should cancel their bonuses," Ben muttered as he left the office. If they ever got bonuses.

*   *   *

"I can't believe this," Baxter said, shifting from one edge of the passenger seat to the other. "Sheila Knight never did anything wrong in her life. Except maybe talk to you."

"Nonetheless," Mike insisted, hands on the steering wheel, "she's lying. Or at the very least, holding something back."

"She told you everything you wanted to know."

"Or seemed to. Trust me on this, Baxter. She's lying."

"And you know this because . . ."

"I just know."

"Of course. So why don't you drag her downtown and give her a lie-detector test?"

"Because there would be no point." Tulsa traffic was not normally an issue, but there were a few exceptions, and Seventy-first on Friday afternoon was one of them. Even after the street had been widened to the size of something you'd expect to see in Dallas, it still clogged, worse and worse the closer you got to the on-ramp for Highway 169. Maybe it was employees fleeing en masse from the chain stores and restaurants that seemed to have sprung up overnight on this boulevard. "She's not a suspect. I don't know that she's a material witness. I can't force her."

"She might comply anyway."

"She might. But the test wouldn't be admissible in court. And frankly, I think polygraphs are unreliable and easily manipulated."

"Easily manipulated?" Baxter waved a hand across her brow. "Is this the sphincter dodge?"

"That works, actually." It was well-known in police circles that tightening the sphincter muscle during the control questions could send the polygraph a false signal, thus disguising subsequent lies. There were several ways, actually. Putting a tack in your shoe and stepping on it at the right time. Anything that elevated the subject's blood pressure could throw off the machine. "But it isn't the easiest way."

"And what is the easiest way, O Great and Powerful Superior Officer?"

"Just lie on the control questions. The test administrator asks control questions, then pertinent questions, then compares the two and looks for a change in the readout. If you lie on the control questions, though, then lie on the rest, there will never be any observable change."

"Fine. If we can't use the polygraph, how do we prove she's lying?"

"We don't have to. I already know."

"Because . . ."

"Did you see her eyes?"

"Yes. Brown. Large."

"Did you notice the crinkling lines? When she smiled?"

"I don't recall that she ever smiled."

"She did. When she talked about how much she used to enjoy going over to the Faulkner home."

"Okay. And you saw crinkling lines?"

"Right here." Mike pointed to the corner of his eye. "An authentic smile engages the whole face, including the crinkling lines, in a generally relaxed expression. A lying smile doesn't. When it doesn't come naturally—when it's being put on for show—the mouth may change, but the face doesn't."

"So you're saying there were no crinkling lines."

"There were, actually, but they were more crow's-feet than laugh lines. It wasn't authentic."

"If you say so."

"I do. And there's more. Just before she smiled, there was a flash of—I don't know. Didn't last for even a second. She wiped it away and manufactured the fake smile. But for a fleeting instant before that, there was . . . something else."

"Which was?"

"Hard to be certain. A frown, a scowl. A grimace. The textbooks call them microexpressions, and they're hard to spot. But that was her true, natural reaction. And that tells me there's something Sheila Knight didn't give us. That perhaps her visits to the Faulkner home weren't all as wonderful as she suggested."

"Are you serious about this? I can't wait to read your report. 'Suspect had suspicious crinkly lines.' "

"Don't laugh, Baxter. Knowing who is and isn't telling you the truth is critical to being an effective homicide investigator."

"Clearly. I'm surprised they don't teach this at the academy. Crinkly Lines 101."

Mike blew air through his teeth. "Look, if you're going to make fun—"

"Perish the thought." She swallowed her smile. "I'm surprised you didn't come down harder on Dr. Bennett. Now she seemed nervous to me."

"Some people are. Especially when the police come calling. That doesn't mean they're lying."

"And she never made eye contact when she was answering your questions."

"Who does?" Mike downshifted and moved into the right-hand lane, hoping to find an escape route from the traffic. "Most people are uncomfortable with extended direct eye contact. Looking away is simply deferential. If you see someone who's killing himself to maintain eye contact, he's either trying to sell you something or lying. Or both."

Baxter laughed. "I did notice Sheila kept doing that thing with her hair. Touching it. Brushing it back."

"True. But don't confuse personal tics with lying. Everybody has a few nervous habits—biting nails, twirling pencils. It's not the same thing. What you look for are discrepancies—differences between what the person is saying and what the person is doing. Saying yes but subtly shaking the head. That sort of thing."

"Speaking of personal tics," Baxter said, "what was all that nonsense about— what was it? Hyperthermal luminous paraffin?"

Mike grinned. "I was just giving her something to worry about."

"So now you think Sheila Knight killed Erin?"

"I don't think anyone killed Erin except Erin. That's your delusion, not mine." He paused, hung a hard right. "Even if there was a murder, it couldn't have been Sheila Knight. She has an airtight alibi."

"She might've had an accomplice."

"And in that unlikely event," Mike said, "she will now be desperate to get to her accomplice and inform him that his hands are coated with hyperthermal luminous paraffin."

"And she won't call, because you fed her all that BS about being able to trace and eavesdrop on her phone conversations." Her head tilted to one side. "Not bad, Morelli. Will Blackwell authorize a stakeout team?"

"For this case? Not a chance. But I called for an unmarked car to watch her office. For her own safety, you know," he said, winking. "That'll get us to sundown. Ben's investigator might take over after that. Mind you—just because Sheila's lying doesn't make her a killer. But if she is working with someone else—we'll find them."

Baxter nodded grudgingly. "It hurts to admit it, but—not bad detective work, Sherlock. You should teach a course."

"I do. Every year. You'd know that if you'd gone to school on the right end of the turnpike."

Baxter gave him a long look. "I never figured you for a teacher. How'd you get started on that?"

"There was an opening at the academy, and frankly, I needed the scratch. Alimony payments were killing me. But I found I enjoyed it. It's a kick, really. Hanging out with the baby cops and wannabes."

"That must require patience. Some of those new recruits are pretty green."

Mike grinned. "Not as green as I was, way back when."

"Oh yeah?"

"Oh yeah. Bright-eyed and bushy-brained, that was me. I thought the world was my private crime lab. Thought I could do no wrong."

"Did that change?"

Mike gave her a wry expression. "Yeah. That changed. All too soon." He hung a left and glided onto the highway. "Sorry. Didn't mean to get all boring and autobiographical on you."

"Not at all. It wasn't—I didn't—" Her hand stretched out, but almost immediately she drew it back. "I'm not complaining. Hey—this is the first time we've talked for more than ten minutes without yelling at each other or threatening bodily harm."

"Well, that calls for a celebration." Mike stopped at a light, then turned to face her. "Sergeant, can you make a decent pot of coffee?"

"I do all right."

"Good. I'll bring the beer nuts."

She looked at him blankly. "Are we going on a date?"

"Something even better." His eyebrows danced. "Stakeout."

"What's your preference, Ben? Free weights or Nautilus equipment?"

"This is your party," Ben answered. He felt distinctly uncomfortable in this workout suit. Could he tell Ben hadn't worn it once since his mother gave it to him for Christmas four years ago? "You pick."

"Good enough. Let's go Nautilus." Peter Rothko was a tall, lean man with a striking shock of burnt-orange hair. "I need to do some serious sweating. I had lunch in the corporate dining room—fabulous food, but so rich!" He patted his stomach, which did not appear extended to Ben. "Thanks for meeting me here. I know it's indulgent, but with my schedule the way it is these days, it was here or not at all."

"I'm grateful to you for meeting me. I feel out of my depth with all this fast-food-and-flavor stuff, and I think it may be important. I needed to talk to someone who really understands the business."

"Well, I might qualify." He led the way to the Nautilus machine. "I like to do the whole circuit in order, starting with the leg presses. Can I show you how it's done?"

"Thanks, I know how it goes." Ben lowered himself onto the black leather seat and wrapped his feet behind the weighted bar.

"You work out?"

"Yeah, I have a membership here, too," Ben said, grunting slightly as he worked his quads. "But don't tell my staff. It would destroy my image."

"You come regularly?"

"A couple, three times a week. Though I don't normally wear this snazzy suit." Ben smiled. "That was just to impress you. I come as often as I can, when I'm not in court. I usually arrive later in the day, though. After work."

"Good for you. How long have you been doing it?"

"A couple of years now. A while back I got the bad end of a scuffle and—well, the result was being pushed off some high-rise refinery scaffolding."

"Ouch."

"Yeah. I was hurt pretty bad—in a coma for days. After that, I decided I needed to do something to improve my physical condition. Before it was too late." Ben finished his leg presses, then vacated the seat. "But you know—I'm supposed to be interviewing you here. How did an amiable guy who's even younger than I am end up the CEO of a huge national fast-food chain?"

"Oh, dumb luck, mostly."

"Yeah, I believe that. Don't be modest, Peter, or we'll never get anywhere."

"It's true. But what is luck, really? Let me tell you—it's when opportunity meets preparation. I'd been preparing for a long time, toiling away in the burger biz. When the opportunity came, I jumped at it."

"What happened?"

Rothko straddled a bench and began doing arm curls. "Like most of America, I grew up working at McDonald's. When I turned twenty-one, I managed to get a little seed money so I could buy an independent burger joint on Peoria that was closing. My parents thought it sounded like a dodgy move, but hey, fast food was all I knew."

"How did it go?"

"Terribly. Disastrously. I lost money by the fistful."

"So why is it my partner thinks you're the richest most eligible bachelor in Tulsa?"

Rothko grinned. "That came later. The first two years were a travesty. Competition was slaughtering me. And then—things began to change."

Ben grabbed an overhead bar and pulled it down behind his head. "What made the difference?"

Rothko released the pull bar with a grunt. "Chemicals."

*　　*　　*

FOR SOMEONE WHO didn't even like to drink that much, he sure spent a lot of time in bars, Loving mused. Maybe it was just his imagination, but he'd been working as Ben's investigator for many years now, and it seemed as if he'd spent about half that time hanging out in saloons, taverns, pubs, and watering holes of all shapes and sizes.

Why did he always draw these assignments? he wondered as he climbed out of his pickup. If the investigation involved some high-tech something or other, Jones would handle it. If it involved anything feminine or upscale, Christina would draw the straw. And if involved anything fun, Ben would do it himself. Why was he always the one who got sent to the bars?

To be fair, bars were generally a good place to get people talking. Whether they thought the alcohol affected them or not, it did, and tongues moved more freely after the third or fourth Bud Light. Just observing people in this environment told Loving more than he could learn in half an hour of sober yakking.

So, he supposed, he drew these assignments because he was good at them. That was what he was going to tell himself, anyway.

As he surveyed the exterior, he realized that this trendy Brookside hangout was considerably more upscale than his usual haunt. He wished he had dressed differently—his white T-shirt and blue jeans might look out of place among the Ralph Lauren pullovers and Miss Jackson originals. But what the heck. He'd make do.

He stepped inside, then caught his breath. Wait a minute. This wasn't a bar. At least not his idea of a bar.

This was a sushi bar.

The fishy aroma wafted down to Loving's nostrils, and he almost instantly felt sick. He didn't like fish even when it was cooked; there was no way he was going to be able to keep this squishy slithery stuff down.

Did Ben know where this woman was going when he handed out this assignment? Was this his idea of humor? Send the big burly redneck to the raw fish joint? Laugh when his face starts to turn white? Watch him try to order chicken fried chicken or something?

Well, it wasn't going to happen. Loving felt a great deal of loyalty and devotion to Ben—but everything had its limits.

To his relief, he spotted the woman he knew to be Sheila Knight sitting up at the front, at the bar. The liquor bar, that is. There were empty seats on either side of her. She appeared to be on at least her second drink, judging by the glasses in front of her. She was wearing a party dress—bright red and rather tight-fitting. No woman would dress like that unless she was going out on a date—or looking for one.

Perfect. This was going to be easier than he thought.

He sidled up to the stool on her left. "Mind if I sit here, ma'am?" He couldn't be less subtle; almost every other seat at the bar was untaken.

To his relief, she didn't object. She gave him the split-second once-over and shrugged. "Sure."

Loving assumed that meant he had passed the sniff test. The bartender asked for his order. "Shot of Bailey's, shot of Kahlúa. Separate glasses."

That got her attention. "Little early to break out the hard stuff, isn't it?"

Loving grinned. "Each to his own poison." After the drinks arrived, Loving pulled his laminated Oklahoma driver's license out of his wallet and plopped it on the top of the bar. "Okay, here's the challenge. Get the Kahlúa into the Bailey's glass, and vice versa. Using only what's on the bar right now."

She arched an eyebrow. "Is this one of those stupid bar tricks?"

"Yup. And since it's so stupid, you shouldn't have any problem."

She gave him a sharp look, then turned her attention to the two drinks. She picked up both shot glasses, as if to pour one into the other. No, that wasn't going to work. She considered the driver's license, but that didn't bring many possibilities to light. She experimented with the salt and pepper, the Tabasco sauce, the menus, the nonfat dairy creamer. But none of it solved the problem.

"All right, wonder boy. I give up. Show me how it's done."

"It's a secret."

"If you weren't planning to tell, why'd you start this thing?"

"I'm not saying I won't tell. I'm just saying you gotta make it worth my while."

She drew back. "Wait a minute, cowboy. Do I look like—"

"Five minutes. That's all I want."

"Five minutes of what?"

"Talking. Like this. Right here. I ask questions, you answer."

"Is this going to be some kind of kinky *Cosmo* test thing?"

"Nope. Just regular gabbing." He lowered his chin. "I'm a very lonely person."

"Why do I not believe that?" She looked at him for a long moment, and when she finally spoke, it appeared to be against her better judgment. "All right. Go for it."

Loving laid the license across the top of the Kahlúa, completely covering it. Gripping the glass firmly, he turned it upside down so that it and the license were on top of the Bailey's shot. Slowly and gently, he slid the license to the side until there was a gap between it and the rim of the glasses. The Kahlúa began to flow through the gap into the bottom glass. And then, like magic, the Bailey's began to flow upward into the top glass. When the two liquids had totally changed places, Loving closed the gap and flipped the top glass upright again.

"That's amazing," Sheila said, truly impressed.

"Yeah," Loving agreed. "Makes a mess of your driver's license, though."

"So I suppose I have to talk to you now, huh?"

Loving returned her smile. "Life is tough sometimes."

BEN READJUSTED THE weights to add twenty more pounds. "So you got a new flavor formula?"

Rothko appeared impressed. "You know about this stuff?"

"I've had the short course. I've toured Prairie Dog Flavors' facility and talked to some of the chemists."

"Then you understand. When I started my operation, I couldn't afford that stuff. My food tasted like what it actually tasted like."

"Horrors."

"Well, it explained why my place was such a flop. You can't compete with the big boys at Burger King and Mickey D's if your food doesn't give customers the same buzz. And I couldn't afford the buzz. Then I got lucky. My grandfather died." He paused. "Wait, that doesn't sound very good, does it?"

"I think I know where you're going."

"He left me some money. Not a fortune, but enough. I spent every penny getting myself a secret formula. Something new. Something better."

"And it worked?"

"Like a dream." Rothko grabbed his towel and wiped his brow. "Have you ever eaten in one of my shops?"

Ben hedged. "Well . . ."

"That's all right. Nothing to be ashamed of. I'll just explain. Every business needs some kind of marketing angle, something to differentiate them from the competition. At Burger Bliss, our gimmick is that we're the high-class outfit. Better-quality food. Sit-down restaurant food delivered with fast-food efficiency."

"How did you come up with that?"

"Like most great ideas throughout history, it was born of sheer necessity. I had a great-tasting product, but that wasn't going to help me unless I could get people in my store. I couldn't underprice McDonald's. Who could? So I had to convince people my food was worth a little extra."

"How did you go about that?"

Rothko shifted to the next machine and started working his triceps. "We advertised that we used a higher-quality meat—which is true. And with the chemicals, my burgers tasted more like beef tenderloin than hamburger. We didn't bury it under mustard or ketchup or secret sauces. We let people taste the meat."

"And this worked?"

Rothko smiled. "Ten years ago I opened the first Burger Bliss. There are now three hundred and forty-three Burger Bliss restaurants in forty-eight states and three foreign countries. Burger Bliss is on the Fortune 500 list and is actively traded on the New York Stock Exchange. Our corporate profits are in the billions." He stopped to catch his breath. "Yeah, I'd say it worked."

"So the key was the flavor."

"That was one of them, certainly."

"You've worked with these flavor people, then. Do you think it's possible there could be rivalry between the chemists?"

"Let me put it to you this way, Ben. The fast-food industry makes over one hundred and ten billion dollars annually in profits."

"So I've heard."

"There's huge money to be made in this business. Huge. And it all hinges on flavor." He moved to a stationary bike and started pedaling. "Of course there's competition among chemists. They all want to be the one who invents the next Big Mac."

"Because that man's going to be the king of the lab?"

He looked at Ben levelly. "Because that man's going to be rich."

LOVING'S FIVE MINUTES turned into a little over a half an hour. Sheila glanced at her watch a few times, but otherwise, she didn't seem to mind, which Loving attributed to his personal charm. And perhaps the fact that he offered to buy the next three rounds of drinks. In that time, he told her stories and anecdotes, never revealing who he worked for, and regaled her with every bad joke he'd heard in the last year. He even explained that since Kahlúa is denser than Bailey's and the empty space in the glasses is finite, the Bailey's is forced upward when the Kahlúa comes rushing down.

"So they put this new guy in as editor in chief," Sheila explained. "He decides which writing assignments I get and which I don't. And he's totally clue-less. I know in a heartbeat he's not from Oklahoma."

"How could you tell?"

"Well, he kept telling me that, now that he was here, there was all this stuff he was going to do. He never once said 'fixin' to do.' "

"A dead giveaway."

"When he talked about Durant, he actually pronounced it Duh-*rant*, in-stead of *Doo*-rant, like everyone else around here."

"And let me guess. He didn't pronounce Miami 'Mi-am-uh,' and he didn't call Oklahoma City 'the City.' "

She nodded. "And he didn't even know where to begin with Eufaula or Okemah."

"Good thing you don't have clients in Gotebo," Loving replied. They both laughed.

The bartender arrived bearing gifts. "Here's your appetizer, ma'am."

"Great."

Loving took a whiff and tried not to gag. "What is it?"

"It's an assortment of their best. Calamari, sushi, eel. Won't you share it with me?"

Loving hesitated.

"We can eat it right here. That way we can continue talking."

Loving drew in his breath. Ben Kincaid, you owe me so bad. . . .

"All right," Sheila said. "Let's start with the eel."

LOVING SURVIVED THE consumption of the appetizer plate, and as much as he hated to admit it, actually enjoyed much of it. The secret, he realized, was not to let Sheila tell him what it was. Better not to know. Just eat in bliss-ful ignorance.

The conversation continued merrily along. Loving kept her going, deftly moving from one subject to the next, guiding without appearing to guide. But none of it was idle chatter. Without ever asking a direct question, Loving man-aged to draw out enough information to write a small biography of Sheila Knight.

After they finished the appetizer plate, he decided it was time to give her a little push—in the direction of Erin Faulkner.

"Must be tough to lose a friend like that," he said sympathetically.

"It was hell. Living hell. I'd known her all my life, practically."

"And then she's gone." Loving shook his head. "You two must've had a lot of happy memories."

"We did."

" 'Specially when you're young, just kids. No worries, no responsibilities. Nothing bad ever happens when you're a kid."

Sheila fell silent. Should he push a little more, or just ride it out? He chose to remain quiet, and a moment later, his patience was rewarded.

"Something bad happened to my friend."

"Yeah?"

"Something horrible. When she was just fifteen."

"I'm sorry. Still, fifteen's practically grown up. At least she had those great fifteen years."

"Those years were . . . not always great." Loving noticed that she was looking at the bar top now more than she looked at him. "Even before the tragedy, she had problems. We both did. We never talked about it, but . . ." She lifted her head. "I'm sorry. You don't want to hear this."

"I don't mind."

"No, we just met. It isn't right."

Loving took her arm. "Listen to me. It's obvious you have something on your mind. You need to talk. I got ears."

Her hands trembled a bit as she ran a finger across the bar top. Her point of vision seemed to recede inward. "Have you ever had a secret so bad, you couldn't tell anyone?"

"Yes," Loving said. "Once."

"Erin and I had a secret like that. And Erin—I think maybe she had another secret. I'm just starting to figure it out, but—I think that may be why she died." Her face saddened. "It's horrible. Having all these secrets and not being able to tell anyone. Even if you really want to. Even if you know you need help. Know you could help others. But still . . . you just can't do it."

"You can," Loving said firmly. "You can tell me." He gripped her wrist all the firmer. "You know you need to get this out of your system."

"Maybe you're right. Maybe . . ."

"I am. You know I am."

Sheila nodded slightly. Her lips parted. "All those years ago, I—"

"*Sheila!* Sorry I'm late!"

Loving swore under his breath. A tall black man in a cashmere coat edged between them.

"There you are," Sheila said, collecting herself. "I was wondering what happened to you."

"Stuck at the office. You know how it goes." He glanced at Loving. "Looks like you weren't bored."

Loving smiled pleasantly. Damn, damn, damn!

The man looked his watch. "We'd better hurry, or we'll be late for the show."

"Right, right. And we can't be out late. I still need to pack." She glanced at Loving. "I'm going to the lake for the weekend."

"How nice."

"Oh, it's nothing fancy. I just need to get away for a spell. I've got a cabin at Grand Lake." She grabbed a few bills from her purse and put them down on the bar. "Okay, James, I'm ready."

James Wesley? Loving wondered. The man who dated Erin Faulkner before she died? He fit the description.

Sheila pushed away from the bar. "Sorry," she said to Loving as she left. "Got to run. Enjoyed it, though."

"Me, too," Loving answered. "Next time I'll show you how to get an olive into a brandy snifter without touching it."

She laughed and departed, Wesley on her arm.

The bartender reappeared. "Something else to drink?"

"Yeah," Loving growled. "And this time, something real."

The bartender glanced at Sheila as she exited. "Looks like you lost out."

"Damn right." He pinched his fingers together. "And I was this close. This close. To something big."

"There'll be other chances."

"I hope you're right. My boss may not be so optimistic."

The bartender appeared puzzled, but decided to let it go. "Say . . . would you show me that bit with the Bailey's and Kahlúa again?"

Loving frowned, growled, then with a great sigh, let it all go. "Why the hell not? You see, it's all in the wrist action. . . ."

"YOU THINK THAT'S possible?" Ben asked as he jogged on the treadmill. "Professional jealousy among chemists?"

"What can I say, Ben?" Rothko answered, pedaling away on his exerbike. "It's not all Ronald McDonald and Dave Thomas in burgerland. It can be a nasty business. And not just at the flavor factory."

"How so?"

"Where to begin? Ever wonder why so much fast-food marketing is targeted toward children?"

"Okay, I'll bite. Why?"

"One word, Ben. Addiction."

Ben did a double take.

"It's true. Little kids get hooked on high-fat food just like teenagers do on nicotine. They're similar, in a way. The tobacco industry used to target their advertising at young people because they knew that someone who started smoking as a teen would have a much harder time quitting than someone who started as an adult. It's not a matter of willpower—it's biochemical. Same for fast food. Hook 'em when they're young, and you've got a customer for life."

"Incredible."

"Burger Bliss, of course, has gone the opposite direction. We've targeted grown-ups. We're the high-class fast food. And that's cost us. Market research has shown that small children often recognize the McDonald's logo before they recognize their own name. The average American kid will have a Happy Meal once every two weeks. We don't get any of that kind of business."

"Too bad."

"Another example. The fast-food biz pays minimum wage to a higher percentage of its employees than any other business. You thought the service was lousy last time you chomped down on a Whopper? There's a reason."

"And that is?"

"Turnover is incredibly high. At McDonald's the average employee lasts three months. But the kids keep coming. One out of eight American workers has been employed by McDonald's at one time or another. Way too many kids give up sports, sacrifice their grades, or drop out all together so they can work. And the pay is pathetic."

"Must create some resentment."

"That's an understatement. Did you read about those fast-food employees who were arrested for putting yummy things like spit and urine and bleach and Easy-Off oven cleaner into the food? They'd been doing it for months. Really—you don't want a bunch of angry, crazy kids running your restaurant. Much better to pay responsible, reliable people decently. That's what we do."

"Probably helps contribute to your image as the high-class fast-food stop, too."

Rothko winked. "Can't hurt. We have a much lower injury rate than the incredibly high rate at most burger joints, too. 'Course, it's in part because our employees aren't total morons. But we've also spent some major money on safety precautions. Nationwide, the injury rate for working teenagers is twice that for adults. But not at Burger Bliss. Statistics are also way high on fast-food robberies—usually by former or current employees. But not at Burger Bliss. And I think it's because we treat our people with respect."

He paused for a moment. His pedaling slowed. "We did have that one horrific incident a few weeks ago. The shooting."

Ben nodded. "I heard about that firsthand, from one of the cops at the scene. Wounded six people, was it?"

"Yeah," Rothko said solemnly. "Killed three. It was a horrible tragedy. And a PR nightmare. We had to close that restaurant."

"I'm sorry."

"But just for the record—our burgers really are the best. You read enough about slaughterhouses, the kind of meat my competitors buy, and you'll under-stand how *E. coli* spreads. But there's never been an *E. coli* outbreak in a Burger Bliss. Never once. We send all our managers to a food safety course. We use re-frigerated delivery trucks equipped with record-keeping thermometers. We cal-ibrate our grills to guarantee the meat is sufficiently cooked. We make our fry chefs use tongs—not their hands. USDA testing is a joke—we do our own mi-crobial testing. I wanted Burger Bliss to be a model of how a fast-food restau-rant could be—and should be—run. We really are a quality restaurant."

"And the amazing thing is," Ben replied, "you haven't gone broke."

"Exactly. Truth is, all these things I've talked about—better salaries, better meat, safety precautions—add very little to our total cost. Like maybe a few pennies per burger. In this billion-dollar business, everyone could be doing it."

"Then why don't they?"

"I think you already know the answer to that question, Ben. Greed." He pushed himself off the bicycle. "They don't do it because they don't have to. And it's taking a toll. All that fatty fast food is. Do you know what the na-tional obesity rates are? It's shocking. Fully fifty percent of our population is overweight. Twenty-five percent of all children. Fifty million Americans are obese—meaning they're over fifty pounds heavier than they should be. It's the second leading cause of mortality—after smoking! And it is directly related to the rise of fast food. That's why Burger Bliss is committed to offering a higher-quality alternative. I'm proud of what we've accomplished."

Ben stepped off the treadmill. He was dripping with sweat, but he felt bet-ter, as he always did after a good workout. He might not be Arnold Schwarz-enegger, but he wasn't total flypaper anymore, either. "You have every right to be proud," Ben replied. "You've taken the high road. And you've made it work."

"Well, thanks. But I have to tell you, Ben—the best part of it is being my own boss. I'm sure you can appreciate that. Have you ever worked for a corporation?"

"As a matter of fact, I have."

"Then you know what corporate competition can be like. When people are competing for their livelihoods—especially when there's a lot of money at stake—anything is possible."

"Like one chemist knocking off a better chemist?"

"Anything, Ben. Absolutely anything."

CHAPTER

21

TRAMP. HARLOT. WHORE. Cheap piece of pussy. That's what she was.

But those eyes. Those dark beautiful eyes.

Gabriel Aravena clenched his fists. Everything was so different now, since he went off the Depo. Everything was changed. This surge of emotions. The confusion. The thoughts flashing through his brain, thoughts he couldn't seem to banish. He had hated being on the medication, watching it change his body, change him. And yet it had brought a certain . . . peace.

That peace was gone now. Gone like a thundercloud that had shot its load and had blown away with the wind. He'd been off the medication for almost a week now. At first, he felt only elation. His body was his own again. All the feelings they had tried to submerge had returned. But only for a little while. When he'd been on the Depo he could entertain all those horrible fantasies. Why not? He couldn't do anything about it. But now it was different. Now he *could* do something about it. Was that what he wanted? He was consumed by desire, obsessed by the irresistible need to take Sheila and throw her down and never stop taking her—

She was a little old for him, true. He had usually preferred his girls . . . younger. But when he looked at the woman he now saw through the restaurant window, he saw the girl of fifteen she had been. And he wanted that girl. Wanted her bad.

He had watched her in that bar, shamelessly flirting with that redneck piece of trash who was putting the moves on her. She had all but thrown herself at him, the cheap little twat. She had all but spread her legs and done him on the bar rail. And no sooner had she finished with him than she took up with the next man who walked up. She wrapped herself around the black man and let him take her away to this place.

He wasn't fooled by the fancy decorating and the high-priced menu. He knew what this was all about. This was about getting her liquored up, maybe slipping her something. Not that it was necessary. Not with her.

And not with him, either.

It was too late tonight, he could see that. This jerk with the hair gel had his finger in it, and there was no getting rid of him. But there would be another time, Gabriel told himself. Another time when it would just be him and her, and then—

Stop! he heard a voice screaming somewhere inside him. *Stop before it's too late!*

But he ignored the voice. He would watch this woman. Yes, that was it. He would follow her wherever she went, no matter how far or how long. And when the opportunity came, he would take her. Over and over again. Even if it killed her.

Over and over again. Until it killed her.

CHAPTER

22

SO, AM I feeling better yet? Sheila Knight wondered as she lit another cigarette. How long is this going to take?

She sucked hard on the ciggy, trying to calm herself. Coming out to the Grand Lake cabin was supposed to comfort her, but it was almost midnight now, and it wasn't working. Maybe she should've talked to the cop. Maybe it was time to come clean. About everything. But she hadn't. She lied, or at any rate didn't tell the truth. Certainly she didn't tell him what she had seen, what she suspected. But she didn't want any more trouble. She wanted to be free of this, not ever more deeply entangled. That was the problem with Erin Faulkner and her family and all the ever-increasing intrigue and horror that surrounded them. Instead of winding down, it just seemed to balloon and grow and become more and more demanding, more complicated, more impossible.

She threw down the cigarette, crushing it in an ashtray. Nicotine was not enough to calm her spirits tonight. She needed a serious drug. The real stuff.

She had not been sure, not until today. Not until she saw the picture in the paper. But now, as she gazed at the photo and let her mind travel backward in time, back to the last time she and Erin had been together . . .

She knew. She put the pieces together, and for once, they made sense. An incredible, horrible sort of sense. A dangerous sort of sense.

She walked to the kitchen, opened a beautiful blue bottle of Skyy vodka, and began drinking it right out of the bottle. Calm yourself, Sheila. Calm yourself. She hated when she got like this. She was turning into Erin—like in some weird way, now that Erin was gone, she felt she had to replace her. She felt as if there was a giant hole in her life, in her soul. Something that could never be filled. Sure, she had friends, family. James.

But she missed Erin. She wasn't sure she could live without her. Or wanted to.

She felt responsible.

She took another swig of the vodka, letting it burn its way down her throat. It hurt, but it hurt good, as they said. She took another drink and started to feel the rosy blanket, the warm sense of . . . fading that came with the onset of drunkenness. It was a good feeling. She wanted more of it. She held the bottle in both hands and drank and drank and . . .

Did she hear something? Outside? This time of night? Way out here?

Couldn't be. She raised the bottle to her lips once more . . .

And heard it again.

She walked to the rear of the cabin, pulled back the shades, and peered out into the darkness. She didn't see anything. But she was certain she heard something. She wasn't so drunk that she would imagine that—

Sheila screamed. Someone had jumped out of nowhere and was on the other side of the window staring at her.

No! she thought as she stared at the all-too-familiar face. That's impossible!

She heard the pounding at the door and knew she had to run. Groping to steady herself, peering through blurred eyes, she made her way to the side door. If she could get out, get down to the lake, she could climb in the boat and speed away. There was no way she could be followed, not across Grand Lake.

But first she had to get there.

She ran outside, plunging into the darkness. The moon was barely a quarter and there were no electric lights way out here. She knew there was a path leading down to the lake, but where was it? Where the hell was it?

She heard footsteps close behind her. She did not have much time. Because it didn't take a vast quantum of imagination to know what would happen if those footsteps caught up to her. The same thing that happened to Erin. And all the others.

BY MIDNIGHT, MIKE and Sergeant Baxter had been sitting in his Trans Am for more than three hours. They had followed Sheila Knight—at a discreet distance, of course, all the way to Grove, then out onto Grand Lake. Sheila parked outside a lakeside cabin, went inside, turned on the lights. She'd been there ever since; no visitors had come to meet her. Mike parked about a hundred feet down the dirt road outside the cabin. It was the perfect vantage point; they could not only see the cabin and Sheila's car, they could monitor the one-way road that led to the cabin.

"The night is long," Mike said, gazing out the car window, "that never finds the day."

Baxter grimaced. "Not with the poetry. Is that Wordsworth again?"

"Shakespeare, actually. From *Macbeth*."

"Puh-lese. If I offer you coffee, will you promise to stop?"

"Distinctly possible." After three hours of watching, Mike could feel the lateness of the hour and the stupor born of inactivity. He took the silver thermos from Baxter, filled his mug, and took a sip.

"Damnation, Baxter. You weren't kidding about your percolating skills." Mike held the mug between his hands, watching the steam rise. It felt good, warming his hands, warming his face. "This is excellent coffee."

"Well, I try to please. Contrary to rumor."

"You succeeded. What is this, some special blend?"

"Uhhh . . . yeah . . ."

"I can tell you're a coffee gourmet. Is it an imported blend? Did you grind the beans yourself?"

" . . . possibly . . ."

"And the flavoring is delicious. What is it? English toffee? French vanilla?"

"Yes."

"Both?"

"Uhhh." Her fingers stiffened. "Look. I didn't make the coffee myself, okay?"

"Where did it come from?"

"Where does coffee ever come from? Starbucks, of course."

Mike whistled. "Wow. The good stuff."

"Well, I wanted—I was—" She puffed out her cheeks in exasperation. "I was trying to make a good impression."

"You?"

"Yeah, I know. Total waste of time."

Mike's head tilted to one side. "To the contrary—I'm honored. Flattered."

"Yeah?"

"Yeah. You got any more of this . . . what is it?"

"White chocolate mocha."

"Heavenly. From now on, I'm inviting you to all my stakeouts."

SHEILA RACED OUT into the darkness, plunging into the thickly treed brush that separated the cabin from the lake. Move, girl, she muttered under her breath. Get to the boat. You haven't got much time.

She didn't have to listen to know the footsteps were right behind her.

Unfortunately, the ground between the cabin and the lake was not only covered with brush but was also on a sharp slope. A cliff, practically. Normally, she would walk down the gravel road out front about fifty feet to an improvised slope that led down to the pier. But she knew she didn't have time for that now, and besides, the footsteps were between her and the path.

If she was going to make it, she was going to have to go straight down.

She plunged into the brush, straining to spot safe places to run. Nonetheless, not three steps down, a tough piece of vine caught her foot and sent her tumbling forward. With a desperate lunge, she managed to grab a branch from a nearby river birch, stopping herself at the last possible moment.

Why hadn't she turned on the back porch light? It might not be brilliant, but it would be better than nothing. The slope was sharp, practically ninety degrees, or so it seemed to Sheila as she tried to get down it much too quickly. The ground was covered with leaves, and thanks to the recent rain, they were slick. She was wearing house shoes, and they constantly slipped out from under her. She took another false step and plunged forward. Once again, a tree branch was all that saved her from falling. She was risking her neck out here, running down the slope so fast.

Of course, if she stopped running, her neck would be in much worse shape.

She had to keep going, whatever the risk. She grabbed another tree, trying to lower herself down a particularly steep place. She slowed, gently descending, one foot at a time, and—

Heard the footsteps. Barely ten feet behind her.

She was scant seconds ahead. She had to get to the boat. Had to get there fast.

She let go of the tree and started running all-out down the slope, hell or high water, staying upright as best she could. A few feet later, she lost her balance. Her feet flew out from under her and she fell down hard, the side of her head slamming down against something that knocked her all but unconscious.

A rock? she wondered groggily. Didn't know. And didn't have time to ponder. Exerting all her strength, she pushed herself up on wobbly legs, tasting the blood trickling down the side of her head. She had to keep moving. *Keep moving . . .*

It was impossible. Only a few seconds later her feet went out from under her again and this time there was no way to control her fall. She went tumbling down the slope, headfirst. Her legs banged up against the rocks and brush and thorns. Her head hit something new, something just as hard, and once again she thought she would lose consciousness. She managed to keep herself awake, but she had lost all control of her descent.

She heard a sudden snap, jolting her awake. What was that? she thought, and a moment later, she realized it was her—her leg, to be specific. She had banged it against something and it had snapped. Had she broken it? She couldn't be sure. She only knew it hurt like hell and she couldn't stop falling. . . .

Until she did. She hit the bottom of the slope with a sharp and painful immediacy. But the descent was over. And just across the muddy bank, not ten feet away, was her boat. And another one she didn't recognize . . .

If only she could get to it. She tried to push herself to her feet, but her injured leg hurt so badly she couldn't steady herself. Her head was swimming, barely able to focus. She fell to the ground again, the cold earth knocking her breath away.

All right then, if she couldn't walk, she'd crawl. It wasn't far. She pushed up onto her hands and knees. The leg still ached, but crawling like an infant, she narrowed the distance between herself and the boat. Closer, closer, closer . . .

"That's about far enough, I think."

Sheila felt a foot pressed against her back, shoving her face into the mud. Too late.

"A little dark for a boating excursion, don't you think?" the voice behind her said. "A girl could get hurt."

THE WHITE CHOCOLATE mocha was gone, but Mike and Baxter were still keeping watch. They hadn't seen anyone else come near the cabin, but they could see that the lights were still on.

"If that woman came all the way out here and she's still up at this hour of the night," Mike ventured, "there must be a reason."

"Like she's going to meet someone?"

"Maybe. Or she's going to do something she doesn't want anyone to see her doing."

"You really think Sheila Knight is the key to this thing?"

Mike waved his hand in the air. "I don't think there is a key. I think Erin killed herself. But Sheila was definitely holding something back. I wonder if I could get Bernie to tap her phone?"

"Look, Morelli, I won't let you do anything improper or illegal."

"You don't have to be any part of it."

"Yeah, but if my partner commits an offense, it could reflect back on me."

"Chill, Baxter."

"Don't tell me to chill. I won't let you screw up my career."

"Baxter, relax."

"Don't patronize me. This is serious!"

"Baxter! Shoosh!" Once she finally quieted, he lowered his voice. "You've got nothing to worry about. I wouldn't do it without a court order. Relax already."

She folded her arms across her chest. "Sorry. I overreacted."

"No joke."

"It's just . . . something I'm sensitive about."

Mike slowly turned to look at her. "You had some trouble in Oklahoma City, didn't you?"

"You know I did."

"I know there's more to it than what I read in your report."

"Which was?"

"Basically, Kate doesn't play well with the other children." He shrugged. "So what? We're cops, not insurance salesmen. There has to be more."

Baxter did not reply.

"The way they hustled you out of OKC and set you up here with Blackwell and the mayor—someone was pulling some major-league strings. Someone who wanted you out of the OKC PD in a big way."

Baxter stared at the floor of the car. She wasn't taking the bait.

Mike continued. "Whatever it was, it probably didn't even directly relate to police work. Otherwise, it would've been in your file."

"Maybe there's nothing to put in the file."

"There is," Mike said firmly. "Something they didn't want to write down. Something you're not telling me about it."

"And how do you know? Is my face making the wrong kind of crinkly lines? Is it because you're such a damn good cop?"

"No. It's because you're such a damn good cop."

Baxter's eyes rose.

"Too good to be cut loose so unceremoniously without a compelling reason."

Baxter's eyes were black, like deep inky wells, neither capturing nor reflecting light. "There was a reason."

"I'm listening."

"And you're right. It had nothing to do with police work. I was . . ." She paused, breathing in and out deeply, several times. "I was involved with someone."

"Another cop."

She nodded.

"Your partner?"

"Worse. The chief."

Mike's eyes widened. "As in, chief of police? Hardesty? The old man?"

She pressed her hand against her forehead. "I can't explain it. It just . . . happened."

"What is he, like eighty-five or something?"

"Just fifty-two, Morelli. And for your information, a very handsome fifty-two."

"Jesus!" Mike stared out the car window. "No wonder you got the boot. Isn't he married?"

"Separated. Still—it wasn't a good idea."

"No kidding. How did it start?"

Baxter receded into her bucket seat. "We were working this case together. It was big—that's why he was personally involved. Corruption in the City Council. Big-time stuff. Late nights. Close quarters. One thing led to another."

Mike remained incredulous. *"Hardesty?"*

"Look, I'm a human being, okay? Haven't you ever had a thing with someone at work?"

"As a matter of fact, no."

"Of course not. Not the Great and All-Powerful Major Morelli."

Mike fell silent for a moment. "Of course, when I started on the force, I was married. After my wife dumped me, I was more an object of pity around the office than anything else. No one was remotely interested."

"She dumped you?"

"Big time."

Baxter inched forward. She was physically closer to him than she had ever been before, not counting the times when they were about to tear out each other's throat. "Tell me about it."

"Not much to tell, really. She didn't feel that my career—not to mention my income—was accelerating as quickly as it should. So she ran off with some rich guy who was in medical school."

"It all came down to money?"

"Yeah." He paused. "Well, that's what I've always said. That's how I've explained it away." Why was he talking about this? He hadn't even told Ben this. But for some bizarre reason, he felt as if he wanted to tell her. "And there's an element of truth in it. But the more time passes, the more I realize I use that explanation—because I like that explanation."

"Why?"

"Because it absolves me. Makes it look as if I didn't do anything wrong. It was all her fault." His eyes turned outward, toward the cabin. "But I think the truth is, I was a pretty sucky husband. I worked too much and gave her too little. It was my job to make her happy, after all. And I didn't. That's why she left. I don't think it was the money so much as just that . . . she was bored. I bored her. Me and the life I was creating. She didn't want any part of it."

"It's not possible to make someone happy all the time," Baxter said. Her voice seemed softer than it had before. "No matter what you do."

"Yeah. But I could've done better. A lot better."

"You will. Next time."

"Next time." Mike laughed, but it was not a happy laugh. "I used to tell myself that. But time keeps on passing, and I become more and more obsessed with my work, and I don't see much happening in my personal life. Julia has gotten on with hers. She's been through several doctor boyfriends, got some highfalutin' nursing job. Even had a kid. A little boy." He drummed his fingers on the steering column. "I love kids. We always talked about having kids. But we never did."

"I'm sorry."

"No, I'm sorry. To waste your time with all this soap-opera crap."

"Don't do that." She reached out and touched him on the shoulder. "If I'm going to be your partner, I have to know . . . who you are. Don't push me away."

Mike looked at the hand still on his shoulder. He could feel heat radiating from it, from her. "I won't."

"And it isn't crap," she continued. "It's your life. My life. Such as they are. We all make mistakes. But we have to push on."

"Yeah?" Her head was moving closer to his, there in the darkness and the close quarters of the car. His head seemed to be closing the gap as well.

"It's too easy to crawl up in your shell and say forget it. It's over. That's not living. You have to take risks. You have to . . . reach out."

Their lips were barely an inch apart.

"Morelli?"

"Yeah?"

"What do you think about cops who engage in intimate relationships with their partners?"

"I think it's stupid. Unprofessional. Usually a sign of serious mental problems."

"Me, too," she whispered. "So are you going to kiss me or what?"

Their lips touched.

And barely an instant later, they heard the shot.

"What the hell was that?" Baxter said, pulling away from him.

"That was a gunshot. And it came from inside the cabin. Come on!"

Mike flew out of the car. He pounded on the front door of the cabin. "Open up! Police!"

No answer.

He looked at Baxter. "You wanna do it, or shall I?"

"Ladies first." She brought up her heel and kicked the door, right beside the knob. The wooden door splintered. Two more well-placed kicks and the door was open.

"Come on." Mike led the way into the front living area, through the kitchen—

Then stopped. They didn't have to go any farther.

Baxter's hand flew up, covering her mouth. "Oh, my God. Oh, no."

Mike stared silently at the grisly—and all-too-familiar—tableau.

The worst of it was that the walls of the cabin were white, so the blood and brains and tissue now splattered all over them stood out with dramatic intensity. It was like a scene from a madman's surgical ward, but the only patient present was Sheila Knight, and the only surgical instrument, such as it was, was the small pistol still clutched in her lifeless hand.

THREE

A Taste of Death

◆ ◆ ◆

CHAPTER

23

BEN STARED GRIMLY at the courtroom doors. "I don't think I should even go in there."

Christina looked at him with a gaze so intense he could not escape it. "C'mon, Ben—we've got a job to do."

"You've got a job to do. I should take a powder."

"Ben, it's been years since you were at Raven, Tucker & Tubb. You can't run from Judge Derek forever."

"I'm not running. At least not for my own benefit. I have to think of Ray. Derek isn't going to like what we have to say. Having me in the courtroom will only make it worse."

"Ben, I handled the last one, but now—"

"C'mon, Christina. Didn't I kill that spider in your office this morning?"

"Yes, but spiders are scary. Judge Derek is just an old egomaniac who's too handsome for his own good."

"You can handle the hearing. You'll be great."

"But your name is on the papers. If you don't show, it could seem as though you thought the case wasn't important. Derek might think you sluffed it off on some second-rate associate." She batted the strawberry-blonde hair tied up behind her head. "Since he doesn't know us well enough to realize that I am, in fact, the brains of the outfit."

"Fine. Then I'll come into the courtroom. But I won't say a word. You're in charge."

From the end of the corridor, they heard a familiar voice. "Is this a power meeting? Can I eavesdrop?" Jerry Weintraub, from the AG's office. Their ursine opponent. "I love this high-level strategic stuff."

"Perfectly ordinary, I can assure you," Ben murmured.

"Hey, I saw that motion you filed to transfer the case to another judge.

What's the deal?" He jabbed Ben in the ribs. "Don't you have confidence in dear old Judge Derek?"

"I have confidence in his ability to railroad anyone he thinks is remotely connected to me."

"Tsk, tsk. Such shocking lack of faith in the judicial system." Weintraub tilted his head toward Christina. "So does that mean it's you and me in there?"

"I guess so. Is that a problem?"

"Not for me. I'd rather have you on the other side anyway."

Christina's eyes narrowed. "Because you enjoy the challenge of going up against a superior legal mind?"

He smiled. "Because I love the way your cheeks flush when you get all worked up."

MIKE AND BAXTER sat on a sofa on the side of the cabin's bedroom while the crime-lab technicians went about their appointed tasks. There was a window just behind them that afforded a breathtaking view of Grand Lake, still and tranquil. But neither of them looked. Mike didn't want to see anything beautiful, anything that would stand in such stark contrast to the grisly scene before him. Which he also couldn't look at.

And he wasn't entirely comfortable looking at Sergeant Baxter, either.

One of the crime-lab tekkies, an emaciated man named Crowley, came over to Mike to report. "We're just about through, sir. Still got to take some photos and video. But the surfaces have been pretty well scoured."

"Find anything?"

"Not really, sir."

"Fingerprints?"

"Just hers."

"Including the weapon?"

"Yes, sir."

"Blood?"

"Only hers. Lots of it."

"What about the gun?"

"Already checked. It's registered to her."

Mike stretched. For some reason, his trench coat felt very uncomfortable all of the sudden. "What about the rest of the cabin?"

"We've found the usual stuff. Hair and fiber. Most of them match her or clothes in her suitcase. A few still unmatched, but nothing suspicious."

He nodded. "Thank you, Crowley."

"Of course, sir." Crowley skittered away.

Leaving Mike and Baxter alone again.

"I guess you know," he said, after a long while, "what this is going to do to our records. Our careers."

"What?" Baxter said, not turning her head. "The fact that we let a suspect we were surveilling die right under our noses?"

"Yeah. That."

"Doesn't seem like the stuff commendations are made of."

"The only thing that's going to piss off Blackwell more than this screwup is the fact that we've already wasted so much time on this case."

"Morelli, don't start. There's no way in hell this was a suicide."

"It sure looks like one."

"There's no note."

"That's not even unusual."

"The gun was in her hand. Again."

"True. But she was dressed this time, so don't go down that road."

"Sheila Knight had no reason to kill herself."

"She may have had the same reason Erin Faulkner did. And dealt with it in exactly the same way."

"You don't know that."

"No. I don't." He pushed himself to his feet. Their eyes met briefly, then both hurriedly looked away. "I don't know anything, right at the moment."

"You must admit, it's a hell of a coincidence."

"That's true," Mike acknowledged. "And I don't believe in coincidences. But what reason would anyone have to rub out Erin Faulkner—*and* her best friend?"

"That's what we have to find out, Morelli. Because if we could answer that question—we could blow this whole case wide open."

"YOUR HONOR," CHRISTINA began, "if you'll examine the attachments to our most recent brief, you'll find a series of affidavits relating to this case."

"If it please the court," Weintraub said, rising to his feet, "the state objects to the use of affidavits. I can't cross-examine an affidavit."

Christina had seen this coming. "Your honor, I'm aware of the evidentiary problem. But given the exigencies of time, I thought it best—"

"Time pressures don't allow her to trample the state's rights," Weintraub cut in.

"If the court would like to extend the execution date," Christina answered, "we can have a full-blown hearing and call witnesses and do the whole dog and pony show. But with the execution date not even a week away, there was only so much we could do. I would implore the court in the name of decency—"

Derek waved his hand. "Relax, counsel. No lecture necessary. I'll allow it. For the limited purposes of this hearing."

"Thank you, your honor."

She watched as Judge Derek fumbled with his stylish bifocals, ran a hand through his all-too-handsome graying temples, then rifled the pages of the brief. "Attachment A?"

"That's the one, your honor."

Derek grunted. "This better be good."

She couldn't resist. "It will be."

Derek peered at her through his half lenses, gave her a few moments of visual sternness, then returned his attention to the brief.

A narrow escape, Christina realized. Her legs were tingling. Did that mean her cheeks were flushing, too? Damn Weintraub—was that remark some strategic mind game, or was she really blotching up like a ink blotter?

"Exhibit One," she began, "is an affidavit from Michael Palmetto, the head of the organ clinic where Erin Faulkner worked before her death. He reports numerous instances of strange and inconsistent behavior on her part. Exhibit Two is from Dr. Hayley Bennett, a psychiatrist."

"I'm familiar with Dr. Bennett," Derek murmured. "She's appeared in this court in criminal matters on several occasions."

"She reports several instances of erratic behavior by Erin Faulkner—and her belief that Erin was hiding some secret."

"That may be, but—"

"The third affidavit is from a man Erin dated, James Wesley. He, too, reports strange behavior on her part. The fourth is from a doctor—of sorts—Erin was seeing. Dr. Jamison Harris."

"He's the candle guy?"

"Uh . . . yes." Christina paused. If Derek knew that, then Derek had actually read the brief before the hearing—quite out of character for him. Why was he so interested? Was it because this was a death-penalty case? Was it because Ben's name was on the pleadings? Or was there something more? "We also have affidavits from several people connected to Erin's father, Frank Faulkner. Two from his coworkers at the chemical plant. Dr. Conrad Reynolds and Chris Hubbard."

Derek closed the brief and removed his glasses. "Counsel . . . what is the point of all this?"

Christina braced herself. Here we go. "The point, your honor, is to make it clear that there are a lot of unanswered questions regarding the Faulkner deaths."

"That could probably be said in every murder case, Ms. McCall."

"Your honor, we can't in good conscience allow an execution to take place when we don't know what really happened."

Derek pinched the bridge of his nose. "Counsel . . . in every criminal case, there will be uncertainties. Because ultimately, other people are unknowable. In any true sense. Are you familiar with Jean-Paul Sartre?"

He pronounced the name Gene Paul Sar-ter. Ben suppressed a grin. For all his vaunted Yale education, his facility with existentialists hadn't improved over the years.

"Yes, your honor," Christina replied. "I'm very fond of the French language."

Yes, Ben thought, but is the French language fond of her?

Derek continued. "Sartre said, 'Hell is other people.' Do you know why he said that, counsel?"

Because he'd had dinner with you? "No, your honor."

"Because ultimately, no matter how much time we spend with someone, no matter how hard we try to get to know them—we can never really know them. It's sad, yes—but very true. Take it from the voice of experience."

Take it from the voice, Ben thought, of a man who's split up and reconciled with his wife about a dozen times.

"Now, I'll grant you, some of these affidavits are interesting. They raise perplexing questions. Questions to which we will probably never know the answers. But imagine what would happen if we halted every criminal prosecution until we knew *all* the answers. We'd never be able to convict anyone."

"Your honor," Christina insisted, "this is a death-penalty case. There should be a higher standard."

"Not in the eyes of the law. The standard is 'beyond a reasonable doubt'— and that's plenty high enough. A jury has already found this man guilty under that exceedingly tough standard. I'm not going to override their judgment based on a few unanswered questions."

"Your honor, that conviction was based primarily on the testimony of a witness who later recanted."

"So you say. But that evidence is not before the court. And frankly, it never will be. Unless you've got something more for me—I'm afraid this hearing is finished."

*　　*　　*

"BAXTER! GET OVER here!"

Baxter didn't much appreciate being yelled at, but she figured this was not the time to make a fuss. She was just pleased he was speaking to her; since that brief lip lock in the car, he'd barely been able to look at her. Why did she always screw everything up?

She hustled around to the back of the cabin. There was a sharp slope that descended to the lake, covered with scrub trees and bramble. Mike was standing at the top. "What is it?"

"Take a look at this," he said, pointing at the slope. "What do you see?"

She shrugged. "Typical Oklahoma backwoods scrub."

"Look again."

Baxter suspected she was being tested, and she didn't want to fail. But she saw nothing extraordinary. A few trees with no leaves. Lots of unidentifiable ivy and bramble. Tall spindly plants with long thorns. You could see it anywhere in the state. What on earth did he think—

Wait a minute. There was a section where everything had been pushed down, just a few feet from where Mike was standing. All the brush had been flattened; there were several broken branches and plants. It was as if someone had started to cut a path about a foot or so wide down the side of the hill.

"Something's been here. Recently."

"That's right," Mike said, hustling toward the slope. "And it went down fast."

Together, they carefully descended the slope. At the base, just off the lake, he showed her a deep impression. "And this is where it landed."

Baxter crouched over the spot. The ground was only slightly muddy, but enough to leave a trace of what had been there. She spotted a small shape, outlined in the mud. It seemed flat at the top, but the bottom was three-sided, like the lower half of a hexagon.

She closed her eyes, letting her mind wander. She'd seen that pattern before. It was common. She saw it all the time. But she couldn't place it. . . .

Until she did. "A pants pocket."

Mike nodded. "A jeans pocket, to be precise."

"Sheila Knight was wearing Levi's when we found her body."

"Damn straight. And look here, where the mud has been scraped. I think something was dragged."

"Like a body?"

Mike didn't comment. "And look over here." He pointed to a place in the mud only a few feet from the jeans pocket.

"A footprint!" Only the top part was visible, but it was still undeniably the imprint of a shoe.

"Not much of one, but enough to make clear it isn't Sheila Knight's foot. And they had a heavy rain out here yesterday around noon."

"So?"

"So this footprint was made after that. In the last twelve hours. As was the jeans pocket imprint."

Baxter's eyes widened appreciatively. "She was down here last night."

"She fell down here," he corrected. "Or was pushed."

"The coroner said there were scrapes and bruises on her body," Baxter recalled. "Her leg was injured. And her clothes were dirty. It didn't seem important, given the big hole in the side of her head. But now—" She pondered a moment. "If there was a second person here, why didn't we see him? We were watching the road all night. And the front door." Baxter felt her heart racing. Did this mean she had been right all along? That Mike finally believed her? "Morelli, are you thinking—"

"It's too soon for thinking. We need to collect all the evidence we can and see what we turn up."

"Yes, but—"

"Baxter—round up the troops. I want every available officer in these woods looking for more traces of an intruder."

"You got it."

"And hurry." Mike jerked his thumb upward. "It's about to rain again."

DEREK SHOOK HIS head vigorously. "I'm sorry, Ms. McCall, but I disagree with you one hundred percent. Did your cocounsel, Mr. Kincaid, suggest to you that this was a strong argument?"

Christina bit her lower lip. Either way she answered that question would give Derek an opening to make a caustic remark. She wasn't taking the bait.

"Because I can assure you it is not," he continued. "A habeas corpus petition is a request for extraordinary relief. And you have presented a most unextraordinary case. Didn't you tell me at the last hearing that you were exploring a new theory? That there were two assailants involved in the Faulkner tragedy?"

Christina tilted her head to one side. "Ye-es . . ."

"So where's the evidence in support of that?"

"I would suggest, your honor, that all of these affidavits . . ."

"Don't play coy with me, young lady. I've read the affidavits. None of them addresses the issue."

"Nonetheless, your honor, as you yourself have said, they raise questions. Serious questions. Not only about Erin Faulkner's death, but about the murder of her entire family."

"And that's as good as it gets?"

Christina paused. Honesty or advocacy? "I will admit we have nothing that directly supports my theory—"

"That's what I thought."

"But it isn't reasonable to expect that someone is going to sashay through our office doors admitting to being an accomplice to one of the worst crimes in the history of the state."

"The bottom line here is that you have nothing."

"I strongly disagree. We may not have anything conclusive, but we have uncovered many intriguing facts. That the police department missed."

Derek clicked his tongue. "And based on that, you expect me to release a convicted man from death row?"

"Not yet, your honor," she said. "All we're asking at this point is that you postpone the execution date. Give us more time."

"I can't do that."

"You must!" Christina implored. "An innocent man is about to be murdered!"

"Don't tell me what I must do," Derek said, rising out of his chair. "I will not tolerate that type of behavior in my courtroom. Maybe your cocounsel thinks that sort of thing is acceptable, but I can assure you it is not."

"Your honor—"

"If you were better informed, you'd realize your advocacy is inadequate and your behavior is appalling."

Christina couldn't hold back any longer. "And if you could get past your decade-old petty grudge against my partner, you'd see that you're about to allow the execution of an innocent man."

Derek's eyes blazed. "Now you listen to me, young lady—"

"And I am sick and tired of this sexist, *young lady* crap. You will address me as you would any other attorney!"

"How dare you—!" He extended a tremulous arm. "You, Ms. McCall, may deposit another five hundred dollars with the clerk of the court on your way out of here. And if I hear another word from you, you'll be spending the night in jail!"

Christina so wanted to speak she could taste it. But she had to think of

Ray first, and she knew that wouldn't be in his best interest. She held her tongue.

"Because of the gravity of the sentence passed, I have given you and your petition an enormous amount of leeway—and you see what my reward for that is. Open the door a crack to lawyers of this caliber, and they kick it wide open. It has always been my policy to go the extra mile with habeas petitions. No one wants to see an innocent executed. But the fact is, we do have the death penalty in this state, and your client was convicted of the first-degree murder of no less than eight human beings, and you have not presented the slightest evidence in support of any of your theories of innocence."

He settled back into his chair. "I am not a jury, and I will not circumvent the decisions of the duly appointed jurors of this state. Not absent extraordinary circumstances." He paused, drawing in his breath. "Accordingly, I rule against the petitioner."

Ben's eyes closed. That was it. The last chance. Gone.

"At least leave the door open," Christina said quietly. "Give us an opening to return if we discover something new."

"I will not," Derek said firmly. "A death-row defendant always has the option to file a new petition based upon newly discovered evidence—"

"We've exhausted our statutory remedies."

"—but I will not continue this hearing. Not a second further. This charade has gone on too long already." He slammed his gavel. "Petition denied. This court is in recess."

FIFTEEN CRIME-SCENE techs spent the rest of the day combing the wooded area behind Sheila Knight's cabin. The area was not that wide or that deep, but micro-scrutinizing every square inch of thick brush was time-consuming. Fortunately, the weather cooperated. A light drizzle fell for half an hour or so, but it was not enough to slow them down. By the time the sun was setting, they had found four different torn scraps of clothing, most of them from Sheila's blouse, but at least one definitely not. They'd found two more partial footprints, both matching the first. Mike and Baxter continued to hunt for something more helpful.

"Mike!"

She slapped her hand across her mouth. She'd called him by his first name! That was a first. Well, she supposed she couldn't be suspended for that. She'd just gotten so excited—

"What is it?" he asked, running beside her.

"Proof positive, that's what." She was holding a small twig—a backwoods substitute for evidence tweezers—and on the end dangled a metal ring with a silver pendent. The pendent bore some sort of stylized engraving.

"Any idea what it is?" Mike asked.

"Looks like part of a key chain to me. Must've broken off. Perhaps during a chase. Or a struggle. Or while hauling a body up the slope back to the cabin."

"Could it be Sheila's?"

Baxter shook her head. "Her keys are in the cabin. With one of those keyless car-lock chains."

"Of course, this could've been here before Sheila took her fall. The rain wouldn't have washed it away."

"But still—"

Mike nodded. "But still. It's our first real clue. Something we can trace." He pushed himself up. "Let's get back to Tulsa. I expect Blackwell is pretty desperate to talk to us. And for that matter—I want to talk to him."

Baxter tried to restrain her excitement and maintain her oh-so-stoic professional exterior. "Does this mean . . . you're not going to try to close the case? That you think I'm right?"

"Let's not jump to any conclusions, Sergeant. Let's just collect the evidence and see what we find."

Her face fell. "Right."

"But Baxter?"

"Yeah?"

He looked at her directly. "Good work."

24

Gabriel Aravena threw the paper down to the floor. Sheila Knight was dead!

He held his hands before him, staring at them as though they were not connected, as though they belonged to someone else. How had all this happened? He never meant to become a monster. But somehow, somewhere along the way, everything got turned around, messed up. Nothing came out the way it was supposed to.

He'd been off the medication for barely a week now. He could feel the changes. And they were beginning to scare him. Sure, his breasts were finally shrinking. His voice had regained its normal pitch. His beard was coming back. But at the same time—the feelings were returning. The . . . bad feelings. The ones he couldn't control. He had thought he would like that.

He had been wrong.

He remembered all those times when he was on the medication, when he had thought evil things, when he had fantasized about sex. Cruel sex. Dreamed about taking women by force and pounding and pounding at them until they couldn't stand it anymore, until they cried out for mercy but didn't get it, just pain and pain and more pain . . .

He closed his eyes, ashamed of himself. It had been different when he was on the medication. He had needed to fight against the drug. It was trying to make him into something he wasn't. But now—now the drug was gone and it was just him and those dreams that he couldn't control and couldn't block out of his mind. He could act on them now. He could do anything. If he wanted to.

Did he? Did he want to?

He was not a monster! He did not want to be a monster!

Because he knew where that would lead. To the same disgusting life he'd had before. The sick thoughts that led to the evil deeds. And . . . that person.

The one who had made him a true monster, for once and always. The one who had taken his life and thrown it into the sewers, ruined it for all time. He couldn't stand that. He just couldn't stand it.

Aravena pushed himself out of his armchair. He had to do something, had to . . . distract himself. Even in this seedy little apartment, there had to be something he could do to take his mind off—

He walked to the west wall and glanced out the window. There was a woman on the street. A jogger. She was not as tall as Sheila Knight, not as pretty as Erin Faulkner. But she was pretty enough. And she was alone. Vulnerable. He could follow her, and then when it got darker, he could take her, throw her down and—

God! He dropped to his knees. What was happening to him? Maybe the doctors were right. Maybe he should be locked up. Maybe he should be on those horrible drugs.

He did not want to be a monster. But the urge was so strong. The need was so great. The voices were talking to him, the ones that came from deep, deep inside. The ones that inhabited his brain. He knew he couldn't resist them forever.

But he had to try. Because he could not go back on the Depo. He couldn't live like that. But he couldn't live like this either.

"I do not want to be a monster!" he cried out, pounding at his closed eyes. *"I do not want to be a monster!"*

But I am.

CHAPTER

25

CHRISTINA SAT IN the office lobby, her arms crossed on Jones's desk, her head bowed.

"I can't believe I folded like that. I can't believe I let that arrogant judge treat me in that manner."

Ben patted her shoulder sympathetically. "You did everything you could."

"I did too much. I totally alienated him."

"At that point, you had nothing to lose. He'd made up his mind."

"Because I blew it." Christina pounded her head against her arms. "I should have backed off when Derek started to get angry. I should've cited more case law."

"Christina, there's no point in sitting around blamestorming. We have to move forward."

"Forward to what? I signed Ray's death warrant."

"Now you're being ridiculous," Ben said, but he knew it wouldn't help. No words would. He'd been in these situations himself. He'd handled Ray's trial, after all, and he'd been toting around guilt about that ever since. She would just have to work through it. "Meeting in the conference room?"

Christina nodded. "Everyone's waiting for you. Although I don't understand what we're—"

"You'll see." He tugged at her arm. "Come on."

"Do I have to?"

"Definitely. I need you, Christina. Now more than ever." He raised her to her feet. "You're the best lawyer I know."

"THINK ABOUT IT," Loving was telling Jones as Ben and Christina entered the conference room. "Who's in a better position to take over the world? They could make it happen overnight."

Ben felt his impatience boiling up. They couldn't waste time on Loving's paranoid delusions. "Who are we talking about this time? The twelve old men who rule the world?"

"No," Loving said.

"The Trilateral Commission?"

"No."

"The CIA? FBI? NSA? KGB?"

"All wrong," Jones answered. "You're going to love this one. This time, the threat to world peace is . . . wait for it . . ."

"Yes?"

"McDonald's," Loving replied.

Ben threw his briefcase onto the table. "We don't have time for this."

"Think about it, Skipper," Loving insisted. "They're strategically placed all over the globe. They got more than twenty-six thousand outposts worldwide. The U.S. Army has fewer than a hundred. McDonald's also has more than a million workers. They're immensely wealthy. They've already brainwashed our children and addicted them to their products. They've destroyed the health of the human species and made us all fat and lazy. They could take over the U.S. in a heartbeat. And after that, the rest of the countries would fall like dominoes."

Ben pressed his hand against his forehead. "Please tell me you're kidding."

A slow, sly smile spread across Loving's face. "Well, of course I'm kiddin'. What do you think I am, crazy?"

Ben did not comment.

"I just thought you could use a laugh right now."

He was certainly right about that. "Listen to me, people. We have work to do."

"But what's the point?" Christina asked. "Our petition was dismissed. Ray's remedies are exhausted."

"I refuse to give up," Ben replied, not missing a beat. "I don't care how grim it looks. Whatever the rules and regulations, this is still America. They won't execute him if we can prove—absolutely prove—he's not the killer. We'll ask the Supreme Court for emergency relief. We'll ask the governor for a pardon. Whatever it takes."

Christina did not appear optimistic.

"We have five days until Ray's execution. Five days. We have to pull out all the stops. All the other cases go on the back burner. I don't care what they are. This takes priority."

"Understood," Jones said quietly. His expression was sad and sympathetic, as if Ben were a pathetic wretch in deep denial who had to be humored. "What can I do?"

"What you've been doing. Only more so."

"Such as?"

"I don't know. You're the resident mouse potato. Hit the Internet. I keep hearing you can find anything on the Internet. Find something that helps Ray."

"I'll try, Boss."

"Loving, I want you or Christina to revisit every potential suspect, witness, or informant on our list. Get something new out of them. Find new connections."

"Got it."

"I don't care if you have to lean on them. Frankly, I don't care if you have to torture them with bamboo shoots under the fingernails. Just so you get something."

"Understood, Skipper."

"Christina?" Ben could tell she was still upset about the hearing. And who could blame her? But he missed her usual effervescence. Her energy was about the only thing that got him through some of these cases. "I want you to pull out all the files, one at a time. All the transcripts, all the witness reports, everything. Read them and reread them and reread them. Find something we've missed. Something everyone has missed."

Her head listed to one side. "I'll try, Ben, but—"

"Good. People, we will not give up. Not while there's any chance, however slight."

"And what will you be doing?" Jones inquired.

"I have about a million tasks to complete before that execution date arrives. But one takes precedence. Unfortunately." His eyes fell to the table. "I have to tell Ray what happened at the hearing."

"WHAT THE HELL was going on out there?"

Chief Blackwell closed his office door, but Mike knew from experience that when his voice hit this decibel range, everyone on the floor could hear. And unless he missed his guess, half of them had their ears pressed against the other side of the door at this very minute.

"You had the woman under surveillance. And you let her die?"

Mike squirmed. "We did not *let* her do anything."

"Right under your noses! She was right under your noses!"

Sergeant Baxter looked no more at ease than Mike. "We thought she was alone, sir," she offered.

"People usually are when they commit suicide, Sergeant." He paced back and forth across the office, apparently so angry he couldn't hold still. "You're sitting in your car, and you don't have a clue what's going on until you hear the gunshot?"

Mike swallowed. "That's about the size of it."

"What were you two doing, anyway?"

Mike looked at Baxter, then quickly looked away. "We were . . . um . . ."

"Not doing anything," Baxter completed. "Just passing the time . . ."

"Right," Blackwell said. "Just passing the time. While this woman puts a gun to her head."

Baxter coughed. "Sir, I'm not at all convinced this was a suicide."

Blackwell marched right in front of her. "Don't start with me, Baxter. I humored you the first time. I won't go down that road again."

"But sir, there are strong indications that another person was present."

"So what? It's a vacation cabin. She probably had people there all the time."

"I mean recently. Just before she died."

"You were supposedly watching the cabin. Did you see anyone?"

"No. But think about it. There was no suicide note. There were cuts and abrasions on her body. A serious blow to her left leg. We found signs that she had fallen down the slope behind the cabin."

"And none of that amounts to a hill of beans!"

Baxter rose to her feet and faced him down. "With all due respect, sir— you're not giving me a chance."

"Why should I give you a chance?" He addressed her more like a drill sergeant than a supervisor. "Maybe I didn't make this clear when I hired you, Sergeant. I expect results. Not theories. Not botched stakeouts. Results!"

"Sir, if you'll just give us a little more time . . ."

"You've wasted too much time already. I've blown a bundle in taxpayer dollars humoring a rookie detective. I should've listened to Major Morelli when he told me to call Faulkner's death a suicide and close the file."

Baxter glared at Mike, her eyes like cold steel.

"And that's exactly what I'm going to do. I assume your opinion hasn't changed any. Not based on this pathetic nonevidence. Right, Morelli?"

Mike sat silently, pursing his lips.

"Well?" Blackwell bore down on him. "Am I right?"

JONES ENTERED CHRISTINA'S office and found her nose buried in a huge pile of files. "You look as if you could use a distraction," he said, holding out a pink message slip.

Christina didn't look up. "I don't want to see your honeymoon pictures again."

"Hardy-har. This is about the Goldman case. Got a call from James Wesley. Erin's sorta boyfriend. He wants someone to come over to his home. Wants to talk."

"What about?"

"Wouldn't say on the phone. But it must relate to Erin Faulkner."

"Shouldn't you tell Ben?"

Jones looked away. "He's busy. And I thought . . . you might like to take it. Might be good for you."

The corner of her lips turned up, just barely. "Yeah, you're right. I need a break." She snatched the message from his hand. "Thanks."

"Oh, no," he said mysteriously, looking away. "Don't thank me till you get back."

"ACTUALLY," MIKE SAID tentatively, "I have . . . somewhat . . . altered my opinion."

"What?" Blackwell looked as if he'd been hit by a bulldozer. "What are you babbling about?"

Mike inhaled deeply. "I'm talking about my initial impression that Erin Faulkner's death was a suicide."

"You have doubts?"

Mike knew this would only further infuriate Blackwell. But he had no choice. "No, I don't have any doubts. I'm sure. These deaths weren't suicides." He paused. "I was wrong."

Baxter turned, her lips parted.

"And when did you arrive at this brilliant revelation, detective?" Blackwell demanded.

"I don't know. I think I've known all along, at least a little bit. I just didn't want to admit it because . . ." His chest rose, then fell again. "I suppose I didn't want to admit that Baxter was right."

"Because she's a woman?"

Mike frowned. "No. Because she's . . . annoying. But I shouldn't've let that affect my judgment. She called this one exactly right."

Baxter gazed at him, her eyes filled with wonder.

Blackwell was not mollified. "And do you by chance have any evidence in support of this sudden epiphany?"

"We're still collecting evidence—"

"Don't stall me, Major."

Mike's jaw clenched. "The cuts and abrasions on Sheila Knight's body can't be explained by the gun wound. There are signs that she rolled or fell down the slope behind her cabin—and perhaps that she was dragged back up it. There are fresh footprints—not hers—also behind the cabin. We've found a key chain—we think it's a key chain—with some strange design on it. I haven't identified it yet, but—"

"Is that all you've got, Morelli? Because, frankly, it sounds pretty feeble to me. And I am sick of this half-baked, amateurish—"

"Just one goddamn minute," Mike said, matching his volume. "I've been on this force a good long time, and I think I've proven I know what a homicide is. I've also proven I can solve one, given enough time and support. And I can't think of any reason why I—or my partner—should have to endure this abusive bullshit!"

The room fell silent. Blackwell took a step back.

"Besides," Mike said, much more quietly, "it isn't good for your heart. You might burst a blood vessel or something."

"Morelli—"

"Look, Chief—just give us a week, okay? That's all I ask. One week to come up with something. If we don't—we'll both agree to close the file."

"One week to do what?"

"Well . . . I'm not totally sure. But my partner is right. Always has been." He glanced at Baxter out the corner of his eye. "And now we're going to prove it."

26

CHRISTINA WAS IMPRESSED to see that James Wesley had a house—and a nice-size one at that. After all, he was a single young man, and as far as she knew, he wasn't the heir to a fortune. The house was nothing fancy—a two-story Federal just north of Fifteenth. But to Christina—who had lived in a two-room apartment for more than a decade—it looked pretty darn good.

She rang the bell, and the door was opened almost immediately—by Michael Palmetto.

"Dr. Palmetto," Christina said. She extended her hand. "Christina McCall. I interviewed you. With Ben Kincaid. About Erin Faulkner's death."

"Of course. You visited shortly after I spoke with the police officers."

She nodded. "I didn't expect to see you here." *Especially since I heard that there was some bad blood between you and James.*

"Well, I've only been here a moment." *Was he distracted, or was it her imagination?* His eyes kept moving toward the door. "Even though James doesn't work at the organ clinic anymore, he still does some occasional freelance work."

"I see."

"He's in the basement. You can go on down."

"In the basement?"

"Yes. He's always in the basement."

Visions of Dracula's coffin flickered through Christina's brain. "May I ask why?"

"Well, that's where he does his work."

"And what work would that be?"

A smile flashed across the Palmetto's face. "You don't know?"

"Sorry. I don't."

"Well . . . then you're in for a big surprise."

Christina didn't much care for the sound of that.

"Let me ask you a question. How do you feel about spiders?"

Her face twisted up. "I hate them. Why?"

Palmetto placed his hand on her shoulder. "Ms. McCall, this is going to be the worst interview of your life."

"JONES IS SO going to pay for this," Christina kept muttering. That was the only comfort she could give herself, right at the moment. He was going to pay dearly.

As Christina descended into James Wesley's basement, she found herself surrounded by more than forty thousand spiders. Yes, forty *thousand*. All alphabetized and secure in lidded plastic cups, neatly arranged on rows and rows of portable shelving.

"It's my life's work," the handsome black man said proudly as he twirled around the center of the basement. "It's what I've always dreamed of doing."

Christina was working hard to comprehend. Not just why anyone would want to be surrounded by these horrible creatures. But how she was going to get through the next two minutes without fainting. "But . . . why?"

"I studied entomology in college, at OSU. Of course I loved all the insects, but I always felt . . . I don't know. A special connection to the arachnids."

"You felt a connection to spiders?"

"Oh yes. I've been an arachnophile since I was a boy. They're wonderful creatures. Diverse. Amazing. I don't know why they've gotten such a bad rap."

"Could it be . . . because they're creepy and they kill people?"

"Well, there is that. But it rarely happens. And there's so much to study. So much to admire. The web making. The sophisticated strategies for catching insects. The complex mating rituals. And the venoms, of course."

Christina felt a chill run up her spine at the word *venom*. "Of course . . . heh . . . none of these spiders are poisonous. Right?"

"Well . . . actually . . . they all are. To varying degrees."

Christina felt her knees wobbling. "Could I . . . possibly . . . sit down somewhere?"

"Is something wrong?"

"I just . . . don't much care for your pets. It's quite a surprise."

"But I warned that man about them. Jones. When I called."

So he had known. This was a put-up job. "If I could just sit . . ."

Wesley quickly pulled out a chair. "They're all safely tucked away. There's no reason to be frightened."

"Frightened? Me? Don't be silly." She lowered herself into the chair. "I'm not frightened."

"I'm glad to hear it."

"I'm terrified."

WESLEY BROUGHT HER a cup of tea and a slice of cinnamon toast. Comfort foods. Although Christina thought a couple shots of tequila were more likely to be effective. Eventually, she felt her stomach settle somewhat and the trembling in her legs subsided. Especially when she stared at the floor and didn't look up at the . . . creatures. All forty thousand of them.

Despite her desire to pretend she was ice skating on Lake Banff, Wesley seemed determined to give her the full tour. "Now this little thing is the *Gramostola spatulata*," he said, pointing at some black beast Christina never came close to looking at. "It comes from Chile. And I have a wide variety of tarantulas—but who doesn't? This light brown number is the ultrarare African king baboon tarantula. And these slick glistening numbers are the western black widows."

"But—why?" Christina managed to say. "Why do you have these . . . things?" She was proud of herself for leaving out the word *hideous*.

"It's a farm, basically," he answered. "I milk them for their venom."

"You want spider venom?"

"Oh yes. It's in great demand. Pharmacologists pay big bucks for the stuff."

"In God's name why?"

"Well, it's hard to explain without getting too technical. Basically, the active compounds in spider venom bind with molecules on the surfaces of living cells. And they do so with great specificity. Because of this selective quality, researchers can use it to develop new medicines and to help them better understand how living cells function. They're used routinely by the National Institute of Health. Most university schools of medicine."

"How do you get the stuff? Do you just ship them the spiders?"

"Oh no. I extract the venom right here. Want me to show you how?"

She didn't, but as bad as she felt, she didn't have the heart to smother his unbridled enthusiasm. He removed a small spider from a plastic cup and took him to the worktable beside a large microscope.

"First, you tranquilize the little beastie with a whiff of carbon-dioxide gas. Once he's groggy—which doesn't take long—you pick him up with these metal tweezers."

Christina noticed that the tweezers were attached to an electrical cord. "What's the juice for?"

"You'll see." He pressed his eye to the microscope while holding the spider beneath the lens. "By pushing this button, I send a mild shock into his system, via the tweezers. And watch what happens."

He pushed the button. Christina forced herself to look—just in time to see the spider spew.

"That's basically everything liquid inside the little guy," Wesley explained. "Venom, and also his stomach's digestive enzymes. I've got a serum that separates the two. Then I freeze-dry the venom and pack it off to the drug companies."

"That's just . . . amazing," Christina said, trying to be kind. "I notice you didn't get that much, though."

"True. It usually takes hundreds of spiders to fill a single order—which explains why I have so many on hand."

"And you actually make a living selling this stuff?"

Wesley beamed. "Sure do. Not a fortune, perhaps. But enough to pay the mortgage. Heck of a lot more than I made working at the pawnshop."

"Pawnshop? I thought you worked at the organ clinic. With Erin."

"That came later. I first met her at the pawnshop. She recommended me to Palmetto at the organ clinic."

"Erin hung out in pawnshops?"

"Not on a regular basis. But she came in on this occasion."

"Why?"

Wesley pulled his chair close. "That why I called. That's what I wanted to tell you." He hesitated for a moment. "She came in to buy a gun."

IN THE SPACE of a sentence, Christina had forgotten all about the fear and sickness that had consumed her since she first stumbled into this house of horrors. Now her mind was focused on one subject alone—a firsthand account of how Erin Faulkner got a gun.

"Did she give you any idea why she wanted a gun?"

"Oh yeah. I'll never forget that. I mean, normally I wasn't that chatty with the customers. Frankly, most of them were the scum of the earth, which is why I eventually left the place. But Erin was different. She was not poor, not poorly groomed, not stupider than dirt. She walked with a limp, sure, but that was intriguing, given her age. And she was extremely attractive, which didn't hurt any."

"So what did she say?" Christina tried to herd him back on topic. "When you asked her why she wanted a gun."

"She said—and get this—she said she was 'haunted by demons.' That's a quote."

"Demons." Christina ruminated for a moment. That sounded uncomfortably like a woman contemplating suicide. She knew Weintraub would see it that way. "Did she specify what kind of demons?"

"No. But later in the conversation, I got her talking about her work. At the organ clinic, you know."

"Right. And?"

"I gathered she was having a bad time. Not only that day, but later, when I worked there. She was not happy at work."

"Then why did she stay? She had options."

Wesley tapped his electric tweezers on the desktop. "I'm filling in a lot of blanks here, but I think she was very conflicted about her job. She believed her work was important—helping sick and injured people find the transplant organs they needed. But there was some other aspect of the job that bothered her."

"Did she ever name any names?"

"Not that I recall. Well, Palmetto."

"Dr. Michael Palmetto? The man I met upstairs?"

"Right. I think she had some problems with him."

"I heard you did, too."

James nodded. "I suspected he was causing Erin unhappiness. Pain. I couldn't work for someone like that."

"What was he doing?"

"Well, he tried to hit on her."

"Was there more?"

"I don't know." He paused. "Maybe."

Christina bit her lip in frustration. She had the unmistakable feeling that she had something on the hook. She just couldn't reel it in. "And so you sold her the gun?"

"Yeah. She wasn't old enough, but . . . well, I falsified the license. And showed her how to use it. I'm quite good with firearms—comes from working in that place so long. Gave her some ammunition."

"And sent her on her way?"

He smiled a little. "And took her to the coffee shop next door. I didn't think she'd go, even as I asked her. But to my surprise, she agreed."

"And you went out a few more times?"

"Right. After I left the clinic. But we never really connected. There was always something between us. Between her and everyone, actually. Something intangible . . . but nonetheless real."

"But you don't know what that was."

"I'm afraid not. I never got to know her well enough. I wanted to." He bowed his head. "It seems as though tragedy strikes everyone I try to get close to."

That triggered a memory. "I understand you were also dating Sheila Knight. Before her . . . untimely death."

"You mean, before her suicide? That's what they say it was, right? Once again, someone I wanted to know, wanted to get close to, finds it preferable to take their own life. You can imagine how that makes me feel."

"I'm sorry," Christina said quietly.

"Oh, don't be. I'm very lucky, really." A smile crossed his face, but Christina found it far from convincing. "After all, I've still got my spiders."

EVERY TIME BEN had spoken to Ray during the last seven years, he had done so through an acrylic wall. But the glass had never seemed so thick as it did today. The distance between them had never been so great.

"So that's it, then," Ray said, with a pronounced note of finality. "It's over."

He was doing an amazing job of controlling his face, Ben thought, of masking what must be his true feelings. He barely twitched. But as Ben gazed into his eyes, he could see all the hurt, all the anguish, all the sunken hopes. The dim light was fading to a dull and ashen gray.

"It isn't over," Ben said firmly. "I won't stop trying."

"Sounds like there's nothing left to try."

"I won't accept that. And I won't give up."

Ray pressed his lips together. "Well . . . four days from now . . . you won't have any choice."

Ben felt a churning in his gut. "Four days is a long time, Ray. We're doing everything imaginable. Talking to everyone. Filing every kind of motion. We won't stop—"

Ray interrupted. "Did you talk to Carrie?"

Ben's heart skipped a beat. "Well . . . yes." Would he want to talk about . . . the incident?

"How does she look?"

"She looks pretty much as she always did."

Ray's eyes softened. "Beautiful, huh?"

"Very."

"I haven't seen her for years, you know. But I've never stopped thinking about her. Not for a single day."

Ben felt an aching in his heart so intense he wasn't sure he could finish the conversation. "Ray . . . if there's any message you'd like me to take to her . . ."

"There is, actually. The same one I sent before. I'd like her to be here."

"You mean, at . . . at . . ."

"I know it sounds crazy. Gruesome. And I know she won't want to do it. But it would make me feel so much better, just knowing there was someone here, someone who likes me. Or once did, anyway."

"I—I can ask her, Ray, but—"

"Tell her she can close her eyes when the needle starts to drop. I just want to know she's in the same room. I want to see her. One more time. Before I go. And I'd like you to be there, too."

Ben felt his mouth go dry.

"See, they give me three seats. All the others are reserved for officials and politicians and victims' relatives. Of which there are precious few. But I still get three seats. So I was hoping you'd take one."

"Ray—"

"I know it's a lot to ask. But I feel as if you're my friend, Ben. I mean, it's been a working relationship. You're doing your job." He paused, pursing his lips. "At the same time, I also know you've gone way beyond the norm for me. You've gone the extra mile and then some. I know it's been a good long time since you got paid, but you haven't slacked off a bit."

Ben shrugged. "I just did what any—"

"And I probably shouldn't personalize this, because I know that a lot of it is just that you're a good, generous person. That all-too-rare breed. But I also like to think that—on some level—we're friends." He paused. "And that's why I want you to be there. When it happens. Will you do that for me?"

Never in his life did Ben recall it being so difficult to speak. "If that's what you want, Ray."

"It is. And here's the really horrible part—would you ask Christina if she'll take the third chair? I know it's dreadful, asking another woman to go through that. But I don't know who else to ask."

"What about your parents?"

"Long gone. My conviction killed them. It really did. I used to fantasize about the celebration we'd have when I was released. When my innocence was proven. But they didn't live to see it." His eyes fell. "And now it looks as though I won't, either."

"Friends?"

"After seven years in the pen? I don't know from friends. Long gone. Unless you include my fellow inmates. A cockroach I'm particularly fond of. But they wouldn't be allowed in."

"Ray . . . I can ask Christina, but I can't guarantee—"

"Sure. I just know that she's worked on this case, too, long and hard, and I appreciate it. I'd like to show my appreciation. And the pathetic truth is—this is the only means left to me. So it's important."

Ben drew up his shoulders. "Then we'll be there," he said, even though he thought it was the most horrible potentiality he had ever contemplated. "Certainly I will be. And I think Christina will be, too."

"And Carrie?"

"I'll ask her."

Ray nodded his head. "If she does refuse, Ben, at least—tell her I love her, okay? Tell her I never stopped loving her. I don't want her to feel guilty. I just want her to know. Okay?"

"I'll tell her," Ben said. His voice was hoarse, and it had a noticeable catch.

"I'm so tired." As his eyes turned downward, Ben sensed that Ray would end it all right then and there if the power were given to him. "So tired."

Ben felt a sharp stinging sensation in his eyes, and he knew if their conversation continued much longer, they would both be crying. "I'd better go now. I've got a lot to do."

Ray nodded, and when his head rose again, he said the three words Ben most dreaded to hear. "See you Monday."

Ben drove all the way back to Tulsa steering with one arm, hugging himself with the other. But he couldn't seem to get warm.

27

MIKE WAS ABOUT ready to scream. He hated paperwork, hated research most of all. And he was buried in it. Was buried and had been buried for more hours than he cared to count. It was a beautiful day out, best in weeks, perfect tennis weather. But instead of being out on the courts or perched on the patio at Crow Creek sipping a tall cool one, he was stuck at a desk piled so high with books that Baxter didn't even see him when she first walked in.

"Can I safely assume these are all poetry books?" Baxter asked, after she finally located him.

Mike gave her a wry look. "Reference books. Of every kind imaginable." It occurred to him that she was looking particularly attractive this morning—not that she had ever not looked attractive. Had she done something to her hair?

Baxter scanned the desktop. "You're trying to trace that key chain, aren't you?"

"You win the Daily Double." Mike lifted a small baggie that held the elusive bit of evidence. "My gut tells me that whoever killed Sheila Knight left this behind. But I can't figure out what it is."

Baxter stared at it, as she had done more or less constantly since they discovered it. "The frustrating thing is, I know I've seen it before."

"I have the same feeling. But I can't remember what it is. I even showed it around the office. And everyone says the same thing. Yeah, that looks familiar. But no one remembers what it is."

"What are those curvy things in the middle? Wings?"

"I thought they were hearts."

"They can't be hearts. They're flat on the bottom. Both of them. And why are they drawn so . . . wispy?" She dropped it back onto the desk. "It's like a Rorschach test, isn't it?"

"Exactly. When you don't know what it's supposed to be, it looks like everything. Or nothing. That's why I've been poring through every pictorial reference I could lay my hands on. And I've sent Penelope to the library for more. When you don't know what you're looking for—you look at everything."

"Sounds like a needle-haystack deal."

"It is." Mike pushed away from the desk and stretched. "But if I could place that design, I might trace it back to our murderer."

"About that." Baxter suddenly seemed nervous, edgy. "I wanted to thank you. For what you did."

"For what *I* did?" There wasn't much room in the cubicle, especially at present. She was standing barely a foot away. Another time, he might complain about cops who invaded his personal space. But at the moment . . .

"In Blackwell's office. When you . . . you know. Stood up for me. I really appreciate it."

Mike waved a hand in the air. "I was just correcting my own mistake. It was nothing."

"It wasn't nothing. It was something. A big something. You didn't have to do it. Certainly not the way you did. It . . ." She began fidgeting with her fingernails. "It meant a lot to me."

Mike shrugged. "Forget about it." Was she wearing some kind of perfume? Because now that he was up close, it seemed as if she was wearing some kind of perfume.

"Can we talk about the other night? The stakeout, I mean. When we were in the car."

"Stop beating yourself up about that, Baxter. We had no way of knowing that some killer would—"

"That's not what I meant." She averted her eyes. "Could we talk about us? What happened." Her hand brushed against her lips.

"Oh. That." Was Penelope messing with the thermostat again? Because it definitely seemed hotter in here. Much hotter than usual. "Sure. If you want to."

"I feel like you've been avoiding me. Ever since we . . . you know."

"Really?"

"Yeah. Really."

Mike shoved his hands into his pockets. "Well, maybe I have. I didn't mean to. It's just . . . you know . . . kind of . . ."

"Awkward."

"Yeah. Awkward." Now he was fidgeting.

"I've felt the same way. But we can't go on being partners if we can't even look at one another."

"That's true."

"I mean, we've got to finish this case. But after that . . ."

"Yeah?"

"After that, maybe we should apply for a transfer. I think Blackwell would allow it now. Particularly if we both requested it."

For some reason, Mike couldn't think of anything remotely intelligent to say. "Yeah. I think he probably would."

"If that's what you want."

"Yeah. I mean, right." He looked up. "Is that what you want?"

"I asked you first."

Mike frowned. "Now this is a bit childish."

"I did. I asked you first."

"I asked you second. So?"

Baxter let out a long exhale. "I have another request."

It was amazing what she did with her mouth when she was nervous. That cute little half-pout thing. How had he never noticed that before? "And that is?"

"Don't tell any of the other guys on the force. About what happened. Between us, I mean."

"Of course not. I would never . . ."

"Stand around in the canteen with the other guys making rude remarks about a female officer? Perish the thought."

Mike tugged at his collar. "I apologized for that."

"Actually, you haven't."

"Well, then I apologize for that. It won't happen again."

"You won't tell anyone?"

His neck stiffened. "What, are you ashamed of it?"

"You know what would happen, if word got around. They'd makes jokes, give me some trashy nickname. Start treating me like I was some kind of tramp."

"We were both there."

"Yeah, but if a woman does it, she's a tramp. If a guy does it, he's Casanova."

Mike took a step toward her. The heat was so intense he felt as if he were standing in the fireplace. "I won't tell anyone."

"Thank you. That's all I wanted," she said, with a note of finality. But she did not step away.

"May I make a request?" Mike asked, inching even closer.

"Fair's fair, I suppose." She was looking up, gazing into his eyes.

"It seems to me . . . we never actually got to finish that kiss."

"And?"

"If I have to keep quiet and forget it happened, it seems as if I ought to at least get to . . . finish."

Baxter didn't answer, but she didn't resist, either. Their heads moved closer together. . . .

"Where do you want it?" A new voice emerged from the doorway.

"Penelope!" Both Mike and Baxter jumped backward, like ionized molecules repelling each other. "I didn't . . . hear you. . . ."

"Am I interrupting something?"

"No!" they both insisted, much too loudly.

"We were just talking about the case," Mike said.

"Yes. The case," Baxter agreed.

Penelope looked at them as if they were wearing their underwear on the outside. "Look, I got those books. You want I should put them on your desk?"

"That would be lovely."

"Fine." She pushed a tall stack back to clear a corner. "And don't forget to go home tonight, Mike. I know how you get when you're on these big research binges."

"I won't."

"Don't forget to eat, either. You want me to send up some sandwiches?"

"I'll manage. Thank you, Penelope." As soon as she left the office, Mike whirled around. "Baxter?"

She was gone.

HIS ENEMY HAD returned.

The one who had taken his life and dirtied it, turned it upside down. The one who had twisted his mind and turned him into something he never wanted to be. Back. Again.

Gabriel Aravena felt his hand shaking as he turned the doorknob and entered his apartment. His neighbor's description of the person who had come by looking for him had not been that specific, but he knew who it was. Some part of him had known it would happen one day. It had happened often enough in his dreams. His nightmares.

What did the visitor want? Whatever it was, it was sure to be evil. Filthy.

Not yet. Please not yet. The old feelings had returned with such power. The bad feelings. The ones he couldn't stop. The ones that rampaged when he saw a small girl with dark eyes, dark coloring. Like Erin Faulkner. Like so many others. That was not what he wanted, was it? He had decided, right? Even without the medication, he was not going to be a monster!

He had never been able to resist this person, and deep down in his heart, he knew this time would be no different. How could it be? The visitor knew so much, so many secrets. How could he resist? Was he stronger now? No, weaker. Barely off the Depo, his body still mutating.

He had to get out, that was all. Run. Go somewhere, do something. He was pretty low on cash just at the moment, but tomorrow was payday. He would go to work at FastTrak, collect his check—and then run.

Just the thought of it filled him with sorrow. He would lose his job. Lose the managerial position he had worked so hard to obtain. He would not see April again. And he had no idea where he would go. But he had to do it. He had to get out, he had to stop the inevitable from happening. Because if he didn't—

Never mind that. He had a plan, a way to prevent himself from turning back, from becoming a monster. And that was something. However feeble it might be, that was something.

He would salvage his life. By running away from it.

"YOU SURE YOU haven't seen this before?" Mike asked.

"Positive," Chris Hubbard replied. "Sorry. To tell the truth—I don't get out of the lab much these days."

Mike dangled the key chain in front of his face. "And you don't know who it belongs to. Or where it might've come from?"

" 'Fraid not." Hubbard leaned back, propping his elbows against the lab table behind him. The young chemist's face seemed utterly without guile. Mike couldn't imagine that he was lying. "What made you think I might in the first place?"

"Oh, I didn't really. I just hoped. I know this thing is the key. If I could just figure out what it is."

"Is there anything I can do?"

Mike looked up and saw the short stocky form of Dr. Conrad Reynolds. "I'm just having a chat with Mr. Hubbard, here."

"Oh?" He seemed immediately interested. "Has there been a development in the Erin Faulkner case?"

"No. That's why I'm here. I'd like to talk to you later, also."

"About anything in particular?"

"Just general stuff. Since you're the head of the plant, and you knew both Ray Goldman and Frank Faulkner. Just to make sure there isn't anything I've missed."

"I see." Mike watched the man carefully. He seemed a bit thrown, but Mike couldn't imagine why. "I'll be in my office. I've got an appointment." He scurried away, more quickly than seemed natural.

As soon as he was gone, Hubbard cocked his head toward Mike and whispered, "Shrink date."

"Dr. Reynolds sees a shrink?"

"Oh yeah. Lot of the people here do. We have a doc who comes by once a week to . . . how do you say it? Commune with the employees. On-site."

"I didn't realize chemistry attracted so many psychological ailments."

"It doesn't attract them. It creates them." Hubbard drummed the eraser end of his pencil on the lab table. "You can't imagine the kind of stress we have, when a new formula can literally mean millions—even billions of dollars in profits. Half the guys in the plant would probably be drooling into a cup right now if it weren't for Dr. Bennett."

"Dr. Bennett?" Mike did a double take. "Dr. Hayley Bennett? She's the company shrink?"

"Yeah. You know her?"

"I sure do. And she never once mentioned to me that she had patients here."

"Guess it never came up."

"Yeah," Mike said, scribbling furiously into his notebook. "I guess it never did. I don't suppose you've had any sudden revelations since the last time we talked. Remembered anything important about Frank Faulkner."

"Sorry, no. I was just Ray's Scrabble buddy. I never knew Frank all that well. Dr. Reynolds would be the one to ask about him."

"They were pretty tight, huh?"

Hubbard hesitated. "Well . . . they knew each other, anyway."

Something about the tone of Hubbard's voice caught Mike's attention. "Does that mean they weren't close?"

"I don't think so. Something was going on between them."

Mike's forehead creased. He tried to remember what Reynolds had told him during his interview, or what he'd read in Ben's report of his interview with the man. "But . . . Reynolds is the boss. How could Frank function if they didn't get along?"

"Reynolds is the boss now. Not seven years ago. Only after Frank was gone. He could never have been the boss when Frank was alive."

"And why is that?"

"Because when Frank was around, Frank was the boss. Of everything. He might not have had the title, but he ran the show. He had the clients, he'd come up with the most successful formulae. He was the big cheese. Acted like it, too."

"That must've created some resentment."

"No doubt. Especially with Dr. Reynolds."

"Why so?"

"Because Reynolds had to work with him every day. Reynolds was Frank's lab assistant, way back then."

"I thought Ray Goldman worked under Frank."

"He did. Well, technically, I think he reported to Reynolds. Doesn't matter, really. We all did whatever Frank wanted. But Reynolds got the worst of it. Frank treated him like a servant. He answered Frank's phone calls, kept his calendar. Acted like a little lapdog."

"Reynolds can't have liked that."

"I'm sure he didn't. But what Frank wanted, Frank got. He was King of the Hill. And deservedly so. He was brilliant, you know. His work as a flavorist was revolutionary. Everyone wanted him to work for them. He was drawing down huge bucks." He paused. "Reynolds was number two. At best."

Mike drummed his fingers. "Dr. Reynolds didn't mention any of this to me when I interviewed him."

"No, I don't expect he would. I've always wondered why the cops didn't talk to him more. I guess they twigged onto Ray right off the bat and became convinced he was their man."

"And you think that was a mistake?"

Hubbard shrugged. "Maybe I'm prejudiced. For all his eccentricities, especially when it came to women, Ray was my friend. But if it was my job to come up with an alternate explanation for what happened . . . I'd give Dr. Reynolds a good hard look."

"THANK YOU FOR coming to see me," Ben said as he showed Dr. Bennett to the chair opposite his desk. "I've been so busy since the hearing I've barely left the office. But I know your schedule is packed, also."

"Oh, not really," she said, waving a palm. "It's my afternoon off. After I finished up this morning, I went home to my butterflies."

"Fascinating hobby."

"You think so? Sometimes I wonder." She chuckled. "I've been holding a stiletto so long I think I'm developing a callous. What can I do for you?"

Ben glanced at the notes he'd made before she arrived. He wanted the interview to seem spontaneous, conversational. So she would be at ease. So she wouldn't see him coming.

"I hope this isn't going to be more about Sheila Knight," she said. "I really can't tell you more than I already did. Especially not now."

Ben followed her meaning. Especially not now that Erin's lifelong friend was just as dead as she was. "No, it isn't about her."

Bennett was wearing her hair down and holding her eyeglasses which, Ben noted, wrought an amazing change in her appearance. She had never been unattractive, but today, she looked downright sexy. "And please don't press me to reveal any more confidences from Erin Faulkner. Or anything about her and her father. I simply can't."

"I understand. It would violate privilege."

"Twice over."

Ben slowed. "Twice over?"

"Right. Since Erin Faulkner was my patient. Just as her father had been."

"Frank Faulkner was your patient?"

"Oh yes. Up to the time of his death."

"You've counseled both Erin and her father? This seems quite a coincidence."

"It wasn't a coincidence at all. I first met Erin at her father's plant. Where I counseled some of the employees. Still do. She remembered me years later when she decided to seek therapy herself."

Ben sat up straight in his chair. "You counseled for the plant where Frank and Ray both worked? Prairie Dog Flavors?"

She nodded. "On a freelance basis. I came in once a week. Helped the eggheads sort out their problems."

"I'm surprised that work interested you."

"Are you kidding? At that point in my career, most of my patients were referrals from the Justice Department. Total scum. Murderers, sex offenders. Lots of sex offenders. Some of the most horrible, twisted people who ever walked the earth. After a few days of that, you'll welcome the chance to talk to some mild-mannered chemists about their impotence."

"Is that what it was, mostly? Domestic problems?"

"Actually, at that place, it was mostly work-related stress. Still is. When I first started there, the place was just taking off. They were getting their first big-bucks clients. Mostly thanks to Frank, who had hit it big as a flavorist. He was bringing in some major accounts."

"That must've made the bosses happy."

"Well, yes and no. That was part of the stress he was experiencing, you see. He wanted to quit and go out on his own. Why should the corporation get all the profits when he was the one doing the work? But he was under contract. Everything he did then and for six years into the future belonged to Prairie Dog Flavors, regardless of how or where he devised it. They owned him."

"I'm beginning to see why he might need a shrink."

"It was tearing him apart. He was generating tons of income—but not getting enough of it himself. And remember—he had a nice house and a large family to support."

"Did he get along with the other people at the plant?"

"He tried, but he was convinced everyone hated him. And acted accordingly, I'm afraid. He thought they were all envious, and not without some justification, I imagine. Anyone who did as well as Frank was bound to engender some ill will."

"What about Dr. Reynolds? Was he one of the jealous ones?"

"He was one of the ones who hated Frank's guts. Familiarity breeds contempt, you know. He was forced to work closely with Frank. Frank told me he tried to treat Conrad well, but it just never worked out. I don't know what the truth is. But I know this—Reynolds had some real problems with Frank."

"When did you last see Frank?"

"The day before the murders. Special session, at his home."

"You make house calls?"

She gave him a wry expression. "I did then. He'd had a severe panic attack. Trouble breathing. I thought he was on the verge of a nervous breakdown."

"Why?"

Bennett considered a moment. "He told me he was working on something—something big. He was having a meeting with someone—had to break away to talk to me. But he wouldn't go into any details."

"Did you tell the police this?"

"Of course I did. And at first, I thought they were interested. Then they tripped onto your client and became convinced he was guilty. And at that point—"

"The investigation stopped. Yeah, I know." Ben reached back and massaged his stiff neck. "I can't get over this idea that the chem lab is a major pressure cooker. I hate to be stereotypical, but I thought they'd all be nerds wearing white lab coats and Coke-bottle glasses who wouldn't know how to spend money if they had it."

"You throw major moolah into any environment, you're going to get stress."

Ben nodded. "That explains my immunity."

Bennett leaned forward, twirling her glasses in a small orbit. "Are you sure about that?"

"About what?"

"Stress. And you."

"I don't know what you mean."

"Well . . . maybe I'm out of line. But I get the impression you're suffering from a fair amount of stress right now yourself."

Ben considered. "I've just had a bad hearing. A bad case gone worse. And my client's about to pay the ultimate price."

"You're talking about Raymond Goldman?"

Ben nodded.

"I can see how that would be emotionally draining. Particularly when it's someone with whom you've worked closely for a number of years."

"Yeah."

"So you're about to lose a case—and a client. What else?"

"What *else*?"

"There must be more. Talk to the doctor."

Ben twisted around in his chair. "Well . . . my office is teetering on the verge of bankruptcy. Again."

"And what else?"

"The repairs on my boardinghouse exceed the monthly income."

"What else?"

"My private life is a disaster. I never do anything but work. I haven't been out on a date for so long I barely remember what they are."

"What else?"

He paused. "My cat is having kittens."

Bennett gave him a long look. "No wonder you're a shambles."

There was a knock on the door. "Come in."

The trim young man at the door took Ben by surprise. "Peter. I didn't expect to see you today."

"I didn't phone ahead. My apologies."

"Dr. Bennett," Ben said, "do you know Peter Rothko? Tulsa's fast-food king?"

"No, but I've read about you, of course." She extended her hand. "Congratulations on your success."

"I've been very fortunate."

"And modest to boot. My, my." Ben wondered if she was thinking the same thing Christina did: *Tulsa's most eligible bachelor.* "If you're done with me, Ben, I'll leave you two alone."

"Certainly. Thanks again for coming." She excused herself. "What brings you here, Peter? Need some help with your bench presses?"

"Nothing that pleasant, I'm afraid." He sat down in the chair Dr. Bennett had vacated. "I know you contacted me to help with the technical background, not the actual investigation. But when I heard about this, I had to bring it to you."

"Heard about what? Something that could affect the case?"

"Affect it?" Rothko nodded solemnly. "What I've got could turn this case upside down."

BAXTER CHECKED HER watch. She really shouldn't be wasting time like this, standing in line. But there was a growling in her stomach that could not be ignored. She craved food, the greasier the better. Large portions.

Not good for her figure. But sometimes, she mused, a girl has to do what a girl has to do.

There was no denying it—this case was starting to get to her. Not the work, not the gruesomeness of the murders. Not even the fight to keep it alive when everyone else wanted to close it. What bothered her was the fact that it wasn't going anywhere. It was a well-known fact that if a murder case wasn't solved in the first six hours, the likelihood that it ever would be solved diminished significantly. In a protracted investigation, it was not at all unusual for a case to hit a stagnant stretch. Sometimes that presaged the breakthrough that resolved the mystery once and for all.

The problem here was, she thought they'd already had the big breakthrough. They just didn't know what to do with it.

She wondered if Mike was still in his office, poring over all those library books. She suspected he was. She had heard—well before she'd even met the man—that he was seriously dedicated, that he had no outside life to speak of, that he was like a feral dog with a bone. He clenched the case between his teeth and refused to release it. Until it had been conquered. And this case was far from conquered.

She couldn't believe she had kissed him. What the hell had come over her? Even now, just thinking about it made her cheeks flush. Not that he wasn't good-looking—he was, big time. Very sexy, even if he was still hung up on his ex. But he was her partner. Her partner! When would she ever learn? She had just bounced back from that screwup in OKC with the chief of police. Was she going to repeat the same mistake on this end of the turnpike?

No, she was not, she silently resolved. From now on, it was probably best that they not be in the same room together, not any more than necessary. But even if they were. No matter how long they were together, no matter how lonely she got, no matter how blue were his eyes or how husky his voice—she couldn't go down that road again. Best to forget it ever happened.

So why did she not think that was going to happen?

Damn everything but the circus! And they say *men* always repeat the same mistakes. Was she doomed to spend the rest of her life screwing everything up, over and over again?

Stay tuned, she muttered under her breath. Same Bat-time, same Bat-channel.

After what seemed like an eternity, she reached the front of the line. Thank heaven. Moral dilemmas could wait. Right now she needed carbos.

"I'd like an extra-large—" She froze in midsentence. Was that what it looked like?

"Pardon me, ma'am," said the well-groomed man in his early thirties. "Is something wrong?"

"What is that . . . thing?" Baxter said, forcing her lips to move. She pointed.

"This lapel pin?"

"Yes, that. What is it?"

And then he told her.

And then she *knew*.

28

BEN LEANED ACROSS his desk, hanging on every word Peter Rothko said.

"So I was at this convention in Kansas City," he explained. "Networking with some of the other fast-food dudes. Carl Breyer. Harlan Woods. And somehow we got to talking about flavorists. Someone asked what was happening down at Prairie Dog. I told them I thought Conrad Reynolds was running the show, but that Chris Hubbard was doing all the work." He paused. "And that's when Harlan's face went white."

"He knew Hubbard?"

"He knew all about Hubbard. And what he knew wasn't good."

Ben felt his heart beating away in his chest. Could this be the break they'd been waiting for? That they needed so desperately? "Like what?"

"Like for starters, Chris Hubbard isn't his real name. He changed it. Correction: he had to change it. After he was arrested. For—get this—indecent exposure."

"You're joking. That kid chemist?"

"I'm as serious as an IRS audit, Ben. Apparently this guy whipped it out and showed it to a nine-year-old girl one day in her front yard. Where he had no business being."

"Was he convicted?"

"Harlan wasn't sure about that. He thought Hubbard—or whatever his name really is—might've copped some sort of plea. But the publicity was so huge he had to move and do the name change."

"How did your friend know this?"

"Apparently Hubbard applied for a job with him, so Harlan had him checked out. Harlan believes in very extensive employee checks. We're talking real Ross Perot–type stuff. A little over-the-top, if you ask me. But I guess it paid off in this case."

"Incredible." Ben reached for the phone. "I've got to get this to my friend at police headquarters. If you're right—" Ben looked up. "You may have saved the life of an innocent man."

"I hope so." Rothko ran a hand through his burnt-orange hair. "By the way, Ben—you play racquetball?"

"Not well."

"Perfect! Let's play a few rounds sometime."

Ben smiled, his right hand already punching Mike's number. "Deal."

GABRIEL ARAVENA OBSESSIVELY checked the clock on the wall of the convenience store. Stupid, he told himself. That will not make the time pass more quickly. Just the opposite, it seemed. But he couldn't help himself. He was so scared. So worried about what he might become. If he didn't get out in time.

April should be back by now. Just as he was not trusted with the proceeds, so he was not trusted to deliver the paychecks. It had never mattered much to him—until now. The seconds seemed to tick away like hours as he desperately waited for her return.

What was taking so long, anyway? Didn't she know how important this was? Didn't she know the danger he was in? Of course—she didn't. She couldn't. Only he knew. He . . . and the other.

He felt damp—on his chest, under his arms. It was showing, too. He saw the woman staring at his shirt as he counted out her change. No matter. He was used to being stared at. Better to be thought a freak for sweating than because you were turning into a woman.

"The eagle has screamed!"

Aravena whirled around. It was April! Waving an oh-so-welcome slip of paper in her hands.

"Payday has arrived, Gabriel. Time to go out and par-tay!"

As he gazed at her, he felt so much affection he almost reached out and embraced her. Why not? He was quitting this job anyway. It was hard to believe that only a few days ago he had been fantasizing about hurting her. Sexually. But he had still been on the Depo back then, or just off it. Ironic, wasn't it? The drug that was supposed to cure him in fact did anything but. It may have suppressed his physical ability to have sex, but it didn't suppress his imagination. It inflamed it. When his body couldn't find release one way, it looked for another. . . .

"Thank you, April. It is much appreciated."

"Don't thank me, Gabe. I'm just the messenger."

"Still—thank you. For everything."

Her brows knitted. "Excuse me?"

"You have always been most kind to me. And I have appreciated it. I always will."

She gave him a strange look. "What's this all about, anyway? Why are you getting all mushy on me?"

Fool! he cursed at himself. You should have kept your mouth shut. "It's just—I thought—you never know. When will we see each other next?"

"That would be . . . tomorrow at nine for the morning shift. Wouldn't it?"

He did not answer.

"Gabe, you're not planning to quit on me, are you? Not just when you finally made manager."

"No, no. Of course not. I just . . ." He tilted his head slightly. "One never knows."

She jabbed him in the side. "Don't go weird on me, Gabe. I like you just the way you are."

As she walked to the back to sign for a milk shipment, it occurred to Aravena that that was quite possibly the kindest thing anyone had ever said to him.

IT WAS FIVE o'clock, quitting time, and Gabriel had the check in his hand. He removed his name tag and headed toward his car. He still had not chosen a destination. But no matter. There were many possibilities, and in his position, one was much the same as another. He was actually looking forward to the drive more than the arrival—being out on the open road, feeling the wind whistling around him, knowing he was on his own and no one and nothing could ever possibly—

"Hello, Gabriel."

His jaw dropped. The check fluttered to the ground. "You."

"Good to see you, too, Gabe. Could we talk?"

"Stay away from me," Aravena said, backing away. "I want nothing to do with you."

"I'm sorry. But that's not an option. I need you."

"I do not want to be a monster!"

"Ah, but it's too late for that, isn't it, Gabe?" The sun was setting, and a shadow clouded Aravena's face. "You already are."

*　　*　　*

HAYLEY BENNETT WAS tearing her office apart, ripping through the files with such speed that a mess was guaranteed. And someone would have to clean up this mess, she told herself. But that did not stop her. She had to know.

She'd been going through the files for a long time, too long, but at last, she found the one she wanted. An old file, but one she still kept, one she likely always would. She pored through it, throwing the pages onto the floor as she finished scanning them.

It took her less than a minute to find what she sought.

How could she have been so stupid? She tossed the file down, disgusted with herself. It had been right in front of her all along, but she had been too stupid to see it. All that time she was talking to the lawyer, anytime in the past seven years, if she had just realized—

But she hadn't. There was nothing she could do about that now. She could make a difference in the future, however. Could and would.

She grabbed the receiver on her desk phone. She would call Kincaid back, then call the police. One way or the other, she would make it right.

"Hello," said the voice on the other end of the line. "Kincaid & McCall."

"This is Dr. Hayley Bennett. I need to talk to Ben Kincaid."

"I'm sorry, he's out of the office at the moment. Could I take a message?"

"Is there someplace I could call him? Because it's really—"

An instantaneous clicking noise, followed by dead space.

"Hello?" she said, furiously pushing the disconnect button. "Hello? What happened?" She tried to hang up and start again. No dial tone. "Hello? Operator? Is anyone there? I have to call—"

"I'm afraid I can't allow you to do that, Hayley."

Bennett looked up—and gasped.

"I was afraid you might do something like this. Something stupid."

Bennett took a defensive position behind her desk. She flipped the receiver of her cordless phone around and brandished it like a club. "I won't let you hurt me."

"You will not have any choice in the matter."

A figure emerged from the shadows.

Bennett's lips parted. "Gabriel?"

He held his arms up, palms outward. "I am sorry, Doctor."

Despite the hormonal influence of the drugs he had been taking, she knew he was a strong man. Powerful. There was no way she could outmuscle him.

Aravena walked slowly toward her until he stood on the opposite side of the desk. "Come."

Bennett's pulse was racing. She felt hot, tired, and more scared than she had ever been before. "Why are you doing this, Gabriel?"

There was a distinct note of sadness in his voice. "Because I have to."

"You don't have to, Gabriel. You don't. You don't have to do anything you don't want to do."

"I have no choice."

Bennett made a break for it. She shoved hard, knocking him backward, then raced toward the door. She never even got close. Aravena grabbed her right arm and jerked her backward. There was a cracking sound. Had he broken her arm? she wondered. It hurt enough.

She tried to club him with the cordless phone receiver, but he deflected the blow easily. He hammered her hand down on his knee, knocking the phone away.

He swung her around again, hard, and Bennett gasped at the pain that radiated up her arm. He pinned the same arm behind her back, causing further agony, then clutched her by the neck, pulling her close to him. She was completely under his control.

"Very good," the other person in the room said. "She's yours now, Gabriel. Do with her as you please. Have fun. I know you want to. It's been a long time, hasn't it? So enjoy yourself." The voice paused, and in that pause, a shudder raced down Bennett's spine and chilled her to the bone. "Just make sure you kill her when you're done."

WHAT THE HELL was that all about? Christina wondered as she hung up the phone.

Dr. Bennett had always struck her as somewhat eccentric, what with the butterflies and all, but that was just weird. Hanging up in the middle of a sentence. Had a patient flashed her or what?

The tone in her voice bothered Christina. She seemed . . . not herself. Distraught.

Or maybe Christina had just imagined it. It was so hard to tell with phone calls. There might've been a bad connection, static on the line, interference, something. . . .

She looked up the number, then dialed Bennett's office. No answer. She didn't have a receptionist, Christina remembered. She was the only one in the office. She tried Bennett's home number, but no one answered.

Not that that meant anything. But it did make Christina . . . concerned.

What had the woman said? She wanted to talk to Ben. Immediately. And then she cut off.

Or had been cut off.

Christina called the operator, pleaded a false emergency, and asked them to check the line.

"The line seems to be dead," came the response, a few minutes later. "Probably damage to the line."

That was enough for Christina. It could be nothing, she realized. But she'd also been in enough tough scrapes to know that if something seems wrong, it just might be. And that you'd better not wait until the last minute to check it out.

She considered calling Mike, but decided that was premature. What would she report—a disconnected phone call? That wasn't even for her? No, he was busy enough. She'd check it out discreetly. Then call if there was anything amiss.

A minute later, Christina was in her car, driving toward downtown. Bennett's office was a little off the beaten track, but the nice thing about Tulsa was that unless it was rush hour, it never took too long to get anywhere. In only a few minutes, she turned onto the street in front of Dr. Bennett's office. . . .

Just in time to see two people piling into a BMW parked outside. One was a dark, strong, dangerous-looking man. Just a glance at him gave her shivers. The other, the driver, she didn't get a good look at.

The sun had all but set, and with her lights dimmed, it was hard to see. But as they started their car, Christina thought she spotted something through the back window. Something brownish, with a trace of red. Auburn.

Hair? Hayley Bennett's hair?

She glanced at the office. The front door was open. She couldn't see much of the interior, but she saw enough to know there was a gigantic mess. A table overturned. Papers strewn all over the floor.

The car was pulling away.

For the first time, Christina really wished she had splurged on a cell phone.

If something had happened to Hayley, and she let that car get away . . .

She shifted into drive. This could be the stupidest thing she had done in her life. But if she'd been stuffed into the back of a car, she'd sure as hell hope someone had the guts to follow.

She just had to make sure she wasn't seen. Because if those two had done something to Dr. Bennett, and they knew she was onto them . . .

Don't go down that road, Christina told herself as she floored the accelerator in pursuit. I am strong, I am invincible. . . .

Just concentrate on the driving.

*   *   *

WHEN BAXTER POKED him in the ribs, Mike jumped almost a foot into the air.

"Wake up, Sherlock. I just busted this case wide open."

Mike blinked his eyes several times rapidly, pushing himself away from his cluttered desk. "I wasn't sleeping. I was just . . . resting my eyes."

"You don't have to make excuses to me, partner. If I'd been scrutinizing all this boring incunabula for the last forty-eight hours straight, I'd be asleep, too."

Mike rose out of his chair, trying to rouse himself. "Did you say something about the case?"

She beamed. "Sure did." She pointed to the evidence bag on the corner of his desk. "I know what that is. Or what it represents, anyway."

"Don't hold out on me, Baxter. How'd you figure it out?"

"I met someone who was wearing the same image on his lapel."

"His lapel?"

"Right. Told me he used to have the key chain, too, but it broke. Must be a flimsy link. Everyone seems to be losing them."

"And it is . . ."

"A club card, basically. A pass. Admittance to one of the city's most prestigious corporate dining suites."

"What's a corporate dining suite?"

"Where have you been all your life, Morelli?" In truth, she hadn't known either, until about fifteen minutes ago, but she might as well milk this one precious moment of one-upmanship for all it was worth. "All the biggest corporate headquarters have private dining rooms. Some of them are four-star restaurants, with private chefs and fancy linen and the works. The Williams Companies have a great one, for example."

"But this doesn't look like the Williams Companies logo."

"It isn't. It isn't anyone's public logo. This was created just for the dining room. Only the top administrators and executives got it."

"And you learned this . . . how?"

All the possible responses ran through Baxter's brain. Vast intelligence. Exhaustive research. Pummeling informants.

Aw, what the hell? He was her partner, after all. "I learned this because the joint was really busy and I happened to get waited on by the district manager."

"What joint?" he asked, grabbing her by the shoulders. "What are you talking about?"

"Haven't you guessed? The two hearts with the flat bottoms are actually *B*s lying sideways. The wispy art style is meant to suggest aroma and the hearts are intended to represent bliss." She paused. "Burger Bliss, to be precise."

PETER ROTHKO TWISTED Hayley Bennett's arm behind her back, sending searing blades of pain cascading through her body. The pain was so intense that tears sprang involuntarily from her eyes. He threw her down onto the floor in a corner, banging her head against a sink. He whipped out a pair of handcuffs and attached one end to her wrist, the other to the pipe beneath the basin.

Behind them, Gabriel Aravena stood like the castle sentry, his face emotionless.

"You must be feeling pretty lucky right now," Rothko muttered, tossing back his orange bangs. He was dripping with sweat.

No, Bennett thought, she was definitely not feeling very lucky.

"If that nosy neighbor of yours hadn't wandered into the office at the wrong time, you'd be dead right now. Wasn't very lucky for him, though." A smile curled across Rothko's face—a smile Bennett did not like in the least. "Don't worry. Your time will come."

"I won't tell anyone," she said, trying to catch her breath. She knew it was probably useless, but she had to try. "I never have."

"You never have because you never figured it out, until today." He reared back the palm of his hand and slapped her, right across the face. "As for the rest, I agree. You won't tell anyone."

Bennett couldn't stop her chest from heaving, couldn't prevent her arms from shaking. "Wh-what are you going to do to me?"

"I won't do anything, my dear. But your friend, Mr. Aravena . . . Well, that is another matter entirely."

"Gabe," she said. "I know you're a good person at heart. I know you *want* to be good. You don't have to do this."

"Oh, but he does," Rothko said, leering. He nudged Aravena. "Don't you, Gabe?"

Aravena obviously would've preferred to remain silent, but forced himself to speak. "I must do as he says, Dr. Bennett."

Tears spilled out of her eyes. "You can take control of your life, Gabe! You can be whoever you want to be."

"Enough of this psychobabble," Rothko said. "Gabriel, perhaps it's best you wait outside. I'll call if I need you again."

Aravena nodded, then slowly trudged out of the tiny room.

Rothko knelt down and squeezed Bennett's face. "I saw what you had in

Frank's file. Your little description of me. That could've been very damaging, you know. Very damaging."

"I would never have told anyone."

"I wish I could believe you, my dear. But you appear to have been doing that very thing when I arrived. I can't trust you."

"You can! I promise—"

"Don't insult my intelligence." He shoved her back against the pipe. Bennett felt as if her head had been split open. She could feel blood trickling from her scalp.

"I'll . . . do . . . whatever you want me to do. . . ." she gasped.

"A generous offer. But there's not really much you can do for me at this point, is there?" He stood and brushed off the front of his exercise suit. "I'm going back to your office now, Doctor, to make sure there aren't any other incriminating bits of information lingering in your files. Maybe I'll just burn down the whole damn place. I'd rather take care of you first, but there's no telling when another of your nosy neighbors might drop by. Don't worry, dear—I'll be back for you."

"Please don't hurt me!"

"I may need to ask you some questions about what I find—which is the only reason you're still alive. But after that—"

She clenched her eyes shut.

"Don't harbor any illusions about being discovered. I shut this place down weeks ago. No one comes here anymore. No one even comes close. You could scream your head off. No one will know—except Gabriel. And do you really want to attract his attention? When you're so lovely and so . . . vulnerable?"

Her stomach was in such turmoil she felt she could be sick at any moment. Her entire body was shaking uncontrollably.

He leaned in close, so near that she could smell his hot breath. "But I will return. Very soon. And when I do . . . it will be time for you to go. Just as it was for Erin. Just as it was for Sheila."

He gave her a kick to the side of the ribs, then left the room, leaving Bennett alone.

Even in her tears, even in the midst of the fear and panic that consumed her, she knew she had to do something. And quickly. Because it was evident Gabriel had not been taking his medication, and she knew him—and his problems—well enough to realize that she was a temptation, an opportunity for vengeance, that he would not be able to resist long.

And even if he did, when Rothko returned, he would kill her. For certain. And with pleasure.

CHAPTER

29

BAXTER AND MIKE were both still in his office. Since Baxter had made the "Burger Bliss" breakthrough, they hadn't paused for a moment.

"Got it," Mike announced, slamming down the phone. "They're going to fax over a list of top executives and managers—everyone who had access to their private dining room."

"At this time of night?" Baxter was hunched over a short bookcase she had turned into a makeshift desk in the corner. "Nice work. How'd you manage that?"

"No biggie. Just proves what my ex-wife taught me."

"Hard work pays off in the end?"

Mike shook his head. "If you yell loud enough, you usually get what you want."

The fax machine in the hallway began to hum. Mike started toward it.

"Not only compliant, but expeditious. You gotta love it. I'll make a copy of the list and—"

"Mike!"

He stopped just inside the doorway. "Yeah?"

"Isn't Peter Rothko the guy who started Burger Bliss? And now he's like the third richest man on earth?"

"Yeah. So?"

She raised her head out of a mess of papers. "I was just reviewing the list you got from the marina. Out at Grand Lake, where Sheila Knight was killed."

"And?"

"Peter Rothko owns a cabin just a short piece down the lake from her." She paused. "And he owns a boat."

Mike stared at her, his eyes widening.

"He could've motored the boat from his cabin to hers," Mike said quietly. "Approached from the rear. That's why we never saw him."

"Hell, at this distance, he could've rowed it over. We wouldn't have heard a thing. Couldn't've." She stared at Mike intensely. "Of course, that doesn't prove anything. Could be a coincidence."

"Wanna hear another coincidence? I talked to Ben just a while ago. Rothko was in his office today. Volunteering information that incriminated Chris Hubbard."

Baxter's brow creased. "Why would he want to—" She stopped short.

Not another word was necessary. In the space of a breath they both had their coats and were halfway to the elevators.

GABRIEL ARAVENA SAT at an empty booth in the dark, trying not to think about what lay just beyond that door, not twenty feet away from him. It was a treasure beyond compare, one that only a few weeks ago he would have consumed with relish. Final vengeance against the woman who had tormented him, had pried into every intimate detail of his personal and private life. His sex life. His dreams and fantasies. The woman who had administered that hideous experimental drug. The satisfaction of taking what he had lusted after for so long. It would be so sweet. . . .

He tried to turn his mind to other things. But nothing worked.

His palms were sweating. He was breathing in deep heavy gulps, like a man fighting nausea. He tried singing songs, reciting verse. No use. All he could think about was how wonderful it would be to take her as she was, chained down on the floor, to rip off her clothes, get what he wanted. She would scream and that would make it all the more delicious. It would be a sweet ecstasy, a rare delight—

He pounded his fists against his forehead. *Stop it!* he told himself. You are not a monster!

What was it Dr. Bennett had said? You can be whoever you want to be. How well she knew him, from all those sessions. How well she understood. She knew exactly how to get to him, to send him into turmoil. How clever she was. How much she deserved to be taken like an animal, to be hurt like—

"Stop!" he screamed.

He covered his mouth with his hand. He had not meant to speak out loud. Not that anyone could possibly hear him. But talking to himself— screaming to himself, actually—that was the sure sign of a madman, wasn't it?

That was proof that he had totally lost what little control he had ever had. That he would not be able to resist—

He could just leave. Rothko was gone and wouldn't return for at least half an hour. But how far could he go? Rothko had found him before; he would simply do it again. And the consequences could be horrible. Rothko had said that if he failed to obey, didn't do every single horrible thing he was told to do—

Then Rothko would reveal all the previous horrible things Aravena had done. He would tell the police, even.

Just as Aravena was finally achieving some measure of freedom, it would be snatched away from him. For something he had done so long ago. For a crime committed when he was sick, when he had all those urges he couldn't control.

But was he any better now? Or did he just like to think so? Here he was, once again, thinking the same old twisted thoughts. Thinking hard. Desperately wanting to open the door and—

And why not? Why the hell not? In this world of sinners, why must he be a saint? Why couldn't he do it? Just do it and do it and do it and—

His head fell, banging against the smooth Formica finish. He was so confused. Tears actually trickled out of his eyes, running down his cheeks and washing his face.

And then, as if the tears had washed away the turmoil, in a moment of brilliant clarity, he knew. He rose to his feet, excited, determined, resolved.

He knew what he was going to do. And he was looking forward to it.

"ARE YOU SURE you don't have any idea where he might be?" Mike barked into his cell phone.

"Sorry," Ben answered on the other end. "I don't."

"What about Christina? She's usually more on top of things than you, anyway."

"She's not around to ask. She's disappeared. Told Jones she wanted to talk to the shrink. Dr. Bennett."

"Blast." Mike pounded his steering wheel. He and Baxter had been driving all over town, looking for Peter Rothko, everywhere they could think that he might be. They'd been to the corporate headquarters, his regional office, his palatial home near Philbrook. He was nowhere to be found. "Did he say anything when he was there? Give any indication of his plans?"

"Not that I recall. He left in kind of a hurry, actually."

"He did? Why?"

"I don't know." Ben pondered. "He did ask me a few questions about Dr. Bennett, though, now that I think about it. Where she worked."

"How does he even know the woman?"

Ben considered. "I don't think he did."

"Then why in the hell—" Mike tried not to get agitated, but it was hard. Be it instinct or premonition, he was getting the distinct feeling that something bad was about to happen. Again. "Why did he say he was leaving? What were his exact words?"

"I think . . ." Ben closed his eyes. "He said he wasn't sure, but he was afraid a problem had just arisen. And he was going to have to eliminate it."

The silence on the phone line was deafening.

"You don't suppose . . ."

"What if he went to her office? Christina was going there, too."

Mike grabbed the detachable siren from behind his seat, slapped it on top of the Trans Am, and turned it on. "Give me Bennett's address." Ben did. "I'll call you as soon as we get there."

"Don't bother. I'm on my way."

CHRISTINA CREPT UP to the darkened restaurant and flattened herself against the side wall. This was quite possibly the stupidest thing she had ever done, and she had a pretty good list of contenders. Certainly Ben would think so, were he here, which unfortunately he was not. She was on her own, and even though she did not understand fully what was going on, she understood enough to know that it was stupid to go in there. When she was by herself.

But then, so was Hayley Bennett.

Two men were victimizing a woman, just as they had probably done to at least two others. It was time for that to stop.

And there were two things of which she was certain. First, that Hayley Bennett had been hurt and that her life was in danger. And second, that the tallish man with the red hair who she had seen drive away would be back soon. She hadn't gotten a clear look at his face, but given his general appearance, and given where they were, she had her suspicions.

And she didn't like them.

If she was going to help, she had to act fast.

She could run, go for help. But how much time did Bennett have? If she could just slip in there and get the good doctor out before the man returned . . .

She was relieved to see that he had left the door unlocked. Christina knew this joint had been closed, so they probably weren't expecting any traffic. Especially not this time of night. But this also told Christina that the man was certain Bennett could not escape. Which meant she must be restrained or incapacitated. Or worse.

The door squeaked a little when she opened it. Just a little, but in this pitch-dark silence, it seemed thunderous. She had seen two men back at Dr. Bennett's office, but had only seen one leave. She wasn't sure what happened to the other. He might've already been in the car waiting; she might've just not seen him. She had been watching many ways at once, and a man on his own moves a lot faster than a woman who's being dragged against her will. She could've missed him.

But it was also possible that he had remained behind.

She removed her shoes so that she could slide across the tile floor, all but soundlessly. Her heart was practically beating its way out of her chest. She couldn't think of a time when she'd been so scared. What a combination: the darkness, the silence, the horror of knowing she was in the vicinity of people who had committed murder, maybe several times over. Being here, on this site of tragedy. Her sweat glands were doing double time and her mouth couldn't be drier if she had just scaled Black Mesa.

But she kept on moving.

This was the sort of thing Ben was always warning her against. Don't be so impulsive, he would tell her. Think before you act. Of course, he was the Prince of Think Before You Act. Sometimes she wondered if he would *ever* act, he was so busy thinking about it. Christina, on the other hand . . . wasn't. For good or ill, she was not the contemplative sort. She liked to get started and get done. She hated to see opportunities get away from her. If she wanted to do something, she did it. And that drove Ben insane. Maybe that was why he had never—

But she didn't need to distract herself with that kind of thinking now. She had to concentrate on what she was doing. On not getting killed.

The moonlight seeping through the windows was not strong, but there did not appear to be anyone in the seating area. At least no one she could see. All the booths and tables were empty. As they should be.

But where was Hayley Bennett?

She slid over the counter and entered the kitchen. So this was where it happened, she thought. The meat, the potatoes, and ten thousand tons of fat. She quickly scanned the grills, the deep-frying apparatuses. There were lots of stainless-steel cabinets, but surely they were too small to conceal a body. A live body anyway.

There was another room in the back. A bathroom? she wondered. A break room for employees? She couldn't be sure. But at this point, it looked like her best shot. She quickened her pace. . . .

She didn't see the pot handle extending from the edge of the stove in time. She ran into it, knocking it off the countertop. It clattered to the floor with a sound that was positively ear-shattering. She jumped into the air, startled, then swept up the pot and clamped it to her chest.

Had anyone heard? How could anyone not have heard? If anyone was here, they would now know they were not alone.

She detected a soft rustling sound coming from the back room. Did she dare? She had no idea what she might be getting into. This could be the dumbest thing she had done in her entire life.

No, the dumbest would be taking all these risks and then backing off when it looked as if she might find something. She had to press on.

Slowly, cautiously, she turned the doorknob. The light was off.

She took a deep breath and flicked the switch.

Hayley Bennett was lying on the floor, pinned beneath the sink. And it was clear that she was in great pain.

Christina rushed forward. "I don't know if you remember me. I'm Christina McCall. I work with Ben Kincaid."

Bennett's face was contorted with agony. "How did you find me?"

"I'll explain later. First we need to get you out of here." She gently pulled the woman forward, trying not to hurt her—then saw that she had been handcuffed to the pipe beneath the sink.

"I don't suppose you know where the key is?" Christina asked.

Bennett shook her head. Tears flew from her cheeks.

"Thought not."

"Rothko will be back any minute."

"I figured as much." Christina examined the pipe. It connected the drain of the basin to the wall. Probably the outside plumbing. It was made of sturdy metal, stainless steel, most likely. But she noticed that the plaster on the wall was flaking.

She pulled on the pipe with all her strength. It gave. Just a bit, but it gave. On close inspection, she saw that the pipe was connected to the wall, not bolted to another pipe. If she could separate the pipe from the wall, it was just possible she could slide the handcuff off the broken end and get Dr. Bennett out of here.

Christina wedged her back against the side wall, then pressed her feet against the pipe. She wished she had her shoes now, but there was no time to go back for them.

"This is probably going to hurt," she said.

Bennett remained silent, but her eyes spoke volumes. Do it.

Christina pulled back, gritted her teeth, and kicked the pipe with all her might. It moved, but it did not break.

"Do it again," Bennett said, her eyes and face crunched shut. Christina was certain the impact had caused her considerable pain. "Quickly."

Christina gave it everything she had. She hit the pipe hard, but it didn't give any more than it had before.

"Again," Bennett said, water streaming down her cheeks. "Hit it again."

Christina started to do just that—but stopped when a creaking sound told her that someone had opened the tiny room's door.

"Who are you?" growled the man in the doorway. "And what do you think you're doing?"

BEN, MIKE, AND Sergeant Baxter stood in the center of what was left of Hayley Bennett's office. They'd managed to put out the fire, but smoke still filled the small area so densely it was difficult to breathe, and ash and soot permeated the room. Her filing cabinets were incinerated. Even beyond the fire damage, the place looked as if Hurricane Hilda had blown through. Paper littered the floor. A coffee table was broken, a bookshelf was upended, a lamp was smashed.

"Some kind of struggle took place here," Baxter said, announcing what was already all too plain. "Before the fire."

"Yeah," Mike said, "and judging by her absence, Dr. Bennett lost."

"Not to mention that man we found unconscious in the entryway. I'm guessing he walked in at the wrong time."

"What about Christina?" Ben asked. The urgency in his voice was unmistakable. "Did Rothko get her, too?"

Mike pondered a moment. "If he had, wouldn't her car still be outside?"

"Maybe. Unless he did something with it."

"He hasn't had time."

"Do you think she might be with him?" Baxter asked. "Or following him? I know that seems insane, but—"

"I don't think it sounds insane at all. Knowing Christina, it's all too possible. Mike, we've got to do something. We've got to find them."

"I know," he said grimly. "But I don't know where they are. Baxter and I have checked his home, his club, his gym, his office. Even the corporate dining room. We've been everywhere he might be expected to be."

"There must be another place," Ben said, "that we haven't thought of yet."

"Easy to say—but where?"

"I don't know where!" Ben shouted. "But we can't waste any more time. We have to find her!"

"Wait, wait, wait." Baxter held up her hands. "Let's all stay calm and think about this rationally. If you were Rothko, and you had killed two people—maybe more—and you wanted to kill again, where would you go?"

Mike grabbed a cushion and flung it onto the sofa. "How the hell should I know where he would go? He killed the last two women in their homes—or left them there, anyway. But for some reason, he seems to have taken Dr. Bennett away with him."

"And there are no signs that she's dead, either. Maybe he didn't have time to set it up. Maybe that man we found unconscious intruded. Maybe he needs to keep Bennett alive, at least for a while. Maybe he just needed to stash her somewhere till he had time to kill her."

"Too many maybes," Mike said. "This isn't helping."

Baxter ignored him. "So he needs a place that's quiet, secluded. Someplace that can be secured. Someplace no one else would go. But it can't be too far away. The longer he's on the road, the more likely he'll be caught or she'll get away."

Ben nodded. "That makes sense."

"So," she continued, "we need a place that's in or near Tulsa, empty or deserted, that Rothko would know about and would able to—"

"I know where he could be," Mike said suddenly. His eyes were dark and fixed. "In fact, I'd bet on it."

"Where?" Ben pleaded.

"The last place on earth I want to return to."

"And that is?"

Mike was already out the door. "We don't have time for chitchat. I'll show you."

"GABRIEL," DR. BENNETT said. Her voice was pleading. "Please don't hurt her."

Aravena stared at them, his face stony.

"Gabriel, listen to me. I know you better than anyone. Better than you know yourself."

"You gave me drugs," he said. His voice was cold and hollow. "You tried to turn me into something I wasn't. Something weak and hideous."

"I tried to help you, Gabriel. I tried to save your life."

Aravena turned his attention back to Christina. "What are you doing?" he repeated. His fists clenched.

"What does it look like? I'm trying to get her free so we can escape before your pal returns." Her honesty was a stall for time. As she spoke, she scanned the room for potential weapons. A scrub brush? A toilet plunger? Somehow she didn't think that was going to do it.

"He will be back very soon," Aravena said.

"I'm hip to that, thank you. So what are you, his personal pet monster?"

She could tell the words stung. His face twitched. "You will never be able to break that pipe."

Christina frowned. "I was beginning to get that idea. But—"

"But I can." Aravena took a step forward.

Christina flinched. Her entire body tensed.

"I will not harm you," Aravena said. He looked at the pipe beneath the basin. "May I?"

Christina didn't understand any of this, but she figured this was not the time for a lengthy cross-examination. She scooted out of the way, letting Aravena slide in.

Aravena crouched beneath the sink and took the pipe in both of his powerful hands. And pulled.

His face turned white with effort. He grunted, sweated, twisted. His muscled arms trembled. And in less than thirty seconds, he had removed the pipe from the wall.

Water began to spew out. Aravena slid the handcuff off the end of the pipe, freeing Dr. Bennett.

"I am sorry I hurt you," he said quietly.

Bennett pushed herself to her feet. It was evident she was in great pain, but she forced herself to move. "We need to get out of here."

"I will help you." Aravena shut off the overhead light, then poked his head out the door. Once he had ascertained that the coast was clear, he waved for them to follow.

They tiptoed through the kitchen, following the path Christina had blazed to get here. First Aravena, then the women, slid across the countertop. Only a few more steps, Christina told herself. Only ten more feet and we'll be out of this hamburger house of horrors. She could call Ben and Mike and get the police out after Rothko and everything would be—

"Where do you think you're going?"

All three froze in their tracks. Christina felt her heart sink.

It was him. Rothko. And he was pointing a gun at them.

"Don't leave the party so soon, my friends," he said, smiling. "I haven't served the cake and ice cream yet."

CHAPTER

30

"CAN'T YOU DRIVE any faster?" Ben said.

Mike's eyes were fixed on the road, his hands tightly gripping the steering wheel. "You know, Ben, most of the time you tell me I drive recklessly and nag at me to slow down."

"This is different," he muttered. "Christina's in there. I know she is. This is just the sort of thing she would do. Brash. Impulsive. Crazy."

"If she's so crazy, why do you work with her?" Baxter asked.

"Damn good question. She never does a thing I tell her."

"Why would you want a partner who never does anything you tell her?"

"Now there's a question," Mike said, eyes still straight ahead. "Why would anyone want a partner who never does anything he tells her?"

Baxter gave him an evil look, but said nothing.

"Can't you do something?" Ben urged. "Radio for backup, maybe?"

"I already did," Mike answered. "On my cell phone. But we'll get there before they do."

"Damn!" Ben's hands gripped the dash tightly.

Baxter leaned forward and laid a hand on his shoulder. "You really like this Christina, huh?"

Ben's head turned. "We've been working together a long time."

"So it's a working relationship?"

"I wouldn't want anything to happen to her," Ben said softly. "I don't know what I'd do without her." He whipped his head around. "Can't you drive any faster, Mike?"

Mike pursed his lips. "I'll see what I can do." He shifted gears and floored it.

* * *

"My friends, you wound me," Rothko said, swinging the gun in the air. "Leaving so soon. Without saying good-bye?" He was smiling the entire time he spoke. Remarkably amiable, for a cold-blooded killer, Christina thought. Almost psychotically so.

"And it appears that you've caused some property damage." His eyes darted momentarily to the back, where water was spilling out of the bathroom. "I'll have to dock your pay, Gabriel."

Aravena's face was set. He did not say a word.

"And who might you be?" he asked, finally turning his attention to Christina. "I don't believe we've met."

"I work for Ben Kincaid," she answered. "And he knows I'm here."

"Does he?" He stepped forward, tossing her strawberry-blonde hair with the point of his gun. "No, I don't believe he does. Because if he did, he'd be here already, wouldn't he?"

"He's slow," Christina replied. "But certain."

"Well, then he will be too late." He pressed the gun against Christina's cheek, tracing a line down the curve of her neck. "I'm afraid I can't let any of you leave."

"You're going to kill us?" Bennett asked. Her face was red and streaked with tear trails. "All of us?"

"I don't see that I have any choice."

Christina tried to think of a way out of this mess. But the man was holding a gun barely inches away. There was nothing she could reach before he drilled her. And she had no doubt that he would do it. Not when she looked into his eyes.

"Why are you doing this?" Christina asked. "Why did you kill those people?"

"Why should I tell you?" He took a step back and smiled. "That's our little secret, isn't it, Gabriel?"

Aravena stiffened.

"You won't get away with this," Christina said. "We'll be missed. Our bodies will be discovered, even here. It'll be traced back to you."

"Ah. Now that's where you're wrong. Nothing has ever been traced back to me. Not for all these years. And your bodies will not be discovered." Keeping the gun trained on them, he reached across the front counter to the nearest stove top. And turned on the gas.

Christina felt a cold chill run down her spine. "You're going to burn the place down."

"It isn't much good to me like this. I had to close it. I don't know why, but after a shooting takes place in a restaurant, no one ever wants to eat there again. I was planning to raze the joint and build a playground or something. This will just accelerate the process."

"You're going to kill us and then burn the bodies?" Bennett said. Her voice was dry and cracked.

"Well, I'm definitely going to burn the place down," Rothko said. "And I'm definitely going to wound you so you can't escape. But I didn't say anything about killing you. That seems unnecessary." A demented grin spread slowly across his face. "You'll enjoy the fire so much more if you're alive."

"IN THERE?" BEN said. "Burger Bliss?"

"In the closed and abandoned Burger Bliss, yes," Mike muttered. "They shut this place down after the shooting incident. The one I botched." He and Baxter exchanged a look. "It's the perfect place for Rothko. He owns it; he controls it. He can restrict access. He undoubtedly has keys. And there's no one else here. No one else even close, this time of night."

"That's Christina's car!" Ben screamed. He pointed to an orange Dodge parked on a side road.

"That's it, then." Mike dimmed his lights and parked his car. "I'm going in."

Baxter grabbed him by the shoulder. "Wait a minute, Mike. Think this out. Let's wait for backup to arrive."

"No way." Mike shrugged her hand away and got out of the car. He quickly strapped on a bulletproof vest. "That's how I played it last time I was here. And we both know how well that turned out."

"Mike, you couldn't have helped—"

"People died, Baxter. Because I screwed up. I tried to deny it, just as I tried to deny that you were right about Erin Faulkner. But the fact is, I blew it." He checked his gun to make sure it was loaded. "I won't let that happen again. Not if I can stop it."

He replaced the gun in its holster, then started moving stealthily toward the restaurant. "Wish me luck."

"WHO WANTS TO go first?" Rothko said, pulling back the hammer on his gun. "I'm thinking a good shot to the kneecap will prevent you from leaving. And then we can start the fireworks."

Christina's brain was racing, trying to formulate a solution to their predicament. But it just wasn't there. Nothing that came to mind was remotely feasible. And Aravena, strong as he was, was just as helpless as she. There was nothing left for them to do. Nothing but to stand here and watch this madman pick them off one after the other.

"You don't want to do this," Dr. Bennett said.

Rothko chuckled. "Oh, I think I do."

"You don't. You just think you do."

"Oh, puh-lese."

"I don't know what happened to you. I don't know what twisted you into the man you are now. Perhaps you were pushed too hard. The need to succeed was too great. Perhaps you have unresolved issues. Sexual problems. Maybe you made one mistake and had to go on making bigger ones to cover it up. I don't know. But I know this—you don't have to do this horrible thing." She extended her hand. "I can help you."

Rothko scowled. "Dr. Bennett, are you trying to psychoanalyze me?"

"I'm trying to help you."

"You're saying I'm crazy."

"I'm not. I don't even know what that word means."

"Well, I'm not crazy!" he shouted. "I'm not!"

"Fine!" She held up her hands, the handcuffs still dangling from one wrist. "But I can help you. If you'll let me."

"You're making me sick." He lifted the gun, eye level. "I've made my decision, Dr. Freud. You're first."

"No!" Aravena shouted.

"Oh, yes," Rothko replied. He pulled the trigger.

"No!" An instant before the shot rang out, Aravena dove in front of Dr. Bennett. The slug hit him in the chest. Blood flew through the air. He crumpled to the floor.

"Gabriel!" Bennett screamed. Christina stared, her mouth gaping.

"This is getting pathetic," Rothko said bitterly. "Do you think you accomplished anything, Gabe? You didn't. All you did was change the order." He raised the gun again. "Say sayonara, Doctor."

Another gunshot rang out. Christina winced. She wrapped her arms around herself, trembling, and waited for Dr. Bennett to fall.

But she did not fall. Peter Rothko did.

"Is everyone all right?"

"Mike!"

Mike raced forward, gun still in his hand.

"He's hurt!" Christina said, pointing to Aravena's motionless body on the floor.

Mike ran to his side. "Goddamn it. Straight to the heart." He whipped out his cell phone and called for an ambulance. "I've already called for backup. They might bring a medic." He moved over to Rothko's side.

"Is he dead?" Bennett asked.

"Unfortunately, no. He'll make it." He collected Rothko's gun and emptied the chamber.

Christina ran to the stove and shut off the gas. "Be careful about firing in here," she warned. "The gas has been on a long time."

"Thought I smelled something." Mike returned to Aravena. His eyes were open, but just barely. He tore the man's shirt and looked more closely at the wound—then grimaced.

Bennett knelt beside Mike. "Will he—?"

Mike looked at her, then shook his head.

Bennett gripped Aravena's hand tightly in both of hers. "Why, Gabriel? Why did you do it?"

Aravena's eyes were almost entirely shut, but he still managed to speak. "I . . . am not . . . a monster."

"No," she said, "you're not," and once again tears poured down her cheeks. "You're a hero. You made yourself who you wanted to be."

FOUR

What's All Around You

◆ ◆ ◆

31

BEN, MIKE, AND Christina were huddled outside the courtroom doors with Ray Goldman, in orange coveralls, his feet shackled, and two marshals standing not four feet behind him.

Mike looked at Christina with concern. "Are you sure you're up to this?"

Christina finessed the question. "I don't have any choice. It's now or never." Her eyes briefly met Ray's. "Tomorrow's the day, you know."

"Speaking for myself," Ray said, "I think we should go for it."

Despite the gravity of the situation, Christina couldn't help smiling. She pulled an outline out of a file folder. "Here's what I thought we'd do, Mike. Start with all the information you've extracted from Rothko, then follow up with the background details you've uncovered. If we handle it right, we'll get a new trial. I thought I would—"

"Wait a minute," Ben said. His voice was quiet but firm. "I'll take the lead on this one."

Christina and Mike looked at each other.

"It is my case," Ben added. "Has been for seven years."

Christina glanced edgily toward the courtroom doors. "Oh, sure. Now that we actually have a case . . ."

"It isn't that. I think . . . it's time I grew up. I'm not a first-year associate anymore and I'm not going to act like one."

"Ben, you don't have to—"

"Yes, I do. All of you have confronted your fears. Especially you, Ray. You've been looking everyone's greatest fear straight in the face for years. So I can damn well face Judge Richard A. Derek."

Christina handed him her file. "I pass the case."

"Well . . . don't go too far."

Her eyes beamed. "You think you might need my support?"

Ben turned toward the courtroom. "Yeah. Especially when my knees give out."

"IN THE END, it all came down to flavor," Mike said, testifying from the witness stand. "Frank Faulkner had it. And Peter Rothko wanted it. Badly. He knew he needed something fabulous to jump-start his floundering restaurant chain and to enable him to compete with the major players in the industry. Faulkner was being hailed as the Einstein of the field; his work was innovative, brilliant. Rothko contacted him about devising a special flavor for Burger Bliss's upscale burgers. And Faulkner was eager to make some extra money. Unfortunately, he was bound by a long-term contract; legally, anything he devised belonged to his employers. So his work for Rothko had to be done on the quiet."

Ben squared himself behind the podium. "And did he, in fact, devise a formula?"

"According to Rothko, he did. But something went wrong. Faulkner demanded more money—much more. More than Rothko could hope to raise. Contrary to what he told you, he never inherited any money, and his restaurant was bleeding cash. So if he wanted the formula, he was going to have to try a different tactic."

"Like murder?"

"Exactly. Rothko enlisted a man named Gabriel Aravena. Aravena had just begun state-ordered therapy with Dr. Hayley Bennett as part of his probation. He had a history of violent sex crimes—especially involving young girls. We believe Rothko essentially hired him to take out Faulkner." He paused. "Apparently hiring a hit man is a lot cheaper than buying a trade secret, these days."

"So Aravena was sent to take out the Faulkner family?" Ben asked.

"According to Rothko, Aravena was only supposed to kill Frank. But something went hideously wrong. The rest of the family came home, much earlier than expected. Aravena couldn't cope with this unexpected complication. He went berserk. He was an unstable, sick man—at that time—with sexual issues and a strong penchant for violence. He ended up torturing and killing all of them—except Erin Faulkner. She fit his profile of sexual desirability and so he restrained her in the basement, apparently with the idea of . . . spending more time with her once the house was secure and the rest of the family was dispatched."

"What happened?"

"Rothko. He arrived at the scene—and found a slaughterhouse. He was incensed. He hadn't wanted this. So he says. He did what he could to make the situation better—took the baby back to its crib, took some money to make it look like a robbery, smoothed Frank's daughter's skirt. He didn't know about Erin being in the basement, and he certainly wouldn't have allowed Aravena to hang around the scene of the crime just to pleasure himself."

"What about the eyes? Why were all the eyes removed?"

Mike took a deep breath. This was not his favorite part of the story. "You've probably wondered why killing Frank would give Rothko the formula. Frank didn't keep it at home, after all. Rothko needed to get into the plant, which had notoriously high security. He collected Frank's ID card, but that wasn't the only thing Rothko needed if he was going to sneak into the lab and steal the formula. As I believe you've experienced, Mr. Kincaid, this lab has a retinal-scan screening device. To get in, he needed Frank's eyes."

Ben had heard all this before, but that didn't make it any less horrific. "That explains the mutilation for Frank. Why the others?"

"Cover. If only Frank's eyes were missing, someone might've figured out the reason. But when it happened to the whole family, it seemed like the work of a sadistic psychopath. Which it was, of course. But it was not random violence. It was violence with a very specific purpose." Mike lowered his chin. "Soon thereafter, the Tulsa PD became convinced that Raymond Goldman was the killer. And he was ultimately convicted, due largely to the eyewitness testimony of Erin Faulkner, who was under great pressure to identify Mr. Goldman as the killer. But it was an ID she was never sure about, and it haunted her thereafter. Her despondency was written off by most who knew her as the grief of a sole survivor. But it was also the guilt of someone who suspected she had been instrumental in the incarceration of an innocent man."

"So at this point," Ben said, "Rothko had his formula. He used it to build his restaurant chain into the great success it is today. Another man had been convicted for his crime. He must've thought he was scot-free."

"Indeed he did," Mike agreed. "Until he ran into Erin Faulkner at the penitentiary in McAlester the night Goldman was almost executed. He had a brief conversation with her and it convinced him that she was about to recant her identification, which of course would reopen the whole case. Rothko couldn't allow that. He killed her—though not before she spoke to you, Mr. Kincaid—and he made it look like suicide, which in Erin's case was always plausible."

"What about Sheila Knight?"

"Sheila was Erin's best friend. She had been with Erin at McAlester, and she'd seen and heard Rothko talking to her. He saw her, too, and he knew who she was. Just to play it safe, after he killed Erin, he kept an eye on her. Sheila had been told that the police suspected Erin was murdered, and that Erin had allegedly recanted her testimony, and when she put that together with the conversation in McAlester, she eventually became convinced that had been the reason Erin was killed. Sheila hadn't recognized Rothko in McAlester, but being a relatively famous person locally"—he glanced at Christina—"and one of Tulsa's most eligible bachelors, it was only a matter of time before she identified him, particularly after the hostage incident in one of his restaurants. His picture was in the *World* the day she died; I think she saw it and recognized him. At any rate, Rothko couldn't take the risk. He followed her to a lakeside cabin—he had a cabin himself nearby—and found the paper open to his picture and Sheila in a frenzy. When she saw him, she panicked. Called him a murderer. Ran away. At that point, he had no choice. Another loose end needed to be tied. She had to die."

"Why did he try to kill Hayley Bennett?"

"Same story, really. She spotted him in your office. She knew she'd seen him before—and not in the society pages. Frank Faulkner was also her patient. He was struggling with office stress—but also, apparently . . ." How to put this? There was no point in destroying the man's reputation now. " . . . also struggling with his feelings for his daughter. And her friends. Anyway, Dr. Bennett had seen Rothko with Frank Faulkner shortly before he died, and she'd made notes about the encounter in Frank's file."

"Why did that seem worth noting?"

"Well, Frank had told her he was working on something big. He was very agitated. And her house call to Frank's home interrupted a business meeting with Rothko—just before Frank was killed. Once Bennett saw him in your office, it didn't take her long to put it all together. Unfortunately, Rothko recognized her, too, and once again, he saw his elaborate plan falling apart. So he rounded up Aravena—who had no choice but to comply, given all that Rothko knew he had done—and grabbed her. The opportune arrival of a neighbor prevented him from killing Bennett on the spot and making it look like suicide, as he'd done with the others. But he surely would've killed her. If we hadn't intervened."

Ben paused, letting all that Mike had said sink in. "Major Morelli, at this time, do you or anyone else at the Tulsa PD have any reason to believe Ray Goldman was involved in the murder of the Faulkner family?"

"No. To the contrary, I'm quite certain he was not. I've not only investigated this in detail—I've also spoken to Mr. Rothko himself. He's been given partial immunity as to the Faulkner family deaths—even if they were instigated by Rothko, they were actually committed by Mr. Aravena, who is now deceased. That still leaves three murders and two attempteds to charge him with." Mike turned to look at Judge Derek. "But Raymond Goldman had nothing to do with any of the murders."

"You're sure of that?"

"I am. The whole department is sure. There really is no doubt. We made a mistake once. But now we want to set things right."

"Thank you, Major Morelli." Ben closed his notebook. "Thank you very much."

THE COURTROOM WAS deathly quiet. Ben had concluded the presentation of his evidence. Weintraub had been all but invisible; he made no real objection to anything Ben said or did. Judge Derek had been silent throughout. Not an unnecessary word had been spoken. And now, minutes passed while the handsome judge sat at his bench, not moving, not speaking.

"What's he doing?" Ray muttered, under his breath.

"I don't know," Ben muttered back. "I wish I did."

"He's going to turn us down, isn't he? Just like the other times. He'll find some excuse."

"We don't know that," Ben said, but in truth, he was thinking the same thing. Had he made a hideous mistake, taking the lead at the hearing? Knowing how intensely Derek hated him, had he sacrificed Ray's chances to his own bravado? "We'll just have to wait. And see."

Mercifully, the interregnum eventually came to an end. "Well," Derek said, massaging the bridge of his nose, "this presents a bit of a dilemma, doesn't it?"

Ben felt Christina's hand dart out for his under the table.

"Your client has exhausted all his appeals. You're aware of that, aren't you, Mr. Kincaid?"

Ben rose to his feet. "Yes, your honor. I am." He was tempted to start arguing. But something told him not to. The man already knows everything you're tempted to tell him. Just keep your mouth shut. See where he's going.

"But as you're also well aware, this court sits both in law and in equity. When newly discovered evidence is brought to light, the court always has the option, in equity, to reopen a case. Most of the newly discovered evidence this court has seen in the past—including in this case—was ridiculously weak and unconvincing." He paused. "But what I've heard today in this courtroom is something else again."

Ben felt Christina's hand squeezing his. Come on, Derek . . . come on. . . .

"It seems apparent to this court that a grave injustice was done seven years ago—an injustice for which Raymond Goldman has paid the price. An impossibly high price. The court cannot return those years to you, sir. All we can do is earnestly offer our condolences, and our apologies. And of course, grant your writ for relief."

Ray slowly rose. His knees were shaking. "Y-you mean—you mean I get a new trial?"

Derek shook his head. "I mean you're free to go." He rapped his gavel. "Marshals, remove those shackles. The writ for habeas corpus relief is granted. Case dismissed."

The courtroom exploded. Ben and Christina threw themselves around Ray, around each other. Flashbulbs ignited the room. "I can't believe it," Ray kept saying. "After all this time. I can't believe it." Everyone in the gallery rushed to the front. Pandemonium ruled.

"There will be order in this court!"

Derek stood at the head of the courtroom, banging his gavel furiously. "We may be out of session, but this is still a court of law and you will behave accordingly!"

He glared at them all for a moment, and then, abruptly, his expression softened. "Take it outside."

"Yes, your honor," Ben said, hurriedly gathering his papers.

"Oh, and one other thing," the judge added.

Ben stiffened. "Yes?"

"Nice job, Mr. Kincaid."

32

AN HOUR LATER, back at the office, a massive celebration ensued. Somehow, in the space of an hour, Christina managed to get the whole lobby area festooned with streamers and ribbons. Champagne flowed. The outer doors were locked; the office was closed for business. Everyone wore silly hats and giggled giddily—Ben and Christina and Jones and his wife, Paula, and even Loving. And at the center of it all was Ray Goldman—looking better than Ben had seen him in seven years. He was wearing street clothes—for the first time in seven years—and even if he hadn't had a chance yet for perfect grooming, the watery glow in his eyes and the amazed smile on his face more than made up for it.

"I still can't believe it," Ray said, a happily befuddled expression on his face.

"Believe it," Ben said. "You're a free man."

"A toast," Christina said, raising her glass. "To Ray Goldman, who the whole world now knows is innocent—as we knew all along."

"Amen!" everyone shouted.

"And let's have a moment for Erin Faulkner, one of the bravest, strongest women I've ever had the pleasure to know. Despite all her troubles, she tried to do the right thing. And in the end—she did."

"Bravo," Ben said quietly.

"And," she went on, glass still raised, "a toast to that great and powerful legal warrior, Ben Kincaid!"

"Hear, hear!" the others concurred.

"Champion of truth, justice, and the American way. Defender of the poor and oppressed. Slayer of the great and toupéed beast Derek."

Ben cleared his throat. "I think you should be sharing in this toast, co-counsel."

She beamed. "If you insist."

"I can't get over how well this case turned out," Loving announced. His huge frame was bobbling—too much bubbly, Ben suspected. "Ben finally won a case in front of Derek. Ray finally wins his get-out-of-jail-free card. And I learned to appreciate sushi."

The rest of the room stared at him.

"Well, I did. It's weird, but I really like that squishy stuff. I've been back to that joint three times."

Jones whispered into Christina's ear. "Soon we'll be hearing about the squid conspiracy to take over the world."

"What happened to Mike?" Ben inquired. "He should be sharing in the accolades."

"Blackwell called," Jones explained. "Yanked him back to headquarters."

"Is he in trouble?"

Jones shrugged his shoulders. "Why else would Blackwell call?"

"FIRST OF ALL," Chief Blackwell said, "I want to extend my congratulations to the two of you on your outstanding detective work."

Mike, sitting in a chair opposite the man's desk, stared at him. You do? Was the old man mellowing, or was he in an extended fantasy fugue state? When Mike caught the Kindergarten Killer, Blackwell barely nodded. When he nailed Detective Sergeant McNaughton's murderer, Blackwell hardly grunted. But now he's getting effusive congratulations?

"I know this case hasn't been easy for either of you. But you stuck with it, and you brought it to a successful conclusion. I'm putting strong commendations into both of your files."

Baxter, sitting in the chair beside Mike, nodded. "That's much appreciated, sir," she said. "But that's not why you called us here, is it?"

Blackwell seemed disconcerted. "No. It isn't."

Mike jumped in. "Chief, if it's about that report I filed on Sergeant Baxter, I withdraw everything I—"

Blackwell waved him away. "No, no. I just—well, I need to know what you two want to do."

Baxter's head tilted. "How do you mean?"

"Look, let's talk turkey. I forced the two of you to work together. Neither of you wanted it. But I thought it was important. I wanted Baxter to get a fair shake—something she didn't get in Oklahoma City, I'm sorry to say. And I thought the best way to accomplish that was to pair her with the best and most open-minded man in homicide."

Mike's eyes widened. Was that a compliment? This was a red-letter day.

"But I know it's been a tempestuous relationship from the start."

Baxter squirmed. "It hasn't been . . . that bad. . . ."

"You're trying to put a good face on it. And I appreciate that. But I know what's what. I've got eyes and ears. All over the place. I know you two have been at war from the start. I hate to think what was going on in the car when that Knight woman was killed."

Mike and Baxter exchanged a look.

"So the bottom line is this—if you want to be reassigned, I'll go along with it. I think this case has given Baxter the cred she needed. There's no need to Super Glue the two of you together forever, if you don't want it. Mind you, I think you make a pretty good team."

Mike nodded. "Do you really?"

"And I think you could learn to work together. But I won't force the issue. If you want to be assigned to new partners, I'll do it."

Baxter's head slowly turned. Mike's did the same. But they seemed to be avoiding each other's eyes.

"So tell me what you want. Will you keep on working together? Or shall I reassign you?"

Slowly, gradually, Mike and Baxter found each other's eyes. But neither spoke.

"Okay," Blackwell said, drumming his fingers on his desk, "do we have a verdict?"

Mike and Baxter continued staring. Silently.

"Well," Blackwell said, his impatience obviously growing. *"What's it going to be?"*

THE PARTY WAS winding down. The last bottle had been uncorked, but no one was drinking anymore. Jones and Loving had both fallen asleep on the sofa. Christina was at Jones's workstation, banging away at his computer keyboard.

"What are you up to?" Ben asked, peering over her shoulder.

"Deleting everything on Jones's hard drive," she answered nonchalantly.

Ben's eyes ballooned. "What! Are you nuts? He'll—"

"Relax. I backed it all up on Zip disks." She smiled. "But he won't know that."

"Christina, have you lost your mind? When Jones sees what you've done, he'll freak! We're talking office-manager meltdown!"

"Yes," she agreed, as she pushed Delete for the final time. "That'll teach him to send me out to interview Spider-Man."

BEN POURED HIMSELF another drink and pulled up a chair beside Ray. Christina had fallen into a chair, and her eyelids were drooping. What an incredible woman she is, Ben thought, not for the first time. How lucky they were to have her. How lucky he was—

Or could be?

"I still can't believe it," Ray said. He had probably drunk too much champagne, but after seven years without, Ben thought he was entitled. "It doesn't seem real."

"It will," Ben assured him. "The first night you sleep in your own bed."

"My own bed? I don't have a bed. I haven't had an apartment for years."

"It'll take a while to get your life jump-started. But we'll be here to help."

"I don't know where to begin. I haven't got a penny."

"I can help there, too," Ben said. "The State of Oklahoma has a trust fund for persons who have been wrongfully convicted. As often as the state has done it, they just about have to. We'll submit some papers, maybe file a friendly suit. We'll take care of it." He smiled. "You won't get wealthy beyond measure, but it'll be enough to get you back on your feet again."

"Will it be enough to let me shop at Miss Jackson's?"

Ben sighed. Ray was thinking of Carrie.

"I know it's crazy," Ray said quietly. "It's been so long. But I can't stop thinking about her. For the last seven years, she's been the object of my every dream, every fantasy. I mean—it's not as if I've had a chance to meet other women. I have to play this one through."

"I understand."

"I don't know what we'll talk about. When I see her again. I mean, I don't know from eye shadow."

Ben nodded. There was no chance that conversation was going to turn out well. But when it was over, perhaps he could begin to move on.

"It's such a relief. Not only to be out of prison, but to have all the loose ends tied up. To have everyone know once and for all that I really did not commit that heinous crime. Including Carrie. I know she had her doubts about me before, but now that she knows—now that she absolutely *knows*— that should make a difference. Shouldn't it?"

"I hope so."

"I know you don't think I have a chance, but so what if I don't? Better to try and flop than to think about it all the time and never do it. If I learned anything during my seven years behind bars, it's this—every day is precious. Every day. You can't waste a single minute."

"Got big plans?"

"Oh, not in the way you mean. I don't want to climb Mount Everest or run with the bulls at Pamplona. That stuff doesn't seem important to me anymore. What really matters—what I missed most—are the little things. Quiet things. Taking a long walk at twilight. Reading a good book. Having fun with someone you love."

The phone rang. Ben picked it up, then half a second later put it down again. "Ray, would you excuse me? I've got to run."

"Sure, why?"

Ben grabbed his coat and headed for the door. "My little girl is about to give birth."

CHAPTER

33

BEN AND CHRISTINA were huddled around a cardboard box in Ben's clothes closet. Joni stood behind them, beaming like a proud midwife.

Ben was mesmerized by Giselle and the spectacle inside the box. "Seven kittens. That's . . . amazing."

Christina grinned. "I can't believe you've never seen a cat have kittens before."

"Or wanted to. But somehow . . . this is different." Ben peered down at the seven smoky-gray kittens nuzzling at their mother's side. "Have I ever mentioned how grateful to you I am for giving me this cat?"

Christina arched an eyebrow. "As I recall, you were pretty grumpy about it at the time."

"I was stupid." You've made my life better, he wanted to add. You always have. You make everyone's life better.

"I was so scared," he said quietly. "When I knew that madman had you. I was terrified."

"Afraid you'd have to do your own legal research?"

"I was afraid of losing you."

Christina looked at him, a strange but not altogether unpleasant expression on her face.

Joni cleared her throat. "Well, I don't think I'm needed here anymore. I'll call you in the morning, Ben. In a few weeks, we can start trying to find homes for these little guys." She left the apartment.

"We're going to give them away?" Ben said.

"Like you were planning to keep all seven kittens?"

"Would that be bad?"

She laughed. "No, Ben. Not if that's what you want."

"Christina . . ."

303

"Yes?"

He swallowed. "Oh, nothing."

He wanted to kick himself. Why was he always so stupid and backward? What was it Ray had said? *If I learned anything, it's that every day is precious. Every day. You can't waste a single minute.*

"Christina," he tried again.

"Ye-es?"

He stared down at the carpet. "This is probably a dumb idea, but you know, they're having a new exhibition of Thomas Moran paintings out at the Gilcrease starting this weekend—"

"I know."

"—and I wondered if you . . . might want to go."

"You mean—with you? This would be like, like a . . ." A slow grin spread across her face. "Are you asking me out?"

He took a deep breath. *Every day is precious.* "Christina, I don't think I've ever told you this, but I—I—"

"Yes?"

He wiped his forehead. "You're really important to me. Really really . . . important to me. I . . . you're . . . very . . . *important.*"

Christina smiled, a smile of mercy. "Be quiet, Ben." She turned away, returning her gaze to the contents of the cardboard box. "You need to pay more attention to what's going on around you."

He knitted his brow. "And that is?"

She scooped up the tiniest of the smoky-gray kittens and held it in her hands. "Life."

ACKNOWLEDGMENTS

READERS INTERESTED IN learning more about the various food and restaurant topics discussed in this book are directed to *Fast Food Nation* by Eric Schlosser and *Kitchen Confidential* by Anthony Bourdain. Both were invaluable to me in researching this book. Similarly, readers wanting to know more about the world of tournament Scrabble (and who doesn't?) should check out *Word Freak* by Stefan Fatsis. Just for the record, my current Scrabble rating is 1353. My wife usually thrashes me, so some nights after the kids are in bed I've been known to play at play.games.com. Care to guess my login name?

Special thanks must go to my federal law expert, Arlene Joplin, and my criminal appeals and death row expert, Vicky Hildebrand, for reviewing the manuscript and advising me on many issues. Thanks to Dave Johnson for being my sure source of information on police procedure. I don't always listen to advice, though, so if you spot anything that looks like a mistake, blame me. Or better yet, assume that like all great artistes, I took dramatic license. Thanks also to Harry for occasionally letting me use my own computer and to Alice for volunteering to help me revise the opening chapters (Maybe when you're older, Princess). And I must thank my wife, Kirsten, editor in chief of Hawk Publishing, always my first reader and an invaluable partner.

By the way, thanks to Christina, Ben really does have a plaque with his name on it at the Polo Grill. Check it out.

Readers can E-mail me at: wb@williambernhardt.com. My official Web site address is www.williambernhardt.com.

William Bernhardt